Stolen Angels

TULSA

ISBN: 978-1-957262-10-9 (Paperback)
Stolen Angels

Copyright © 2022 by Calvin Fisher
All rights reserved.

No part of this publication may be reproduced, distributed, or transmitted in any form or by any means, including photocopying, recording, or other electronic or mechanical methods, without the prior written permission of the publisher, except in the case of brief quotations embodied in critical reviews and certain other noncommercial uses permitted by copyright law.

For permission requests, write to the publisher at the address below.

Yorkshire Publishing
1425 E 41st Pl
Tulsa, OK 74105
www.YorkshirePublishing.com
918.394.2665

Published in the USA

Stolen Angels

Calvin Fisher

To the family who kept me safe through all these years,
and the friends who helped me broaden my horizons.
This book would not be what it is without you all.

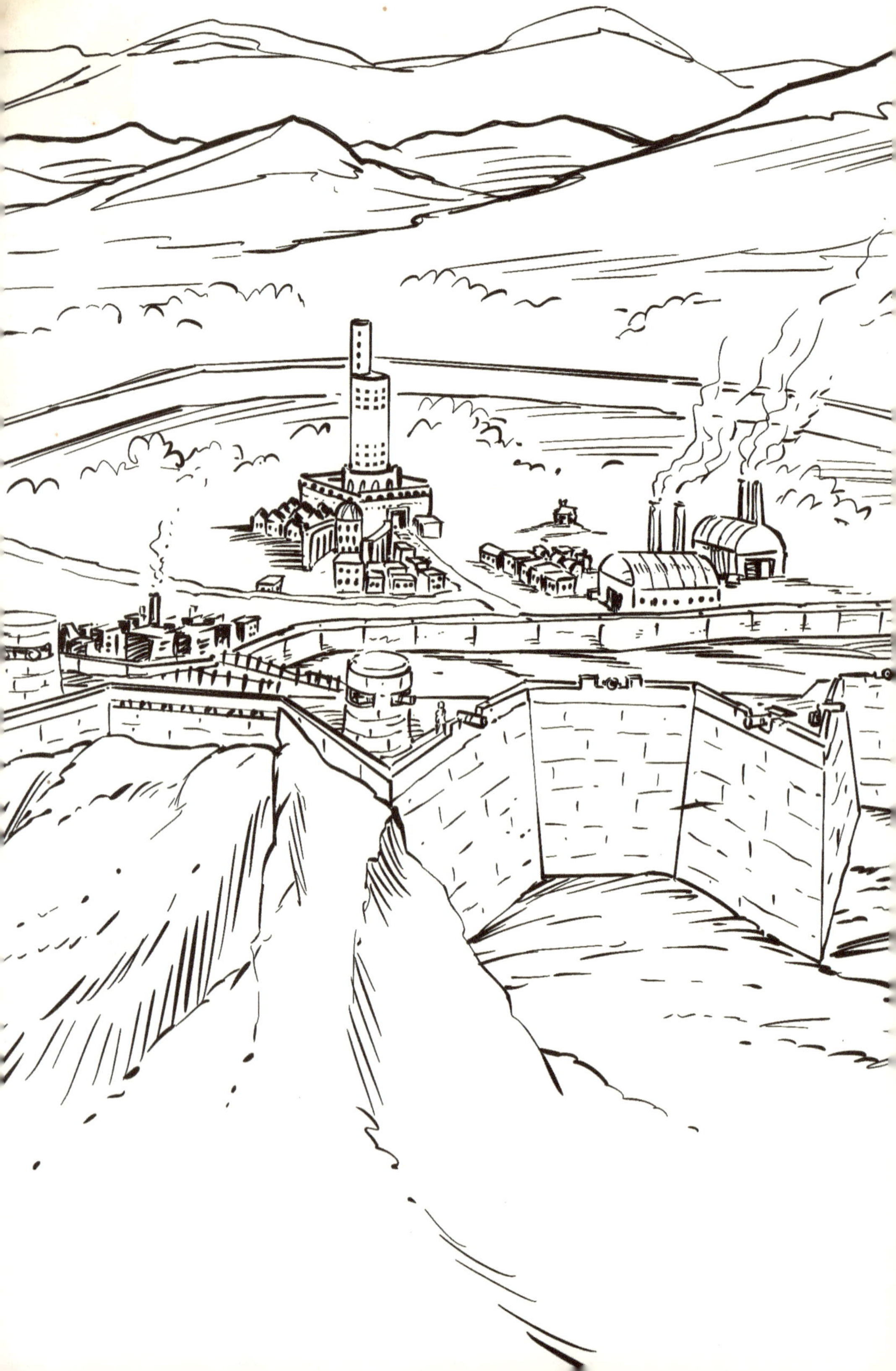

CHAPTER 1

All things eventually end. Each and every thing created has been created before and will succumb to the passage of time. Entropy is the natural state of life, yet Quintin always felt this fact could be circumvented. Glancing up at the hundred-foot wall, crafted from stones larger than most houses out east, Isel seemed in direct defiance of time itself.

Quintin smiled, nudging the sleeping figure seated in the cart beside him. "Hey, sleepy-head, we're here."

He nudged the girl harder, the small figure grumbling as she swatted away the pestering hand.

"I'm awake now. Can you stop that constant poking?" Fre sat up, grumbling.

"Trust me; you don't want to miss this." Quintin urged her.

Fre rubbed the sleep from her eyes, squinting as she poked her head out from under the wagon's canvas into the sunlight. Quintin followed her gaze, sharing a moment of awe as they approached the city wall. The format wasn't unlike many of the fortress cities found out east, only here the star design had been scaled beyond what Quintin thought possible.

Each wall held bunkers on each point, with blaze cannons lining the parapets, creating a devastating kill zone for anyone foolish enough to challenge its defenses.

"How long do you think it took them to make?" Fre asked, seemingly less inspired than Quintin.

He shrugged, "I have no clue. With conventional tools, it would take millennia, but this is the city of angels. The most skilled Heirs of their time probably built it in a year."

Fre scrunched her nose at the thought, "That's an unhealthy use of Resonance. How could anyone keep up with that pace?"

Quintin raised an eyebrow but didn't say anything. The truth was it wasn't fair. That's what built Isel into an empire when others had failed. The wagon approached the gateway, the steel portcullis hanging over the group like a guillotine waiting to drop. The wagon driver slowed as he approached the checkpoint. A registrar stepped out to meet the group, walking with his ratchet bow slung over his shoulder, preoccupied with the register in hand.

"Do you have your proof of shipment with you?" The registrar asked, glancing up at the wagon's driver.

The greying farmer nodded, pulling out a small handbook and handing it down. The registrar glanced at the receipt inside the book.

"This doesn't mention any passengers with you, is that correct?"

The farmer nodded, "I picked up these two at the last town, offered to pay fare to Isel."

The soldier nodded. "I'm going to need you two to put your names down along with your date of birth."

He handed the register to Quintin along with the pen. Quintin nodded taking the book. He scanned the page before finding two blank spaces, his hand thrumming as the pen scraped along the heavy paper.

As he handed the book back to the registrar, the man raised his eyebrow, "Your friend not going to sign?"

Quintin shook his head. "Sorry, sir, she doesn't read Thean, I'm sure you understand."

The man glanced to Fre, eyes noting the coral hair and blue eyes, "Bit of a ways from home, I see." he mumbled, "Head on through, you're all cleared."

The farmer nodded his thanks, as did Quintin. The wagon lurched forward, the draft horses straining under the weight of grain. Quintin felt a brief moment of cool air as they traveled up the tunnel into the city.

"Thea protect us," Quintin gasped as the wagon opened up to the vast cityscape of Isel. Thousands of people milled about the merchant district, sellers shouting and holding up their wares to anyone who would listen. Nobility stuck out like flowers in a sea of dirt. Their reds, greens, and purples were a stark contrast to the muted grays and browns of the working class.

Quintin lurched as the wagon halted, the elderly farmer pulling the break, "This is as far as my wagon goes. You'll have to walk the rest of the way."

The elderly man watched keenly as Quintin grabbed his bag, followed by Fre, and they hopped off onto the cobbled streets.

"Now, don't you two get into any trouble; my name is sitting right next to yours on that ledger, you hear."

Quintin waved at the man in acknowledgment as he walked away. *Two years of searching, let's hope it's worth it.* Quintin looked around, gauging their surroundings. The city was daunting. Stone mansions stood in the distance taking bites out of the skyline and even those were dwarfed by the Spire. Built well before the end of Heaven's War, it stood as a message for a bygone era, a lance ready to pierce heaven itself. Quintin noted the smoothed paving stones as they walked. Even in the industrial district, the roads were nice.

Fre nudged his arm, drawing attention to a large glass line running through the center of the road. "Shia, they've even protected the lower quarters with Leys. Just how rich is this city?"

He glanced at Fre, who raised an eyebrow, "So, we're here. What are we looking for again?"

Quintin rubbed his chin, looking at the rows of buildings. "I'm not sure. A districting office, a local treasury, any place where they've got records on hand for the local businesses."

Fre sighed, "That was a lot easier done in our last few cities. This place winds worse than the Arvarian Laberythn."

Quintin nodded; he'd never heard of such a place, but he understood the idea. This place was a maze. He grumbled, a little unsure of where to start. Fre's stomach rumbled, giving him pause.

"Would you like to find a place to stay before we look? Maybe ask around for information?"

Fre grasped her stomach at the request, thinking a moment before nodding.

Quintin smiled as his hand moved down to the heavy purse on his side, "Where do you want to stay? It's not like we lack options."

Fre smiled, "Then let's head upwards; all the good food is in the upper districts."

Quintin led the way upward, eyes glancing over every sign and advertisement available from the road. Food seemed to dominate the commercial scene, with only the occasional furniture store or clothier dotting the landscape.

"Thea help us," Quintin grumbled, thinking of the amount of time that would be needed to scour this place just to find a district office.

Fre nudged him, gathering his attention, pointing to a large stone building across the road. "That place looks fancy; you think anyone there can help us with directions?"

Quintin scanned the building over. They had money from the last town, enough that they didn't look like urchins coming here, but kids were normally looked down upon.

"We can try. Seems like they may have some hemasti steak. We can always enjoy lunch if nothing else."

Walking up to the tavern, Quintin felt the cool air indicating glyph cooling, an oddity in many places in the empire. He did a quick scan of the patrons, noting most were above the age of a hundred, with greying hair, and dressed in plain but well-tailored clothes.

"I don't see any old people here," Fre said. "Looks like mostly seasoned merchants."

Quintin nodded in agreement. No one here looked like they were older than most middle-aged merchants, meaning information would be high and scrutiny low. The last thing they wanted were nobles and Thean Heirs poking into their business. The tender led them to a table in the corner. Quintin nodded his thanks. It felt odd.

The 'kid' was probably twice Quintin's age if he had to guess, though you couldn't tell until a person hit sixty to see any real difference.

"Can I get you two anything to start?" the tender asked, "We have some great options for drinks."

Quintin shook his head, "I'll just have a water."

He looked to Fre. "I'll have some ale if that's okay. Your cheapest option will do."

The tender nodded. "I'll get those right out to you both. Will there be any food today?"

"Some lizard steaks will do fine," Quintin said.

The tender nodded, "I'll tell the cook to get two cuts of hemasti onto the grill."

Quintin sat back as the tender receded to the kitchen with his little pad of paper. "Well now, all we need to do is figure out who to talk to in this place."

Fre glanced over to the bar by the kitchen. "Don't look like much of a talkative crowd, eh?"

Quintin nodded, "Not really. We'll see what we can do, but first, let's eat."

The pair watched as the tender arrived from the kitchen with their drinks. "Your food will be out in a moment. Anything I can get you?"

The man glanced at the pair expectantly.

"Yes, actually," Quintin said, "We're looking for the districting office in the city. Do you know where I can find it?"

The tender shook his head, "Sorry, I don't really have any experience with that. I'd check the local inns. They'd have more information than I."

Quintin nodded as he ran his fingers through his hair. "Ok then. We'll be sure to check there. Thanks."

The server nodded nervously, clearly unsure of how to take the visible disappointment on Quintin's face. The man moved a table over to talk to another customer, leaving the pair to sit with their drinks. Quintin gulped down half his water in one go before watching Fre do the same to her ale.

"You should be careful with that," Quintin said, concerned, "Your tolerance is worse than a child's."

Fre waved him off, downing the second half, "The food will dampen it," pausing as she burped, "Besides, it's so cheap it could just be spiced water."

They stopped the conversation as the food arrived; their attention turned to the steaming plates of food in front of them. Quintin ate his food silently. The sound of the surrounding booths faded into a white blanket as he cut up the gamey steak. The tender came by, and Quintin passed off the silver.

Glancing over to Fre, he smiled, "You look tired."

Fre sighed, sitting up and leaning forward, "I feel like I've eaten a balloon full of sand."

Quintin raised an eyebrow. He hadn't heard that one yet. "We'll get a room here momentarily. Able to walk?"

Fre pulled her chair out and stood, teetering for a moment before righting herself. "I'll be fine; let's go." She pointed, walking clumsily towards the door.

Stepping out into the street, Quintin scanned the shops. The upper citizenry was prime territory for safe information. Getting a place to stay here would offer greater safety, though it would cost more. Quintin's hand traveled to the purse at his waist.

"We're going to need some extra cash." Quintin looked over to Fre, "Can you set up a place for us to stay? I need to get us some silver."

He tossed the purse to Fre. She glanced at him, "Meet back here at midnight?"

Quintin nodded, "If I'm not back by then, consider leaving town."

Fre nodded, "Catch you then."

She turned as Quintin waved, her slight frame vanishing quickly into the crowd. *It's amazing how she does that,* Quintin thought. He brushed his pants off, composing himself for what came next. They needed some silver, and the docks had plenty of scraps to collect. Not the most legal thing one could do. Though, with success so close, Quintin was willing to take the risk.

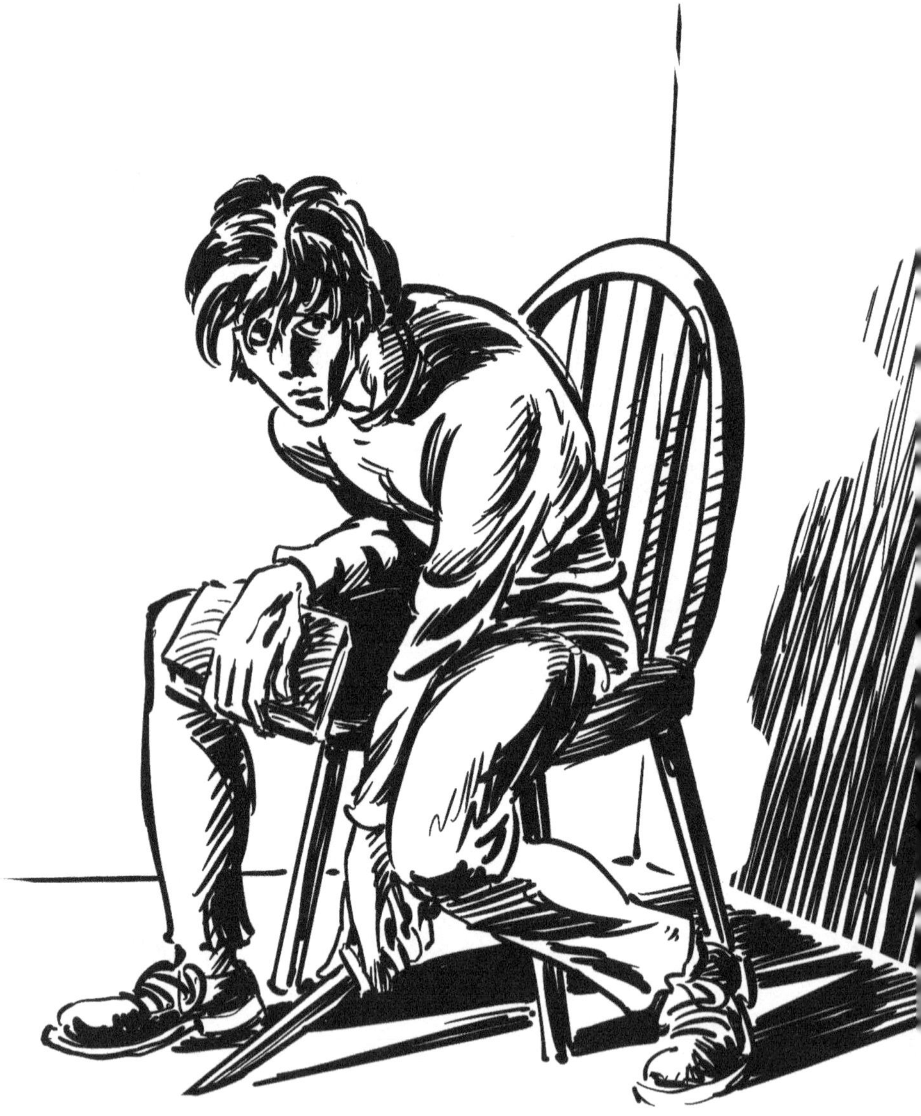

CHAPTER 2

The air grew cool as the sun began to relinquish its hold on the world. The summer heat faded like a bad dream. Quintin looked at the sunset. All it meant to him was the cover the darkness provided. The docks were unlike many places in the city where commercial and urban sectors began to empty as it grew dark.

The mills, and the adjacent docks, continued their relentless business. Ducking into an alley, Quintin wove through the small spaces between storage buildings. Coming out to the water's edge, he began to creep towards the lights of the mills. Quintin felt the rumble of machinery and the clatter of carts as he drew near.

The docks stirred with men hurling boxes of unprocessed ore and tools from one area to another, the rhyme or reason lost to Quintin as he watched. Isel stood as the only place in the Empire legally allowed to process the nation's silver – a byproduct of imperial expansion over the last century. It was at these docks that raw ore would come in, and refined silver would be shipped to the imperial mint and weapons manufacturers around the nation. Quintin scanned the dock. The mills were overpopulated as expected, making salvaging scrap metal nigh impossible. He was looking for something a little quieter. His gaze fell upon a small building offset from the rest with a sign displaying the imperial signet hanging above the door.

"Bingo." Quintin smiled.

Crouching in the shadows, he slipped across the cobbled street. The building had a small smokestack along with several windows. He located some empty crates. Propping them up against the wall, he peeked into the workshop below. A rudimentary glance over the workbenches and small furnace confirmed his suspicion. In such a large city full of nobles and royalty, the demand for pure silver would be huge. A silversmith would be in charge of such requests.

The care required to ensure a set of lockplate could be supplied or a family heirloom repaired meant passing the work over to a more trustworthy and responsible professional. Quintin glanced over to the smithy's staff. There were three people – two assistants, a young woman and man – and an elderly man Quintin assumed to be the smith. Quintin cracked the window, the chatter of conversation traveling up from the group.

"Watch the hilt, Shia, boy. This isn't a race!"

The old man grimaced as the younger man poured glass from a ceramic pot onto a piece of silver. Globs of white-hot glass splattered, causing the woman to jump back in surprise.

"Goodness boy, is that how you plan to handle all your commissions?"

The elder man took the piece of silver, the shape of which Quintin now recognized as an unfinished sword. The older man sat the proto-sword into a vice.

Careful not to put pressure on the glass lattice his apprentice just poured, the smith wiped his forehead, sighing. "That's all for today. We'll sand down this mess tomorrow and get a handle put on it."

He turned to his assistants, "Sheri, if you can, write up a receipt when you get home. Arbur, you can calculate our expenses."

The pair nodded. They paused a moment, the two waiting for the smith to say something.

"Get out, the both of you!" The smith waved his hands, shooing them away.

The pair jumped, scrambling out the door. The smith sighed as he turned to the unfinished weapon.

"What am I going to do about you? Seems you always come out wrong."

The old man threw a cloth over the project as if laying a loved one to rest. "I'm getting a meal from the mess hall. You stay here till I can finish you."

The elderly smith shuffled over to the door. He turned to look at the shop before turning out the light. Quintin waited for the door to click shut. He moved immediately, sliding the window open even further, squeezing through the gap. His feet hit the floor with a thud. Quintin winced, pausing to see if the sound had caused interest outside. Quintin didn't wait any longer, moving to the workbench and rummaging through the projects on the table. He pocketed handfuls of unfinished jewelry. His eyes landed on a long piece of silver in the back. Pulling it out from a pile of cloth, his eyes lit up as he recognized the four edges tapering up to a point.

A dockworker yelled something outside, reminding Quintin that he was on a time limit. Tucking the unfinished weapon into his belt, he moved to the smith's most recent project. Fre had gone months without her own weapon, breaking her last one during an altercation with a town's guard.

This one wouldn't do that. Pulling the cloth off the glass encrusted blade, it looked even less completed than the sword that had broken. Quintin felt Fre could make it work. Pulling the unwieldy object from its vice, Quintin tucked it beside the other.

"Looks like I'm finding us a place to clean these up."

Satisfied with the amount of silver in his pockets and purse, he turned to leave. The window wasn't an option; the space was too cluttered with sharp objects to safely climb or jump. Quintin needed to slip out quickly without being noticed. "Should be possible. It's dark enough the dock workers won't make out faces, just act like you belong…"

He adjusted the blades so they'd be obstructed by his legs while walking. Quintin stepped up to the door, preparing his escape. Pulling the latch, he swung the door outward. His eyes met those of the elderly smith, several feet away, frozen in place as he registered what was happening.

"Shia, I took too long." Quintin gave the man a smile before turning and racing down the cobbled street.

"Oy!" the smith yelled, "Thief! Guards, we have a thief!"

Quintin continued to run, not daring to turn to look. He could hear the clatter of steel-shod boots on stone behind him. The air cracked, and a bolt flew past Quintin's head, followed by cursing as one guard slowed his pace in order to reprime his ratchet bow. Quintin didn't wait for the rest of his pursuers to fire a bolt, ducking between two buildings.

The upper citizenry had far more symmetrical alley layouts, making losing the guards difficult. Shots echoed behind him. Either they were calling more guards, or they planned to cut Quintin off. His eyes raced over his surroundings, and time began to slow around him as his adrenaline spiked.

Keeping to the streets is a bad idea. I need a way up.

He looked to the buildings, almost none of which had peaked roofs. His eyes rested on a large trash bin pushed against a building. "That will work."

The world began to return to normal. Quintin's mind started slowing down. Racing to the bin, Quintin hurdled himself onto it before leaping five feet to the roof above. His hands met the gutters, iron digging uncomfortably into his palms. Throwing himself onto the roof, Quintin didn't stop running. He could hear soldiers below him, armor clattering as they searched.

The danger faded with each alley he crossed without being noticed by the guards below. Quintin grew calm, slowing to a mild joy as he lazily leapt from building to building. The upper citizenry sat above the slums. There was a stark contrast of the well-lit streets, which ended abruptly at the divide between the two. The slums were Quintin's first destination. There he could find an abandoned building where silver would be processed away from prying eyes.

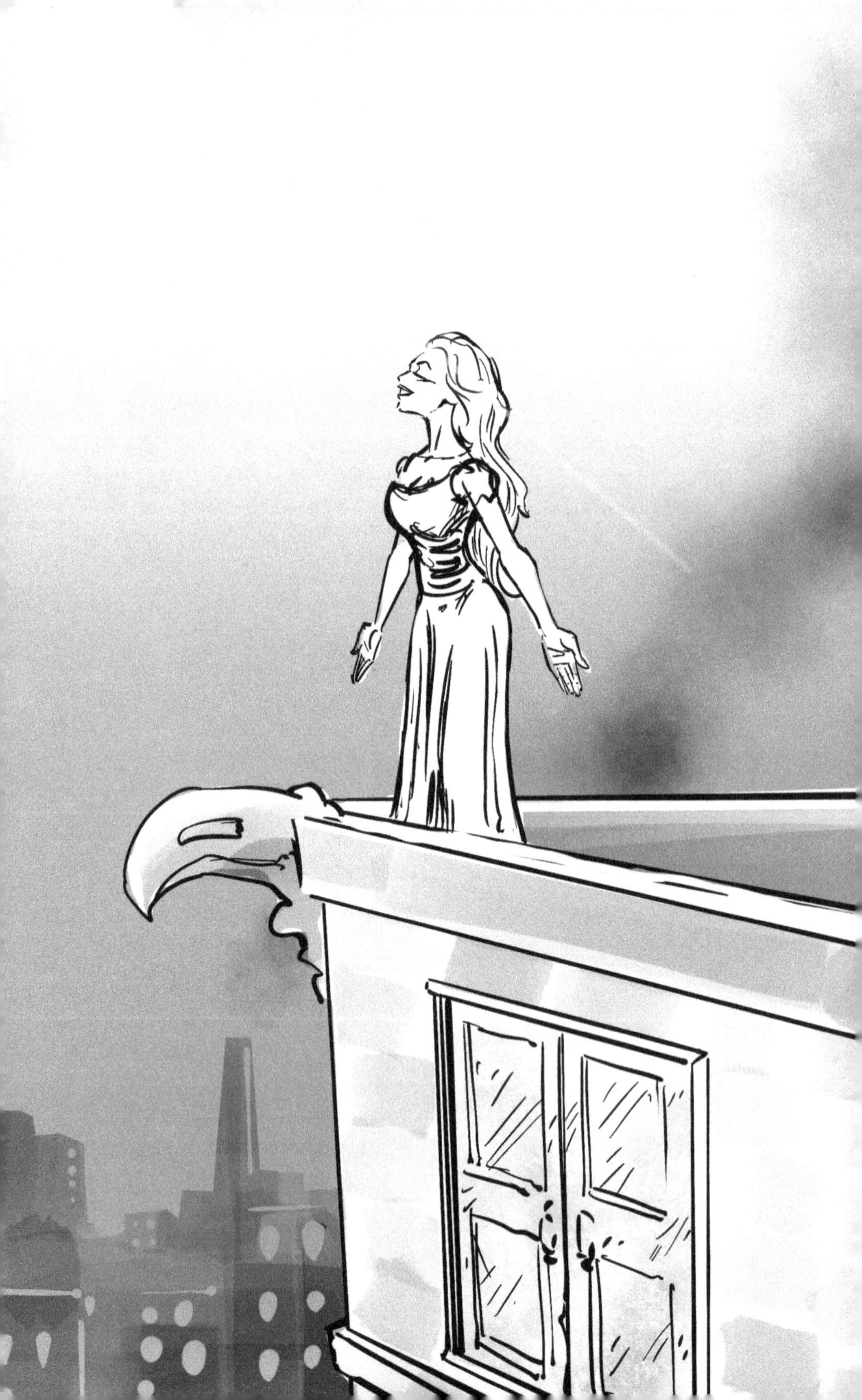

CHAPTER 3

Selyne leaned forward, brushing aside her hair as she stared at the page in front of her. Grasping her pen in her hand, she pressed the nib into the sheet and began to write. She sat a moment, ink bleeding into the page, creating a blot on the paper.

She stared, hands not moving. "Shia, this is stupid."

Selyne grumbled, tossing aside the paper. The crumpled page fell beside the small waste bin, joining the dozen other pages Selyne had tossed away. She leaned back in the chair, tossing the pen aside, grabbing the sheet of paper her mother had left for her. It had to be the most infuriating list of chores she'd ever been given. Seriously, why was she writing invitations to the local nobility, wasn't that a job better left to the secretaries?

Footsteps echoed up the stairwell of the Spire, alerting Selyne of a visitor. *What does she want now?* Selyne sighed as a knock came at the door.

"Come in," she called, voice resigned.

The door creaked open slowly, and Selyne's mother poked her head in. "Am I disrupting anything?"

She looked at the crumpled pages littering the floor.

Selyne shook her head, "It's no issue. What did you want?"

Her mother slid the door closed and pulled up Selyne's extra chair, never a good sign.

"Something happened at the silversmiths. There was a break-in. The royal guard is looking into it." Her mother wrung her hands nervously – she was leading to something.

"Ok, sounds bad. Why are you telling me this? It's almost bedtime." Selyne leaned forward as her mother composed herself.

"The objects stolen weren't just simple jewelry. Several state-of-the-art weapons, your Imperator included, were taken deliberately." she paused. "I talked to your father just an hour ago, and we think it would be best if you have someone with you while we sort this out."

Selyne grew cold as the words sank in. "So we're now resorting to babysitting. That's ridiculous."

"It's nothing like that," her mother reassured, "Just with what the seer said and now this. We need you protected, especially with the potential of syndicate involvement. Our common escorts will not be able to keep you safe."

Selyne rolled her eyes. They didn't need her. They needed the title. "Heaven forbid they need to elect a new imperial line."

Her mother stared at her critically. "Are we clear on this matter?"

"Yes," Selyne said sharply.

Her mother nodded, though her expression still seemed dissatisfied. "Well then, expect us to find someone within this week. We'll also be restarting your schooling. The Thean Universities are going to prove much safer until we sort this out."

Selyne hardly acknowledged her mother's words. She was tired more than anything. Talking to her mother always did that. The pair sat in silence for a minute, waiting for something to break the impasse.

"I'll be going now," her mother said gently, "Try to sleep tonight."

Selyne nodded, "I'll try."

Her mother left the door cracked, but Selyne shut it promptly.

"This is bloody horrid. Why does she even bother talking to me? Could just as well leave a note on my door." Selyne grumbled as she dragged herself from her chair, wandering over to her wardrobe, scanning her selection of coats.

"I imagine Lawrence and Aril are at the pub about now. Maybe I should send a runner." She paused the thought.

Her mother would probably catch a courier leaving the Spire. She didn't want that talk again, at least not until tomorrow. She grabbed a heavy brown coat that would hide stains well and slipped on her heavy leather boots. Next, Selyne pulled out the ornate clips holding her hair back, choosing instead some of her older jewelry.

Her typical pub sat in the noble sector of the city, but she had found rather quickly that the difference in the attire was palpable. Feeling comfortable with the way she looked, Selyne cracked open her window, crawling out onto the balcony overlooking the city. Selyne caught her breath as she leaned over.

It was several hundred feet to the ground, a fall that would kill even the strongest man. *Let's hope our private seer isn't wrong about this.* Selyne took a deep breath, focusing on the air around her. The process was said to get easier with time, though Selyne wasn't so sure. The air around her started to change. Many Heirs had a sense for the threads they could control around them, and Selyne was no different. Her eyes focused on the tangled mess of threads that moved in infinitely complex swirls. Resonance didn't make any sense, and there was no amount of training you could do to learn its secrets. Either you were blessed with it or you weren't, according to the seers.

Selyne could not only perceive the threads but harness them. She reached out, her body beginning to hum gently as it began to resonate with the threads, almost like a tuning fork. Selyne felt a gentle warmth as the threads around her intertwined with hers. The air began to spin erratically, curling around her arms and resting in her hands.

Selyne smiled at the feeling, "Now it's time for the big one."

She stared dubiously at the ground below her. This was supposed to work instantly if she heard correctly, "Guess all that's left to do is jump?"

Placing her hands on the railing, Selyne shoved herself into the open air. The panic didn't come as she had expected. Instead, there was only calm, like a martial artist performing a form for the thousandth time. The air began to coalesce around her, distributing itself unevenly over her body, positioning her to land feet first.

Pressure began to increase underneath her arms, causing Selyne to wince as her arms strained at the pull of air. The sensation only lasted a moment as her feet contacted the marble paving stones. Selyne released the air around her, feeling as if she'd just come out of a daze.

Blinking, she looked around her. She had made it over the wall surrounding the Spire without the guards noticing. Judging from the paving stones, she had also landed in the noble sector.

"Now then, let's see if Aril is at the pub. Maybe I can steal a drink off her."

Pulling her coat close and surveying the roads for spectators, Selyne began the walk down the paved roads. Walking through the noble district always made her feel lonely. Its ornate parks and fountains were unable to compensate for the desolate streets. The rigid atmosphere was the reason she avoided the bars in the upper districts. Selyne couldn't drink in such a solemn place.

Fortunately, the walk to the citizen's district wasn't long. Selyne took another turn, a smile creeping onto the edges of her mouth as the noise of normal life echoed through the stone building. Her feet began to quicken their pace, eager to join the masses. Selyne moved automatically, her legs knowing instinctively where she wanted to go. It wasn't long before she stood at the doors of Cern's Bar.

She didn't waste any time pushing open the doors. Her eyes scanned the room, resting upon a tall figure behind the bar. The man met her gaze, returning a warm smile to her. Selyne sauntered over to a barstool, seating herself in front of him.

"Quiet night, huh, Cairn?" she asked, staring at the hushed customers huddled in corners of the room.

Cairn Cern, the owner of the establishment, shrugged. "It is after dinner. Currently I expect only a trickle of late workers and bored nobility."

Selyne sniffed in disinterest, "No sign of Aril anywhere."

She sighed – it was going to be a lonely night.

"Hey Cairn," Selyne asked, "what's the strangest thing you have on tap tonight?"

Cairn gave her a critical look. Selyne picked some lint off the front of her jacket.

He sighed, "I've got some Thailian beer which will put a grown Rhinil out after one pint. Though I should warn you, it's not cheap."

Selyne rolled her eyes. He always gave her that warning, and he knew how little she cared. She laid a silver quarter on the table, "I'll take three to begin. I'm not leaving until I can't remember this tomorrow."

* * * * * *

Fre glanced nervously at the clock. Quintin was late. Again. *He went to the mills. Chances are he's looking for a place we can work in the lower quarter.*

The door to the inn opened, and Fre glanced to see who it was. A soldier stepped in, dressed in lockplate, and took a seat next to Fre at the bar.

It wouldn't be so concerning if we hadn't picked up the worst possible inn in the city to meet, she thought. Fre glanced to her other companion at the bar. The lady dressed in an indistinct coat over a faded blue dress with trousers underneath. It looked normal, but the cut was wrong.

Fre watched as the woman chatted with the barkeep, wondering if maybe she was nobility looking to burn off some steam. Fre snorted with derision into her mug. *It wasn't an uncommon sight, though if you were going to try to use a disguise, at least find a seamstress in the citizenry to make you the right clothes.*

Their eyes met for a moment. Fre averted her gaze a moment too late as the intoxicated woman scooted closer. *Shia, leave me alone.*

The woman downed the last of her drink, "Are you new here? I haven't seen your face around before."

Fre smiled faintly, "I just arrived this morning."

The woman's eyes gleamed in what seemed to be a genuine interest, "Really? Tell me what it's like out east. Is it really as wild as they say?"

Fre raised an eyebrow, reasoning that she must not have been completely oblivious to the situation despite her intoxication. Looking at the woman's flushed face, Fre marveled at an Ithean's ability to drink themselves senseless.

Given the woman's heritage, she'd probably been drinking hours before Fre had arrived.

Fre laughed wryly, "Trust me, this place feels like a hospital for how clean everything is. Even your words feel sterile."

The woman nodded, "It's so dumb. Seriously, I can't say anything without my mother coming for me."

She picked up her glass before realizing it was empty and cussing. Fre glanced at the door, irritated at Quintin's tardiness and mentally begging him to hurry up. Fre turned back to the woman, smiling and nodding absently as she continued.

"She wants me indoors all day, surrounded by stuffy scribes at the university, all because of some petty theft."

The woman was coming close to shouting or crying. Fre couldn't tell which.

"Shia, it hasn't even been a day, and she's made that decision." The woman waved to the barkeep, who hesitated. She glared, and the man sighed before going to the back.

The woman fiddled with her cup, "Listen, kid, don't ever let anyone load you with more responsibility than you need. It'll squash you."

The woman held out her glass and let the barkeep refill it. *The way she's acting,* Fre thought, *one would think she just lost a loved one.*

Fre sipped her own drink. It wasn't anything she needed to care for.

"Am I interrupting something?" a voice asked behind Fre.

She turned, along with her inebriated companion.

"Shia, look at those eyes!" the woman gasped at the figure standing behind her.

Fre almost choked as her eyes went to the uniform the man wore. It had royal markers. Her mind immediately wondered what Quintin had done and why this man was here. She took a sip of her drink to hide her face.

"No sir," she said as she shook her head, "She was just giving me some advice. I haven't met her before tonight."

The man raised an eyebrow, the lights catching on his eyes.

"Those really are remarkable eyes."

The woman fumbled with her drink, sloshing it everywhere.

He smiled, "An interesting choice to accept advice from."

Smiling nervously, Fre wondered if he knew something she didn't.

He turned to the woman, "However, tonight, you're my concern. I'm sure you recognize my uniform?"

The woman wrinkled her nose in disgust as she looked at the pins on his chest, "Bloody hell, mother. I'm guessing you're my babysitter for tonight?"

The man shrugged, "Something like that."

Fre couldn't process the conversation – royal guard? Babysitter? Mother?

The context of the situation was growing more concerning as the conversation went on. Fre's attention was brought back as the woman let out a loud sigh.

"At least she had the decency to send someone pretty."

Fre sat back, watching as the man offered his hand, "I'm flattered, but a little pressed for time. Let's go."

The woman downed her glass and took his hand, "Well, by all means, don't let me get you into trouble."

Fre watched as the woman nearly tumbled out of her chair. The man propped her up with his arm.

"There we are. Let's get you home."

Fre watched as he led her out the door, shaken by the whole ordeal. Now that that was complete, her mind went back to Quintin, who was still absent. She glared at the time on the clock. She sat, watching the room; had this been the right place?

Finally, her worries were assuaged. Quintin pushed aside the front door, his slight frame and unkempt hair unmistakable. He glanced around the room until his eyes met hers. Weaving through the dinner time crowd, he pushed between customers, trying his best not to be smothered by the masses. He gave a wary glance towards the guard as he sat beside Fre at the bar.

She sipped her newly refilled glass looking at Quintin critically and speaking in a voice equally so, "You're late."

Quintin waved the bartender near, raising three fingers to indicate which tap he wanted. Fre watched, eyebrow raised, as she waited for his response. Quintin waited until the man served his drink before saying anything. He did one last check with his eyes, causing Fre to wonder exactly how big of a stir he had caused to be this nervous. Fre opened her mouth to say something, but he started before she could.

"I ran into some trouble down in the lower quarters," he said suddenly, "I got what we needed plus a little extra."

Fre closed her mouth, recalculating what she wanted to say. "So, do we have a place to work down there?"

She took a small sip as she started to feel the heat in her face, reminding herself to stop before regretting the decision the next day. Fre's mind turned to the woman she had met earlier. She wondered if she would talk so openly if she ever got inebriated? A lot of the drunks she'd met had either yelled in anger or cried. She pushed the glass away, convicted by prior observances.

Quintin downed his first glass in one titanic gulp, an action that was betrayed by his slight frame. He gasped, setting the cup to the side and turned his attention to Fre.

"I found an old warehouse on the canal. I've put all our stuff there." He seemed distracted as he spoke.

"Did you get spotted?" Fre asked. "You look on edge."

Quintin didn't say anything but nodded. Fre sighed, staring at the drink. It wouldn't be safe for her to drink anymore. She glanced at Quintin ordering his next glass.

"Burn the Ithean constitution and their over-distilled alcohol along with it," Fre sighed, thinking about the issue at hand. "It's going to be okay."

He nodded, "We're okay, but staying in the upper citizenry may not favor us these next few days."

His eyes lit up as a thought occurred, "Hey, did you manage to find any records on my father's company?"

Fre had to resist cringing at the question. She had asked around, going so far as the slums for intel. The response had been conclusive.

"Quintin," she looked at him with a pained expression, "The company dissolved the branch here eight months ago."

The spark in Quintin's eye dimmed. He didn't look upset, though Fre found the lack of concentration far more troublesome. He felt less human when he withdrew behind that face.

"Did you hear what happened?" he asked.

"I talked to some peers in the slums. They mentioned a crack down from Emerald Syphon. They're the criminal syndicate ruling this city. Apparently, they forcibly removed hundreds of businesses around the same time."

Fre watched as Quintin put pieces together in his head. "I presume my father's business wasn't going well."

He looked to Fre, and she confirmed his query with a nod, "They stopped receiving resources from the business network, making it impossible to sustain business under the pressures of taxation and criminal extortion."

Fre shrugged, "If it's any consolation, the records strongly suggest your parents didn't set foot on this side of the continent."

Quintin's brow furrowed at the statement, "What exactly are you implying?"

He sipped his third glass while Fre sniffed in indifference at the injustice, "I went to several district offices and tax firms. None of them could explain what had happened. Though they mentioned that the syndicate had sabotaged each business."

Quintin scratched his chin; an action Fre found silly. He didn't have any facial hair, nor would he ever.

"You think they had something to do with our predicament out east?" he asked, a twinge of venom in his voice.

Fre shrugged, "The timelines are a stretch, though looking at the examples laid out in the city's records, I found several assassinations, arson, and ransoms of loved ones."

Quintin nodded at the last one and smiled. "You've been busy today. All I did was point a target on our back."

Fre dismissed the statement, "Trust me after you see the fees I had to pay, you'll reconsider the value of your work."

Quintin's smile grew as he downed his third glass, and Fre returned the gesture. He needed to stay in a sound state. She had seen him retreat into himself before. The whole thing had eaten him up. Worse, Fre couldn't survive in a place so far from home without someone.

"I'll have to show you the place I set up. It's got a lot of space to work."

Quintin's eyes got a dangerous sheen as he grinned in a predatory fashion, "It also will put me in the perfect position to figure out just who runs this city. Emerald Syphon was the name, correct?"

Fre nodded. It had been a while since she'd worked on silver. It was a pastime she quite enjoyed. "We should get to bed. Best to get some rest while we can."

Quintin tossed some silver onto the bar, scooting out of his chair. "I hope you got us two beds this time. I've gotten sick of wooden floors this last month. My back is about to riot."

Fre gave him a dirty look, "Hey, I'm not the one concerned about funds. You better enjoy the bed. It's the last of our cash."

Quintin chuckled, "Trust me. I do."

Fre almost said more but held herself back. It was late, better to leave it for tomorrow. She let the comment rest as a future issue.

CHAPTER 4

Selyne sat up, head pounding from the night before. She winced, recoiling from the sunlight, trying desperately to recollect the night prior. *You know it's a fruitless endeavor. Figure out what we are supposed to do today.*

She didn't like the thought, though she knew it wasn't wrong. Best not to dwell on it. Fumbling, eyes refusing to adjust to the light, she searched her nightstand for her daily schedule. Her hands landed upon a paper sheet along with a glass of water. *Thank Thea for servants. Heaven knows how I would manage without them.*

Selyne sat facing her door, blocking the sunlight with her own shadow, scanning the page as she drank her water. *Mother's being rather lenient today. I would've expected retribution for direct disobedience on the scale of last night.* She scanned the page for anything abnormal. Her prerequisite classes were there as always. Social functions were the same for lunch and dinner. Selyne furrowed her brow as she realized other social functions were less than usual.

"No meetings with any local authorities. I know marriage proposals were off the table after my last attempt, but mother wouldn't leave me a day without some political practice."

Selyne stared at the suspiciously blank space on the page, attempting to pry out the secret behind its occurrence. Her eyes drifted down, focusing on the only other thing on the page. "Meeting with your mother after lunch." Selyne read the sentence aloud.

"Does she expect this meeting to take up the day?" she mused.

The idea was unnerving, to say the least. Selyne gulped down the rest of her water. She felt like she was finally able to prepare for the day. The process of getting ready moved along at a methodical rhythm. Selyne checked her pocket watch before slipping it into her dress pocket. She stepped out into the hall moments later. She'd have several minutes before anyone needed her. A sigh of relief escaped her lungs at the realization.

Turning away from the downward stairwell and her problems by proxy, Selyne turned to the stairs behind her and began her trek upwards. The Spire was immense in height, making it difficult for anyone to truly utilize all of its potential space. That hadn't stopped Selyne's father. Coming into the royal family as a promise from another kingdom, he had set about doing what he did best, establishing himself as the strongest person in the room, only the room had been the size of a continent.

Selyne's mother had utilized this perfectly, doing what she did best and establishing herself as the smartest person in the room. Suffice to say, Selyne was going up to what could effectively be called a glorified storage closet; only this storage closet housed an empire's worth of stuff. Selyne found her parents excessive to an extreme. Though Selyne acknowledged the solitude their years of collection allowed.

She passed the last of the servant housing on floor twenty. Here, tapestries began to appear hanging on walls, along with paintings from bygone nations. Selyne passed her first room. This one held several locks on its door. Her father claimed it housed his private collection of armor, though Selyne had never seen its interior.

She continued to pass similarly locked doorways, many of which she didn't know the contents of. The stairwells grew ever tighter as she continued up higher. Selyne slowed as she reached the bend leading to the fiftieth floor, stopping in front of a secluded door in between floors.

The room was considered an oddity, and the royal masons would talk about its implications for hours if asked. Selyne didn't bother; it was far more valuable than that. She turned the handle easily. This room would never be locked. It had remained this way since she was a child.

The door swung inward, revealing shadows draping the cramped interior of the room. Selyne reached a hand to the side of the wall, finding a small switch on the side and flipping it upwards. Light hummed to life as the small crystalline lattices transmitted Resonance throughout, saturating the place in a comfortable white glow. Selyne let herself have a small smile as she stared at the wall lined with dozens of books, games, and childhood projects. The study wasn't a true library. The Spire had a library on the eighth floor, which was more befitting of the title.

No, this was a place that now only held value for Selyne alone. She seated herself on one of the dust-covered chairs, breathing in the memories. Selyne turned to the small table beside the chair. The dust on its surface was disturbed, the majority of space taken up by a recent pile of books. Selyne rummaged through the stack, coming up with a small leather book. Its red leather cover was worn with use. Selyne cracked open the pages, the book's aged binding creaking with the movement.

Fingering through several pages, Selyne came to her place marked by a receipt from last week. *A Brief Summary of Thea's Local Deities and Their Respective Mythos.* Selyne read the title of the book at the top of the page. The manuscript wasn't a difficult read, designed as a primer for preteens. That was much of why Selyne loved the book, along with the dozens of others lining the shelves. Their beauty was in the simplicity in which they described the world.

Selyne started reading, beginning halfway through a chapter. Her headache receded as she continued through the pages, hours passing as Selyne lost herself to the story of Solus and the Thailian pilgrims, El and his miracles, even Shia and her terrible beauty.

"Imagine, I'm supposed to be related to these stories." Selyne shook her head at the sheer insanity of the notion. "Clearly, divinity isn't what it's dressed up to be, or our theologians are horribly wrong."

Selyne smiled to herself, thinking of what the implications would be if she joined the Church of Solus. "I couldn't step back into a Thean church ever again – the empress denied from the State religion."

Selyne paused in her amusement, a thought muddying her mood.

She pulled out her watch, glancing at the time. Selyne had missed lunch while reading. Unfortunately, her mother wouldn't be happy about that, and she was next up on her schedule in thirty minutes. "It's not the greatest start to a potentially dangerous conversation," Selyne sighed as she thought of her mother's look of disapproval. "Putting it off won't get us anything useful. Better to get it off and done with as soon as possible."

Selyne placed her book gently onto the top of the stack, "I'll be back tonight, don't you worry." She closed the door gently behind her and walked quickly down to the tenth floor.

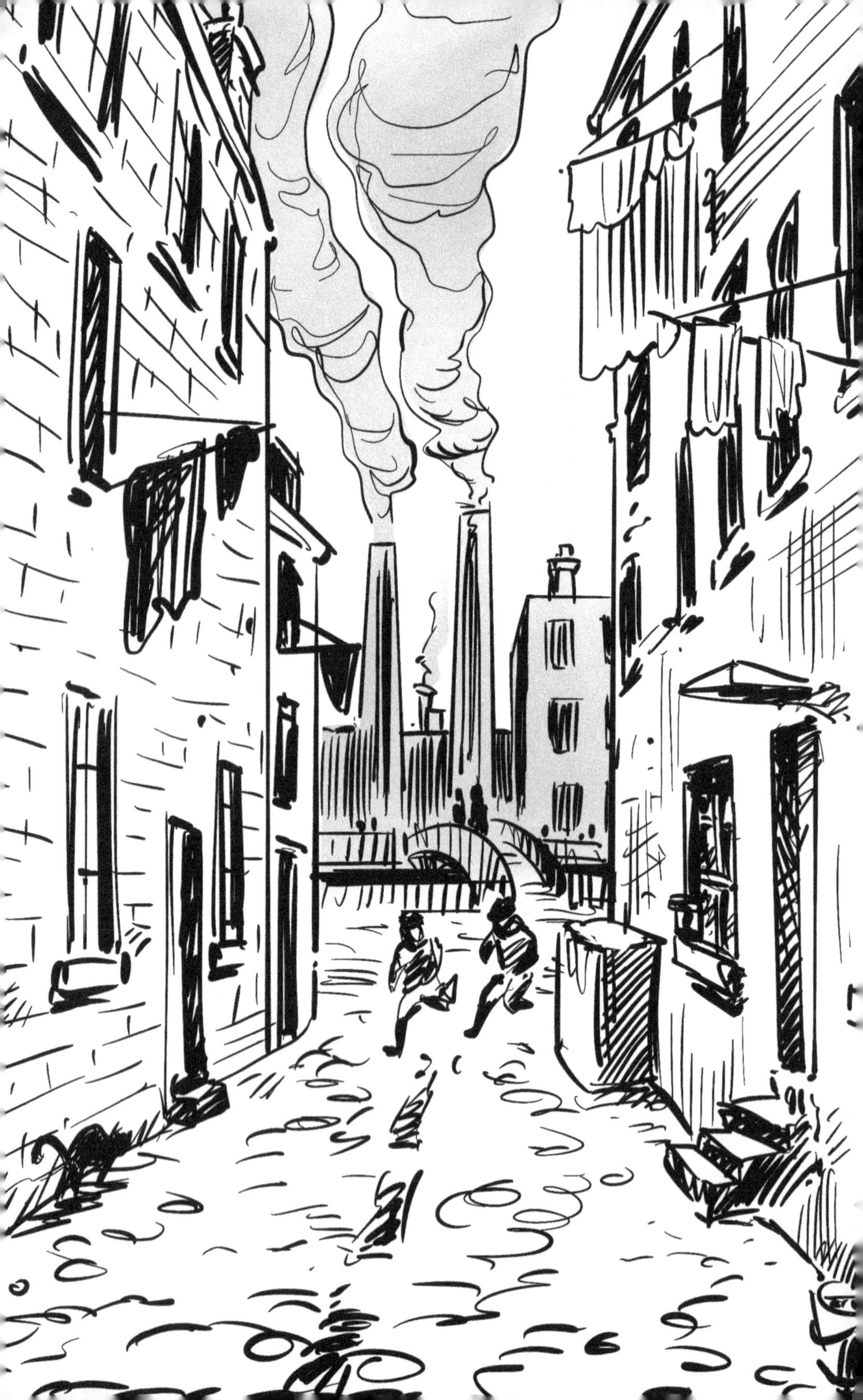

CHAPTER 5

The morning sun didn't reach the streets of the lower citizenry of Isel. The city had been built into a hill, the walls reinforced by the tons of dirt and rock they retained, all while letting the civilians build upon an elevated base looking over the surrounding land. However, when stones had been laid on the surface of the hill to create a base for the city, the builders had neglected to properly level the earth. Quintin wasn't sure if they'd intended for the city to slope downwards from its center, but he appreciated the shade the buildings offered.

He walked through the winding streets, Fre trailing close behind. The pair worked their way to the slums. The night prior had found Quintin in a rush. Despite this, he figured he'd found an above-par place to set up shop. The pair turned off the streets onto the canal walkway.

"Which one is ours?" Fre asked, glancing over the decrepit buildings lining the canal.

Quintin smiled, pointing to an old factory building across the water. "I looked it over last night and found no evidence of squatters. Also, it still has several tables and a back room with a functioning lock."

His voice echoed with satisfaction as he recalled the interior of the abandoned factory.

Fre nodded, smiling as she noticed Quintin's smug expression. "Sounds like it's worth a look."

She gestured to a bridge leading over the canal. Quintin followed Fre as she tested it. Unlike the bridges further west, these didn't have government funding to maintain them. The wooden beams creaked uneasily as they inched across, Quintin wincing at each loose board. After a few hour-like minutes, Quintin breathed a sigh of relief, feet planting themselves firmly on the other side.

Fre didn't pause, strolling over to the old building. She tapped the small side door, and it swung inward, rust flaking off the hinges as the door protested its use. Fre raised an eyebrow, glancing down at the red dust powdering her trousers.

"It's a work in progress," Quintin reassured.

She rolled her eyes and stepped inside. Quintin stepped in after her, careful to close the door behind him so that he would hear anyone should they enter. He surveyed the interior, eyes scanning over the derelict furniture. What had been vague shadows the night before now revealed themselves to be dozens of abandoned workstations, each one stripped of their equipment years ago and in various states of disrepair.

Quintin pointed to a door located at the back of the room, "That room over there is what really sells the place."

"I don't think you need to sell me on anything," Fre said, her words carrying the hint of condescension that often tinted Fre's words when she thought Quintin was being silly.

He shrugged it off. Regardless of what was needed, his peace of mind wouldn't be set until he knew his eggs were all in the basket. The backroom had once been the office for whichever merchant had control over these silver-steel mills in the years before the emperor's insistence on all silver being processed in royal facilities.

Unlike the other door, this one's hinges didn't spew oxidized iron everywhere, the chrome plating remaining intact after all these years. A single window filtered a greyish-white light from the alleyway outside, creating an atmosphere that fit the tired feel of the old office. Fre stepped up to one of the workbenches, opening up the various drawers and leaning firmly on it to check its strength.

She nodded, "Honestly, I'm surprised the tables haven't been taken considering their condition."

Fre set a small bag onto the table, removing various tools from within.

"Would you like to see what we're working with?" Quintin asked, "I got us some real ankle biters."

Fre watched as Quintin almost ran into the small closet fitted into the back of the room. He emerged a moment later, a small bag in his left hand and a large bundle tucked into his right.

"Have you checked the streets for wanted posters?" Fre asked, shocked by the sheer amount of metal he had grabbed, "Several nobles are probably frothing at the mouth to get their hands on you."

The words only seemed to bolster Quintin's excitement, a grin appearing on his face as he set the pile onto the table. Fre picked through the folded cloth, revealing the blued steel underneath. She pulled each blade out from their storage, inspecting the color of both. Her eyes landed on the second one's surface, noting the globules of glass coating it.

"This is not what I think it is," Fre said in disbelief, turning to Quintin, searching for any sign of deception or mischief.

His previous grin expanded even further, simply shrugging at the question. "I figured this would be a good pastime, something to do while I'm walking the slums tonight."

Fre paused, looking at him critically. "You're really going out today?"

She seemed to deflate as she asked the question. Quintin nodded, though he felt like he'd done something wrong,

"Better to gather information as quickly as possible. The less time we spend in this city, the better."

Fre nodded, though she didn't seem completely convinced.

Quintin grabbed his bag, along with the plate-breaker dagger from off the pile of silver bangles.

"Make sure that weapon is finished. The handle looks a little loose?" Fre asked.

Quintin shrugged, "I'll take the chance; I have my short in the back if things go wrong."

Fre sighed but didn't say anything more on the subject. "When do you plan to be back?" she asked.

Quintin paused, thinking for a moment. "Expect me back by dark. I won't want to stay on unfamiliar streets after sunset."

Fre nodded, "I guess I'll see you then."

Quintin smiled, opening the door. "I'll be sure to see you first."

Fre watched as the door closed behind Quintin with a soft click. A moment later, she heard the grinding of rusted hinges as he left the complex. She turned back towards the pile of silver on the table, "Shia, he really did go overboard this time."

Fre pushed aside the smaller bits of jewelry. Those would be melted down later, focusing instead on the sword in front of her. The weapon was nearly completed, missing only a handle; the glass globbed onto the edge would need removal. Fre pulled a file out of the bag she'd brought with her and began to grind down the glass. The process was tedious. If she used too much force or a tool with too much bite, she risked shattering the lattice, rending the glyphs engraved onto the blade useless.

Fre dwelled in the little details, enjoying the care required with each section of the blade. *I hope he's okay.* Fre knew just how confident Quintin sat in his own ability. These last few years, he'd been sure of success in finding his parents. The look on his face when they hit another dead end made her worried. *It doesn't help that he's being reckless. Honestly what kind of hair-brained thought process made him want to go out today.*

Fre set down her file, moving to some sandpaper for the finer details. She noted the glyph lattice underneath, confused, "Odd, I don't think I recognize this design."

Glyphs were difficult to work with, and making multiples work together to create a functional lattice required years of knowledge and practice. Generally, this meant silversmiths followed a set pattern for their swords as it guaranteed their functionality. To find an unfamiliar pattern was rare, to say the least. Fre ran the abrasive paper down the length of the lattice for several minutes before moving to a finer grain. The lattice looked most like those found on blaze-swords, though it contained far more electrical glyphs than expected, each one reinforced in hardened steel.

"What did they make this out of?" Fre ran a file down the edge of the sword, which didn't help clear anything up.

She pulled her knife out of its sheath, testing the steel on its edge. Fre shivered. Her knife was well made, forged from high-grade carbon steel; still, it didn't ring like the weapon laid out in front of her. Picking up the unfinished weapon, feeling as if she held something magical, she turned it over and began working on the other side. This would be a weapon like no other, and Fre was going to make sure it looked the part.

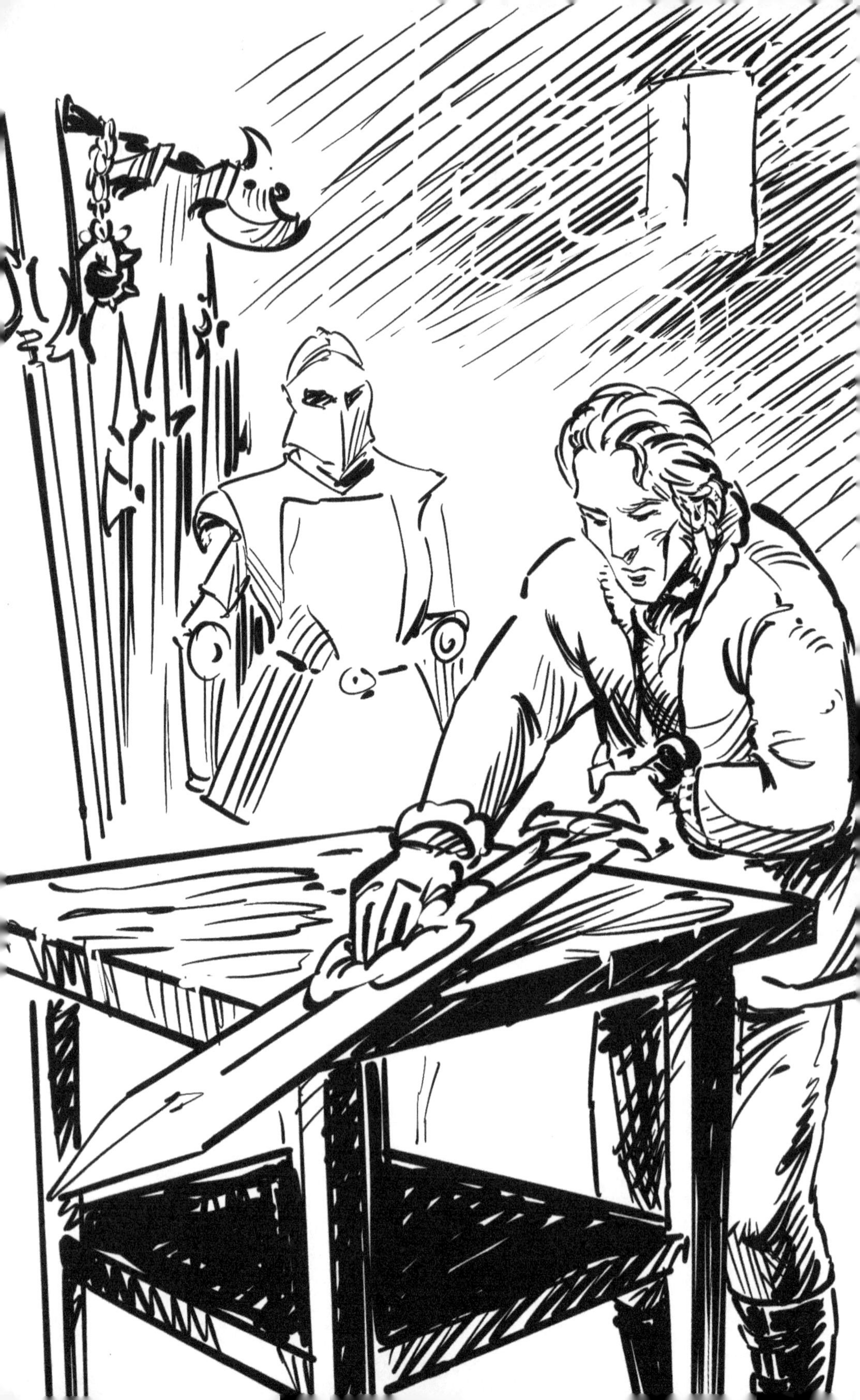

CHAPTER 6

Quintin stepped out into the afternoon sun. He winced, lamenting the loss of shade. Working his way to the back of the abandoned factory, Quintin began his excursion into the slums of Isel. He found it remarkable how a city could have such a divide in the living conditions from section to section. Rats crawled along the gutters in the alleys, seemingly undeterred by Quintin's presence. The critters were used to people traveling through their territory.

He stared uncertainly at the winding pathways in front of him. One couldn't figure out the rules of a new city in a day or even a month; it made the job of finding people to talk to rather difficult. Stepping out onto a small dirt street, Quintin surveyed the small clumps of people gathering around the few shops. His eyes landed on a group of kids, not much younger than himself, huddled around one of the smaller buildings. Quintin wandered across the street, casually making his way up towards the group. People here refused to meet his eyes, and he noted more than one person crossing the street as he passed by.

Quintin came up to the group, judging their reaction to his presence. No hostility appeared in their posture, but more than one of them stood up straighter as Quintin caught their attention.

"Can I help you?" one of the boys asked, looking Quintin up and down.

"I'm not entirely sure," Quintin said, shrugging slightly, "I'm looking for anyone who can get me in touch with the Emerald Syphon. I've got some information on a massive raid on their storehouses tonight. I'm willing to pay for any information you have."

The atmosphere dropped as Quintin noticed several of the boys stiffen at the syndicate's name.

The boy Quintin now presumed to be the leader, raised an eyebrow, "People don't just throw that name around here. Are you some kind of enforcer?"

Quintin recognized the slang commonly used in reference to the imperial police force. He'd expected this – he didn't know this place.

"Sorry," Quintin said, "I just got into the city several days ago. My name is Quintin."

The boy snorted, "What makes you think we can even get you what you want?"

Quintin pulled the last of his coins and offered them to the boy, "I'm not sure you can," he said, "but I don't know these streets as you do. I'm sure if you can't get in touch with them, you will know who can."

Quintin held the coins out, "Please."

The boy rolled his eyes and took them, "I'll do what I can, but don't expect too much."

Quintin nodded his thanks, "I'll be at the Inn on the main street, the one with the hemasti skull on its sign."

The boy nodded, "Yeah, yeah, I got it." he said, pocketing the money and gesturing for his mates to follow him.

Quintin let them go, remaining silent as they turned into an alley and vanished. "They aren't going to help."

The thought was painfully true, but that didn't matter. Quintin just needed to find some more people to ask the same favor. He'd gotten several documents during his travel uptown to meet with Fre, most of them coming from the enforcer's office. Quintin rummaged through his bag, pulling out a list he'd written before bed last night. It was a list of several buildings around the slums confirmed to be places where stolen goods were shipped out of the city.

Emerald Syphon will never talk to someone like me, so I'm going to create a problem that will lead back to me. Quintin needed to find some more people. He needed to tell them about the upcoming thefts, and then he was going to go and commit several robberies. Why spend months searching when he could let the syndicate come to him?

* * * * *

Selyne pushed open the heavy ironwood door leading into the Spire's library. She entered, brushing past a flock of servants busy with the afternoon cleaning, making her way to the sitting area in the back. She found her mother seated there with several people she didn't recognize. Astania didn't notice her daughter's entrance immediately, engrossed in a discussion of international importance, a perfect image of an Ithean empress. The power of Selyne's mother sat in perfect contrast with her father.

He commanded the room with a shining passion common amongst his people. His wife was a little different, approaching everything with the quiet intelligence expected from the empress of Ithea. Astania glanced up, eyes catching Selyne's. Selyne stood a little straighter as her mother's attention turned to her, growing self-conscious under her gaze. The conversation grew quiet as more people looked to Selyne, their eyes following Astania's interest. Selyne felt herself grow red under the group's scrutiny.

"I'm so glad you've joined us, Selyne," her mother said, gesturing to a chair, "please take a seat."

Her voice sounded genuinely interested in Selyne's presence, which made Selyne all the more concerned. Astania never spoke that way. Selyne tucked herself into the cushioned seat, giving a halfhearted smile to the people around her.

Astania cleared her throat, "Now that everyone is here, can we move on?"

Selyne glanced around the group, acknowledging who exactly she was sitting with. Three people sat beside her mother – a woman not much older than Selyne herself, an elderly man who somehow looked older than her mother, and the soldier who Selyne recognized from last night.

"Selyne, I'd like to introduce some of the people I've found to watch over you these next few days." Astania turned to the group, pointing to each in turn. "This young woman is currently standing in for Alfear Angel-Kin. Expect her to help in your studies from now on."

She pointed to the elderly man, "This man is the Head of the Thean Heirs department; he's keeping the logistical matters of your heritage together as we try to get you into the university."

She pointed to the final person, "This is Willem. He's retired as of last year, but he is part of the royal military and will be your protection during your next few months."

Selyne looked at each person in turn. Why did there have to be so many? "Am I going to need to change classes? I don't really want that."

Selyne tried to keep her irritation hidden.

"I know you don't like this," her mother said. "None of this is going to prevent you from pursuing your previous interests. They're simply going to be providing extra teaching and protection for you."

The elderly man sitting beside Selyne's mother cleared his throat, pulling his chair up, indicating his entrance into the conversation. "Princess," he said, his voice strained with centuries of age. "I'm sure you're aware of the interest the Thean institutions have in someone such as yourself. While, as an heir to the throne, you lay outside of our jurisdiction, it would be a waste not to give your abilities every opportunity to grow."

He glanced to the empress for confirmation before turning back to Selyne. "As such, we want to allow you to work with our senior Heirs and scientists, under your mother's supervision, of course."

The old man leaned back into his chair, watching Selyne for a response. Selyne wasn't sure how to take the suggestion. School had always been private; what would the university even look like?

"So, it's just a single extracurricular class?"

Her mother nodded, "It would be a little more extensive than most classes you take, covering larger swaths of information," Her mother pointed to the other woman in the group, "Kalli is the one who will be teaching you. I imagine she may be able to spread some light on any obscure questions you may have."

The woman seemed to come to attention at the sound of her name, looking up from a page she had been writing in.

"Yes? Did you have something to ask me?" she looked around the room as if unsure of whom she was addressing.

Selyne looked at the woman, confused. *Is this really someone who should be teaching? She looks like she should be sorting documents in an office somewhere.*

Selyne shook her head dismissively, "I've got nothing to ask at the moment, though I'm sure that will change as time continues."

She looked to the soldier standing in the back. He hadn't moved since they'd been talking, seemingly ok with resting on a heavy wood cane throughout the conversation.

"How is he supposed to work?" Selyne asked, looking at her mother.

Astania glanced up to the man, "He'll simply be following you anytime you leave the Spire, don't worry about his schedule. He's being paid very well to keep tabs on you."

Selyne wasn't sure if that answered her question. "I need some time to think on this. Right now, I'd like to spend some time alone."

Her mother nodded, "You are all free to go," she said, turning to the guests. "I'll contact you in the next few days, and we will talk about further plans."

The group stood, giving some quiet thanks and awkward bows as they excused themselves. Selyne watched them leave. She couldn't imagine getting to know these people. She looked at her mother, the older woman's frame relaxing as the group left.

Astania returned Selyne's gaze, smiling despite apparent fatigue. "So, what do you think?"

Selyne shrugged, "I don't think this will help anything, but I don't expect to change your opinion on the matter."

Her mother sighed, "You have a lot of problems for someone your age. You like to act as if you can handle this, but I haven't seen anything that says that's true."

Selyne groaned internally. This was always the thing that came up during these conversations, "It would be easier if you'd let me use some funds for projects. It feels like you want me to sit here in my room and study history all day."

Selyne spoke with an edge in her voice, sharpened by years of resentment.

"You say that," her mother said, "but I've said many times that action, the way you carry yourself, has to come first if you want me to trust you."

She massaged her temples. "I can't deal with this right now," she stood as she spoke, dusting herself off and turning to leave.

"Can I expect to see you at dinner?" her mother called out as Selyne walked away.

Selyne raised her arms and shrugged, "Don't expect anything. Right now, I just don't want to talk."

Exiting the library, she didn't bother waiting for her mother's response. She turned towards the downward stairwell. "Next week is going to be bloody miserable."

Selyne grumbled and pulled out her pocket watch. The hands read half a cycle past the sun's zenith, the golden hands of the clock obscuring the topaz, which indicated recession. The pub felt like a good option. Nobody would be working at this time.

"Maybe I'll go visit Aril. She's always open for a drink."

The idea was appealing, though at this point, Selyne would settle for anything that allowed her to ignore her mother.

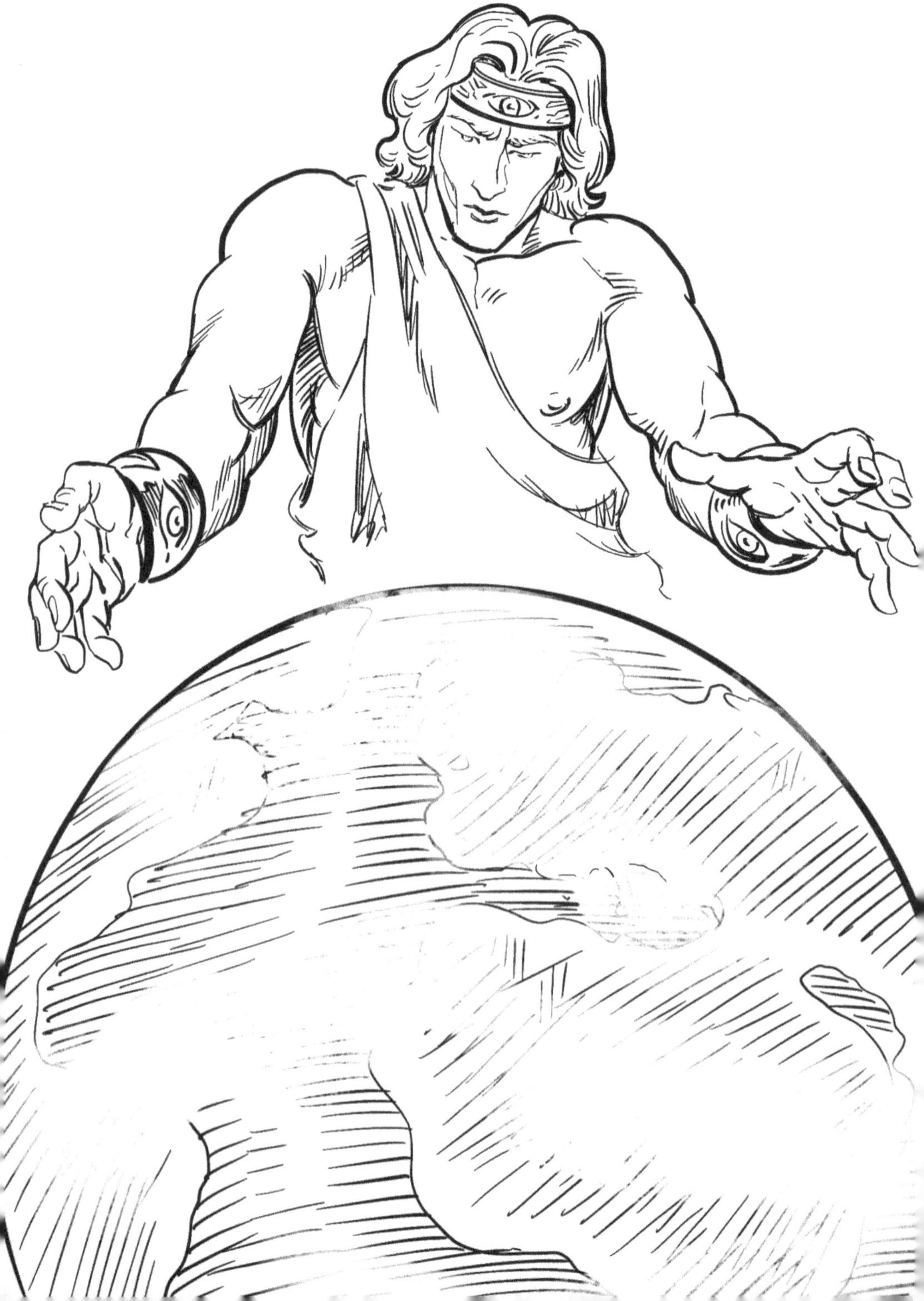

CHAPTER 7

Quintin had never considered himself a full-time thief, but it was some bloody good fun to steal from criminals. Turning down one of the larger streets of the lower city leading toward the industrial sector, Quintin took care not to rush; he was supposed to be here. He carried a large bag over his shoulder that he'd found at a failing tailor's shop for half price. It now carried a thousand times its price in trinkets, coins, and clothing.

That last group had confused Quintin a lot – why would you need a facility dedicated to housing dozens of designer outfits in a city as rich as this? Quintin didn't really want an answer; having extra clothes that would fit and look good wouldn't be questioned. He looked to the sun, trying to judge the time he'd spent gathering his treasure.

The slums took longer than expected – perhaps they keep most of their resources here for protection. It wasn't uncommon for criminal activity to be organized under a single group in most cities of the empire. Often, this was done to avoid conflict with imperial law enforcement, creating a unified infrastructure that became integral to the everyday lives of poorer citizens. Working from that general rule, keeping your power in the place where it was founded made sense. Spreading to wealthier areas put the balance of power into question.

Quintin caught a glimpse of the abandoned factories above the houses, feeling relieved at being somewhere safe. *I wonder if Fre has finished working for the day.* The prospect of seeing her sword finished gave Quintin a thrill; it wasn't every day you had an opportunity to see a glyph brand up close. Feeling at liberty with the empty streets, Quintin cut through the road, making a straight line towards his destination. The interior of the factory building was dark, with the sun waning. Quintin stepped gingerly around ancient workstations, making his way to the thin line of light outlining the back room.

The door opened smoothly, revealing chaos beyond. Fre had taken to her work seriously. Tools lay strewn about the office, a pile of small hammers sat beside Fre, in front of a small furnace. Quintin came up behind her, glancing at the small pile of silver coins piled on her right, along with dozens of small precious stones.

"You've been busy," he said, picking up a small diamond and studying it, "Did you even eat today?"

He looked at Fre, who was busy putting away the few molds and smelting tools they were able to carry in their travels. She set her space in order before looking up at Quintin. It always shocked him how easy it was to read her physical and mental state just from her face.

Her pale face lacked even more color than usual, and redness was appearing at the edges of her eyes, indicating overuse.

"You look like Shia took a bite out of you," he said, chuckling.

Fre leaned back in her chair, stretching her hunched back. "All for a good purpose," she said, yawning, "Judging by the bag on your shoulder, I would guess you had similar success?"

Quintin smiled, setting the bag on the table and opening it to reveal the contents within. "The crime here was stuffed with sweets." Quintin pulled out the piles of clothes and silver coins, "keep in mind; this is only from the lower city."

Fre began to dig through the items.

"And you're sure this will gather his attention?" Fre said, looking dubiously at the pile of clothing beside the other objects.

Quintin shrugged, "Hopefully. That isn't a small amount of silver in the bag."

Fre looked at the pile. It was more than enough for a savvy person to live off for half a lifetime. Something close to a hundred years' worth of taxes and food, condensed into a bag full of metal.

"It is what it is, I guess," she said, "at the very least, we won't have trouble paying fees while staying here."

Quintin smiled, "Hopefully, it does more than that. I worked hard today."

Fre raised her arms in resignation, "Despite that, we'll just have to wait and see."

She looked to the pile of outfits sitting on the table, "In the meantime, how about a look around the better parts of town? All of this has gotten me into the mood for some sightseeing."

Ithea was an empire that prided itself on heritage. Many of the buildings and cities throughout the empire could be directly traced back to the end of Heaven's War. Thean universities also talked constantly about the number of texts passed down to them by one warrior or king from eons past, many collecting thousands of artifacts simply to outdo one another in the grand heritage contest.

Isel was different. You could, of course, trace the Spire and the university back to before Heaven's War, but the city itself was only created approximately a thousand years ago, making it only five or six generations old. Quintin could feel the difference in the people as well. Having travelled through dozens of cities throughout the empire during his search, none stood out quite as much as the capital. Here colors were brighter, and faces smiled more, even in the slums. The whole thing oozed with an optimism only found in the economic boom of a new city.

Quintin walked along, passing by shops with large glass windows revealing whatever wares they were selling inside. He looked over to where Fre stood talking with an elderly woman selling books. She laughed as the elderly lady whispered something to her before handing

Fre the small notebook she'd just purchased. Quintin smiled as Fre skipped back across the street to where he stood. She took everything so optimistically, something Quintin felt he could learn from her.

"Where to next?" he asked, glancing up at the crowded storefronts.

Fre flipped open her newly acquired notebook, producing a graphite pencil from her trouser pockets. "We can start with makeup and maybe a wig if we can find it."

She put the graphite down on the paper. "We don't have a cooler in our hotel room, so food seems like a bad idea. We may also need some new tools for the weapons. My abrasives and oil have been almost out since cleaning up those blades you got."

Fre pursed her lips, furrowing her eyebrows as she thought.

Quintin looked down at the notebook, raising an eyebrow before asking, amused, "You didn't write any of that down?"

The page had been filled with rough sketches of flowers and mountains, along with a few people-shaped outlines. Fre flushed, closing the book.

"Not like you could've read any of it," she muttered. "Besides, it's a short list."

"Can't argue with that," Quintin said, shrugging off Fre's scowl.

"I'll grab the abrasives and oil from the smithy," Fre said, "You grab the makeup and any other items from the pharmacy."

Quintin nodded, "Meet back in an hour?"

Fre pulled out her watch, flipping the lid open. "Make it an hour and a half. It takes about seventy-two minutes just to walk there from here."

Quintin nodded, "An hour and a half then. Take care. Hopefully, this all goes over as we planned."

Fre turned away into the crowd. Quintin watched her go for a minute before focusing on his own tasks. Despite the cacophony of the thousands of people around him, Quintin felt isolated. Hopefully, his little endeavor with Emerald Syphon would go off without any issues, and they could be out of town by next week. The prospect of this being all over in a few months sent a shiver down Quintin's spine. How long had it been since he'd seen his father? A year? Two years? If this went as planned, his and Fre's problems would be solved. He'd have his old life back, and with the help of his parents' connections, it would only be a matter of time before Fre could reunite as well.

Quintin felt his legs move a little bit faster as the prospect filled him with excitement. He stepped into the entrance of a small pharmacy on his side of the street. There were fewer people perusing the aisles, which is what he preferred. He marched over to the makeup section, scanning the wooden cupboards for the items he was looking for.

He assumed this purchase would be a means to conceal Fre's facial features. People from the islands of Anglis tended to get remembered by the people they interacted with - a byproduct of their rarity in the empire and the infamy their heritage brought. Undoubtedly an Anglis buying the means to conceal themselves would gain the ire of whomever they bought from, which wasn't something Quintin or Fre wanted considering what they were about to attempt.

Quintin walked out from the makeup aisle, now in search of a wig. Fortunately, it wasn't uncommon for nobility to simply shave their heads, opting for the convenience of never needing to worry about style or head lice ever again. Quintin arrived at the clerk's desk a moment later carrying a handful of assorted powders and creams, topped by a dark black wig. The clerk raised an eyebrow but didn't say anything as Quintin exchanged silver.

"Would you like a bag for all that?" the clerk asked.

Quintin nodded, "It would be appreciated."

The clerk handed Quintin the cloth bag full of makeup. Quintin nodded his thanks and hurried out the door. He glanced at his pocket watch. He'd need to head back soon if he wanted to make it across town before the deadline.

Stuffing his watch into his pocket, Quintin hurried down the street. With the supplies collected, they could lay low and simply wait for the day they would meet with Emerald Syphon. Quintin felt a nagging at the back of his mind as if he'd forgotten something. He pushed the feeling away. He would not have any more hesitation this close to getting the answers he had been seeking for so long.

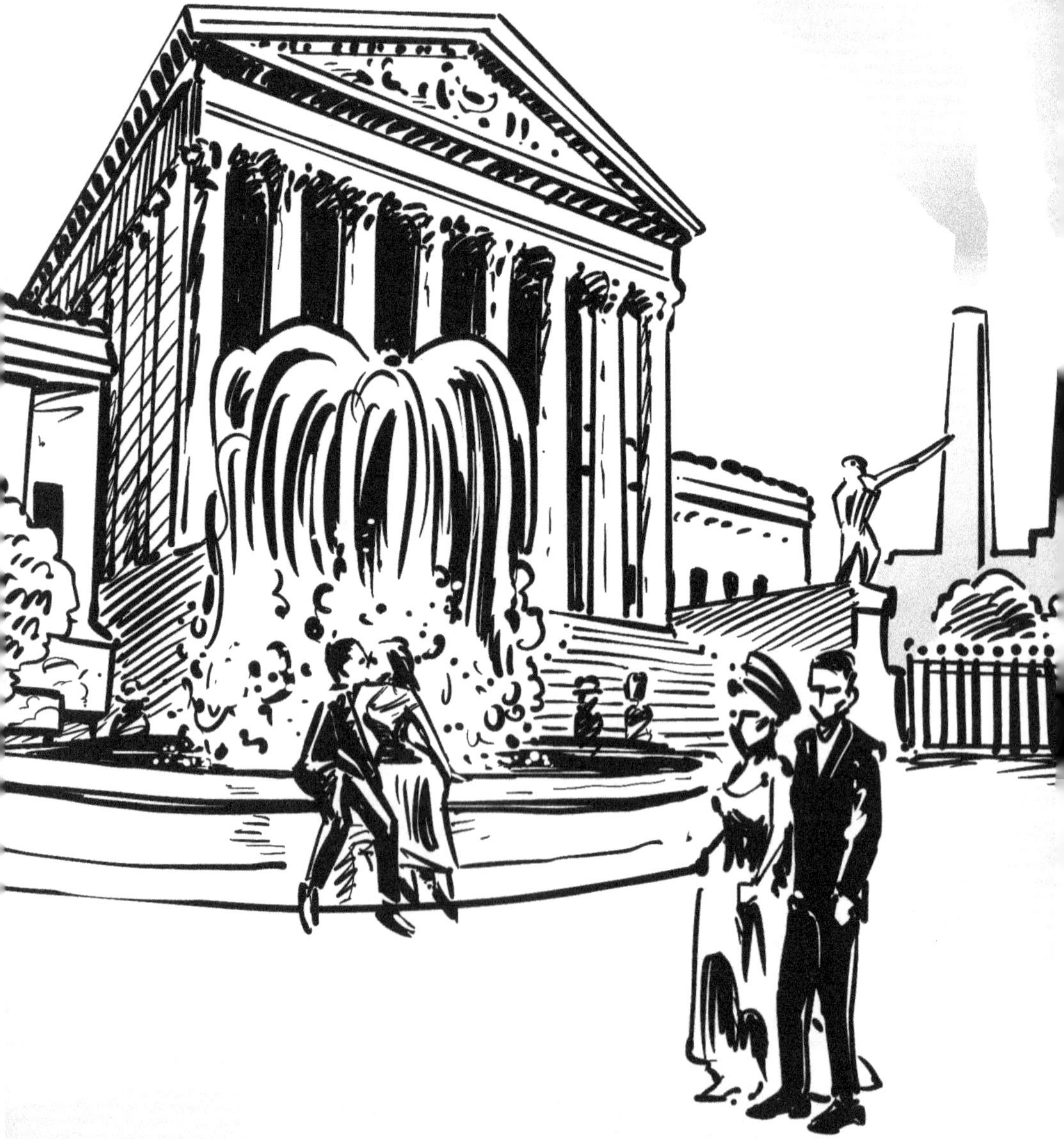

CHAPTER 8

The Midnoon sun blazed down onto the busy streets of Isel, its heat creating mirages across the marble paving stones. The glass Leys cast a prism of color up and down the street as it refracted light in every direction. Quintin looked out from his cramped alleyway, peering through the thousands of citizens on their way to lunch towards the large building across the throughway. The structure felt dark even when bathed in the full glory of the afternoon sun. With its deeply stained wood and pitch-black slate devouring the daylight, it was truly an imposing image.

Quintin looked up at the sundial hanging on the front of the building, making out the time, five past absolute noon, on its face. Fre was behind schedule. A droplet of sweat rolled down his temple. Quintin cursed the overwhelming heat of the day, making his current situation miserable. The droplet reached the corner of his eye, and Quintin brushed it away in irritation. Another minute passed as he sat there, fear creeping closer as he continued to wait. Fre was still nowhere to be seen in the swarms of businessmen and women bustling about the street.

The situation was all too familiar for Quintin – the constant fear every time he sent Fre into a dangerous place to scout ahead. The fear was becoming commonplace the more time they spent in this city. A hundred scenarios floated through his head, each more hopeless than the last. It didn't help that he'd chosen a meeting place where weapons weren't allowed. It was necessary. Criminals tend to get nervous around someone carrying a sword on their belt.

Time continued to weigh on Quintin as he sat in the stuffy alleyway. He felt he should be doing something other than sitting; perhaps he could find Fre over by the marketplace several blocks down the road? Quintin dashed the thought before it managed to get too much of a foothold. Fre was perfectly capable of handling herself. Quintin knew she would remove herself from a situation if it happened to get dangerous, and Jaymes wouldn't be looking out for a small girl; the truth didn't help his confidence very much.

Something moved in the entrance of the tavern bringing Quintin out of his head as he looked at the entrance under the pavilion.

"In the name of Shia, it took her long enough."

Fre had exited out the main entrance, her face hidden in the shadow of the outdoor pavilion, making her way to the railing facing the street. Wearing a pale blue dress with a maroon cloak framing her small features, she looked more like an average merchant's daughter than a street urchin. The wig and makeup also helped with the illusion.

Fre scanned the street, her eyes searching until they rested upon Quintin, staring at her from the shadow of his little alleyway. Her movement was urgent as she beckoned for him to come. Quintin leaped up from his position, glad to be freed from the stifling heat of the enclosed alley, weaving through the waves of foot traffic. Careful not to trip on the glass Leys as he continued forward, Quintin was able to avoid the carriages with their drivers cursing at him to move. He finally got through the last few groups of people to where Fre waited, leaning up against the railing of the pavilion.

Coming up the stairs onto the roof of the outdoor cafe, Quintin was hit with a sudden rush of cool air on his face. A glance around the perimeter revealed the cooling patterns hidden on the wooden support beams holding up the awning. Quintin took in a deep breath, glad to be free from the blistering gaze of the sun. It was time to get to work. Fre prowled across the deck, acting nothing like the lady she looked to be, sidling up next to Quintin, glass in hand.

"What's been taking you so long? I've been watching the front door for an hour. Is Jaymes waiting for me there?" Irritation and worry painted his words as the tirade of questions poured from his mouth.

Fre sipped whatever she held in her glass, remaining unperturbed by the outburst. She waited for Quintin to finish before answering.

"He's waiting for you inside," she said, taking another sip before continuing, "quite impatiently if you ask me. I overheard him talking with his men; you've probably got ten minutes before he leaves. He's one of the most paranoid men I've seen in a while, and he seems to think you have something up your sleeve."

Quintin nodded. Criminals like Jaymes didn't get very far if they weren't just a little paranoid. Hell, paranoia was the only reason they'd managed to survive for so long in such a large city, where crime ruled more than half of the population.

"Well, either we do this now or not at all. I believe you know the way?" Quintin gestured towards the doors leading to the interior building as he spoke.

Fre took the invitation, leading them both into the interior of the building. Stepping through the door, Quintin was hit by the stark contrast of the aesthetic. Where the outside felt like a scar on the landscape of the upper citizenry, the inside was brightly lit with gambling tables and booths for customers to eat, giving Quintin a strange sense of vertigo as his mind reeled under the dazzling lights and the chaos of servers running amongst the tables.

Fre led him past the tables towards the back of the large room to a booth situated in the far corner filled with three men. The man in the middle looked up from the conversation he was having with one of the men on the side, eyes darting from Quintin to Fre. His features narrowed as they approached.

"Am I supposed to know who you are?" Jaymes asked, his guards putting themselves in between Quintin and their leader.

Quintin gave the large man a bow in respect. "Sir, I believe I scheduled this meeting with you today?"

He searched the man's eyes for any signs of recognition. "I wanted to trade some information on the recent thefts in the city?"

Jaymes waved off his guards and gestured to Quintin to take a seat. "Please, pull up a chair. Feel free to order anything you'd like from the menu; it's all on me."

Quintin obliged, pulling up a chair, but declined the menu the waiter offered, receiving several looks of suspicion as he did so.

Jaymes nodded, folding his hands as he leaned forward. "Well then, if we've both come here to bargain, why not begin with some introductions?"

The large man offered his hand out, "I'm Jaymes."

Quintin grasped the hand, "And I'm Quintin."

"So what's with this information you claim to have? I've never heard your name around this city before. Are you an informant?"

Quintin laughed wryly. "No, no, nothing like that, just a guy who has kept his ears to the ground in hopes of finding something of value."

Jaymes took a gulp of his wine, wiping off the droplet with his napkin. "Cut to the chase, kid. I'm down hundreds of Alums worth of silver these last few days, and I'm not in the mood for any shenanigans."

Quintin nodded. "Understood. First, I want to set my terms."

Jaymes clenched his jaw in irritation. Clearly, Quintin had stolen enough to make this man angry, and his patience was growing thin. The big man took a deep breath before replying.

"I'll listen, but know if you ask for anything unreasonable, it's going to get messy."

Quintin nodded understandingly. "I don't need anything too large, though I'm not sure you can provide what I'm looking for."

He reached into his coat pocket, pulling out a small piece of thick paper. He unfolded the page and set it to face up on the table. The

Stolen Angels

document wasn't too complicated, with several lines of cursive followed by several signatures and an official seal at its base.

"These are my family documents," Quintin explained, "I know my father had business in the city until a few months ago, and I wanted to know if you could tell me what happened to it."

Jaymes picked up the letter, taking care to read over its contents fully. He raised an eyebrow, looking over to Quintin. "Are you some kind of Tinman?" he asked.

Quintin recoiled, a look of indignation on his face. "What makes you ask that sort of question?" he exclaimed, "I assure you that I am in no way affiliated with the police!"

"Well, you're asking a lot of incriminating questions." Jaymes said, narrowing his eyes, "It's liable to make me suspicious."

Quintin rubbed his hands on his trousers nervously. Obviously, the man would be skeptical. It made a lot of sense for the law enforcement to orchestrate a large-scale robbery, only to pretend to be someone from out of town offering to oust the thieves in return for nothing more than information. *It's not far from the truth, unfortunately.* Quintin grimaced.

"Is there anything I can do to prove that I'm legitimate?"

Jaymes shook his head. "It's not information I'm free to share," he said flatly, "if you want to work out a payment of silver, we can talk."

Quintin shook his head. "I'm not in any financial need at the moment. If you can't can't give me the information I need, then I'll go somewhere else."

Jayme clenched his teeth, trying to maintain his temper. "Listen, well boy, if you leave here now, you can expect life to get a lot more dangerous."

Quintin shrugged, "I'll take my chances elsewhere."

He stood up to leave, giving the kingpin a bow of respect before turning around to leave. Jaymes watched him go. He was silent, though Quintin could feel the anger radiating off of him.

Quintin looked over to Fre. She gave him a knowing look and nodded as they exited the door. The pair made their way down the street in silence, Quintin occasionally glancing back to get confirmation from Fre. They'd poked the hornet's nest; now, they just needed to wait for the hornets to begin pursuit. He felt a tug on the corner of his long coat, and immediately he sprang into action, moving into a quick walking pace, taking turns off the main road, weaving in and out of the small side streets most common in Isel. They found a small street just shy of being an alley whose only occupants were a trash bin and some rats.

Turning in, Quintin and Fre stopped up against the wall to catch their breath. Fre had given the signal for a tailing individual, one they hoped had followed them from the tavern. Now the plan was to look panicked so that he would give chase. Quintin listened, waiting for the sounds of footsteps around the corner. Silence met his ears as he waited. Several moments passed with nothing happening at all, yet Quintin could feel the tension growing by the second. A slight scuffing sound came from around the corner, only a few feet from where Quintin stood. It was the sound of someone's foot sliding across the paving stones, a misstep where one meant to land squarely on the ground. Adrenaline began to flow in Quintin. Even now, he could feel the buzz of blood in his ears. Still, he waited.

The man came around the corner, coming on the outside as to avoid an ambush. It was a fruitless endeavor, as Quintin moved faster than his eyes could track. The sound of blood exploded in his ears as he moved to the right and swung his fist. There was a thud, and the possible snap of ribs as his fist met the left side of the man's rib cage, burying it in and driving it all the way through, sending the man flying up against the building in a cloud of dust.

It was over in an instant. Quintin stumbled backward as the world began to spin, contracting and expanding, as his eyes tried to adjust to the rapid changes in speed. His knees almost gave way, forcing him to prop himself up against the wall next to his newly acquired catch.

Fre stepped out from her position on the other side of the small street, looking at the nearly unconscious man lying against the building.

"Are you sure he's not dead?" her voice was a mix of awe and concern as she spoke.

Quintin crouched down, placing a finger under the unconscious man's nose, and nodded, "He's alive. I'd ask you for something to tie him with but, considering his physical state, I don't think that will be a problem."

Fre crouched down beside him, looking at the person he'd laid out only seconds before, "Poor sod, you never stood a chance."

"He's not dead. Here feel his breath," Quintin's voice grew defensive as he guided her hand to his nose.

The man stirred, groaning as he tried to move into a sitting position. Quintin moved quickly, rummaging through the man's pockets for any sort of clue. Surely he'd have a place to meet with his superiors after the job was done.

"Find anything?" Fre asked, leaning over his shoulder to get a look at the dazed man.

Quintin shook his head in irritation. "He's got nothing on him, excluding the knife."

He sat back, preparing for his next move. The man was coming to his senses, and he'd be coherent enough to speak any moment. Quintin pulled out his short, a small knife about three inches in length with a blade curving upwards into a vicious point. Quintin leaned forward, holding the edge of his knife to the man's throat. The criminal's eyes grew wide as they focused on the hand that threatened to end his life.

"What do you want?" the man gasped, panicking as he tried to move away.

Quintin leaned in closer, pinning the man between the building and himself. "It's simple, really. I just need to know where I can find the person who sent you."

The man stiffened at the request, "I can't do that," he said, shaking his head weakly, "It would mean my death."

Quintin shrugged, "Your silence will get you killed here soon enough."

He pushed the knife closer, drawing blood. The man hesitated, now unsure of his next move.

"Look," Quintin prodded, "if this goes over well, I can promise your safety, or you could die here with no hope of survival."

The man seemed close to tears, clearly unprepared for this sort of situation.

"Have you heard of the clothier's shop just off the king's road?"

Quintin shook his head; he hadn't found time to explore the royal sector of the city.

The man sighed, "If you manage to find it, you simply need to go towards the warehouse in the back. Jaymes runs his business from there."

Quintin nodded, releasing the pressure on his knife. "I appreciate the cooperation."

The man didn't have time to react before Quintin slammed the hilt of his knife into his skull, knocking out cold once more.

"Goodness," Fre gasped, "If you didn't kill him before, you probably did just now!"

She crouched down, testing to see if the man was still breathing. Quintin stood up, glad to be done with the encounter.

"Do you think he was being honest?" he asked Fre as she finished up her examination of the unconscious man.

She shrugged, "Can't really tell with him out stone cold, now can we?"

Quintin looked down, embarrassed.

Fre sighed in resignation, "No matter, let's get back to our room at the hotel and clean up, I feel tonight is going to be something special."

Quintin nodded, turning away from the alley. It was only a matter of time, but he would get his answers regardless.

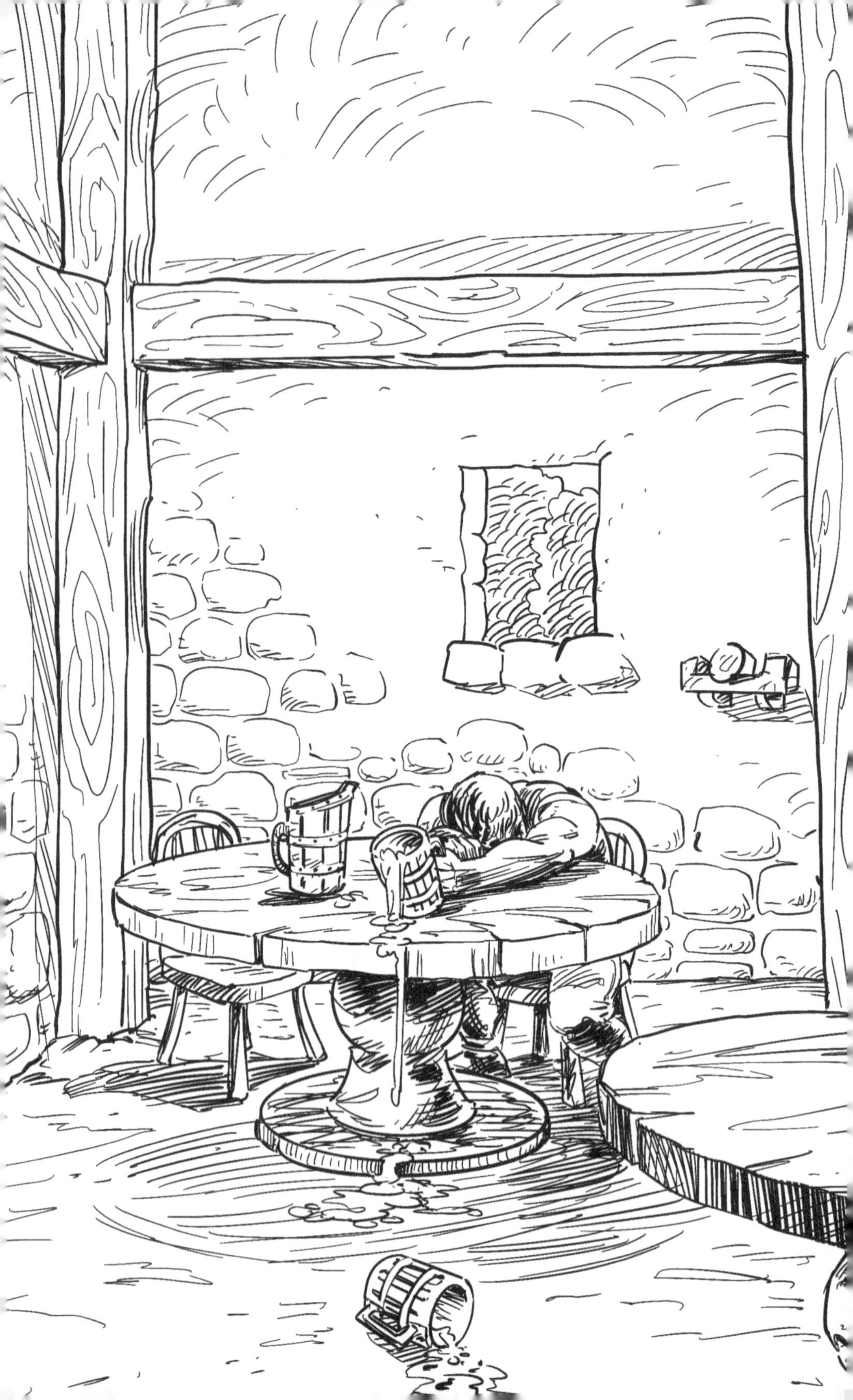

CHAPTER 9

Quintin didn't relax until the door closed in their room. The walk back had been uneventful, but he could never be certain another tail hadn't picked up their trail. Fortunately, the establishment Fre had chosen was wealthy enough that nobody could get access to their room without Quintin and Fre knowing beforehand.

Quintin took a deep breath, collecting his thoughts. They needed to begin to prepare for tonight if they wanted to succeed with this plan. Fre broke away and headed for the bathroom, presumably to remove her ridiculous wig and the layers of makeup plastered to her face.

He walked over to one of the beds where a large trunk sat. Pulling out the key the landlord had given him, he slid it into the lock, turning it until he heard the signature click. Unhooking the now open lock from the chest, he opened the lid revealing two scabbards, a pair of cloaks, and a change of clothes for Fre.

Pulling the wider scabbard out along with a pair of clothes and a cloak, he placed it on a chair next to the bathroom door for Fre. Quintin then grabbed the remaining cloak and his sword out of the chest, closing it behind him. He took off the jacket he'd worn to his failed deal with Jaymes, trading it out for the cloak.

With that done, he moved to the mirror, making sure the cloak hid his sword as he attached it to his belt. The latch to the washroom clicked, and Quintin turned to see the clothes now vanished. Fre exited a moment later, looking like her usual self. She'd donned the ashen-colored cloak, obscuring her slight frame within its shadows.

Quintin smiled, stretching out his arms to reveal his outfit, "Well, how do I look?"

She gave him a once over. "Moody."

Quintin waited for more before he realized he wouldn't be getting anything else from her. "Is that all you have to say? I worked a whole four minutes picking out this cloak. I even got it in a lighter shade to make it less 'moody.'"

Fre moved to the mirror in the corner, checking her face. "You kept the shirt, not to mention the shoes?"

Quintin looked down to find he had indeed chosen a dark grey shirt and a pair of black leather boots. Out of the dozens of outfits he'd stolen the prior week, the decision would certainly seem intentional.

"She makes a point." Quintin stopped staring at his feet and glanced over to Fre like she was one to talk. He could tell from Fre's expression that she'd realized her own predicament.

"Anyway," he said, quick to change the subject, "you ready to move?"

Fre took one final glance in the mirror, "I'm as ready as you are."

"Well then, I think we need another week's preparation."

She gave him a scowl, and he laughed, "I'm only kidding. Let's get going."

"Yes, let's." Fre replied, still scowling at him for a moment before turning away and moving towards the door.

Quintin followed behind, closing the door behind them, locking it. They walked down the hallway, little globes of glass illuminating the brightly painted corridor. It hit Quintin once again just how wealthy this part of town really was, with Resonance heating water and lighting rooms. They even had running water, and it had been the cheapest place Quintin had been able to find. A twinge of disgust floated through his mind as he thought about how nice it was here. It just made the disparity between here and the lower streets more prominent than Quintin had a taste for. They went down a flight of stairs and turned down yet another hallway leading out into the commons. Here was where many of the wealthier travelers spent their time drinking, gambling, and taking advantage of the money Thea had blessed upon them.

Quintin wobbled past all the laughter and chatter to the island, where a woman sat reading a book. As he drew near, she looked up and placed her book page down on the desk. "So, the young Noble returns. I'm not gonna lie; I thought you may not be showing up."

"I wouldn't dream of it," Quintin said, digging through the pockets in his cloak, coming up with three-inch-wide coins made of solid silver. He handed them to the lady who took them and set them on the desk face up, the likeness of the emperor looking up at them with indifference.

The lady rummaged through several drawers before producing a bar of silver, about an inch long and half an inch wide. Silver, so long as it was true silver and not some similar material like Argentum, carried with it some interesting properties. Silver was the only known substance on the planet that could absorb Resonant energy. This was why it was incorporated into almost every weapon, as it gave the wearer a semblance of protection from any Heir's attack at the cost of some of the alloy's durability. This trait of silver also meant nobody could actually replicate it using Resonance, making it extremely valuable.

The bar the lady used now would have enough silver in it that if Quintin had tried to stuff his silver with Resonant counterfeit, the two should stick together like a magnet. Without it, there would be no way for the common man to tell what was real and what was simply an illusion created by an Heir.

The lady ran the piece of silver over the three coins, lightly tapping each one as she reached it, "Well, nothing's sticking. I believe that means you're free to go. Just need the lock to your chest and both of your keys."

"Of course," Quintin dug into another one of his cloak's pockets and produced the two silver keys and the lock.

She waved a dismissive hand as she walked to the cabinets in the back, each numbered with their corresponding rooms.

"Thank you," Quintin said before turning around and walking towards the large wooden doors leading to the outside world.

Stepping outside, Quintin was met with the fading light of the sun. There weren't many people out at this time, most choosing the safety of their homes over the darkening streets. Quintin stepped out onto the glass Ley on the edge of the street. He dug into yet another one of his pockets, pulling out a crumpled piece of paper where he had written down the criminal's instructions on where to go. Hopefully, it wouldn't be far.

Quintin looked up and down the streets, lost on where to start. He glanced down at Fre, "You have any ideas where to start? I don't even know where the Emperor's Lane is."

Fre pointed to the tower as if it was obvious. "I think we start there. That is where the emperor lives, after all."

Quintin furrowed his brow, unconvinced, "Are you sure about that?"

Fre rolled her eyes and let out a sigh of exasperation, "You're hopeless."

She snatched the paper from his hand, looking it over before flipping it over and studying for another few minutes. Quintin began to grow impatient, looking up at the clock hanging outside the Inn.

Finally, Fre moved, pointing to the left, down the large street.

"We'll travel around the edge of the Spire," Fre said, "using it as a reference will keep us going the right way until we reach the Emperor's lane."

Quintin nodded, leaning over Fre's shoulder as if the piece of paper would reveal a map in her hands.

Fre glanced back at him, scowling and stepping to the side, "Do you mind not breathing over my shoulder? It's weirding me out."

Quintin coughed, embarrassed, as he stood up straight. The pair continued walking. The streets were growing cramped as they moved away from the main thoroughfare into the urban centers of the city. They were nearing the noble sector. Quintin could tell by the marble paving stones slowly taking over the cobble beneath their feet.

Fre paused as they approached a new intersection. "I think this is what we're looking for."

Quintin pulled himself out of the small sidestreet and was nearly struck dumb by the street before him. The road had been built wide enough to fit six carts side by side with room for the sidewalks. Down its center sat a massive Ley worn smooth by centuries of travel, its power lighting the lamps on either side of the street. Quintin conferred with Fre's earlier assessment. Nothing except this could be considered a royal highway.

They continued down the now lamp-lit street, their boots making the only sound around. Quintin felt a tug at his cloak and looked back to see Fre gesturing towards a large clothier's shop with her hand. Quintin followed her down the path, around to the side of the large building. His eyes readjusted to even less light as lamps had not been placed on such a tiny path. Fre slowed down, taking more care, choosing where to turn and when to go straight. The space between buildings was getting smaller, and Quintin feared if it grew any smaller, he would have difficulty drawing his weapon.

Fre suddenly stopped short, causing Quintin to nearly trip over his feet. Pulling himself steady, he looked to where Fre was standing. She had stopped at an intersection and was peeking around the corner. She waved for Quintin, who stepped as close as he could.

"That's where we're going."

Fre pointed to a large building on the opposite side of the street from the building they were hiding behind. Quintin could have mistaken it for an inn if it weren't for the lack of a sign and the absence of windows. The whole place reeked of an industriousness that wasn't found in any of the buildings around it.

"Do you think they would come to the door if we knocked?" Quintin asked as he scanned for any other way in.

Fre shrugged, "I think they might. Or I could just take the door off its hinges and let you take care of what is on the other side."

Quintin thought about it for a moment. Either way, they would be alerting anyone inside, and sneaking in was also impossible.

He sighed, "Let's do this, while we're still young."

Fre hummed her agreement and swung around the corner, running silently towards the door. Quintin came up behind her. There was a quiet rasp of silver steel as Fre drew her sword. A glow suddenly filled the cramped street as the intricate patterns of glass running throughout her blade began to resonate. They didn't know what the thing did exactly. Hopefully, it worked like most glyph brands. She closed the remaining distance from the door. The air buzzed as she swung her blade. Quintin averted his eyes as the blade made contact. There was a loud hiss, and a massive intake of air as the blade vaporized the hinges in two swift strikes.

For a moment, there was a layer of silence while they both stared, dumbfounded by the weapon's performance. Then, a loud crack echoed throughout the city as the door began to topple over, tearing the large frame out with the lock. Quintin shook himself back to reality, preparing for the fight to come, hand resting on the handle of his sword. The door made its final crash as it hit the ground, sending a cloud of dust into the air.

Quintin detected movement in the interior of the building, and the glow of yet another Resonant blade shone forth from inside. A large man came out, wearing plated armor and carrying a large blade that created a red haze as it heated the air around it. The man stumbled his way over the carcass of the door, making his way toward Quintin's shadowy form, standing at center stage, calling all attention to himself.

It worked as one of the remaining men standing behind the big one moved to the left in an attempt to flank. Quintin remained where he stood, waiting for the large man to make the first move. His opponent was happy to oblige, moving in to attack Quintin's unprotected side. Making a quick horizontal cut, the large man had exposed a weakness in his form.

CHAPTER 10

Quintin took a deep breath in. The pounding of his heart felt like a hammer banging inside his chest, growing faster with each beat. He looked up at the crimson blade, now seeming to move with the speed of molten iron. He turned his gaze to the man on his left, who was moving at a similarly slow speed, his silver steel blade not having completely left its sheath.

Quintin gripped his sword with a grip of death, pulling his blade out in one smooth motion. Its full length reflected the moonlight. It was a vicious weapon with four sharpened edges running up the three feet of silver steel and culminating in a point at the top. It was a weapon used to punch through armor and break the edge of a blade. Perfect for the situation at hand.

He took a step outward, his opponent's blade slicing empty air. Quintin then pivoted his whole body, pushing past the man's weapon inside his guard. The point of his weapon encountered the man's breastplate. It was normal steel and not built as thick as many Imperial designs. It simply caved instead of shattering as his sword barreled through the layers of steel and into the man's stomach. Quintin didn't stop moving and pushed the man through the open doorway, using his falling body to pull his blade from his center mass. He turned to the other man who had cleared his sword from his sheath. The man's face had turned to one of shock and fear. Quintin took a step clearing the broken door. Then, in a single motion, he brought the blade back into position and lunged.

There was no need to get in close. He had no fear of the man's blade, and without any semblance of armor, it made any spot a kill shot. It was over in a moment, the man sinking to the ground, dead from the hole created in his heart only milliseconds ago. The blood suddenly drained from Quintin's head, and he stumbled at the sudden dizziness he felt. He took a step and nearly toppled over as his legs screamed in protest.

He looked around, trying to spot Fre on the darkened street. He found her on the other side of the road, standing over what he presumed was the third man who had come out, though he couldn't tell as Fre's sword had dismantled so many parts of him that all that was left was a pile of charred cloth and flesh. Walking over to her, he winced as the smell of burned flesh hit his nose. She looked up at him and sheathed her blade, removing what little light was left.

"You okay?" Fre asked, a whisper of concern touching her voice as she looked him up and down.

He rolled his shoulders, his muscles screeching in protest at the movement. "What on earth happened to him?"

Fre shuddered, staring at the sword in her hand, "I'm not sure I want to know," she whispered

Wincing, he conceded. "I've certainly felt better, not that I can't continue our mission."

Quintin couldn't see her face in the darkness, but he could feel her gaze on him.

"Very well," Fre spoke, walking past him into the empty doorway across the street. "Did he give you any trouble?"

Quintin turned to see Fre poking the big one laying inside the doorway, "No. If this is the best Jaymes has to protect his wares, we have nothing to worry about."

The rest of the building was mostly empty, with a small entryway leading to a hallway going left and right into darkness.

"Could you draw your sword for a moment," Quintin asked, keeping his voice level.

There was again the soft sound of steel as Fre complied with his request. The interior was bathed in soft white light. The sword was really an oddity. It seemed to act like some warped form of a glyph brand. Normally a glyph brand would burn on contact, maybe melt some steel. This blade was different. Its fire consumed everything, vaporizing it in an instant. It had been unfinished, with a lot of material needing to be polished and a lot of counterbalance being required before it could be considered a blade – and not a very good one at that. Quintin didn't want to imagine what it could've done if a professional had been given the opportunity to work on it.

Resonant pattern work was difficult. It was a process that, when done properly, would grant even a common person the ability to wield Resonance. Quintin didn't really understand how it worked and could only identify one or two types of weapons that used glyphs. Whatever that blacksmith had done to the glyphwork had created a weapon unlike any other.

Using the light from the blade, Quintin looked around the entrance until he found a lamp sitting on a small table. Turning the key, the lamp glowed for a moment as the resonant patterns activated on its base until the oil caught fire, creating the familiar glow.

With the ability to see restored, the pair made their way into the building. They chose to take the left path first, making their way down the narrow corridor, passing by empty rooms with their doors hanging ajar. Reaching the end of the hallway, they came to a dead end.

"Well, that's unfortunate," Quintin said in a matter-of-fact way.

He turned back to Fre and pointed back down the hallway, "It seems we went the wrong direction."

Fre looked over his shoulder at the blank wall behind him and said optimistically, "Depends on what we're looking for."

"We're not looking for a wall nor an empty room to stay the night," Quintin said in a dry voice, "Jaymes should be here."

"Then it seems we've gone the wrong direction." Fre retorted before walking away from Quintin back the way they had come.

He rolled his eyes and followed behind Fre. They continued on past the hallway on the right. It looked very much the same, but as they came closer to the end of the hallway, Quintin could just make out a thin line of light coming from a door on the left. He stepped up to the lit door frame and tried the handle. It opened and revealed a well-lit staircase leading to the upper levels of the building.

The staircase was old, and Quintin winced every time his feet caused the entire thing to creak. He stopped a moment on the landing, making sure there wasn't anyone waiting to ambush him at the top. Pulling out his small mirror from the folds of his cloak, he held it up and angled it until he had a view of the stairwell.

What he saw was a clear stairway with a door wide open, revealing another hallway. Satisfied that it was clear, Quintin turned the corner and continued up the final steps to the top. Light bathed the second story causing Quintin to squint. There were only three doors in the small hallway. One hung open, and Quintin could see a table with six chairs placed around and cards scattered on its surface.

Quintin stepped inside, glancing over the cluttered space. "It seems this was where our friends outside were staying," Quintin mused.

Fre nodded in agreement, navigating around the table over to the wall.

"These seemed like the only people in the building," she said, rummaging through a leftover coat.

Quintin shrugged. He'd hoped to find his quarry here. If these were the only people here, then where was Jaymes? Quintin considered the idea that he'd been lied to. Shia, this could be an imperial storehouse for all he knew. He heard Fre hiss out a string of curses in her native tongue that he didn't understand.

"What is it?" he asked.

Fre stood in the corner holding a piece of paper Quintin recognized all too well. Fre looked over at him, holding up his papers of nobility.

"Did you get a look at the tall guy's face before you killed him?" Fre asked as if she knew the answer.

Quintin slumped as he realized the predicament they were in.

"What do we do?" Fre asked.

Quintin took one of the seats at the card table. He'd hoped to force some information out of Jaymes, perhaps get access to legal records, anything that could help with his search. If he was dead, then they were up a river without a paddle.

"We should make sure he's not still in the building," Quintin said, "he may have tried escaping or hiding. I didn't see my opponent's face- maybe it wasn't him."

Fre didn't object to the proposition. Tucking the official document into one of her pockets, she marched over to the door.

"You get the left, and I'll get the right." Quintin pointed loosely with his hand as he turned to the door in front of him.

It had a basic lock, one that he could pick with relative ease; however, there was a faster option. He moved his hands to the other side of the door, closing his fingers over one of the hinges. The building must have once been a form of an inn, as much of its design reflected that purpose. These hinges were a good example, being designed to pull loose if anyone were to lock it in an attempt to bar entry.

Quintin pulled both pins loose, thanking Jaymes silently for his shortsighted decisions while simultaneously cursing his own. It was to be expected of someone like Jaymes, who'd sat on top for so long. It was lit just like the other rooms on the second story with a small resonant lamp in the center of the room, casting shadows on the walls.

He looked around for anything that looked important, his eyes passing over the desk and chairs to a large closet in the corner. He walked forward, the floor creaking as it settled under his feet. As he reached the closet, he knew immediately it held something worth finding. It was newer than the rest of the building, with silver steel lining its surface to protect against any resonant attack. Quintin looked down at the dozen reinforced locks dotting the surface.

It didn't look like he would be able to pull a few pins to open this door. He needed Fre. Hopefully, her sword could make it through the door without too much resistance. He turned around, taking strides back through the way he came, poking his head out into the hallway.

"Fre, I found something."

There was a shuffle and the sound of furniture clattering from the other room. Another moment passed before Fre appeared in the doorway with a satchel resting on her shoulder and a piece of bread stuffed in her mouth.

Quintin raised his brow as Fre continued to chew on the piece of bread, "I need you to come open this door—if you're finished, of course."

Fre nodded, casually making her way down the hall with the bag still tossed over her back. Passing Quintin, Fre set down the bag, readjusting her cloak and turning her attention to the large silver steel monolith standing in front of her.

"This may take a pretty minute to get through," Fre said, stepping forward with her hand on her sword handle. "Here's hoping this works a second time."

"Be careful," Quintin said, "that thing could blow up in your hands for all we know."

Fre nodded and tossed the remainder of her bread to Quintin, "You chew on that; sit back and watch an unqualified person do their job."

Quintin caught the mostly stale piece of food, giving a wicked grin in return. Sometimes the utility of one's tools would compensate for the lack of experience one had—just look at the typical Thean Heir— but when paired with an intelligent user, a good tool could do almost anything. Fre tended to be more talk than reality, especially where work was involved. There was a rasp as the sword left its scabbard. Griping the weapon in two hands, Fre carefully scanned the metal surface, planning her means of assault.

The room grew quiet, the intake and exhalation of air being the only sounds filling the space. Quintin watched as Fre steadied herself, taking one more deep breath before swinging. Arms and blades moved in a blur, flashing bright white as the energy released from the weapon swallowed the silver steel hinges with a hiss. Fre continued the mad flurry, working her way around the entirety of the door, consuming the various locks still holding on to the frame. The cacophony of ringing steel and burning energy finally ceased as Fre disintegrated the final bolt holding the door.

She stepped to the side as the large mass of metal fell outward, making contact with the floor in a deafening boom. Quintin squinted through the dust at the dark interior of the large safe room, raising his lantern and walking forward to explore its depths. Various bags lined the shelves accompanied by a number of wooden crates, many of which were labeled. Quintin scanned each one quickly. He didn't want to waste time opening locks if the contents held no use to him.

"Hey Fre, how many more swings are left in that arm of yours?"

Quintin turned to face Fre, sitting propped against the wall. She touched the handle of her sword.

"It's getting hot. I wouldn't trust it not to burn me if I don't let it rest."

He sighed. This job was starting to wear out its welcome.

"You keep watch out the window in case any Thean enforcers come to investigate the little light show we put on while getting here. I'll do this the old-fashioned way."

Quintin reached into one of his cloak pockets as he spoke, turning back to the locked crates. Each one of the little tags on the crates was written in the strange script commonly used in Thean universities, meaning all the education Quintin's father had worked so hard to put into his head would be effectively useless in this situation.

"When in doubt, luck and one's gut feeling is the best way to create change." He mumbled, wincing as he followed the voice in his head.

Quintin wasted no time grabbing any documents he could find. They wouldn't be useful anytime soon, but he could sort through them while they traveled through to the next city. He stepped up to one of the larger crates he felt had some potential. Its lock was some sort of gold and silver alloy, inlaid with an intricate pattern. Its previous owners clearly had some money to spare, and if he got anything out of this endeavor, it would be money. Quintin picked up the lock in his hand, relieved when a small keyhole stared back at him, instead of a glass indentation. His key ring rattled as Quintin sifted through the dozens of different lock picks at his disposal.

He shoved a jagged pick into the hole, jostling it around until he heard the hallmark click of the pins falling into place. Quintin tossed aside the now open lid, placing the lantern on the lip of the crate, allowing him to sift through its contents with both hands.

Quintin pulled out several pounds of hay before his lantern began to reflect off the surface of something inside the crate. Reaching in with his left hand, he grasped the shiny object and brought it up to the surface. It was a small silver box about five inches tall and three inches deep. Scanning the side, Quintin could see no visible locking mechanism.

He was not disappointed when the lid came loose with a little coaxing of his thumb. A devilish grin crossed Quintin's face as he looked at the contents within. A noise coming from outside drew Quintin back to the small room. He looked to see Fre standing next to the window, peering out through a slit in one of the curtains.

"I got everything useful from the safe. Are our guests from the university or downtown?" Quintin's words came out in a whisper as he spoke.

"Downtown," Fre responded, "Looks like Jaymes made multiple meetings with his people tonight."

Quintin sighed; he really wasn't up for another fight tonight.

"You didn't happen to see a file cabinet in that other room, did you?"

Fre shook her head at the question. "Just a few coin purses and some food. Also, a blanket or two. Why?"

Quintin shook his head, "It's nothing. You up to climbing on some rooftops?"

"Well, I'm not fighting through another three men if that's your question," Fre said as she buckled her sword back into its place on her hip.

The pair turned and hurried out into the hallway. Their boots scuffled on the floor as they rushed up the stairs into the attic. Here they found the only window in the entire building facing out over the alley. Quintin dug into his pocket, gripping his knife to calm himself as he watched Fre pry the window open.

Steps could be heard downstairs, and Quintin urged Fre to go first before he climbed out onto the ledge. They shimmied along until Fre reached the gutter riveted to the side of the building. She slung her bag of loot over her shoulder and climbed up the metal rungs to the rooftop. Quintin followed close behind, tucking the silver box into his cloak and clambering up.

The moon cast a pale blue light across the rooftops of the massive organism that was Isel. Quintin took a deep breath of crisp night air, taking a moment to admire the Spire rising out of the center of the city. The otherwise beautiful sight was tainted with the gloom of tonight's adventures. Quintin clutched the bag containing everything he'd gotten. His only hope was that this night wouldn't spell a total failure for himself and Fre.

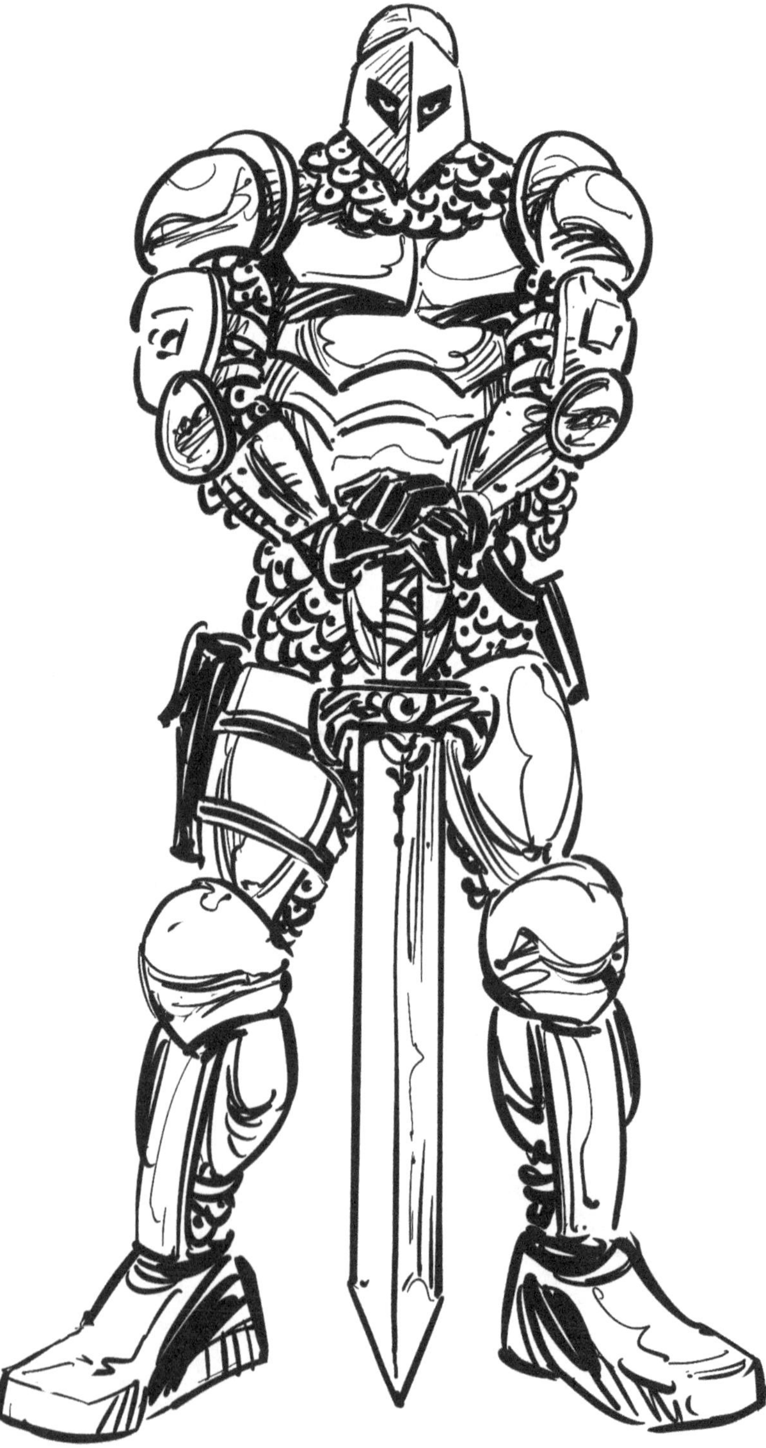

CHAPTER 11

Steam wafted off the top of the mug, bringing the warm scent of cocoa up to Alfear. The morning was a sacred time for the man. It existed as an opportunity to find some peace before marching off to deal with the bureaucracy of Enforcement. Today peace was broken, shattered by work that had followed him home. The large man sighed, looking over the brief letter to ensure it was real.

"A break-in of the royal smithy, a killing of prominent criminals, both tied to what?"

He looked up to see Kalli sitting in the corner. She'd forgotten the food he'd put beside her, more intent with the bits of metal in front of her. Alfear stood, dusting off some crumbs leftover from breakfast.

"You leaving already?" Kalli asked, glancing up at Alfear as he walked to the door.

He nodded, grabbing his sword on his way out. "Seems like the imperials have a mess to settle with the lower city."

Kalli rolled her eyes. "You shouldn't be cleaning up those types of messes."

Alfear shrugged haplessly. "Unfortunately, the Heads think I should probably find a way to get jurisdiction over the matter."

"You better be in before dark," Kalli said, giving him a critical eye.

Alfear raised his hands, helpless. "Sadly, you can neither issue nor enforce that order."

"I know." Kalli didn't say anything more than that.

"That's going to be a conversation," Alfear sighed. "I'll be back tomorrow. That I can promise you."

She nodded, her mind returning to her work. Alfear opened the door and stepped out into the mist-covered streets of Isel. Something told him this was going to be a long week.

The Office of Hierarchal Affairs was a swirl of paranoid panicked scribes. Alfear waded through the chaos, trying to reach his desk at the back of the room. The notorious crime lord by the name of Jaymes had turned up dead this morning with a hole through his chest, and his storeroom looted.

Naturally, this was throwing the underground society into a frenzy, with each crime syndicate pointing the finger at the other. Tensions were mounting daily. With the reported kills within the past six hours, it seemed that a spat between the syndicates would be inevitable. That, however, was what the Capitol Law Enforcement was to take care of. Currently, the only thing he needed to find was the one responsible for the killing.

Alfear continued onward, passing his desk and the mountain of papers that had accumulated in his absence, focusing instead on the man leafing through the books on the shelves in the back. Alfear came up beside him, peering vaguely at the hundreds of books centered on them. The man standing beside him glanced over, giving him a once over before returning to his searching.

"So, what exactly did I miss which was so important that it required you to send me a letter on my day with Kalli?"

He finally pulled a book from the shelf and turned toward Alfear, "You hear about Jaymes?"

Alfear nodded, "I've heard enough to know he's dead. Which means our job has gotten considerably more complicated."

"You're damn straight it's gotten more complicated. I've been here since dawn sifting through ledger after ledger trying to figure out who could possibly be behind this. All while you've been following after Kalli with your heart on your forehead."

Alfear shrugged off the comment. He had been indisposed this morning helping Kalli sort out her current housing situation in the city. The woman had a curious ability to collect the most obscure material to use in her various experiments and research. Alfear smiled at the thought of her soot-covered face as she had explained the situation. It had been one such experiment utilizing military-grade spark power which had led to an explosion in the west wing of her family manor and an eviction from her parent's estate.

"All I can say," Alefar focused his eyes on Rala "Is that a man simply cannot refuse the love of his life, nor can he ignore the call of his responsibilities, even if one happens to be a beautiful and intelligent woman and the other is a middle-aged man."

"I assume that's why you're here now?" Rala queried, "to fulfill your responsibility to order in this town?"

Alfear grinned at that statement and gestured around himself to the books and people bustling about. "Do you see any beautiful woman here, Rala?"

Rala chuckled at the comment, "No, I don't. Not with Sirus and Dele gone to study in our universities in the far east. Alas, this place is much duller without them to bring some life to these dusty shelves."

Alfear gave Rala a gentle pat on the back, "I don't feel your pain, Rala, but I can help you with your paperwork."

Rala gave Alfear a side glance but decided not to follow up on it.

"Yes, well, this way then." Rala stepped back to his desk, Alfear following behind.

After digging through the mass of papers on his desk, he pulled a single sheet from the chaos.

Rala took a look at the crest on the paper and gestured with the scroll in his hand, "Let's take this to your desk; more room to work with."

They both walked to the other corner of the room where Alfear's desk sat. It was a completely different picture from Rala's, with all the papers folded away in the drawers and his pens ordered by size and color. Rala pressed his thumb against the seal, and it glowed before popping off and floating to the desktop. Rala spread the pieces of paper that fell from the scroll, placing each into ordered piles.

"You know the story the public has been telling since yesterday noon, but that's not why we're here." He leafed through the pages on the desk, pulling one from a stack and laying it in the center.

It was an official letter judging by the numerous signatures and seals dotting the bottom of the paper. Taking a closer look, Alfear noted that some big names were on the list.

"What exactly is this?"

"It's a trade deal." Rala said, "Signed by the First Heir, the Nobles, Council, at least one Royal Officer, and the emperor himself."

Alfear raised an eyebrow at that, "What kind of trade were we doing with a crime boss from the lower township?"

Rala began to leaf through another pile of papers lying on the desk, "You know, those shipments which are sometimes sent from the universities on the edge of the Empire?"

"Yes?" Alfear said, more as a query than an affirmation. "I know it happens, but I spend far less time in this office than you do, Rala."

"These shipments," Rala said, continuing his previous statement, "contain anything found by our Seekers that is either too valuable or too complex to be researched and protected at one of the smaller universities."

Alfear took the piece of paper Rala was holding in his hand and began to scan the page. He had formed a pretty good, albeit incomplete, idea of what was going on based on what Rala had told him so far.

"So, our dead man got his hands on some dangerous objects, and his acquisition of said objects is what got him killed."

Alfear tossed the paper he held. It hadn't been anything but a cost analysis of the whole failed trade project and the subsequent killing. Leave it to Rala to focus on details better left to the scribes and secretaries.

"Do you have a list of the stolen objects and a list of potential suspects responsible?"

"Of course." Rala began to once again rummage through one of the stacks, pulling out two pieces of paper. "These are the names of our current suspects as well as each of their relations to Jaymes. They are organized by those with the greatest motive to least motive."

Alfear scanned the two pages, each filled front and back with enemies and affiliates Jaymes would have had contact with during his plans.

"And the list of items lost?"

"That would be the paper you tossed over there," Rala pointed to the paper Alfear had tossed to the corner of the desk.

"Ah, of course."

Rala snorted as Alfear picked up the paper again, making a mental note to actually read the fine print before he made a judgement on a piece of paper.

"It's in the bottom right under accessories and property."

Alfear looked at the small list of items. He then looked at the cost of reparations, and his eyes lit up. "Hey, what are the two items labeled with a thousand pounds of silver each?"

Rala looked up from the map he was annotating and peeked over at the page in Alfear's hand, "That would be the two angel hearts that were kept at the vault at Ial. Plans for their transport began during the Heston assault on the South Western territories. How can you not know this?"

Alfear shrugged. It never seemed all that important to keep the more obscure knowledge in his head. He could leave that to Rala or

Lian; both kept random facts about the internal affairs of the Thean bureaucracy.

Alfear's mind wandered a little longer – where was Lian – someone had killed a man for a set of angel's hearts…

An idea snapped into his mind. He glanced up at Rala, who was looking back at him, "What?"

Rala poked him on the cheek, "Just wondering where you had gone for a moment."

Alfear brushed aside Rala's hand, "I just got an idea."

Rala shook his head. "Heaven help us."

A look of hurt crossed Alfear's face, "Don't be like that. This idea should save us a lot of time sifting through suspects."

An intense spark gleamed in Rala's eye, "What have you got?"

Alfear tapped the page in his hand, "An angel's heart is a pretty rare item, with only two others under Thean protection."

Puzzled by that statement, Rala gave him a look, and Alfear paused before continuing, "Each of these items creates a very unique resonant signature."

Rala nodded, following Alfear's thought process, "You thinking of getting a seer to find the culprit?"

Al thought about it a little more – a seer could detect the use of resonant frequency by a human; they could also detect any latent strings inside a human or object; a good seer could find an Heir from within a crowd of regular people. A great seer could not only detect an Heir but could give a detailed description of how strong their power was as well as how they could use that power. Alfear needed the best seer he could find.

"Do you know anybody good?" he asked.

Rala pulled at his ear as he thought for a moment. He nodded as a thought came to him, "I think I know of someone – a Seeker by the name of Orion. He's currently working for the Department of War, but he should be willing to help a comrade given the levity of the situation."

"And you think he's up to the challenge we have at hand?"

Rala responded, "Having seen this man work during the last Thailian Border War, I believe we could have no better seer for this task."

Alfear shrugged. If Rala was willing to give the man such a standing compliment, then that was good enough. He rolled up the list of items he held in his hands. He straightened himself out and paused, however, when he remembered the mass of confidential documents strewn about his desk and overflowing onto the floor. He glanced back toward Rala.

"You have a plan for this clean-up?" he asked as he nudged the pile with the scroll in his hands, causing some of the pages to topple down onto the floor.

"Hey!" Rala jumped at Alfear's wanton antagonizing of his documents, kneeling down to pick up the fallen pieces as if the floor might burn them if they sat on it too long.

Rala ran his hands over the pages to remove any creases in the paper. Once he was certain his papers were safe, he turned toward Alfear, a scowl shadowing his blue eyes and grey beard.

"What?" Alfear asked, with a feign of innocence in both his voice and face.

It did little to calm Rala, who still had a scowl on his face, but had moved from Alfear and began to compile the papers from the many stacks cluttering the desk. He moved the now toppled stacks into one unified pile. Though he seemed busy, he still glanced back at Alfear every few moments to make sure he wasn't making any more moves against his work. The lack of conversation was unnerving for Alfear, though not uncommon.

In fact, this picture was more familiar to him than he would like to admit. He continued to watch Rala as he aligned the last few papers, and pulled out the small seal that he had held. Using Resonance, an Heir or skilled glyph worker could make material from thin air. There were drawbacks to the process. Most things made in this manner broke down back into the resonant threads that made them over time, and the item would vanish entirely if the person who made it happened to meet an untimely end. The benefit was you got an object which could be manipulated freely using one's own inheritance or a seal with a glyph like Rala had now.

The older man glanced over to Alfear. "You have that page I handed you earlier?"

Alfear nodded, holding it up for Rala to see.

"Good," Rala nodded.

As he activated the glyphs, the seal seemed to adhere to the pages on the desk. Alfear watched in awe as the pages compressed far more than any scroll or book ever could, until only a small white cylinder laid on the desk in front of him. "Someday, boy, you will need to come to understand the importance of this information, or else you will be very lost when I no longer care for you."

"Perhaps." Alfear shrugged. "But…"

Rala held up his hand to Alfear's mouth, "I don't need your convoluted reasons right now, mate."

Rala looked up at Alfear's somber face, sighing at the dampened mood.

"You like it?" Rala asked, holding up the tiny block of papers in his hand. He expected and enjoyed the gawking Alfear was giving his newest toy. Bringing attention to it would hopefully lighten the mood.

Alfear peeled his eyes away from the strange little device and looked at Rala's face, "How in all that is good in the world did you get your hands on that impossible device? I swear I'll never get over that resonant ability."

Rala shrugged and pulled on his ear while a smile remained on his face, "I happen to know a Professor in the Seekers Department. He had those little things on his desk and needed a way to test the new glyphwork he put into it. I was happy to oblige him."

"But how does it work?"

Alfear was completely enamored. The compression had shrunk the pages down to half their previous size.

Rala pointed to the piece of paper clutched in Alfear's hand.

"If you look closely at that piece, you'll see threads of metal woven into the paper. Those were created by a resident Heir here in the city, and they react to the glyphs on the seal, causing them to compress against each other."

Alfear opened his hand and pulled the page closer to his face. It was whiter than any other paper he had ever seen before. It looked more similar to a piece of cloth with threads woven together rather than tree pulp and glue.

"What is truly remarkable about that material," Rala spoke as Alfear continued his study of the page, "is that one does not need to worry about the information being stolen, since as long as you know the creator of the paper, you can always have them release the steel in the paper, and it falls apart into a thousand unreadable shreds. I'd show you, but I kind of need this paper."

"Don't worry," Alfear said dismissively, "I would never ask you to destroy such a masterpiece of craftsmanship unless it was absolutely necessary."

They both fell quiet with thoughts rushing through their heads as the world moved on around them. A moment passed before Rala snapped back into action.

He turned back toward Alfear, "Well, boy, we should probably get going to the Department of War. The Imperial University doesn't pay us to stare at fanciful devices. That job is for the Learners Department. Say, do you have a place to store this for a moment?"

The barrage of words brought Alfear to attention. He noted the scroll Rala was proffering, and immediately his hands began to pat down his jacket. "Of course. Just give me a moment."

Alfear's brain continued catching up as he dug out his keys and unlocked the silver steel box on the foot of his desk, "Here we are."

He stood and turned while taking the scroll from Rala, placing it amongst the other papers in the box before locking the trunk.

Rala stood up. "Daylight continues to burn while we sit here jabbering like a bunch of old ladies during the Summer Solstice."

Alfear chuckled at the comment. "Personally, I feel like you always jabber like an old gossip."

Rala ignored the statement, either deliberately or not; Alfear couldn't tell. He looked to the clock on the wall catching the time.

"Shia, it is well past eight."

"We should probably go."

Alfear was ready to get on the move. Rala looked at the clock as well, "Aye, if we don't get that done soon, you may have to cancel your plans with your lady friend."

Alfear gave Rala a withering glare which only broadened the elder man's grin all the more.

"Let's just go," Alfear said, ready to change the subject as he made his way through the desks, dodging around clerics and scribes who were rushing to and fro with files piled high in their arms.

The walk to the courtyard wasn't a long one. The Affairs office was ground level, tucked into a corner of one of the bow arms of the University. Alfear stepped out into the late afternoon sun shining down onto the university courtyard. It was an impressive sight, always managing to inspire awe in Alfear every time he saw it. The University consisted of three larger buildings which stood for the three colleges. There was the large domed center building which was where the Learning and Seeking Department hosted classes. The central library was located there as well as the laboratories. Curving out from either side of the Center Dome were two curved buildings often referred to as the bow arms. These were designated to the Enforcers corps and the Law Department. It was also where Alfear usually worked.

He winced as the large brass dome of the central building reflected the full fury of the summer sun down on him. Alfear walked out from under the pillars in the entry of the bow arm, out into the field of flowers. He was careful not to leave the small, cobbled path as he made his way across.

The sun was blazing hot, warming Alfear's skin and causing him to sweat. He ignored it, with his eyes still on the monoliths around him. These buildings weren't just old; they were ancient. Each building had been reclaimed by his ancestor at the end of Heaven's War, the rest of the campus growing up around them as time progressed. The Spire had a very similar origin – a monolith reclaimed as the Itheans spread out to become the greatest empire the world had ever seen. Alfear wondered if their age was the reason each building reached heights that were hard to achieve with the tools available to them. They'd been built in a time when angels had walked the earth.

It was, however, what lay underneath the University that was really inspiring. Miles and miles of tunnels with rooms filled with knowledge and research that much of the world didn't know about. Even the people who worked down there didn't understand a quarter of what they should. Alfear stepped off the small path onto the island that held the center building.

The center building, unlike the two arms, was freely open to the public. It contained every book that had been written in the last seven thousand years. The Seekers and Learners were always keen to share their knowledge with the world. Alfear found it funny how fanatical their quest for knowledge seemed at times.

Stepping into the building, Alfear was hit with a wave of cold air. It seemed that they were running the absorbers on high today. Alfear walked past the front desks taking a right turn to a large circular staircase mirror on the other side of the room. Bookcases lined the walls as he walked around the balcony until he finally reached a door wedged in between the shelves. He pulled his keys out of his jacket and flipped through them until he found the one he was looking for. He slid it into the lock and twisted it, listening for the click before turning the knob leading to the hallway beyond. There were offices tucked in on either side. Their occupants, along with their positions, were displayed on small brass tags on the door.

"Which office is the one we want?" Alfear turned to face Rala, who he had almost forgotten was following him a moment ago.

Rala stepped ahead, and Alfear turned parallel to the wall in order to let him through. Moving forward, Rala lead them to an office on the right. He didn't care to knock and simply opened the door and pushed himself into the room. Alfear almost said something until he saw the man sitting behind the desk. He was big with a dark black beard that matched his jet-black hair cut in a military-style.

He looked like a younger, stronger version of Rala. The man looked up, startled by the noise, and smiled when he saw his visitors.

"What in Thea's good world are you doing here?"

His voice even sounded like Rala's.

Rala returned the smile, "To see my little brother, of course…and to ask you for a favor."

"Feel free to ask me anything, Rala. You know I'm always willing to give you a hand." He gestured to a seat, "Please sit down and talk. I believe there are also some introductions to be made?"

Rala glanced back at Alfear as if remembering he was still standing in the doorway. "Of course. Alfear, I'd like you to meet my brother, Orion. Orion, meet my coworker, Alfear."

Orion stood up from his desk and extended his hand, "Pleased to meet you, Alfear."

Alfear clasped his hand, "Please to meet you as well. I hear you may be able to help us."

He nodded, "Yes, of course. What exactly are you looking for?"

Alfear pulled the piece of paper from within his coat pocket and spread it out for Orion to see. Orion took the paper in his hand and sat back in his chair, studying the page intently.

Looking around, Alfear noticed he was the only one still standing. He glanced around the room until he found an empty chair and took a seat. Orion scratched his beard in contemplation as he continued reading.

"So, I take it that this favor is a little more complicated than a cup of sugar for your pantry?"

Rala shook his head, looking sheepish as he fidgeted nervously with the end of his collar, "I'm sorry to spring this on you so quickly. Normally we have a few weeks to sort out a plan of action, but with the entire city in an uproar, the Affair's office needs answers now. Any chance you can help?"

There was a moment of silence as the pair waited for a response.

"You said this was urgent?" Orion asked.

"Within the span of today is optimal if possible," Alfear replied.

Orion opened up his small pocket watch and glanced at a chart on his desk, "Well, I'm busy with several important meetings for the rest of today. I can't let our soldiers starve, but if you stop by here around eleven tonight, we can begin our search for your little angel hearts. Sound cheery?"

Rala smiled, "Sounds good to me. Just don't ever use cheery in a sentence like that again. It makes you sound like an old kingdom's man born last millennia."

Orion chuckled, "Some of the people I work with come close to being born this last millennium, so I guess it just grows on a person. Now, I'll see you both tonight?"

"I do believe so," Alfear replied.

Orion nodded, "Good now, get out of my office. I have a meeting with the head of our learning department in a few minutes. We'll pick this up tonight."

Orion ushered the pair out into the hallway, closing the door behind them. Alfear turned to Rala with a grin on his face.

Rala returned a scowl, "Don't be getting cocky, boy. Just focus on preparing yourself for a night of traveling through the slums."

Alfear nodded in agreement. Tonight would be busy. His mind drifted to Kalli as he followed Rala down the hallway back to the stairs.

He was going to have to explain why he wouldn't be making dinner tonight. A sigh escaped his lips. Sometimes you just needed to face the rain as it approached.

CHAPTER 12

Alfear breathed deeply, letting the hum of Resonance flow throughout his body. Many discounted the resonant frequency of heat due to its common occurrence in the wider world. On frigid nights like this, however, it offered some much-needed warmth. Orion shivered next to him, rubbing his gloved hands together. The man was getting on in years, coming up on a hundred soon; his hair had begun showing signs of greying.

The man paused for a moment, presumably testing the threads around him. Alfear watched ponderously as his companion stood nearly motionless. Seers were unlike other Resonant users. Alfear never could sense any influence on the threads coming from them like other Heirs. Orion had described it as being a blind man whose had his ability to hear increased. Seers couldn't touch the threads around them, leading to a heightened ability to see them as compensation.

Orion looked up from his concentration, pointing east further into the lower city.

"You're sure they're that way?" Alfear asked, following Orion down a backstreet.

"I do not doubt in my mind," the older man replied, "Angel-kin are easy to locate."

"Really?" Alfear asked, intrigued, "Why is that?"

Orion looked at Alfear as if he was joking.

"Seriously?" Orion said, "You guys have one frequency of threads radiating out from you like a lighthouse," the man snorted in derision. "Honestly, you stick out like an Anglis man in a Thailian court."

Alfear scrunched his face in disdain, and it wasn't that obvious surely. The sound of shoes clattered in the alley as urchins tried to escape the ire of an enforcer in full lockplate. Orion sniffed in disgust as he walked past an inebriated man in the street. "this place grows worse with each decade," the man grumbled.

Alfear shrugged; the sight was commonplace in his line of work. "How close do you think we are?"

"Patience," Orion murmured, "we'll be here longer if you distract me."

The older man continued down another alleyway. Alfear glanced at his watch. The hand sat just short of the amethyst stone, indicating the sun's ascent.

"Another sleepless night as expected." Alfear sighed, following Orion down the alley. Hopefully, they could be done before breakfast. Otherwise, Kalli was going to have words.

* * * * * *

Fre ducked into the small workshop. Quintin had told her that the lower city had hundreds of empty industrial buildings abandoned when the emperor had decreed a consolidation of the silver and steel production in an effort to stem the sale of illegal weapons and the minting of counterfeit coins.

It was pointless information, really. To Fre, the building was a place to work and sleep, but Quintin had seemed so interested in the subject, so Fre had naturally filed it away in the back of her mind. Quintin walked over to the workbench, with Fre following closely behind. He pulled out the pouch he had filled with various objects from Jaymes's strong room and dumped its contents onto the tabletop.

It really wasn't much, just a few scrolls, a large coin with some foreign language on it and two small egg-shaped pieces of silver. Quintin scooped up the scrolls and the coin and handed them to Fre. He pushed the two silver eggs to the side.

"Could you put these with the other Thean goods?"

Fre grabbed the items from his hand and walked to the small room in the back, where they kept their cots. Moving to a corner of the room, she came to a small cabinet that had been left when the operation had been shut down years ago. It had several drawers each one tagged with a piece of paper labelling its contents tacked to it with some small nails she had found while trawling this place when they first arrived. She took the bundle of stuff Quintin had given her and crouched down to place them into the drawer labeled *Resonant Goods*.

"Hey, Fre! Come look at this!" Quintin's excited voice filled the cramped interior of their home.

She stood up and rushed out into the other room to see what it was exactly that had gotten him so excited. He was seated at his desk with some small hammers and pliers littered about him, peering at something in the middle of the mess. Fre drew closer, trying to get a better look. Quintin was holding a jeweler's glass, looking into the large crystallized structure glowing faintly.

"Where did that come from?" Fre spoke with an excited and almost reverent voice.

Quintin looked up for a moment. "It was inside one of these things."

He nudged what looked to be the remains of one of the small metal eggs. "I was about to go at it with a hammer when suddenly I pulled out a pin at the top. Then it just sort of fell apart."

Fre leaned in closer. The gem was clear; however, it seemed to reflect more light than was being produced by the few candles Quintin had lit in the room. Her attention then was drawn to the second silver egg laying on the table.

"Do you think the other one has another stone in it?" she whispered.

Quintin's eyes followed hers. "It wouldn't make sense to use the same method of storage for two different items. Then again, maybe it would."

He shrugged the question off and handed her a pair of small pliers, "Just be sure not to break the stone. It may lose value if it's damaged. Remember, look for a pin at the top. If you remove that, it should just come apart."

Fre nodded and snatched the pliers from his hands. She grabbed the little silver egg before rushing over to her bench to begin disassembly. Pulling up a stool, she sat down and began a more thorough investigation of the specimen. At a glance, the object looked almost smooth. As she peered closer, she began to see that it wasn't, and instead, an intricate puzzle formed out of dozens of rings and plates placed flush against each other. There were two pieces on its surface that didn't quite rest perfectly against their neighboring plates. One was at the top, where there seemed to be some kind of keyhole. The other came out of the lower side of the egg at an odd angle.

Fre grabbed the pair of pliers Quintin had given her, gripping the top protrusion as tightly as possible. She pulled and twisted in an attempt to pull it loose. Another minute passed as she continued working. It didn't seem to want to come out, but she had been able to coax it out just a little bit. Wiping off the little bit of sweat that had formed on her forehead, she went back to it. She pulled and pried until her fingers ached and began to feel like blisters might form.

Slowly the pin continued to come out little by little until it finally popped out with a jolt, pulling the pliers out of Fre's weakened fingers and onto the floor. With the pin pulled, it was as if a mass tension had been released, and just like Quintin said, the rings and plates came loose and slid away to reveal a glowing heart within.

It wasn't quite like the one Quintin had pulled from his. Where his had a brilliant clear glow, this one was tinted with a blue glow. It was beautiful and completely foreign to Fre's eyes. Unsure of what to do next, Fre stood up from her stool – she needed a break.

"I'm going to go clean up. Work like this tends to burn one's hands, and I think the river calls my name. When can we look back at what we've done and say it was worth what we have gained? I fear we paid the ultimate price for the empire now."

Fre dusted herself and did a once over of her desk before walking to the door leading to the outer factory building.

"Could you bring in the jeweler's book when you come back in? We may need it to figure out how small we need to cut these down in order to avoid suspicion." Quintin said as Fre opened the door to leave.

"I can do that, but I'm not sure these even have an acceptable size that would avoid suspicion. I mean, the way they shine isn't normal."

Quintin sighed, "I'm afraid you're probably right. We may have stolen something too expensive."

He stopped talking as his eyes rested on the almost eerie light coming from the stones.

"I'll get the book." Her voice was calm, without a tinge of regret.

"Thanks," Quintin said, his voice laced with irritation.

Feeling just a little dejected, Fre stepped out of the small interior into the larger building complex. It looked much creepier at night, with the moon casting shadows across the abandoned worktables leaving the edges of the large complex in complete darkness. Then there was the massive smelter, a dark body made of iron and stone curled up against the opposite side of the complex like a slumbering behemoth one would regret waking up. It was ironic, really, considering how much time Fre spent walking the darkened streets and back alleys, that she would fear that very thing that so often kept her safe from danger.

Making her way through the workstation to the large sliding doors at the other end of the complex, she was careful to cut her feet or legs on the piles of wood and metal strewn across the floor. As she reached the door, she grabbed it by the large handle. It squealed in protest as she pulled back on the rusty rollers, creating a space just large enough for her to fit her thin frame through.

Squeezing through the opening, Fre stepped out into a large courtyard. The moon was bright. Its light reflected off the cobbled space. It was a quiet, large space compared to much of the city, with the large open square leading down to the riverside. Basking in the cool light of the moon, Fre moved into the center of the courtyard.

There was no fear – the light chased away enough of the shadows creating a safe place to stand. Fre continued, making her way down to the water's edge. Normally, one wouldn't swim in the river water, as much of the sludge coming from the factories filled it with stuff known to make a person sick, but here the water entered the city still clear and untainted by the waste of progress.

Fre noticed some urchins at the water's edge, cleaning what seemed to be clothing. She didn't pay them any attention as she finally got to the very edge of the water. She stared at the dark surface as she pulled off her shoes and sat down beside the bank. Closing her eyes, she let the sensation of cold water take up her consciousness.

There were few things in the world that Fre could find peace in, and taking even just a moment to leave behind any worry, pain, or sorrow she held seemed like something that would help any man. Of course, Quintin never seemed to need time to stop and think. Fre had always just assumed he never stopped resting. He was a constant, not just to her but to himself as well. Fre looked at the moon. It appeared that about ten minutes had passed since she had first stepped out here. It was probably best if she started back.

Pulling her feet up, Fre scooted away from the river. She stood, brushing the dust off herself. Satisfied, she knelt down and submerged her hands in the cold flow of the river. Immediately, they felt better, and the water slowed the blood and relaxed the hand. She had to be careful, her skin was prone to breaking if she wasn't careful, and if she did get cut, it would be a nightmare to try and stop the bleeding.

Here, lineage was everything, and with good reason. Itheans prided themselves on their ability to use Resonance to manipulate reality, something her people couldn't do. Finished, Fre stood up and grabbed her shoes, turning back to the darkness of the large warehouse. She took a different route inside this time, walking around to the other side of the building. Going in, she made sure to take a left to a pile of books in the corner. There were only four of them, so it was not hard picking out the smallest and taking it with her inside the office she called home.

As she came inside, she noticed Quintin looking over the other objects they had obtained on their most recent excursion.

Quintin glanced up at her, "You feeling better?"

She nodded.

"Good. I didn't want you getting yourself hurt over something as trivial as a stone. The last time you got hurt, I nearly died from panic."

Fre could tell from the way he spoke that his head had improved while she'd been out. That made two of them.

She handed him the book, "I got this on my way in."

Quintin took the book and began leafing through its pages.

"You know you still haven't taken care of the books. I found them laying on the ground where they have been sitting for the past week." Her voice had a critical tone to it.

Quintin held up the book in his hand and tapped the worn-out leather cover. "You think any urchin or self-respecting criminal would steal a book that looked like this?"

Fre gave him a dangerous look, resting her arm on her side. "You know that there are a dozen holes in that roof, not to mention the hundreds of rodents that would love to take a piece out of them if given a chance."

Exasperation edged in her voice, catching Quintin's attention, causing him to look up, concerned.

"I'll get it done tomorrow, okay? Can you find a spot in the back room where I can fit them?"

Fre exhaled loudly, venting her irritation into the rest of the room before going to the back to throw around some things in order to make space. It was infuriating living alongside Quintin. He was one of the smartest people she knew, and yet there were times he was too dumb to realize just how much he knew. Then again, maybe she expected too much from someone only two years her senior.

She picked up several bags that had been propped up against the wall. She looked into each. They contained clothes in numerous states of wear. Why had Quintin stolen so many?

She tried balancing them on the top of the cabinet but, after seeing the way they teetered precariously over one of the cots, decided it was best to find a better place. She looked around the room.

She shrugged her shoulders and finally decided they could be piled on top of the rest of the bags on the other side of the room.

At least then, when they fall, they'd fall on their feet rather than their heads. Stepping back, she looked at the piles of bags and determined that they may need to start expansion out into the larger complex.

"I've got it!" Quintin's excited voice came from the other room.

Fre turned from her work, taking quick strides to the other room. She found Quintin at his desk peering at a page in the book. He turned his head to her and gestured excitedly for her to come. She came over and peered over his shoulder.

"I almost began to believe that we wouldn't be able to sell these things off, but then I found this." Quintin pointed to the bottom of the page titled *Sapphire*. It was a small passage, almost a footnote, talking about some strange variation that the stone could have.

"Some sapphires dug up from the mines around Iso have been said to have amazing reflective properties. Many who have seen one describe them as almost luminous in the sunlight."

Fre read the passage and looked over at the small stone sitting on the table. Could that light coming from it really be a product of the torchlight?

Quintin tapped her on the shoulder and handed her a small jeweler's hammer. "You want to get started?"

She turned her head and looked up at him, taking the hammer, "Any particular size you want for these?"

"Not really. It seems most stones found are about 3 centimeters across, so that should be fine, give or take a few."

Quintin's voice was dismissive as he spoke, which didn't really reassure Fre very much. Sitting down with hammer in hand, Fre prepared to cut. She reached over to grab her gloves off a hook on the side of the bench while also procuring a few other tools and a pair of goggles from a drawer on her left. She was finally ready. Picking up the stone, she brought it close, searching for points that would be good places to start. Meanwhile, behind her, Quintin was preparing for his first strike, lining up the stone on his table. He swung his hammer. There was a resounding ring as it slammed into the hard surface.

Fre covered her ears at the sound, spinning around to see what had made such a loud noise. Just as she turned, she could see a blinding light coming from the crack Quintin had created. The stone began to vibrate violently as the crack expanded. Quintin stumbled away from the rock. Fre had no time to process what she was looking at before the rock broke apart, completely flooding the room with a blinding light, and then all went dark.

CHAPTER 13

A brisk breeze from the south began to blow, clearing the clouds from the sky and bringing a cool wind into an open window in the royal Spire. It blew the piles of paper, causing them to fall off their perch, creating a loud rustle as it drifted down to the floor in droves. The noise caused Selyne to jolt out of her slumber.

Pulling up from her desk, she peered around to see what it was that had awakened her. Scanning the room, she noticed the pile of paper on the floor. From there, her eyes trailed to the open window, blowing in the cold night air. As she stood to close the window, an overwhelming ache crashed into the back of her skull, causing the room to reel around her.

"Shia, I really overdid it last night." Selyne looked around her, trying her best to keep the contents of her stomach at bay as the room spun around her.

She surveyed the room and counted one, two, three, four, five, six, seven, eight total empty bottles and a half-empty one still sitting beside where she had fallen unconscious. Cursing under her breath, she decided to leave the mess of bottles and paper on the floor. Instead, she walked to the washroom on the other side of the room. She turned the spigot for cold water, cupping the ice-cold water in the palms of her hands and pressing it onto her face. The cold liquid helped calm her headache as the dizziness receded just a little bit.

Feeling more like herself, Selyne decided to try and take stock of the situation. Her face was a mess, with makeup smeared across it from her last engagement with the nobility that afternoon. She looked down at her dress, which was not in much better shape, alcohol stains and ink splotches covered the front. She sighed. Her mother's plans had raised Selyne's stress to greater heights than usual, and Selyne feared she wasn't coping very well. She blamed the stress on her mother's most recent plans. Though if she was honest, this was just another turn in a cycle that had begun last year.

Soaking her face once again in an attempt to remove the rest of her makeup and alleviate the ache that still persisted behind her eyes, she grabbed the towel hanging to her right, patting her face dry. With that finished, all that was left to do was take care of her clothing situation and the mess that had once been called her room.

She started on the dress, reaching to unbutton the back. It was not a comfortable task, and the migraine sitting at the back of her head was not helping. The thought crossed her mind to call for one of the servants, though she decided against it. No need to make a scene, and having someone see her in this state was not something Selyne enjoyed.

Leaning back, she pushed her shoulder blades together as she tried her best to reach the bottom two buttons. This was not something she wanted to do at half-past one in the morning, hungover with a migraine eating at the back of her eyes. Eventually, the trouble became too much, and Selyne decided it would be better to squeeze out of the thing and leave the buttons to burn for all she cared. It was a tight fit but not impossible as she managed to wiggle out, letting the dress fall to the floor like an exoskeleton.

In nothing but her undergarments, she walked to her wardrobe and picked out a new set of undergarments and a blue nightgown. It took several minutes of curses and fumbling around before she managed to remove the remnants of her trashed laundry and replace them with the cleaner alternative.

Selyne finally turned to the mess strewn across the floor of her study. Starting with the bottles, she gathered up each one, including the half-finished bottle on her desk. Tossing the lot into her waste bin, Selyne continued picking up the room bit by bit, throwing dirty laundry into her hamper for the servants to get later. She then began the arduous process of sorting out her desk, gathering up her pens, and putting them back into their cases before tucking them into her desk's drawers.

As she reached the papers, however, she slowed, taking her time to look through them before deciding whether or not to keep or throw them out. Many of the pages were incoherent, with ideas going on for a sentence before shifting to a completely different subject in the next. The whole mess strung together in a glorious melody of chaos on the pages. Selyne placed all of those in one pile to be thrown out later. She glanced at the pages she had left. Her writing was far from scholarly in its content; mostly she wrote of fairytales and daily life. Selyne considered tossing those as well. She paused, staring at the pile of unfinished work. Sighing, she set the mess of notes down on her desk. She'd look through them when her head didn't ache.

Her eyes drifted from the pile of pages, focusing on a different document. The paper was tucked under the miscellaneous objects populating Selyne's desk. It was made of thicker paper than the stock Selyne used. It was the type often used for official documents. Selyne took a seat, pulling the document out of the mess of clutter, careful not to disturb the precarious equilibrium on her desk. This had been the document that started everything.

Most people figured out whether or not they had a Resonant inheritance by the time they were three, around the time a child began truly remembering the world around them. However, there was always the odd exception. Most researchers guessed that the occurrence of late inheritance had something to do with trauma, or simply the power had no other suitable hosts to inherit the Resonance.

Reasons aside, Selyne had to deal with the results. Selyne recalled the examination as if it happened yesterday. The seers had been called in after she had shattered her window. Her maid had dropped a tray of glassware, prompting the incident. They'd spent several hours poking and prodding Selyne, going so far as to gather a blood sample from her. The results had been concrete; Selyne was the benefactor of a late-stage inheritance.

"This is stupid," Selyne whispered as the memory soured her mood.

She shivered, looking around the room. "I need to take a walk."

Selyne walked back over to her wardrobe, finding a large coat and pulling it on. She grabbed a pair of soft slippers, sliding her feet into them before stepping out into the hall. Selyne inched her bedroom door open, hands squeezing the handle tightly as she tried her best to prevent the door's hinges from squeaking. Night had consumed the Spire. It was late, and Selyne didn't want to wake up anyone else at this unholy hour.

She peeked out into the hallway. Shadows covered the stairwell, the beam of light coming from her room only deepening the night's darkness. Slipping out into the darkness, Selyne began the trek upstairs, neglecting to close her door. She didn't want to risk the noise that the latch would make. Silence could be eerie, but Selyne didn't mind it. No, what she hated could be considered as almost silent. The stairwell was hollow, empty, but when Selyne began walking, everything changed. It was as if the sound of her own footsteps invited something else to come along as well, a spectre brought to life by the noise.

Selyne continued upwards, breathing a sigh of relief as she reached the small library at the top of the Spire. She stepped into the room, fumbling around with the wall until her hands found the small switch. White light burst to life in the glyph bulbs as she flipped the switch. Selyne let out a sigh of relief. The light burned away the darkness of night and all the fears it brought with it. She scanned the hundreds of novels covering the walls, looking for something that would catch her interest.

Despite having grown up reading the books on these shelves, Selyne only recognized a small fraction of the literature they contained, making each visit an adventure to discover something new. Selyne ran her fingers along the rows of books, stopping at a small yellow book. Selyne pulled it out from the shelf, reading the title embroidered in gold onto the cloth cover. *Classic Tales of Angels and Heaven's War.* The cover didn't reveal the author. Selyne took a seat, cracking open the dusty novel. Her mind struggled to focus, the remnants of her headache still causing discomfort as she read.

Still, Selyne was determined to continue onward with the novel. Time distorted as Selyne was lost in the pages, her mind unaware of the hours that may or may not have passed while it focused on the pages in front of it. Selyne was unfamiliar with the stories. Most compilation works of old stories focused on the iconic stories. You would expect to hear of Amie Angel-kin's reunification of the great kings or Azaahar's duel with the eldest ancestor. Instead, the small yellow book focused on tales Selyne had never heard of. Her current story involved the Angel Elin and the goddess of death Shial. The story consisted of an argument between the two, ending with the Angel and goddess approaching a farmer to resolve the conundrum. The farmer sides with Elin and receives his blessing. However, his wife is cursed by Shial and doomed never to have children so long as she lived. Selyne found the story rather tedious. It seemed whenever an ordinary person dealt with divinity, it always ended poorly.

Selyne had to wonder what that meant for her. Inheriting the power of an Angel couldn't bode well for her health and prosperity. The hinges on the door squeaked, drawing Selyne out from the novel.

"Hello?" Selyne called nervously. *Who'd be awake at this time?*

The door creaked open. The man Selyne's mother had introduced days earlier stood in the doorway,

"Hey," Selyne said, surprised by the intrusion. "Is something wrong? I'm not sure I remember your name."

Wil glanced around the room before settling on Selyne. "My name is Willem; we met earlier."

"Right," Selyne said slowly, "Still, what are you doing here at this hour?"

"Your door was open, and your room was empty." Wil leaned against the doorframe as he spoke. "Your servant sent me up here to look while she checked the pub next door."

The man seemed sincere with his explanation.

"Oh, heavens above," Selyne gasped as a thought occurred to her, "What time is it?"

Wil scrunched his brow, thinking for a moment. "I'd say about half-past revival. The servants just woke up for the day."

Selyne groaned. She'd been up for half the night burying herself in a book. Her headache hadn't even vanished completely. "This should prove to be a difficult day."

Willem shrugged, "It may not be so bad."

He pulled at his ear, glancing at the book in her hand, "So, what were you reading?"

Selyne laughed in embarrassment, tucking the book to the side. "It's nothing. Just some fables I found on the shelf."

"It's not a bad way to begin a day," he said frankly, "Nothing like a good hero story to get you motivated."

"There weren't many heroes to be found in this book," Selyne snorted mockingly, "Mostly just regular people at the wrong place at the right time, you know."

"I often wandered into the forest as a child," Wil said, shrugging. "Sometimes, you aren't blessed with knowledge or power. Sometimes you have to search the forgotten places for it."

Selyne cocked her head, confused. "How often has that plan worked out for you? Just for curiosity's sake."

Wil paused, eyes growing distant as if recalling something long past. "There was one time," he said quietly.

He looked at Selyne, coming back to reality, "but it only takes one encounter to change one's life. Not every journey will bring answers. However, I don't think you can learn anything new by remaining in the same place."

"Too bad we don't have an enchanted forest here in the city," Selyne said wistfully, "Heavens know I could use one right about now."

"Don't feel too disenfranchised," Wil said as he pulled open the door. "You're beginning classes today. Some would consider university to be a special sort of forest."

Selyne gave a halfhearted smile. It would be only a few hours before she began lessons. The irritation was still there, the whole thing seemed silly, but Selyne couldn't suppress the excitement of the unknown completely.

"Are you ready to go?" Wil asked, gesturing out the door with his thumb. "I'm pretty sure your servant is waiting for you downstairs."

Selyne stood up, setting the book down on the table and glancing about the room. She still had a headache, and already she could feel the weight of a sleepless night on her shoulders. It was far from an ideal way to begin a new chapter.

Selyne sighed. She walked over to Wil, stepping out into the hall.

"Best not to keep her waiting," she said, glancing at Wil. "She is the one who's going to stitch me together for today after all."

Wil smiled quietly, "Makes my job much simpler if she does," he whispered under his breath.

Selyne ignored the remark. She had a new wave of motivation, and she didn't want anything dampening it before she got through her day, or at least the morning.

CHAPTER 14

Quintin awoke to a maelstrom of light filling his vision and a fiery buzz coursing through his veins. He looked around the room and was bombarded with swirling patterns of white light everywhere he turned. His mind reeled with the patterns of light, confused by the incomprehensible landscape glowing in front of him. The memory of the last few hours eluded Quintin's mind, still, he tried his best to remember what exactly it was he had been doing before he had lost consciousness, moving up through the pathways of his mind trying to retrace his steps.

He'd made a promise.

No, that wasn't correct; Quintin wasn't sure why his mind made that conclusion.

We killed Jaymes and robbed his storehouse.

That sounded correct. He'd been in the office taking stock of the things they had picked up during their midnight raid.

Quintin's memory dropped off after that. There was nothing to indicate his current predicament, his mind hitting a wall of white as he tried to see the last few scenes before his current situation. The world continued to shake, tremors running through his veins. The sensation became unbearable as it tried its best to shake Quintin's body apart from the inside out. All this happened as the constant swirling of patterns began to drive Quintin towards insanity. He tried closing his eyes, but it had no effect on the swirling lights as the darkness eluded him.

He sat there for only Thea knows how long, losing his mind in the alien patterns around him. As Quintin sat in this strange state of purgatory, something akin to words began to rise out of the chaos. Quintin called the noises words, but that was not entirely accurate – he couldn't understand what was being said, nor did it sound like any human voice Quintin had ever heard, but he could sense a pattern in the rhythm of the vibrations. Even as they threatened to tear him limb from limb, the light combined itself with the rhythm to reveal the truth of these words that they spoke.

It hurt Quintin's head as he tried to understand the cacophony, but for some reason trying to reach out to the alien symphony with his mind lessened the pain he felt throughout his body. Quintin tried opening his eyes once more. This time, however, it was as if someone had flipped a switch in his mind. What had once been a confusing swirl of chaos now had definable features.

"What in the name of Shia is going on here?" Quintin turned his head side to side; the swirling patterns shifted and contorted as he looked around.

A flicker appeared at the edge of Quintin's vision, drawing his attention. It was a different kind of light, with an orange and red tint; it swirled in one direction, remaining in place as it danced around. The light continued to dance for a moment before realization smacked the front side of Quintin's brain – it was the lamp he had been using to work this evening.

Though he could not make out the base or cage, the motion and color were unmistakable to his eyes. Quintin stared at the light; its glow was unmistakable, though its shape seemed distorted as the swirl of lights covered Quintin's vision. How had it gotten here? In this world where nothing looked normal, why was the light the one thing that remained the same? An idea formed in Quintin's mind. Moving his arms, he brought his hand up to his face, the pain returning as he moved his body through the strange lights. It no longer felt like he was falling apart, but his body ached as if he had worked in a quarry all day then went home and plowed a field.

Working through the pain, Quintin positioned his hand in front of his face. The swirling lights grew agitated, compressing their pattern as they tried to avoid Quintin's hand. His focus didn't remain on the swirling lights for long as his attention turned towards his hands. Quintin shivered as the eerie sight took hold of him. His hands were gone, their flesh and blood now replaced by a lacework of shimmering blue light. A quick glance down confirmed that it wasn't just his hands that were no longer normal. Quintin moved his hand, and the blue lacework followed suit, the swirling patterns recoiling as he moved his arm through them.

It felt like moving through honey, and Quintin got the sense that the swirling lights were pushing off his body, not unlike how a magnet would repel another magnet of the same type. Quintin sat there, watching the swirling patterns dance around him in lazy circles.

I wonder what on earth this place is? Quintin thought. He could be dead, but that didn't seem right; this all felt too real. The world began to tremble, drawing Quintin's attention back to the present. Something seemed to be pulling on the swirling patterns, bending them into unfamiliar shapes. Quintin glanced around the room. Using the lantern light as a point of reference, Quintin was successfully able to locate where in the room the disturbance was coming from.

A blue glow was emanating across the room, originating from a small latticework of blue light positioned on what Quintin assumed was the workshop floor.

"Fre!" The realization hit Quintin like a sledgehammer.

He lunged forward, gasping as his body pushed up against the swirling energy around him. Quintin inched forward, his limbs straining as if they were moving through packed sand – *come on, MOVE* – Quintin screamed in his mind as he frantically tried to pull himself closer. Fre's body didn't seem to be moving. The swirling patterns seemed to have surrounded her, creating a rigid prison around her.

"Please just let me go!" Quintin was getting desperate as he began to tear his body apart in his attempts to reach her.

The tremors stopped suddenly, and Quintin felt the rhythm fade from his ears. Everything began to grow dim as Quintin continued on. His inner ear began to go haywire, and, looking around, Quintin could see the storm of lights begin to fade as the sensation that he was falling began to overtake everything else. Quintin spun violently through the darkened void, breaking apart into a million pieces as he began to lose consciousness once again.

There was a pop, and Quintin fell face down onto the concrete floor of the workshop. He rolled over and immediately threw up the contents of his stomach. Everything roiled around him as Quintin did his best to regain his bearings. His eyes kept readjusting to what looked to be a room spinning in two directions at once. It took a moment, but the warm interior of the workshop began to take shape around him. Quintin wiggled his fingers. He hadn't realized at the moment, but he hadn't felt anything while in that world of swirling shapes. Glad for the return of sensation in his extremities, Quintin pressed his hands against the stone floor, pushing himself up off the ground.

As Quintin got to his feet, he was finally able to survey the area around him clearly, his eyes focusing first on the lamp in the corner, then he noticed the body on the floor.

"Fre!" Quintin's mind raced as panic over her current condition.

She seemed to have fallen from her chair sometime last night, presumably for the same reason Quintin had been knocked unconscious. Though she looked unharmed, the air around her shimmered unnaturally as if it were made from diamond.

Quintin raised a tentative hand towards Fre. His attempt was halted abruptly as he came into contact with the distorted air. A searing pain erupted from his hand, causing him to pull back. Looking down at his hand, Quintin noticed a clean, paper-thin cut, slicing down through the membrane between his fingers and into the center of his hand. Blood began to pool in the wound, moving slowly as it began its coagulation process.

Quintin's stomach twisted at the sight, and it took the entirety of his willpower to keep from passing out at the pain. He breathed deeply, trying to control the pain – he had bigger problems to worry about at the moment. He stared at shimmering air, unsure of how to proceed.

He noted that while he and Fre had been knocked from their chairs by whatever happened, the room remained in its usual state, untouched by whatever unseen force had hit them. Quintin stumbled over to the chair, clutching his hand in a sorry effort to alleviate the pain of moving. Taking a seat, Quintin rested his injured hand in his lap as he tried to gauge the situation.

Fre lay huddled next to the chair she had been sitting on earlier. Despite his earlier assessment, Quintin noticed her body was trembling as if fevered. He didn't want to attempt to reach her as long as that distortion in the air remained. He'd lost function in one hand; he didn't want to risk losing the other.

I need to get closer, Quintin thought, *but how in the loving world am I supposed to do that?*

Quintin moved carefully, approaching the strange prismatic phenomenon in the air. He crouched down, moving slowly as he approached what seemed to be the edge of the barrier.

"What in Shial below is this?" Quintin whispered in fear.

Reality seemed to shatter, with panes of shimmering air crisscrossing each other in unknowable patterns. Quintin found a trapezoidal pane somewhat separated from the distorted mess. He pivoted around the strange shape. The space didn't seem to exist in three-dimensional space, the reflective surface disappearing entirely whenever Quintin looked at it from the side. Quintin grimaced, an edge that fine would explain the burning cut on his hand.

He grabbed the lamp, watching the light scattering on the prismatic surfaces in the air. They seemed to be surrounding Fre, making any attempt to help her impossible. The feeling of helplessness drove a cold tendril into Quintin's heart. Clearly, he'd made a mistake somewhere. Quintin pulled his hands into a fist as the frustration grew.

If I could just remember what in Shial happened here. He grimaced as the pain in his hand grew unbearable.

They had stumbled into the realm of Thean witchcraft. That much was clear. Now Fre was suffering from the consequences.

Quintin began to fall forward as he lost balance, panicking as the crystalline lattice blurred. As he fell towards his face, he threw out his injured hand, catching himself only inches from the razor-sharp edges of the lattice. Letting out a groan at the burning pain that exploded in his right hand, he pushed back, falling into a sitting position a few feet away. He took a precautionary glance to make sure he hadn't lost any part of his body and froze as he came to his left hand.

The lantern he'd been holding was cleanly cut three-quarters of the way through its center. The only thing keeping it together was two wires that had avoided the cut. Quintin swallowed, imagining his hand in place of the wire cage. At a loss for ideas, Quintin set down the disfigured lantern and began to acknowledge his own wound. The edge of the lattice had created a very clean inch and a half cut through the membrane between his ring and middle finger. The pain had faded to the back of his mind, turning into a dull throb. Fortunately, the bleeding had stopped entirely, and the wound was already scabbing over.

Using the reflection still cast by the lantern, Quintin worked around the dangerous area on his floor to the back room. The room was dimly lit – the only light was coming from the lantern in the other room, making it difficult to distinguish the bags piled up against the wall. Quintin got to work, using his good hand to pull the bags out of the pile, digging through each one in search of their medical supplies. He trawled through four bags coming up empty in each of them. Why did he steal so many clothes anyway?

Finally, there was only one bag left. Quintin pulled it out of the corner and worked the leather straps with his one good hand, opening the flap and digging through the contents inside. Surely it had to be in here. Quintin dug deeper with his hand, moving past all the empty vials, makeup bottles, and lock picks reaching to the bottom of the bag, his hands came into contact with a leather container, and Quintin smiled. He pulled his arm out, revealing his catch, a small leather box painted red with the word for health inlaid in black ink across its cover.

Quintin clutched the box in his wounded hand while returning to the other room, where he could use the light. He used his good hand to stabilize himself in the doorway, and his vision grew blurry as the pain began to get to his head. Quintin quickened his pace, pushing himself off the doorway, lurching across the room, and collapsing into the back of his chair.

He dropped the box of equipment onto the table and got to work. Quickly, he unlatched the lid, revealing the contents inside. He grabbed the roll of bandages, a small vial of numbing ointment, and some Everwood root. The ointment would act quicker, killing the pain almost instantly. However, the effects wouldn't last very long – hence the Everwood root. Quintin didn't waste any time jamming the Everwood root into his mouth and chewing heavily.

With the pain now under control, Quintin finally got his first good look at the damage that had been done. The cut was deep, probably in need of stitches. Quintin winced. He wouldn't be able to stitch the thing up, not with the weak painkillers at his disposal. He decided to do what he could, grabbing a bandage out from the bag of medical supplies, doing his best to wrap the cut using his good hand. Quintin poured some extra numbing ointment on the bandage before finishing the bandage. He winced as the chemical came into contact with the wound, Though the sensation faded a moment later. Quintin sighed as he tied the knot on the bandage. It was rudimentary, but he hoped the added ointment would glue the whole thing together somewhat. Quintin relaxed his hand, glad for the alleviation of the immediate pain.

Quintin leaned back and let out a breath he hadn't realized he'd been holding. That was one problem taken care of, and now he just needed to figure out how to solve the crisis with Fre. He turned his chair, looking back at the situation occurring on the workshop floor. The lattice of crystals was still there, keeping him from Fre. Its strange angles reflected in the lantern light. Those edges had cut through his hand as well as his lantern. It hadn't even cracked the glass as it cut the thing almost completely in half.

Coming at this issue directly would only end in his injury. He needed to find a more roundabout way to handle this. Quintin scanned his workbench for anything that could be of use. His eyes fell upon the small hammer. Snatching the small tool in his good hand, Quintin got down into a prone position, coming level with the floor. He scooted the lantern closer. Quintin didn't know what had created the strange phenomena, though he wasn't going to wait around for something to change. Finding another surface that was separated from the more hazardous lattice, Quintin brought the small hammer close. He started simple, tapping the flat surface of the structure, testing its structural integrity. The surface was completely unyielding. He slammed on the surface with some more force, his hand jarring from the effort. Still, the surface remained unfazed.

Quintin stood up, scanning the workbench for a chisel. He managed to find one in a drawer. Gripping the metal spike gingerly in his wounded hand, he began pounding on the surface again. His pain eventually grew unbearable, and Quintin stopped, cradling his damaged hand. His attempts had been fruitless, leaving nothing to indicate that he had been hammering into the surface for the past twenty minutes. Whatever the lattice surrounding Fre was made of wouldn't be broken through using any of the tools at Quintin's disposal.

This is going nowhere, thought Quintin as he stared at the unyielding barrier between himself and Fre. It could go burn in Shia's fire for all he cared. Anger mounted in Quintin's chest as he sat there. The world was bad enough as it was; he didn't need some stupid curse coming out from the depths and biting him in the hand. He threw the small hammer at the unyielding wall separating him from Fre, the last bit of his defiance leaving his body with it.

The small hammer bounced off the surface, flew through the air, and froze a foot from the ground, hanging as if held by some invisible force. Quintin stared for a moment, his brain already given up on the whole situation. He found it hard to be shocked by the impossible sight.

"Bloody Thean witchcraft," Quintin grumbled before attempting to rise.

As he came to his feet, he was hit with the futility of it all, a tear beginning to form as he slowly lost his composure over the situation. He wanted to scream, to find whoever had done this and tear their heart out. Instead, he just sat there, his thoughts eating away at his mind. Quintin didn't know how much time had passed, enough to let the light of day come streaming in under the crack of the door leading to the outside warehouse. Frankly, he couldn't care less. There was a loud clatter inside the office, causing Quintin to jolt out of his stupor, desperately trying to locate the source of the noise.

"That's weird."

The room was empty, and Quintin relaxed, "Probably just a rat rummaging through all the food supplies I left open last night."

Quintin groaned as last night's failure came crashing back down on him again. It was just another city without answers, any hope of getting a clue about his parents dead along with a man Quintin accidentally killed. At this point, he couldn't care less about rats in the food. Another noise filled the little space, a quiet groan resounding in the silence; this time, it sounded human. Quintin looked up from the patch of concrete he'd been staring blankly at, his eyes catching movement on the floor. Fre was moving.

Fre rolled sideways as she slowly regained consciousness, her body on a path towards the impossibly sharp edges of her prison. Quintin watched in horror, unable to muster enough energy to try and stop her from hurting herself. He couldn't do anything from out here anyway. Fre stopped on her side, completely unscathed, and curled up on the floor, falling back to sleep. Quintin leaped from his chair, knocking it over as he scrambled over to where she lay, completely overwhelmed by what was happening.

His outburst startled Fre, who jolted out of her slumber, her head twisting suddenly as she tried to locate the noise. Her eyes focused on Quintin, squinting between her eyes at the light from the lantern.

"Hi Quin, what are you doing working so early in the morning? Did I sleep on the floor last night?"

Quintin said nothing, his mind unable to comprehend what was happening in front of him.

"Hey, hey, have you been crying?" Fre's voice grew concerned as she took in Quintin's sallow complexion and teary eyes, "Are you ok?"

Strained laughter echoed throughout the room as Quintin finally snapped under the weight of the last night.

Fre grew defensive as the laughter continued, "Quintin, you're starting to scare me."

She sat up and turned all her attention towards the spectacle in front of her. Quintin brushed the tears from his eyes, "I'm sorry, Fre, I was just worried, that's all."

His voice came out a croak as he tried his best to quiet himself.

"Strange way for you to show worry," Fre said as she continued to watch Quintin, an unnerved look still on her face.

Quintin finally managed to get his breathing under control, shuddering once as he exhaled the final feelings of panic from his body, "I know, I can't remember much from last night, but something unnatural happened, and for a moment, I thought we were both dead. I'm just glad you're ok."

Fre rubbed her temples, "I wouldn't go so far as ok, my mind is trying to split out of my head, and the room has been blurry for the last minute."

She looked at Quintin, "Did I drink too much last night?"

Quintin leaned in, getting ready to explain, when the sound of screeching iron sounded from the outer building complex, drawing the attention of Quintin and Fre as it echoed throughout the building. The two sat motionless, trying their best to detect any other hints of sound. Quintin was not disappointed when the clattering of old machinery echoed once again throughout the building.

Moving quickly to snatch his sword from where he'd placed it yesterday evening, he stood. Fre pushed herself up off the floor, teetering precariously as she stood up. She closed her eyes as she was bombarded with a thundering pain in the back of her head. Quintin turned to see Fre collapse forward, catching herself on her workbench as she toppled back into her chair.

He walked up, scanning Fre's sweating face and unfocused vision, "You don't look like you're going to die, but you sure as death can't stand, stay here, and I'll check outside."

Quintin's voice came out steely as he spoke, a mixture of calm analysis and fear.

Fre gave little resistance to his prompting and sat back, holding her head. Quintin turned back to the door, looping his scabbard onto his belt, preparing himself as he stood with a door looming in front of him. Taking a deep breath to focus himself, Quintin lifted the latch on the door and carefully peeked out into the large outer complex. The large space was brightly lit, the light of the rising sun coming in through the large industrial windows lining the top of the walls, dispelling the shadows lurking among the piles of metal and rotten wood strewn about the area.

A flash of steel caught Quintin's eyes. His reaction was immediate, shifting his body to the left as the flat side of a sword blinked past his face only inches away. Quintin drew in another breath, his mind racing as the blood rushed to his head. Now in control of himself, Quintin surveyed the near motionless world around him. A soldier stood to his left wearing full lockplate's and carrying the sword that almost smacked

Quintin a moment earlier. Drawing his sword, Quintin was unable to hear the rasp of steel as the rush of blood filled his ears.

Taking a broad stance, Quintin stepped forward, putting his entire weight behind his blade, moving faster than the enforcer could react as he drove the point of his blade forward into the lockplate's chest piece. Steel ground on silver steel as plate met sword point, sending a shockwave throughout Quintin's entire body. The metal buckled as Quintin continued to push forward, trying to break through the plate. There was a sudden release of tension, and Quintin's sword pierced through the man's armor. Determined to put the enforcer down, Quintin aimed for the heart, hoping to end this with a single blow.

The sword stopped short, coming to a grinding halt as it hit yet another plate of steel underneath. The world began to speed up, and the enforcer stumbled back in real-time, taking Quintin's sword with him. Quintin fell forward, pulled by his weapon, his face coming only inches away from the face of the enforcer. A pair of dark brown eyes looked at Quintin from within the glass eye slits of the lock plate's helmet. The man brought up his longsword, pulling it back from its swing with blinding speed, bringing the serrated edge up towards Quintin's chest in a moment.

Quintin's mind raced in a mad panic as it tried desperately to move his body faster; his eyes darted back and forth manically as he looked for any salvation. The glint of steel caught Quintin's eyes, and silence filled the void where his heartbeat had been earlier.

The sensation of falling filled Quintin, his ears popping as if they were rapidly changing altitude

Time passed in agonizing moments as Quintin waited for the sword to strike his side. The sword didn't come. He opened his eyes. The world that had been present was now replaced by the swirling maelstrom of energy he had experienced the night before. Quintin groaned internally at the ever-changing patterns taking place before his eyes, and he swore that if this was someone's sick idea of an afterlife, he was going to ask Shia to take his soul. Looking down at himself,

Quintin was met with the same lattice of blue making up his body that he'd seen prior. He then looked to the right where the man trying to kill him stood.

He looked considerably hazier than Quintin's own form, his blue lattice smudging into itself, creating a single blob of color rather than individual strands. Quintin attempted to move, reflexively activating the signals leading to his muscles in hopes of lifting a leg off the ground. His lattice pulsed a brilliant blue as he tried, and pain flared immediately in his lower torso, causing him to halt. It seemed he was at an impasse. Currently, the sword seemed to pass right through his chest, leaving him unscathed, but Quintin wasn't liking his chances once he left this strange dimension. Of course, there was the chance that he was dead, and this was just a vision of pre-afterlife lucidity felt by the newly deceased. If only he could move. Quintin tried to move once more to little success. Clearly, that wasn't going to work any time soon. The energy creating the world around Quintin began to thrum with energy, and he suddenly felt as if he was plummeting at a blinding speed, pushing his stomach into his throat, his vision condensing into a single point as he fell out of consciousness.

Air rushed outwards with a bang, and Quintin slammed onto the factory floor. The enforcer looked taken aback by the sudden reappearance of the man he had tried to cut in half a second earlier. Quintin looked up at the looming figure, whose eyes were hidden behind the reflective eyepieces, sword poised for a kill point. Quintin began to stand, his body trembling as he did so. The enforcer stood back as if hesitant to engage his opponent again. Quintin looked the man in his eyes. His body had used up every last drop of energy it had stored up, and pain began to take over as Quintin's adrenaline ran out. He looked at the enforcer, gritting his teeth in frustration. Quintin's legs gave out a second later, and he was enveloped in darkness as he fell unconscious.

Alfear leaned back to catch his breath as the kid collapsed to the ground. A night's worth of time spent searching the lower city only to end with this. Orion stepped out of the shadows where he'd remained hidden during the fight.

"Are you ok?" Orion asked, gesturing awkwardly towards him, "You've got something sticking out."

Alfear looked down at his chest where the kid's weapon had lodged itself. "Thea above that kid had a powerful arm. I'm going to have a bruise from this."

He looked at the pierced piece of lockplate. The weapon had avoided the glyph work remarkably, going through the entire piece of steel before being stopped by the second layer of armor beneath. Alfear deactivated the plate's glyphs, pulling it away from the rest of the suit and setting it aside to be dealt with later.

Appreciating the removal of the extra weight, Alfear turned back to the issue at hand. "You brought us here, Orion. Mind showing me what we're looking for?"

Alfear turned to Orion, who seemed to have taken an interest in the unconscious boy. Alfear stepped forward, watching as his partner rummaged through the kids' pockets.

"Now is not the time to look for loose change," Alfear said jokingly.

Orion ignored him, growing more concerned as he continued searching.

"Ah, this is bad," Orion groaned, "How on earth am I going to explain this to the department?"

"What's the matter, Orion?" Alfear asked, growing concerned, "Is this kid important?"

Orion snorted, "More than you could imagine. Heaven above, we're in a mess."

"I'm not sure I understand what's going on. Could you explain what's so upsetting?"

Orion sighed. "You saw the kid vanish when you tried to apprehend him?"

Alfear nodded, "I've never seen anything like it."

Orion laughed wryly. "No, I couldn't imagine you would. It's an inheritance that's been lost for millennia."

"Are you telling me this kid has the Angel's heart?" Alfear asked, realization coming to him.

Orion nodded with a sigh, "I checked all over his body for any sign of the heart. He didn't possess it anywhere on his body. I'm sure you're familiar with what that means."

Alfear's gaze turned to the unconscious thief on the ground, dread taking him over as the implications of Orion's words sank in.

"The kid made a pact that quickly?" Alfear asked.

The idea seemed impossible, though he trusted Orion's judgment.

"We'll need to take him in just to be sure," Orion said, standing up, "If you would check the room he came from to see if the other Heart is in there. We'll start collecting evidence and hopefully gauge the size of this mess."

Alfear nodded and walked over to the door the kid had come from. The interior of the room was cozy, though a little messy, with lamplight illuminating the workbenches lined with tools. Alfear detected movement in the corner of his eye, his focus turning to the other person in the room. It was a small girl, probably no older than her compatriot, her coral hair and pale skin indicating she was probably Anglis in descent. The young girl seemed sick as she stared dizzily at Alfear.

"Hi," Alfear said, trying to sound non-threatening. "I'm an enforcer with the Thean institute. We found your friend outside, and we're going to need you to come with us."

The young woman groaned, sitting back in the chair. "Feel free to take me in. I'm in no condition to run."

Alfear nodded, "We'll get you all sorted soon enough, though you may not like the results."

The girl shrugged, though was unresponsive otherwise. Alfear stepped outside, confident the girl wasn't going anywhere. He groaned, the lack of sleep beginning to agitate him. Hopefully, he could be done with this by tonight, but Alfear suspected that wouldn't be the case.

CHAPTER 15

Quintin regained consciousness with his ears pounding. Fortunately, he could remember what happened last night. He opened his eyes. The state of his body was regrettable. His muscles were burning from overuse and his head pounding from his constant shift in and out of reality. Glancing around the room, he was met with the barren surface of a prison wall. Quintin sat up as he began to search his surroundings. Pacing around the edge of his cell, he was met with solid stone walls with not a crack or window to speak of. The door was solid steel, with a silver lining around all of its edges to prevent someone with an inheritance from using their power to break through. Escape was impossible; Quintin knew that without any tools or weapons to speak of. He was completely at the mercy of whichever Thean department had sent an enforcer to retrieve him.

Quintin looked down at his hands. He had done something yesterday during his fight with the enforcer – was it Resonance? Quintin didn't have a clue what else he could ascribe his actions to. One of the men who had taken him into custody mentioned something about agitated threads in the air of their workshop; maybe that had something to do with his current abilities?

Quintin looked down at his hands, they didn't look any different, but Quintin could feel something different under the surface, like a hundred grains of sand were shaking gently while they traveled through his bloodstream. It wasn't painful per se, just an unnatural experience. Quintin felt like reaching out and touching his newfound power. The bolt on his door screeched, pulling Quintin out of his mind. He turned to see the door swing open, revealing a broad figure standing in the hallway beyond.

It was the man who had brought him in only hours ago, though now he was no longer dressed in full plate. His stance and shape were familiar.

The man gestured with his hand, "Come, there are some people who wish to speak to you."

Quintin paused in thought for a moment. Obviously, he didn't have a say in what he did and did not get to do in this situation, but he still wanted to consider all his options before proceeding. Quintin glanced up at the man. He had taken no moves to forcibly remove him from the cell, but that didn't mean he wouldn't if Quintin refused.

"What if I say no?" Quintin finally spoke.

The man thought for a moment, "Do you want to stay in here? Because I can arrange for that."

Shia, the man had gotten him there. Quintin let out a heavy sigh, "No, I don't suppose I do."

The man nodded, "Then right this way, young sir."

The man stepped back from the door, and Quintin stepped forward into the hallway. The large man stood behind him, blocking the hallway to the right, leaving the left for Quintin to proceed. The hall was well lit, with Resonant lamps lining the walls giving off a comfortable glow as they continued down the cell block. Despite the warm glow of the lanterns, Quintin couldn't sway the feeling that a thousand pounds lay above his head. They reached the end of the hall, where a flight of stairs led towards the upper levels awaiting them.

Quintin quickly made his way up the stairwell, the large man following close behind as they proceeded up the twisting stairway.

"You're going to want to take a left once we reach the top," the man spoke from behind Quintin, his voice resonating throughout the enclosed space of the stairwell.

Quintin nodded in acknowledgment. They came to the peak of the stairwell, the small hallway expanding into a large corridor snaking out in three branches. Quintin took a left as he'd been instructed. Escape crossed Quintin's mind for a moment. With the enforcer behind him, he could try and vanish like he had before. Quintin discarded the idea as he recalled the previous night. He'd been able to vanish from the world twice, and both times he'd been stuck in one place as he'd done so. That wasn't even considering what traps or defenses this place contained built for people like him. The Thean institutes were built by people with inheritance. If anyone knew how to contain someone like Quintin, it would be them. Quintin sighed, the irritation of being contained growing. The pair walked down the hallway for another few minutes before the man told Quintin to stop at the door on their right.

The door looked just like the other half dozen they had passed during their journey through the complex, with an unassuming face and a simple brass latch holding it shut. The man knocked, and a muffled voice came from the other side, beckoning them to come in. Hearing the confirmation, the man lifted the latch and pushed the door gently inward, revealing the interior within. The office was cozy, with an orange resonant lamp creating a soft glow to saturate the room, and despite the small size, it didn't feel cramped due to the clean surfaces and well-planned placement of all the furniture.

A man sat behind the desk, with a well-trimmed beard and clean suit marking him as someone who took care of everything he put his mind to. The man looked up from a report he had been drawn from by the knock on his door.

"Alfear!" the man spoke with a clean accent as he addressed Quintin's escort, "I'm so glad you could come and resolve this today. You wouldn't believe the number of people breathing down my neck waiting for an update on this whole situation."

The man stood up from his chair as he and Quintin's escort, Alfear, embraced each other in a handshake. An awkward feeling came over Quintin as he watched the two interact – he felt like a homeless man who had walked in on a family reunion during a holiday, making him very uncomfortable.

"Well then, shall we get to the business at hand?" Alfear spoke with such casual levity one would think they were making plans for their next tea party.

"Indeed, no point in burning more daylight than necessary."

The two sat down, their attention turning towards Quintin. "Well then, how about I begin this meeting by asking your name, young man?"

The man sitting behind the desk looked at Quintin as he spoke, his eyes traversing Quintin's face taking in every detail.

Quintin cleared his throat and readjusted himself nervously in his chair, "Quintin sir, Quintin Velar."

The man nodded, "Nice to meet you, Mr. Velar. My name is Turian, the man next to you is Alfear, though you may have already caught that earlier. I want to talk to you about the sticky situation you have created for us here at the university."

Quintin let out a sigh of resignation. He understood the risks of getting caught in his line of work and had made his peace with the consequences.

He shrugged, "I'm not sure it matters anymore."

Turian raised an eyebrow at his comment, "It may not matter to you, but it sure as Shial matters to us, kid. Tell me, do you know what exactly you stole two nights ago?"

Quintin paused at the comment. Turian's gaze was still on him, his expression unchanged, yet Quintin got the idea that he was not taking this conversation where he originally thought.

He readjusted himself in his chair, the curiosity inside him becoming unbearable, "What exactly did I steal?"

Turian laughed, leaning back in his chair. "I'm so glad you asked; perhaps I can show how much of an issue you've become."

He pulled up a piece of paper laying on his desk, its handwriting and seal looking unfamiliar to Quintin, "I have run diagnostics and can verify that the results of seer Orion's investigations are correct. I am sorry to inform you that the inheritance contained within Angelheart Nihil has been taken and is currently in the possession of the child."

Turian stopped reading the paper, "There are several names here at the bottom. All people who I know and trust with my life, verifying that the words on these pages are true."

He looked up to where Quintin sat on the other side of the desk, "So tell me, Quintin Velar – what do you think of your newly acquired power?"

Quintin's mind raced, trying desperately to sort everything he had just learned. These people were spouting words and names Quintin had never heard before. However, they also seemed to know what it was that had happened to him.

"I'm not sure what it is you're trying to say?" Quintin's voice came out in a stammer as his brain shorted out and words began to cross in his mind.

"It's quite simple, really," Turian said, "You stole something that you simply cannot return, leaving us with limited options."

Turian sat back in his chair, tossing the paper aside, "However, while we could charge you for your crimes, the theft of Thean property punishable by death, I feel like that would simply make a bad situation worse?"

Alfear leaned forward, "An inheritance isn't something we can control. It's a power that chooses whomever it pleases to gift with abilities. Upon your death, the inheritance chooses someone else, and we would be tasked with searching for the next person who inherits it. This could be anyone, spanning the entire empire, or even, heaven forbid, someone from Thailia inherits your ability. We want to avoid that, which means we are essentially, for lack of better words, stuck with you."

Alfear seemed as if he would say more, but Turian cleared his throat, interjecting himself back into the conversation, "Alfear, I believe I was still speaking with the young sir."

Alfear came out of his rant, looking a bit sheepish as he reclined back into his chair, "Sorry for the interruption, Sir."

Turian waved the comment, "You're forgiven, kid. Besides, you've said much of what needs to be said," he turned to Quintin, a softer expression on his face, "We'd rather not charge a child with imperial theft. It's not something that fits with what I or anyone else here believes in. We also don't want to risk losing the inheritance, but if we cannot trust you to maintain stability at the expense of others, then we will stop you, child, or not."

Quintin listened, finally catching up with everything they had been saying. At least they didn't want him dead; they wanted to talk first. "So, you're willing to pardon me, us, in exchange for us paying off our debt?"

"Presumably, you'd be working for us, utilizing your new abilities how we see fit." Turian said matter-of-factly, "Essentially, you'd be fulfilling the role planned for those we intended to give your power, a servant working for the betterment of the empire."

Turian ended in silence, letting his words hang in the open air. He waited for a reply as Quintin debated the options before him in his head.

"If I agree, would I be expected to fight? It may not look it given what you've seen me do, but I truly hate the idea of fighting." Quintin posed the question to Turian while glancing warily at Alfear's frame slouched in the corner.

Turian followed Quintin's gaze, nodding as he grasped the situation. "Don't worry about that. Despite what the public tends to think of the Thean Heirs, only about ten percent of the people under our care end up in any sort of combat. Considering your abilities, it would be unlikely you'd ever see any combat."

Turian said all of this in the most reassuring voice he could manage. Quintin sat back in his chair, silent. Frankly, he already knew which answer he'd be choosing, yet he still hesitated. Agreeing to this would mean no more searching for his parents. He wasn't sure he wanted to let that go yet. Quintin grimaced as he prepared for what he was about to do. He hated the decision, but when it came down to it, he'd rather be alive than dead.

Quintin shook his head, looking up at the man sitting behind the desk, giving him a wry grin, "Not like I have a choice, but I'll agree to join if that means anything."

Turian raised an eyebrow but decided to continue, digging into one of his desk drawers for a piece of paper and placing it onto the desk in front of Quintin. "We found your official letter of identification during our search of your hideout, so all we need is a mandatory blood test."

Quintin filed the comment away for later as he looked over the document. It was a general medical form asking for heritage, age, and weight, a common thing found in most hospitals located in the east and apparently inside the Thean universities. Quintin filled out the document with near-automatic procedure, filling in each of the blank areas with information before handing it back to Turian.

The man took it and handed him yet another piece of paper, "It's a confirmation form. It states your agreement to work with us and learn at our university until the day it is deemed fit, or the contract is terminated by either party."

Quintin took the form; he knew plenty about such agreements. His father had made sure of that. He handed the paper back, his newly written signature still sinking into the page. *It's for Fre – that's all, and this should keep her safe.*

Turian gave a grin at the sight of the signature. "Congratulations, you have now become an official acolyte of the Thean university. It's an honor not many ever get."

Turian's words fell on a disinterested mind. It had been the right call, right? Quintin gave his best smile back, "I'm glad for the honor."

Let's just hope I don't end up regretting it as time continues.

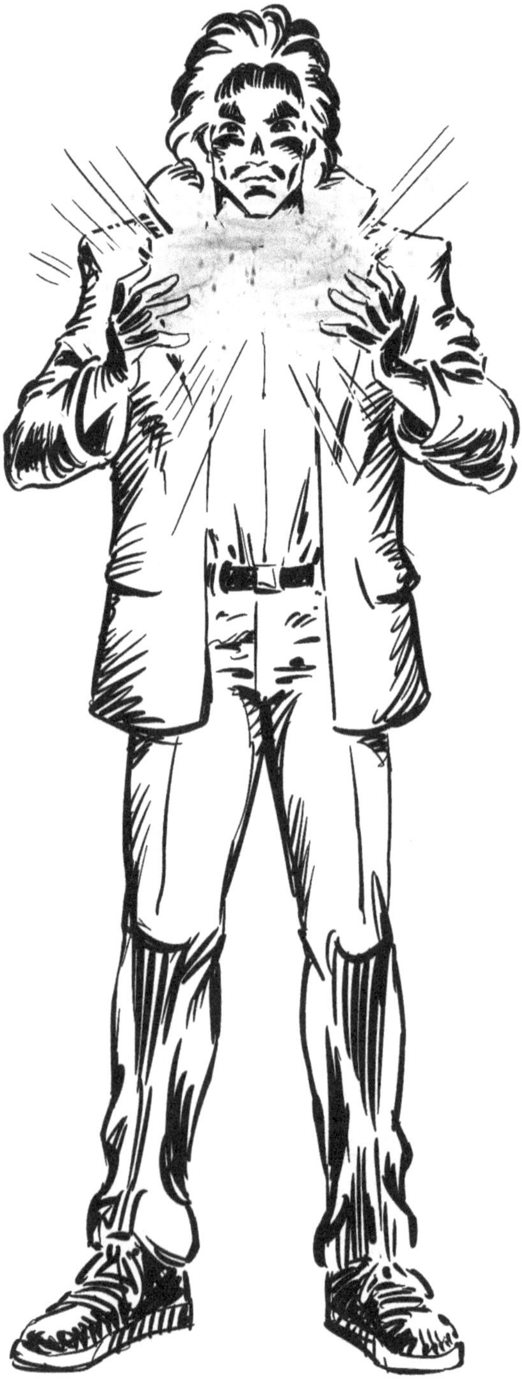

CHAPTER 16

Fre walked the winding pathways inside the left bow arm. It felt strange that people didn't give her so much as a glance as they passed by. Only hours ago, these people had been considering her execution. Now she was walking free without so much as an escort following. Fre looked back at her hand, where she kept a small piece of paper containing instructions. The bearded man, Rala – if her mind served her correctly – had given it to her after receiving orders to release her.

It was a basic type of instruction, just a series of L's and R's preceded by a number. The letters were obviously designated for left and right. The numbers indicated the number of doors on Fre's right side she would need to pass before turning. Fre continued through the winding halls, taking care not to run into anyone as she stared at her hand.

The halls grew quieter, and Fre stopped, looking left at the door. The office looked like any of the dozens she had passed, but considering this was the end of the list, it would be a waste not to enter after coming so far. She knocked gently and waited. A voice came from inside a moment later, the muffled voice beckoning Fre to enter.

She cracked the door slowly, moving headfirst as she slipped silently into the room. She was greeted by a remarkably tiny office, lit dimly by a lamp and single heater sitting on the desk. It reminded Fre somewhat of her desk back at the factory. The man behind the desk was another matter entirely.

His demeanor wasn't anything like the others. While the enforcer had looked at her with an unwavering force, Rala's smile reminded Fre of her grandparents. This man's demeanor seemed to ask a question. He looked her up and down for a moment, and Fre shuffled at the awkward situation. He looked like most of the other Ithean people Fre had met, with brown eyes and black hair, though his hair seemed streaked with gold which refracted in the lamplight.

"I presume you would be Fre?" the man said calmly, "Alfear said you'd be by some time this afternoon. Have a seat. Please?"

Fre grew overwhelmed at the torrent of words, nodding her head at the question before scrambling for the chair in front of her. She took a seat and dug into her pocket. She probably should have done that earlier, as she was forced to stand, digging into the depths of her trousers to retrieve the note and hand it to the man.

"Rala told me to give this to you when we met. He said it would help with our conversation today."

The man took the letter and opened it, glancing at it for only a second before placing it face down on the table. Fre doubted he could have read it that fast.

The man held out his hand and gave a small smile, "My name is Lian. I would like to welcome you to the Thean University here in Isel. I'd first like to congratulate you on your entry into the university. I hear the process was rather unorthodox."

Fre once again was caught off guard by the man's overflow of words, and the smile seemed to appear all too quickly out of nowhere. Still, she took the hand and gave her best attempt to smile back.

"Hello, Lian. My name is Fre, though I believe you already knew that."

Lian nodded and released her hand.

"You and your friend have made lots of noise here at the university. You won't find many Heirs here who will not know your names by the end of today."

That was a concerning prospect. Fre didn't want that kind of attention, but she kept the smile on her face.

"Hopefully, that's not a bad thing," she said, "I really don't want any trouble, and I'm sure Quintin doesn't either."

She could feel her own insecurities coming from her mouth as she spoke.

Lian simply brushed the comments away with a chuckle, "Relax, Fre. The other bureaucrats can handle those problems. I'm here to talk about something far more important."

He gestured towards the paper he'd left face down on the desk, "Those pages contain an in-depth analysis of your blood's mineral makeup. This is a very detailed copy, but the preliminary results I gathered this morning were more than enough to require my attention."

Fre grew uncomfortable at the mention of blood. It was a ghost that followed her throughout the entirety of Ithea, refusing to let her be. The Ithean Empire was the only place in the world that inherited Resonance. Places like the Confederated kingdoms of Thailia actively took measures to avoid inheritances for religious and military purposes, but that wasn't the case for the Anglis isles. Something often looked over when considering the idea of inheritance was the way it interacted with the human body. People born in Thailia or Ithea contained metallic and crystalline structures that aided in the absorption and processing of resonant energy. The Anglis lacked any such structures, making inheritance a death sentence for most.

"How bad is it?" Fre asked. Her own voice shook nervously as she asked.

Lian shrugged at the question. "It's bad enough that many here won't like it. But you didn't die back then, and you're alive now, so you're not in too much danger."

Fre thought back to yesterday morning. She'd been so sick as to be incapable of combat for the rest of the day. Even in her cell, it had made her sick whenever she tried to activate it.

"Is there any chance that this power will kill me? My body seems ill-suited for this."

Fre felt like an imposter. She'd stolen this power, and now it was effectively null. It wasn't like she would lose a part of her soul if she never used whatever it was inside her, but the guilt of her actions made her want to cry.

Lian shook his head vigorously at the words, "It's not nearly as bad as you seem to think. Understand it takes time for your body to acclimate to its ability, and while you will always have to be careful, I'm sure I can train you into a very effective Heir in no time."

His words seemed like they wanted to help, but they were dwarfed by Fre's concerns; like a rock in the middle of a river, the comments flowed around and away like so many others before it.

"Hey!" Lian's voice shook Fre as it caught her by surprise. She focused on his face as he looked at her with a sharp eye. "You seem to have some misconceptions about yourself. I don't like that. Alfear gave you to me for teaching, bless that man's overworked soul, and I'm not about to let you quit before we try."

Lian sighed, "Mind humoring me for a second?"

He held out his hand, encouraging Fre to do the same. She complied, but whatever this man had planned...her thoughts were cut short as the air around her began to buzz. Fre recognized the sensation. It mimicked the feeling she'd had with her own power, excluding incessant nausea. There was a pop, and Fre jumped as a spark exploded from Lian's hand. It was followed by several more bangs before the lights coalesced into a single unbroken string of white light.

"It's a piece of lighting," Lian said, holding up the glowing thread, "My inheritance allows me to make as much of it as I ever could need."

The sight resonated with Fre. It was a primal feeling – a mixture of fear and familiarity never experienced before. Lian smiled at the sight of Fre's awestruck expression and gestured with his free hand.

"An inheritance comes naturally to those who receive it. If you want, it will work for you also."

The words seemed stupid; logically this type of power would take years to learn. She couldn't imagine doing any such thing. Even as she hesitated, her mind began to stir, encouraging her to try in spite of her reason. It was an intuition coming straight from her very soul. A comfortable buzz arose from within her, and a shimmer appeared in the palm of her hand. The strange haze she created refracted the light of the lamp in a warped way.

Lian's smile grew, and a laugh escaped his mouth, "Not so impossible, is it?"

Fre laughed as well, "It doesn't hurt like I thought it would. No ache and nothing in the way of sickness."

Lian nodded, "What you have felt these past few days is common for most. An explosive amount of energy escapes when someone inherits powers. It's a way for the body to adjust. This is much milder in comparison."

Fre looked at her hand. The sensation was completely alien, persisting through sheer instinct alone. Lian closed his hand, extinguishing the glow, and Fre reluctantly followed suit. The strange buzz receded as the power faded back into her subconscious. The room grew dim, taking the sense of wonder with it.

"I understand that you are not a native to any of the outlander fiefdoms?" Lian asked as he looked over the chart.

Fre nodded, "My mother was a native, but my father was a Thailian merchant. The affair got him kicked from the Thailian citizenry. He made a home in the south, selling silk."

Lian raised his eyebrows in disbelief at the statement, "I wouldn't have guessed Thailian heritage. I guess your complexion comes from your mother. Still, this should work in our favor."

Lian continued taking notes on the page. Fre felt strange. It felt wrong as he continued, almost offensive that one would put so much value in the blood of her father. It was the thing keeping Fre alive, so could she really blame the man? Lian finished his scribbling and placed the paper on the desk.

"I'll get this sent down to the Archives today," he said, turning his attention towards Fre. "Did Rala explain what we would do from here?"

Fre shook her head at the question, which elicited an exhale of exasperation from Lian.

"Someday, I would love to see that man actually finish a job he starts," Lian grumbled in a quiet voice.

He turned back to his desk and pulled a piece of paper from the top drawer, handing it to Fre. She took it and glanced at its contents.

"That should contain everything you need to know. I'll be the one overseeing your training, so please tell me if anything or anyone causes you trouble." Lian trailed off as he realized Fre was blushing.

"Is something wrong, Fre?" Lian asked.

Her face grew even more flushed at the question. Her hand slowly handed the paper back to Lian. He stared, clearly confused.

"Is there a problem?" he asked again as he took the paper.

Fre's discomfort continued to grow, "Um, I can't read this."

She returned the paper as her voice threatened to crack.

"Oh!" Surprise overtook Lian's face as he took the piece of paper from her hand and tucked it back into one of his desk drawers, and began digging through the other drawers as he spoke, "Well then, is there an alphabet you can read on paper?"

"I've talked with people from most reaches of Ithea and have a copy for each of their dialects."

He laid out several new papers, each written in different shapes and formats. Each was as unreadable as the last. Fre looked over each one last time.

"Do you have anything in Anglis? It's a small island nation bordering the sea your own empire borders. My dad taught me how to read."

Lian scrunched his eyebrows at the statement. The Islands of Anglis weren't a common trade partner here on the other side of the globe, on the western seaside maybe, but not in the center of the empire.

"I don't think I've got that on hand," he shuffled through his drawer, producing a blank page of paper. "Let me send a letter to the scribes here in the office, and we'll get that sorted within a week."

Fre sat back and watched the young man scribble furiously onto the paper. *You'd think an organization in charge of an empire's entire Resonant power would spend more time tossing threads about.* Reliance on basic paperwork seemed the most alien thing in the situation. Fre looked down at her hand. She was one of them.

Lian's pen stopped, and Fre looked up to see him fold up the letter. Her eyes followed the careful movement of his hands as he placed symmetrical creases into the paper.

"So, what…" Fre stopped herself short. Honestly, she couldn't finish that statement, or rather, she couldn't choose what to end it with. Life had changed on such a fundamental level that everything needed answers. Lian looked up from the now sealed letter in his hand. His oddly clear gaze grew cloudy as fluid began to well up in Fre's eyes.

Lian stood up from his desk, "Would you mind walking with me to the scribe's office? It seems you could use from fresh air."

Fre nodded and swallowed down the lump in her throat. How did he remain so calm in this situation? Lian led her out of his office, following close behind as they walked the halls, giving direction whenever they reached a break in the hallway. The walk seemed to help, and the stress of the last few days lessened as Fre continued to walk, as if the pressure went into her legs instead of her eyes. Lian pointed to a door on their right, and the pair stepped through into a large room with a vaulted ceiling and rows of desks filling its center and bookshelves lining the walls.

It wasn't what Fre imagined when she thought about a scribe's office. Chatter filled the room, and a person sitting still seemed to be an oddity among the swarms of men and women carrying paper or climbing ladders amongst the shelves. Lian grabbed her hand and led them to the back of the room, parting the crowd.

They drew close to a large man sitting at his desk shuffling through a pile of papers. Fre recognized the bearded man as the one who she'd gotten directions from hours before. The man looked up from his work. His eyes came to life at the sight of Lian.

"Well, I didn't expect to see you here anytime soon. You also brought the child."

Lian smiled, "Yes, we're actually here because we need your help."

Rala nodded, "What do you need with an old scholar? Or do you need my brother perhaps? It seems most people make meetings through me instead of just walking to his office these days."

Lian chuckled, "Don't worry, we just need a scribe to write up some legal papers. Our friend here doesn't read Imperial script."

"That would pose a problem," Rala nodded, "What language are we looking for?"

Taken aback by the sudden attention, Fre scrambled to gather her thoughts. "My native dialect is Anglis. My father never taught me to read anything else, and Quintin had just started teaching me a few weeks ago."

"So, you want me to write up a confirmation form in Anlgis before we proceed? Should prove easy enough."

"Thank you for this," Lian said, clearly relieved. "When can we expect to see that finished?"

Rala glanced towards the clock and then to the pile of paper on his desk, "Normally, I'd put it at the end of my week, but considering the value of this work, I'll put it ahead of most of this. Let's say a day or two?"

"Perfect. If we've settled that, how are you for lunch?"

Rala's eyes widened at the prospect of leaving his desk for a few hours, and he shook his head, "Sorry, kid, but the paperwork comes first. Heaven knows you've created most of it."

Fre wondered who Rala spoke of with that comment.

Lian simply shrugged the comment off with remarkable ease, "Sorry to hear that. We need to go out. Do try to take care and get some food."

Rala paused, looking up from the busy work he'd begun, "You know, a year ago, you'd have insisted I go with you."

"What can I say," Lian said, "You've worn down my will. Soon I'll be just as dry as you."

Rala snorted in derision, "Maybe. Though at the moment, I believe you have a very bored girl desperate for some company."

Fre blushed as both pairs of eyes landed on her. Really, waiting was no trouble. In fact, it was common when dealing with adults.

"Sorry, you are always so demanding, Rala, I…"

"Stuff it, kid. I don't need any more of your vain banter, just get the girl some food, or I'll do it myself."

Lian shut his mouth and instead turned to Fre, "What kind of food do you like?"

Fre thought for a moment. She hadn't had the luxury to sit and try the food for somewhere close to a year.

"I've been gone for so long I honestly had no idea of the scope of change that occurred during that time."

The thought brought a childhood memory out from the depths of Fre's mind, sparking an idea. "Do you know any restaurants that sell shellfish? It's been a very long time since I've eaten something from home."

Lian ran his fingers through his hair, thinking, "I believe we could find something in the upper citizenry. If we leave now, we could get there before lunch passes."

Lian turned to Rala, "I'll be by later to pick up that paper."

Rala waved him off without looking up. Satisfied, Lian turned back to Fre and gestured for her to follow. The pair walked through the crowded halls and into the sunlight. Fre finally felt a weight fall from her shoulders as the eyes of the world grew distant. Lian continued to walk down the road, making his way to the upper citizenry. Fre ran to catch up. The past night was fading with every step taken away from the university.

The world is at my fingertips, and change lays on the horizon. The thought came to Fre with welcome optimism.

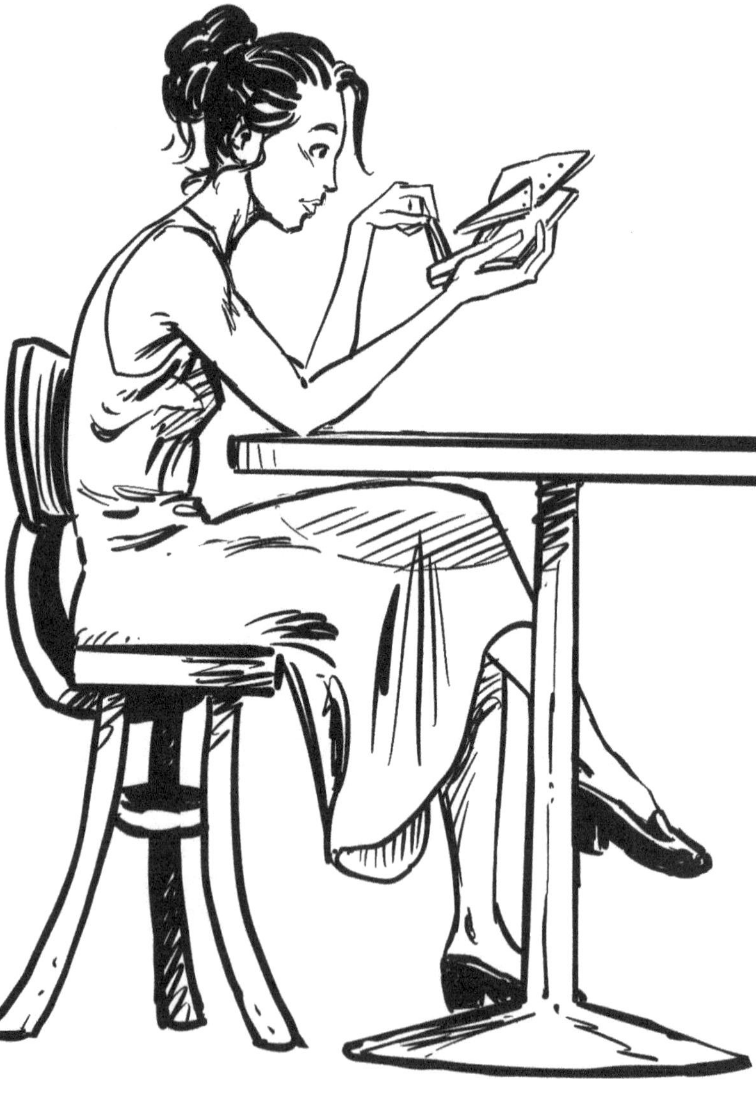

CHAPTER 17

Selyne slammed her head into the table. Someone probably wanted her gone from all the noise and melodrama she had caused in the university's library that morning. From her irate cursing early this morning, to her irate cursing now, it was a wonder that no one had asked her to leave sooner.

The idea had gone over well at first. Selyne's first day of introductions offered an optimistic view of things to come. That idea had died with the ever-increasing number of required textbooks Kalli insisted she read. The day had been nothing but digging through theoretical papers full of notes from long-dead scholars, and the drudgery had begun to get to Selyne.

It was dryer than the bottle of whiskey she had started that morning. Selyne looked down at the page in front of her. It was filled with information about the many different ways one could use Resonant fire – naming the various glyphs and their functions – a truly tedious subject.

It didn't matter whether or not one couldn't use a firebrand for something or what new glyphs were being tested. Selyne wanted something concrete that applied to her current needs. It was infuriating knowing that nobody cared about your power. Her ability to move air and change pressure seemed to lack any application in the eyes of the world other than to be used to move factory machinery.

The whole thing is silly, Selyne thought. *I should be flying through the sky, not wasting time here.*

She looked down at the book and cursed again, drawing more than a few glares from passersby. These were the upper floors; after all, they expected you to be quiet. It didn't help that Selyne had been asking for this for years, with the weight of royalty growing heavier every year her father grew older, hoping that the chance to work on something outside of her family would give her a little extra freedom.

She hadn't expected hours of note-taking and memorizing, all while a private security guard stared down her back to prevent her from getting hurt. Selyne shifted in her booth to look back at where Wil sat. He hadn't moved since they had gotten here, sitting in one of the many lounge chairs, completely engrossed with the book he was reading. In all fairness, he seemed nice enough, keeping quiet as they traversed through the sprawling city streets and small walks of the university. Mostly he just let Selyne do what she wanted. He hadn't spoken since their time in the Spire. The only time he seemed to speak was when Kalli was around.

Selyne grumbled as she thought about the pair. They always managed to talk about something that made no sense to Selyne. They never excluded her from the dialogue, but whenever Resonant theory began to get tossed around, Selyne ended up completely lost.

Wil looked up, perhaps feeling her stare focused on him. Selyne looked at him with a blank stare, her mind elsewhere. Wil closed his book, pulled himself out of his chair, and strode casually over to where she sat. Selyne broke out of her stupor, looking up at the wiry frame of her bodyguard.

"What do you want?" Selyne asked casually.

Wil patted his left jacket, "Have you checked the time? Kalli gave us an hour to study before we needed to be at the right bow arm for glyph working."

Selyne dug into the inside of the vest she had put on over her dress at the start of the day, pulling out a small silver pocket watch and checking the time, drawing more than a few glances as she did so. She eyed the tool's silver hands hanging off an inlay of gemstones used to indicate the time.

"We're about halfway until we reach noon," Selyne said, noting the small hand hanging between the ruby indicating the sun's zenith and the topaz standing in for the first half sun.

Wil peered over her shoulder in an attempt to see the surface of the watch, "Your next class is at twelve, right?"

Selyne nodded.

"Well, then we should probably get ready to leave. I take it that your mother wouldn't take kindly to you missing your first field day." He stood up and began to pick up the pile of books strewn about their small alcove.

Selyne let out a sigh before finally standing up to help. Again, it wasn't this man's fault her mother had decided to throw her into the deep end, talking to members at the Thean university and enrolling Selyne before even having the nerve to speak with her face to face. The pair carried their used books over to a drop-off table and began their trek downstairs.

Despite the sour mood the entire situation had put Selyne in, she couldn't help but admire the sheer grandeur of the Thean library. Its vaulted ceilings reached well over three hundred feet in height, crowned by a glass ceiling and supported by massive marble columns lining the inner circle of the layered levels connected by large curving staircases. What's more, the place was old, almost as old as the Spire, with its sprawling architecture covering hundreds of thousands of feet underground and on the surface, a feat only found in buildings built before Heaven's War. It was a place she'd rarely bothered visiting during her childhood, her family relying on their own personal collection of books. Stoneworks and history were never two subjects Selyne had found interesting. Reaching the bottom floor with Wil in tow, Selyne made her way to the outer bow arm. Despite the large size of this central building, many of the departments were located in the two curved wings of the university, and Selyne needed to meet Kalli in the wing of Thean Affairs before the sun reached its peak.

A hot gust of wind blasted Selyne in the face as she stepped outside into the large stone courtyard. The summer heat still persisted in these latter months, baking the marble pavers and radiating onto the skin of anyone unfortunate enough to walk across campus.

"Should have taken the catacombs," Selyne mumbled to herself as she hurried across the lawn.

Wil grinned at the statement but neglected to say anything.

Odd, you think he would have remarked at that, Selyne thought, deciding it was best to ignore the man's smug face as he winced at the light surrounding them. She chose instead to shadow her eyes with her hand and finish this walk as soon as possible. The cool interior of the Thean office felt amazing, and Selyne thanked Thea for whoever had created the glyph for cooling as it renewed her charred soul.

"Now then," Selyne said, uncertainty tinging her voice, "where to go from here?"

The foyer was devoid of people, and unlike the library, there weren't any signs indicating where anything was or where they should go. Selyne surveyed the room, her glance resting on Kalli seated in a small alcove in the corner. Selyne must have missed her when walking in, but she was clearly staring back at her from above the top of her book. Selyne realized she'd been staring and blinked before turning away to look elsewhere.

The small interaction was enough, and Selyne sighed internally as the woman closed her book and stood from her chair, dusting herself off before walking towards Selyne. Selyne took a deep breath, preparing herself for what was about to come. The last day had been a tedious affair of lectures and introductions. Selyne wasn't sure if she could go through it again. At least Kalli seemed nice enough. Her dark brown hair was barely maintained within a braid, and her dress was made of blue satin, a decision that seemed deliberately subtle. There was an implication that this woman knew the face she put out to everyone.

Kalli stepped in front of the pair, hands on her hips. "So, are we ready to get started?"

Selyne wanted to say anything but yes, however, she doubted Kalli would accept that as an answer. Irritation nagged at the back of Selyne's mind. For a moment, she wanted to just tell the pair off and walk out.

She sighed, trying her best to suppress the urge. Walking out now wouldn't resolve any of her problems.

"What are we doing today?" Selyne asked in her most optimistic voice, "yesterday was dry enough to put me to bed, so hopefully, today won't be a repeat."

Kalli laughed gently. "Don't worry. Your teaching right now is to acclimate you to the university climate. I'm going to have a far more hands-on experience."

Let's hope you hold to that statement. Selyne smiled, "Well then, should we get started?"

Kalli walked over to one of the side doors, opening up into a hallway beyond. She entered first, followed by Selyne, with Wil taking up the rear. Selyne got the sense that she was being escorted, not unlike a prisoner. She didn't know what to think of that.

Kalli halted at one of the doors recessed into the hall; turning around, she made sure her two followers were still there, "I've got everything set up already, so feel free to take a seat anywhere."

Selyne stepped past Wil and stared into the room. It was relatively tame, unlike many of the study halls she'd seen throughout the library, which lacked the copious amounts of chiseled marble or granite ornamentation. Instead, she saw heavy wood panels and a dark grey stone floor filled with dozens of tables. Selyne found the atmosphere to be quite familiar, the muted colors reminding her of the deeper levels found in the Spire, though logically that would make sense considering the origins of the two structures were the same.

"This will be the room we'll meet in throughout the week," Kalli's voice broke through the silence, bringing Selyne back to reality. "Currently, I've leased out the lab on the third, fourth, and sixth days of the week, but we can obviously make any accommodations to suit your needs."

Kalli fidgeted as she spoke, and Selyne got the feeling that this woman didn't like human interaction on a daily basis.

"Sure beats your typical class at least," Selyne stated, "Wil if you could sit outside, it would be nice to have some privacy."

Selyne looked over her shoulder at the guardsmen. Wil nodded, giving Kalli a nod as well before finding a seat in the hall.

"With that sorted, let's get started." Kalli beckoned Selyne into the lab.

The laboratory was a large space with rows of desks extending towards the back of the room. There was an odd assortment of tools set on top of the cabinets, many of which Selyne didn't recognize. She also noted that many of the desks had some form of damage done to them, with many having burn marks or gouges taken from them.

Kalli pulled up a chair, "Kindly take a seat. Please know this is my first-time teaching anything, so feel free to ask any questions if I fail to make myself clear."

Selyne gave a small smile, taking the seat. She really didn't know how to react to Kalli's presence. The woman didn't exude the pompous ignorance that so many of the nobles Selyne grew up with possesed. It was quite the opposite, in fact. Kalli acted out of some form of optimistic joy. Everything that came out of her mouth seemed invested. Selyne just wished she'd stop. There came the point when that sort of conversation grew to be too much.

"Now, I went over your file the other day before coming here, and I've come up with a lesson plan which should accommodate your specific skills." Kalli opened one of the notebooks, its pages already full of pen marks, "You've probably noticed that there isn't much research on your given inheritance, so I thought we would focus our teaching on shoring up those deficiencies and do a little experimentation along the way."

Kalli handed the book over to Selyne. The messy handwriting within outlined the entirety of Kalli's plan. Selyne flipped through several pages, groaning internally as the number of filled pages grew from five to twenty to Thea knew how many. Closing the book before it could get any worse, Selyne focused on the other oddities strewn about the table.

"So... what's all this for?"

Once again, Kalli seemed oblivious to Selyne's absolute disinterest in whatever it was she had to offer. Instead, she grabbed one of the pieces of metal she'd placed on the table earlier, handing it to Selyne to look at.

"These were something my own teacher gave me to hone my own inheritance; each one contains the glyph correlating to the given resonant frequency along with a brief description of their designated uses in modern times."

Selyne looked over the tablet she held in her own hand, letting the light reflect off its metallic surface, revealing the curves and dots that made up the glyph. It was a round shape with a dot in the center with four others placed equidistant from each other on its outer edge. Selyne looked at the name underneath the pattern; naturally, it would be the glyph for pressure, just another grain of salt to throw on an already sore wound. She flipped the coin to look at the description for its uses. "Used commonly among engineers in the factory and mines. An industrial staple to Ithea's infrastructure." Two sentences that didn't bode well for Selyne's future prospects.

"How many of these do you have?" Selyne said, already disinterested with the first one.

"Currently, we have six known base glyphs. One for pressure or air depending on your upbringing, one for heat, another for electricity, matter, polarity, and strength." Kalli spread out the few she had in front of her looking them over with undeniable enjoyment, "Though with the advent of two more Angel-kin being discovered, we can expect two more types to be coming to fruition in a matter of months."

Selyne grew confused at the last statement, "How could we get a 'new type of glyph? Aren't those kind of predetermined by nature itself?"

Kalli nodded at the statement, "Yes, it's true that glyphs exist only for the forms of energy found in nature."

She dug into her bag and produced a large piece of parchment full of descriptions and images. "However, potential information never defines reality."

Selyne looked over the images. The information was very similar to that found on the back of the little info tabs Kalli had handed her earlier. The difference was quite a few descriptions for powers that were devoid of any glyph whatsoever.

"Glyphs are not a natural phenomenon." Kalli began, "They do not appear in nature and are instead passed down by Heirs who possess the ability of the glyphs. This is all fine and dandy until you realize there are some powers so rare as to be unobtainable by our scholars."

"So, we know these exist?" Selyne asked, looking the sheet over, "but we don't have any examples of their glyphs. How would an 'Angel-kin' change this?"

"Good question," Kalli said, "Angel-kin is the term we use to refer to powers such as your own."

Selyne shrugged, "That doesn't help with my question in the slightest."

Kalli raised her hand, cutting off Selyne, "We'll get there; rest assured."

Her voice was calm, which only brought Selyne more frustration at the lack of a quick answer; still, she held her questions.

Kalli continued, "Angel-kin is a term relegated to a very, very small group of individuals who possess only one resonant frequency out of the total eighteen. They differ from lesser Heirs in that the loss of those other powers does not reduce the actual amount of internal

Resonance which could be stored into one's body, quite the contrary actually. Each Angel-kin we've discovered in the past two thousand years has possessed far greater amounts of internal Resonance. History denotes such power as being those of the Angels who fought during Heaven's War. Thus, the name Angel-kin was created to denote the relation each person had with the power."

Selyne blinked twice, the glaze leaving her eyes as she began to process everything that was just said, "Heavens, that was more information than I wanted. Still, an interesting tidbit to keep for future use."

Selyne's mind sparked for a minute, another question taking shape. A knock sounded on the lab door, Interrupting Selyne's fleeting thought.

Wil peeked his head through the cracked door, "I hate to interrupt, but it's currently an hour past the sun's zenith, and we have a lunch date with your mother, which she was very clear you were not to miss."

Kalli sighed, and Selyne rolled her eyes. "Well, I guess we won't be getting to any serious work," Kalli said, not sounding all that perturbed by the prospect.

Selyne shrugged, she really didn't have an opinion either way, and frankly, she'd probably be more comfortable talking to Kalli than her mother. Kalli, however, had no such trepidation, pulling several of the items into her bag,

"We'll just treat this as an introductory lesson. Here," she handed Selyne the pile of little tablets now contained in a little pouch Kalli had removed from her bag along with the journal. "Try to read some of the stuff I put into that book and see if you can come back tomorrow with some serious questions."

Selyne took the objects; she wasn't finding time to read them, "So is that all we'll be doing? I thought you would teach me how to use an inheritance. This is just trivia."

Kalli snorted at the comment, "If I could teach you how to use your powers, I would gladly; unfortunately, I am not very good with my own inheritance. Rather I am teaching how you should work around the shortcomings that come with these powers."

Great, Selyne thought, *as if my time wasn't wasted enough with this class.*

For once, Kalli actually seemed to recognize the feelings written on Selyne's face, "Don't worry, we'll have plenty of time to work over your abilities soon enough. Trust me, hands-on experience is the best form of learning for an Heir, and I'm going to make sure you get plenty of it in these next few months."

Selyne wasn't assured by the words in the slightest. Wil had stepped into the room, his strained patience causing his eyes to dart around the room.

"We really need to go," he said, approaching the desk standing beside Selyne, hoping his presence would urge her to move. He really didn't need to do that, but he was running on her mother's time, so Selyne couldn't really blame the man. Selyne stood up, dusting off the two halves of her dress instinctively, grabbing the small bag and the book before stuffing them into her dress pockets.

She presented herself, arms out to Wil, "Lead the way. I honestly have no clue where my mom wants to meet."

Wil gave a slight bow in Kalli's direction, which she responded with a wave. Satisfied with the paltry farewell, Wil turned to leave. Selyne once again followed in tow.

I have a year of this to look forward to, two if they find me incompetent. Selyne sighed; the noise caused Wil to glance back. *Let the man worry,* Selyne thought. She was sure he'd had his fair share of poor seasons, and Selyne didn't feel like allaying his concern over hers.

CHAPTER 18

Quintin winced as the summer sun glared down from its perch in the noonday sky. He grew up in more arid climates than this, though he still felt like the sun should take a break for a few days and leave him alone. *Though now that I think about it, isn't that just winter?* Quintin sighed. He hadn't gotten enough sleep last night to handle today. His eyes glanced over to where the large man stood. Alfear had asked to see Quintin and Fre this morning. A day had barely passed, and he was already moving forward. Quintin wasn't sure if it was out of desperation, naivety, or trust, but he had to admire the speed at which the man acted.

Alfear scanned the pair of children as if making sure he hadn't missed anyone. "Alright then, I'm glad you could both make it out here today considering the circumstances, but with that said, I think we can get started. Why don't we start with names?"

Alfear looked at Quintin, gesturing with his hand for the boy to begin.

"My name is Quintin, sir," Quintin stammered, "I'm not sure if you need anything else."

Alfear shrugged before turning his glance to Fre, "Works enough for me, now how about you?"

"My name is Freaziah, but everyone who knows me just calls me Fre" Fre shuffled nervously as she gave her answer.

"I'll try to remember your names," Alfear said, "but with how much we'll be spending time together, I think it's only a matter of time. Now then, who here knows what an heir is?"

The question was dropped without so much of a warning, leaving Quintin to scramble for an answer. "Aren't they people who can resonate without the use of glyphs?"

He didn't know much, but it was nearly impossible not to hear talk about Heirs and their abilities if you lived any amount of time in Ithea.

"That's not a bad answer, though a bit rudimentary." He looked to Fre, "what about you, any ideas?"

"I've only learned what Quintin has told me," she said sheepishly.

"That's alright. I want an accurate measure of what you know so I can start you at the right level. We'll be keeping it basic today." Alfear turned to Quintin. "You were correct to assume that glyphs and Heirs work the same way. However, there are some important things that apply to living humans and inanimate objects that need to be taken into account."

Quintin felt the air begin to buzz gently. He glanced over at Fre, who looked as confused as he did. Clearly, she felt whatever was in the air.

"Resonance is the term we use for our abilities," Alfear said. "The world has thousands of threads which make up its fabric. An Heir is someone who can interact with this energy, causing it to resonate, which can produce almost any natural phenomena on the planet."

A flash of fire burst from Alfear's hand as if to emphasize his point.

Quintin jumped slightly at the outburst. He recovered quickly as his curiosity began to get the better of him.

"There are some rules to this," Alfear continued, "It's kind of in the name, but Heirs only receive an ability which is passed down through unknown means. This means an Heir cannot learn new abilities, only expound on the power they already have." Alfear let the fire appear in his hand once more. "We Angel-kin generally only receive a single inheritance, mine being fire, but we make up for it in other ways which brings me to my next point."

Alfear extinguished his fire once again. He dug into his back pockets for a moment before retrieving two different objects from his pocket.

They were small flat silvery objects, their surfaces engraved and inlaid with glass. Alfear tossed one to Fre and Quintin, respectively. Quint fumbled for a moment as the object tried to escape his grasp.

"On each of those pieces of steel is the same glyph set," Alfear said. "However, one is far superior to the other, I want you to try and figure out which is which."

He crossed his arms as he watched the pair of students examine the glyphs. Quintin leaned into Fre, holding out his glyph for examination. Fre did the same, giving a clear picture of their differences. *Well, Shia,* Quintin groaned internally; *they look exactly the same.*

"Do you see anything?" He asked, looking to Fre.

She took the pair in her hands, studying them for a few moments. "This one is lighter. Also, it seems to have less glass inlaid in its grooves."

The large man smirked.

"You have a very good eye, young lady," Alfear said, "could you tell me which one is a better glyph?"

Fre paused for a moment in thought. "My intuition says something heavier is generally sturdier. I don't know about the glass, though, I'm guessing this one is the better glyph."

Alfear nodded. "That would be a correct assumption. The body of both glyphs and humans are what store threads that can be used to resonate. The stronger the body, the more energy you can store. The glass acts as a sort of conduit, something our blood also does. The better the conductor, the easier it is to release Resonance into the outside world."

Quintin nodded. It made sense. "So why are Angel-kin so special?"

Alfear nodded. "Good question. Despite what you may think, your physical body is not the body that houses your threads. It's actually the conduit. The body which keeps your threads actually comes with your inheritance."

"So you inherit energy reserves?" Quintin asked.

"Along with the information needed to use it," Alfear said, nodding. "It's what makes Angel-kin so dangerous. We have enough energy stored in our bodies to level a small city, though we may not be able to use it like that depending on our inheritance."

"Are you serious?" Quintin stammered.

He didn't feel any different, not like he had a bomb buried inside his chest. "I feel pretty normal."

"We're not sure how it works either," Alfear admitted, "there have been a lot of theories about how we store so much energy, but that doesn't change the reality of the situation. Angel-kin are an extremely valuable resource, and it is generally an indicator of change when we find new ones. Anyway, my job is to make sure you don't hurt yourself while you learn how to use this newfound ability. Over the next few months, we'll learn how to regulate our usage to avoid hurting yourselves, along with some more complex techniques like ignition and glyph-work."

Alfear looked over the pair of dumbfounded kids. "Ask any questions you want."

Fre shook her head. Quintin followed suit as he registered the question. *Enough power to level a city?* The prospect seemed insane to him.

"If you don't have any questions, then I believe you two can go. Today you'll be free to tour the campus and rest. Starting this weekend, we'll begin seriously with your training." Alfear waved the pair away, looking down at his watch and cursing under his breath. "I need to be somewhere else soon, and I trust you can find your way back?"

The pair nodded. The large man didn't wait for any other indicator from the pair before walking briskly across the university lawns towards the left bow arm.

Quintin watched the man as he walked away. He didn't know how on earth he was supposed to handle all this. *Just what have I gotten us into?*

CHAPTER 19

Alfear beckoned to Quintin. He was wearing his lockplate. His helmet was tucked under his left arm. Lian stood next to him along with some people Quintin didn't recognize.

"You look bloody miserable," Alfear said. "That's probably going to get worse today."

He turned away before Quintin had an option to respond.

"It looks like we're all here," Alfear said, looking for confirmation from Lian.

There was a series of nods from the adults.

"Alright then. Lian, do you want to explain what we're doing today?"

Lian excused himself from his conversation with the man from the other group. "Yes. Let's go. If you would all line up next to each other, we'll begin."

Quintin followed the order, lining up next to Fre and another lady. They stood silently, waiting for Lian to speak.

He cleared his throat. "Most of you have spent the majority of your time learning a plethora of theory and conduct. Today we will have some fun with some real-life practice."

Lian pointed to Alfear, "Alfear has brought his set of lockplate. You will be allowed to test your abilities on him or me as soon as I get armored."

The woman standing next to Lian spoke up. "I know in Quintin's case; the inheritance has an internal effect. You'll be paired with me. Selyne and Fre, you'll have to choose between one of the guys."

The pairs split. Fre naturally gravitated to Lian, leaving Alfear to take Selyne.

"Now then," Lian said, clapping his hands together.

His lockplate fit together like a puzzle held together by electric Resonance.

"This lockplate," Lian continued, "is lined with pure silver on the outside. While we wear this, you will be able to test your abilities without fear of hurting us."

Lian connected the last helmet pieces, obstructing his face. "With that said, feel free to begin."

He gestured to Fre to follow him to another section of the dirt plot on the green.

Alfear sighed, glancing to Selyne, "I guess you're stuck with me."

Selyne shrugged, "I'm hardly partial in this decision."

She tossed aside the tiny rocks she had been fidgeting with.

"This way then," Alfear said, "We've got our own test pit to use."

Quintin watched the pair walk away, leaving himself with Kalli.

The woman had set her book bag aside. "So, have you had any time to practice before now?"

Quintin shook his head. The university didn't offer a good place to use inheritance and punished improper use with overwhelming zeal.

Kalli sighed as if she'd expected this. "Well, there's no time like the present, I suppose."

She knelt down and began rummaging in her bag, retrieving a smaller book from within.

"Usually," Kalli continued, "A person receiving an inheritance won't need any assistance activating their power. Generally, we attribute this innate knowledge as obtained once one receives an inheritance."

She paused, settling on a page. "This, however, doesn't mean a person knows the full extent of their abilities which is where I'm going to help. Tell me, have you tried projecting your Resonance outward?"

The question seemed odd to Quintin. *Outward relative to what?*

"I'm not sure how far out is it supposed to go?"

The air began to buzz in Quintin's ears. Kalli had activated her Resonance. He felt the world warp as energy coalesced in her hand.

"This is the Resonance of matter," Kalli said. A small piece of granite formed in her hand. "It has an extremely long distance of projection due to the stable form the energy takes."

She tossed the stone to Quintin, who fumbled to catch it. He marveled as he picked up the solid object, pulling his knife out and scratching at the surface.

"How long will this be here?" Quintin asked, feeling a little uneasy by the unnatural phenomenon.

Kalli shrugged, "As long as I want, the only thing limiting its existence is my lifespan. Anything we create with our inheritance will fade when we die. It is one of the few laws that cannot be circumvented."

Quintin pondered the idea. He couldn't do anything like this. Not even remotely.

"So, projection is the distance and duration that my inheritance can manifest itself?"

Kalli nodded, "That's a good enough explanation to start with. Your ability seems to affect your own body. So don't expect it to go far."

Quintin looked down at his hands in trepidation. The power was there; he could feel it just beneath the surface. The thrum of energy began to grow as Quintin focused his mind on it.

He felt it travel through his body, coming from the center of his chest, moving outward to his arms and legs.

"Good to know you have an inheritance," Kalli said, unimpressed. "Let's see what it can do."

Quintin looked at the impatient woman, preparing himself for the side effects of what he was about to do. The world lurched as Quintin's vision went dark. His perception shifted to his other sense.

He looked to the blue web of threads that indicated Kalli. He saw her breath echo in the threads.

"Can you hear me?" Kalli asked.

Quintin couldn't hear the words though he understood the waves they created in the threads.

An inherited trait? he wondered.

Alfear had mentioned such things.

"I can hear you," Quintin replied.

Kalli didn't respond, standing unchanged.

"Hello?" Quintin asked, watching his voice travel through the threads. "This is a stupid place to be."

Quintin watched though Kalli didn't seem to register any of it. A thought came to Quintin – he needed to talk to her.

His vision lurched, the sense of a sudden descent churning his stomach. His feet touching sod. The sudden weight of standing on solid ground feeling oppressive after the freedom of being nothing. Nausea hit him like a barge, though he managed to keep it in.

"Welcome back," Kalli said. "You look like a ghost."

Quintin glared at her as he sat back in the grass.

She chuckled, "That was impressive, really. Though not being able to communicate makes it tricky."

"I could hear you talking," Quintin asserted, "Talking back didn't work."

Kalli furrowed her brow, confused, "Interesting. How easy is it for you to move while invisible?"

Quintin thought back to his fight with Alfear. "It's doable. Though you don't move like normal."

Kalli nodded, taking in his words, "Have you considered trying to fly?"

Quintin groaned at the prospect. "I'm not feeling good after that last shift. I'll be sick if I go again."

"I'm sure you'll be fine," Kalli said dismissively.

"I doubt it." He grumbled as he picked himself off the ground.

"See?" Kalli exclaimed, "You're already standing. Now get to it."

Quintin glared before fading into nothingness. The dizziness vanished along with his body. Quintin let out an instinctive breath of relief.

Kalli stood in front of him, crossing her arms as she waited for Quintin to return. He reminded himself he was supposed to be learning.

Looking at the glowing landscape, he tried his first steps. Quintin moved up in front of Kalli. The movement didn't feel anything like walking, taking little to no effort. Quintin hadn't even moved his legs.

He felt more confident, looking up at the sky. *Let's see if I can go up.*

Quintin tried to climb upwards. Immediately his body felt like it was swimming through syrup. Quintin looked down. He hadn't gotten much more than a foot off the ground. He tested moving his arms and moved freely without any resistance. Something felt like it was pulling him down.

He let himself lower back to the ground, coming face to face with Kalli. "I wonder…"

Quintin reached out his hand. A jolt of energy flew through Quintin's body as he touched her face. He yelped in surprise, recoiling from the sensation. "I hope she didn't feel that."

He gulped nervously. He felt he should return to the real world, but the prospect of throwing up gave him pause.

Taking a deep breath, Quintin shifted. The world spun, his vision exploding into sensory overload. Light and threads combined into an impossible image for a split second. He felt his feet land on the ground, stumbling as the chaos of his body staggered him.

"Watch yourself," Kalli exclaimed, stepping forward to catch him.

Quintin grasped her hand, thankful for the support.

"I think we'll call it a day."

"Sounds good," he said, nodding weakly.

Moments passed spent adjusting to the shift in reality. Quintin blinked. His vision mostly returned to normal.

Kalli tore out a page of her book, handing it to Quintin. "I've got some notes for you. Take it easy for the rest of the day. Though take these into account when it comes to experimenting with your inheritance."

He took the page from her hand, looking over its contents. Each point was marked by a number.

"Just a few things I noticed while you worked," Kalli remarked.

Quintin tucked the page into his pocket for later. "When do you think they'll be done?"

The princess was floating a couple of feet off the ground. She seemed to be throwing something at Alfear. Kalli pulled out her watch.

"We've only been working for thirty minutes." She said, "Perhaps another half before they stop."

Quintin laid back, closing his eyes. "If it's ok, I'd like to spend that time resting,"

"By all means," Kalli said, chuckling quietly.

The afternoon sun drifted down, warming Quintin's body as he let the simple sensation of existing take over.

Fre gasped, Resonance flaring as Lian threw another ball at the pane she'd created. The ball smacked into the clear wall of energy, cracking loudly as it rebounded off the surface, flying into the distance. Fre shook her arms out, trying to dispel the tingling feeling coming from them.

"Do we need to rest?" she heard Lian call from his position across from her.

Fre shook her head. She'd been learning the limits of her abilities the past week; this wasn't her maximum by a longshot. Lian grabbed another ball, tossing it carelessly in his hand.

"Try and catch this one. See if you can avoid any marks."

Fre concentrated, watching the ball intently. Lian gave a gentle underhanded throw. Fre ignited her reserves. She would need to create a cage around the object to prevent it from bouncing away. It seemed simple; however, complications arose when trying to close the gaps. Fre moved on instinct, igniting the air around the ball. Barriers formed as Fre visualized them in her mind, forming a polyhedron around the ball.

The ball bounced off the sides of the cage wildly, causing more strain for Fre, slowly coming to rest at the bottom of the invisible cage. Fre released the threads, letting the ball fall to the ground. Her arms now burned, a dull ache starting to form in her bones.

Lian leaned down, grabbing the ball and examining its surfaces. "It seems like sketching in three dimensions has helped a lot," he said, tossing Fre the ball, "Your visualization of what you want to create has gotten increasingly better."

Fre caught the ball, smiling as she inspected the untouched surface.

Lian pulled out his watch, looking down at the singular hand surrounded by gemstones. "We've just hit the sun's decline. The others should be finishing up here soon."

Fre nodded, relieved that she wouldn't have to ask for a break.

"You're shaping up quite well," Lian said, sipping his cylinder of water, "I expect you'll be able to move onto even finer actions here soon enough."

Fre leaned over and grabbed her water, twisting off the lid. She'd become something she imagined to be unobtainable. She glanced over to where the princess was training. The woman flowed through the air like an angel, unfettered from the bonds of the earth. Fre hoped to get to that level of control; until then, she'd be grounded.

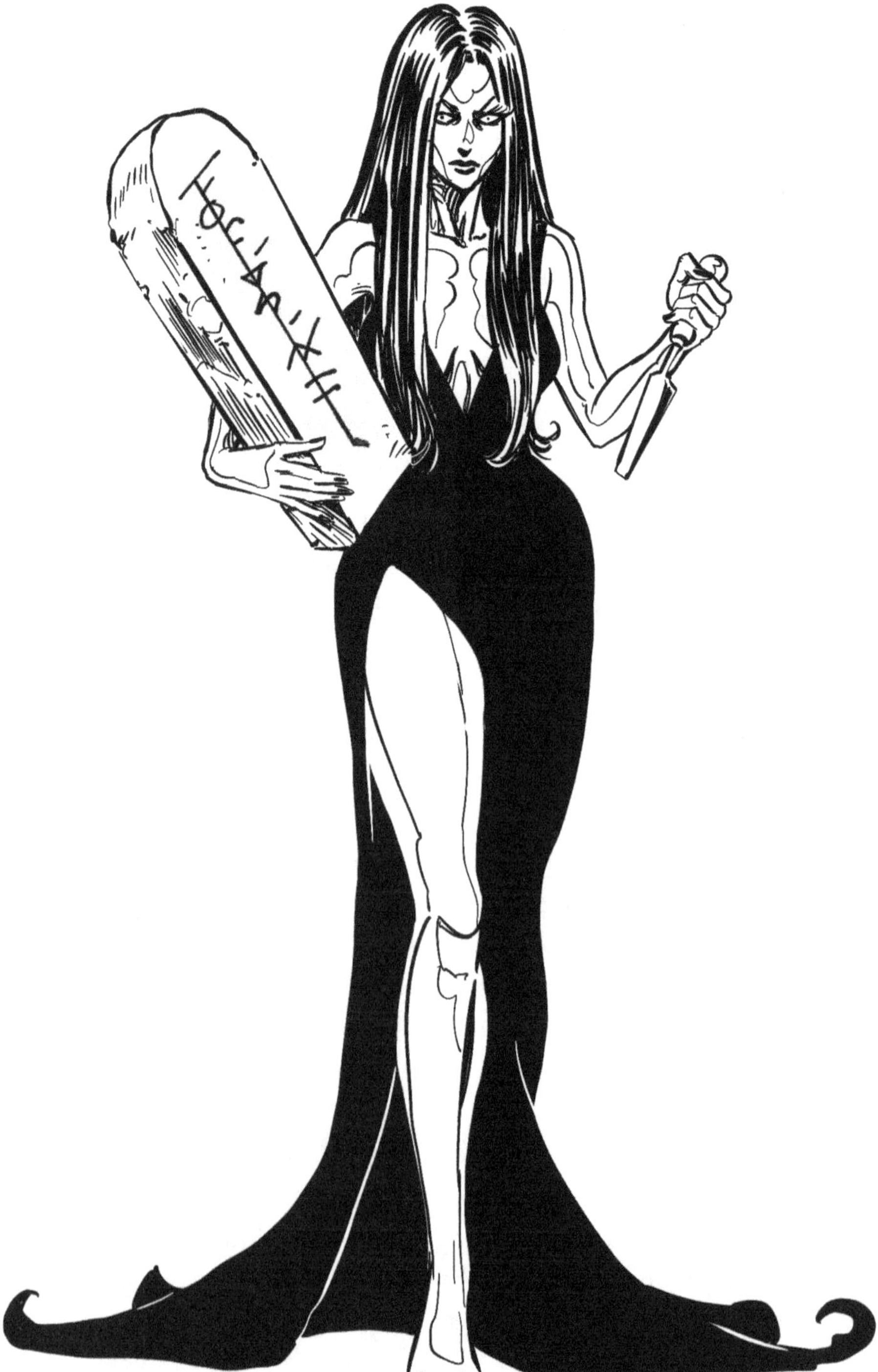

CHAPTER 20

Wil walked the quiet halls of the nighttime Spire. Unlike the hubbub of the day, which created a constant rumble throughout its interior, the quiet covered everything like an enormous quilt, creating peace in its warmth. Wil continued down the stairs from the royal quarters where he'd dropped Selyne off minutes ago, making his way downwards into the belly of the structure where the guardsmen slept.

Wil passed a few servants in the halls, receiving bows of respect and looks of conflicted disdain. Honestly, the bows disturbed him, more so than the glares. He didn't like the expectation that came with someone revering him. Honestly, who did they think he was?

Wil passed by one of the kitchens where they were cleaning up for the night. He winced at the clatter of pots and pans being cleaned as he walked by.

"Heavens, that's uncomfortable," he grumbled, regaining his composure as he continued downward.

He gripped his cane tighter and continued onward. He passed several off-duty guardsmen coming up the other direction. They didn't bow or glare, and they simply walked onward.

It was a common practice amongst the military. Ignoring a living legend meant you didn't have to acknowledge their flaws; nobody wanted a hero who'd lost his taste for glory. In their minds, Wil no longer existed. Wil pondered the idea – in two hundred years, once he'd passed on, they'd probably spout his name from the rooftops, the only man to survive for six months by himself in Rhinil infested territory and come back unscathed.

Not completely unscathed, Wil corrected himself wryly.

Wil continued past the pair of soldiers, reaching the basement levels of the Imperial Spire. Here rested the barracks for the Royal Guard along with the Armory. Wil moved past the dozens of rooms filled with guardsmen putting away their uniforms for the night, making his way silently like a spectre towards the deepest floors of the spire. The walls were barren, with only torches giving light to the damp hallway. A large iron door came to light at the end of the hallway. Wil pushed the door aside with one arm and entered the Armory.

The walls were studded with hundreds of iron and silver steel spears. Sets of armor rested on their stands with swords and shields resting amongst the hundreds of shelves of weapons. It felt like getting lost among the shelves of a library. Wil walked to a newer portion of the room where some guards were doing maintenance on their chainmail. He moved to a rack of swords opposite the two soldiers.

The pair spoke in hushed whispers, and Wil made a mental effort to ignore the conversation, focusing on finding the spot they'd archived his sword. Silently, he tabbed through the tags on each weapon until he came to his own. Wil ran his hand over the familiar feel of hardened leather reinforced by silver steel.

It was a relic from a time now gone. The dull rasp of silver steel echoed through the room as Wil unsheathed the weapon, its deep gray coloration reflecting faintly in the torchlight. The conversation stopped momentarily, and Wil felt the two soldiers' gaze as he drew the entire length of the blade free from its scabbard. The weapon totaled four feet in length with a handle designed for two hands, and half of one edge had been replaced by spaced slots one would find on a parrying dagger. To the average eye, it seemed to be a rather impractical weapon and for the average soldier. They'd be better off using a halberd or blaze spear; however, Wil knew just how deadly this weapon could be in the right hands. Even just holding it brought back images of the soldiers killed by this weapon. Men who looked in disbelief as a monster tore through sword and plate like an immovable force of nature.

The conversation began again behind him as the pair of soldiers lost interest in him. Wil continued his work. He grabbed a nearby cloth along with a small bottle of oil kept on the shelf for public use.

"It's unfortunate, really. I heard at this point there that nobody in the nobility was left who will even entertain The Girl anymore."

Wil paused as the conversation behind him caught his attention.

"Well, if they really can't stand her antics, they can remove her from the throne. Ow!"

The soldier was cut off by an elbow from his compatriot.

He rubbed his rib cage in affliction, "What was that about?"

"Don't give me that."

The soldier's friend gave a nervous glance towards Wil in the corner, "You know that's not the type of thing you say if you want to keep your job here."

The soldier grumbled, "I serve under the current King. If that child takes the throne, they won't need to take my badge."

His partner shrugged. "You're done. Let's head to bed. Some sleep would do you some good."

They moved away down the halls of weapons and armor, their conversation fading into echoes before disappearing behind the clap of the iron door coming to a close. Wil continued his work on his sword, making sure to remove any excess grease left of the blade and in between the teeth. The conversation didn't cause any sort of surprise. Anyone could hear the same sentiment all through the Spire's staff and out into the nobility.

Wil sheathed his sword with a snap and turned to leave. The sentiments of guardsmen held no sway in his own life. They were simply the words of someone who didn't like the failure of institutes they held so close to their heart. Wil hurried through the hundreds of shelves, moving further and further away from the miles of storage that made up the imperial armory.

Wil came to the large iron door. It hung slightly ajar. The two guards had forgotten to close it on their way out. Honestly, the quality of some of these men was severely lacking. Wil let out a sigh and closed the door behind him.

The sound of the bells banging into place as Wil latched it shut echoed down the long corridor, repeating and resonating off the walls, creating a cacophony. Wil grit his teeth at the noise, his hands instinctively moving to his ears to block it out. He'd forgotten just how loud the door was. Suddenly the idea of leaving it open seemed more reasonable.

The echoes began to recede, and Wil finally eased his eyes open. The corridor was exactly as it had been a moment earlier. Wil shivered nervously, his anxiety remaining despite the now quiet corridor. Shaking his head and doing his best to ignore the ringing in his ears he turned to head back upstairs. Wil looked down at the door handle. It had been bent out of shape where his hand had smacked into it. The iron handle was hanging on by a sliver of metal.

Wil sighed as he stared at the damaged handle. He tested the latch, relieved when it lifted and closed as intended.

"Thank you, Shia, that works," Wil said, relieved. He turned to leave; *hopefully, that's all for tonight. I'm not sure I can take much more.*

* * * * * *

Sunlight filtered through the deep green leaves. This orchard had once been a common summer home for the emperor in the early years, a safe place to vacation with the family. Later Selyne's eldest brother would come to own it, a gift from their father for obtaining the title of First Prince of Ithea. How long had it been since Selyne stood under these trees and felt the gentle breeze carry the scent of parmon blossoms through its currents?

You know we haven't been here in years. The thought sullied Selyne's mood.

She'd grown apart as each of her older brothers had taken more and more responsibility in the Empire. It had started with Sirius, being the oldest, he'd been quick to leave home in hopes of making a name for himself. The others had followed a few years later. Selyne pushed past the recollections. She was here, and she might as well enjoy the time she had here. The trees hadn't grown since she'd last been here. The fruit also had yet to come, an oddity to be sure, but with how the weather was these days, Selyne felt this was nominal.

Selyne walked down the rows of trees stretching outward for miles. "Where is everyone?"

She grew cold as a feeling of loneliness began to take hold. This place had grown dead since she'd been gone; all that was left were ghosts in these woods. The world began to grow cold around Selyne. She couldn't help but feel sad walking through this orchard, like staring at the last pages of an unfinished novel, nothing left but an unfinished work to indicate the writer ever existed.

Selyne wanted to cry at the tragedy of it all, though she didn't seem to be able to.

Thoughts of her brothers flittered past in her mind. It all seemed so vivid, the memories seeming to take shape in the orchard.

Laughter echoed through the trees. Selyne could remember watching her brothers race about the orchard. She'd hardly been old enough to remember, but seeing them had given her so much pride at the time.

Ladri beckoned to the other two brothers before disappearing into the trees.

The orchard went silent, leaving Selyne in the present.

Selyne shivered, "Why did we come here? We knew he'd be here, so why?"

She looked frantically at the trees around her, hoping to retrieve the memories she'd just lost. A shadow moved behind one of the larger parmon trees.

"It's truly a heartbreaking thing, isn't it? To see such a great lineage reduced to nothing. It always happens, but to think you'd be the last is just pitiful."

The voice echoed out from the forest, traveling throughout the miles of trees and into Selyne's very core. Selyne turned again as the shadows shifted yet again.

"Who's there?" Selyne shouted, "who said that?"

Anger roiled inside Selyne as she searched the forest, mixing with sadness and loneliness. She wanted to scream, maybe cry, but she remained there watching as the darkness grew.

A woman stepped out from behind one of the trees. Her skin was an unnatural metallic color as if made of blued steel. Her hair and dress were a coinciding deep black.

The woman stared at Selyne, glowing eyes shining through waves of hair.

"Shia!" Selyne gasped, recoiling from the woman.

The woman gave a slight bow, "Yours truly, I'm surprised you recognize me."

Shia gave a wicked smile as if she'd said something devious.

"What? No," Selyne stammered, "you're not even real. You shouldn't…"

Selyne lost the words to say – this didn't seem right.

Shia laughed, "Look, I'm not sure why you called me here either. I don't do favors for traitors." She thought about it for a while before shrugging. "Honestly, I'm just here to watch it all burn down."

Selyne stared at the Angel in front of her in disbelief. "You came here to watch me suffer? Angels do that?"

Shia shrugged, "I'm not Solus or Elin. I don't hand out favors." She looked at Selyne with a predatory gaze, "I watch and wait to take what is mine by right. Death comes for everyone, so sit tight. I'll be around soon enough, Selyne."

"Selyne?"

"Selyne?"

The voice changed, fading into a voice Selyne knew very well. She opened her eyes to find the dim light of the sun floating through the curtains in her windows.

"Selyne?" Mara's voice was quiet as she gently prodded the sleeping princess's shoulder.

"I'm awake, Mara. No need to worry."

The maid pulled back quickly as Selyne sat up from her covers. Had she actually slept here?

Mara gave a gentle bow, "Sorry, Princess. I know you hate being disturbed in the morning. I was going to leave, but then the clocks hit noon, and I began to grow concerned."

Selyne gave the girl an appreciative nod, "It's okay. I appreciate the concern. Though I assure you I'm fine."

Mara nodded, though the girl didn't seem all that convinced.

"So, there's no longer a need to be concerned," Selyne said in the gentlest voice she could manage after waking up. "Why don't we get ready to leave. I can't imagine Wil is okay with me breaking plans this much."

Mara pulled her hand away. "I'll let you wash up. I'll get the clothes ready. Do you have a preference today?"

Selyne pushed the covers off and made herself get up from the bed. *No headache. When was the last time I drank?*

Moving over to the window, Selyne pulled open the curtains. *I believe it has been two nights since I've touched a bottle.*

That would explain the nightmares.

Mara fiddled nervously with her shirt, "Ma'am?"

Selyne remembered the girl standing in the corner, "Ah, yes. Clothes. Let's go with something bright. It's a clear sky outside. Let's take advantage of that."

Mara nodded sharply, "I'll see to it, ma'am."

Mara moved to the second room of the suite and stopped before closing the door, turning to Selyne. "Ma'am?"

Selyne looked back, growing irate at the girl's persistence.

Her voice grew on edge as it spoke, "What is it?"

"I got the water hot a few minutes ago. Just wanted to be sure you got in before it got cold."

Selyne nodded, "Thank you. I'll be sure not to forget."

The girl smiled and closed the door. Selyne released an irritated sigh. She knew the girl meant well, but Selyne was getting anxious. If she couldn't find a bottle soon, there would be problems.

"The water will be cold."

The thought alone caused Selyne to shiver. "A drink in a cold bath would be worse than a warm one without one. Shia!"

Selyne turned around in a cloud of irritation, walking to the washroom door next to the wardrobe, "I need something to settle my nerves before I say something I'll regret."

The bath proved to be the right choice, the moderate temperature of the water relieving the tension of sleep without being overwhelming. A knock came at the door, interrupting Selyne from combing her now damp hair in the mirror.

"Yes?" Selyne called, not turning from the thick strands of soggy auburn hair covering her face.

"Ma'am, the clothes are ready when you come out. Would you like any help putting them on?"

Selyne turned away from the mirror, "I'll be okay. You can go, Mara."

She listened and could hear the soft footfalls, presumably Mara, receding away from the door. Selyne turned back to her face staring at her from the other side of the mirror. When had the circles faded from her eyes? Selyne stepped from the washroom, still combing her nearly dry hair.

Mara had left her selected clothing on a newly made bed where Selyne would be able to find them easily. Selyne looked over the objects; the girl definitely had adequate taste. She had selected a pale blue blouse, a heavy riding skirt, and a pair of slacks to go underneath. The girl had even selected a pair of boots to go with the outfit.

"I'm going to need to hang on to this one," Selyne thought, slipping her head through the top of the blouse, "She'd be at least worth what we pay her monthly."

Selyne stepped out of her room into the empty hallway. Here, the top of the keep's Spire garnered little to no foot traffic even on the busiest of days. The soles of her boots padded softly on the marble floor. The hall rounded gently until Selyne came to a flight of stairs. There were close to two hundred of these she needed to descend in order which was why most people used the elevator. However, Selyne needed to pick up her effort before leaving for the consulate.

Making her way down the flight, Selyne could see an increase in people. The servants moved to prepare what looked to be lunch for the royalty and nobles of the upper tower. Selyne passed by the maids carrying food up to the upper suites. She ignored their nervous bows as she stepped into the Spire's highest kitchen.

The place was a frenzy of motion as cooks stirred pots and checked ovens, plating the food and sending it with a maid at breakneck speed. Selyne hugged the wall, trying her best to scan the room without getting trampled by the mass stampede of servants.

Her eyes locked onto a large man with a jet-black beard currently working on a plank of meat with a knife larger than Selyne's forearm. Selyne waved and bounced on her feet as she attempted to get his attention.

"Chef, Chef Tamra!" Selyne yelled into the cacophony around her.

Fortunately, the man must have the ears of an angel, looking up from his work at her call. Selyne gave him another wave. This time his eyes caught hers, Tamra's face breaking into a smile as he recognized who was calling him.

Putting down his knife, the big man waded through the mess of fellow cooks parting them like a boulder in a river, "Hallo Princess, what brings my honored customer to this humble kitchen?"

The big man's deep voice caused dissonance as Selyne stared into the wrinkles created by Tamra's pure white grin.

"I'm here looking for my escort. Has he dropped in today?"

Why was she feeling so anxious? Selyne remembered she hadn't gotten her bottle this morning.

Tamra glanced around the room. "He was here earlier today. Let's check the back. I'm sure he's still here."

Selyne followed Tamra back through the swarm of people in the large man's wake as they made to the back of the kitchen. Here the lights were dim, and the kitchen noise was muffled, creating a stark contrast to the chaotic environment of the kitchen outside.

Tamra placed a hand on Selyne's shoulder and pointed to a table in the middle of the room, "I believe that's your man, yes?"

Selyne followed his finger to its destination, landing on the tall figure and brown hair that shimmered golden in the light. Wil looked up from his glass of ale. His emerald eyes met Selyne's in the small space.

"That's him. Thanks, Tamra. I'll be okay from here."

Selyne stepped towards the table, leaving behind a disconcerted Tamra as she sat down across from Wil.

He put his glass down and leaned back in his chair, "So, did you have a good sleep last night? I met your maid in the hall this morning. She said you looked like you were dead."

Selyne felt her hands begin to shake violently. This was not the time for small talk, "Yes, well, yesterday was taxing. So, you wouldn't happen to know where I can get a drink around here?"

Wil raised an eyebrow at the frantic way the words came out of her mouth, looking over the situation he was in with a warrior's eye. Finally, he gave up trying to come up with the correct answer.

"Just take what's left of mine," he mumbled and pushed the glass towards her.

Selyne scrunched her nose but took it anyway. It felt like the bottles were growing sparser as the days passed – a ploy of her mother's machination more than likely. Selyne took a swig of the fermented liquid, relishing the bite of alcohol on her lips. Shia, it was good.

Wil pulled something from his pocket, drawing Selyne's attention. She looked over to see a brass pocket watch nestled in the palm of his hand. The piece was ornate, easily worth several months of a soldier's pay. Why would Wil own such a thing?

Selyne downed the half-full mug and gestured with the glass, "Where did you get something so valuable? A family heirloom? Or is my mother pandering to a new endeavor?"

Contempt slipped out as she thought about her mother. Wil seemed unaffected, however, closing the lid and sliding the timepiece back into his coat pocket.

"Your mother figured I should be able to help with scheduling. The watch is only a tool to aid in that. You also have a meeting in an hour with the Department heads at Thean University. Get ready."

CHAPTER 21

Light flittered through the dust motes drifting down from the ceiling, creating a rather calming atmosphere. Alfear sat back in his chair, staring at the person sitting across from him. Selyne leaned on her elbow. She fiddled with her pocket watch as she ignored the people talking around her,

"We can't rely on the Imperial troops to manage the growth in Rhinil activity in the southern regions. They simply lack the human resources to do such a thing." Rayal bristled with annoyance as she spoke; repeating the same thing four times in four different ways had that effect.

Beril leaned forward, standing up as he looked Rayal in the eyes, his gaze steely. "I understand your concern. Shia, woman, it's all you've been concerned about this evening. I understand as the head of Ithea's military logistics that this would be at the forefront of your agenda, however as the Thean Head of the Department of Economics here in the central empire, I have a duty to maintain trade throughout the four corners of Ithea. All I ask is a redistribution of troops from the Thailian border to vital arteries of Ithea's commerce."

Rayal opened her mouth to speak but was interrupted by the third Thean head raising his hand.

"Before we continue this discussion, can we please focus on the question we brought our guests here for?" He turned towards Alfear, ignoring the glares from Beril and Rayal.

Alfear straightened in his chair, glancing around the room to the council around him – the three heads of the Central Thean Departments. The commander of troop distribution in central Ithea, was on his right and the spokesman for the merchant's guild, and Selyne on his left.

Alfear cleared his throat, "Currently, we have obtained three people who have inherited some form of angelic inheritance. These include the patrons' Angels of Deception, Freedom, Discord, Justice, and Wrath."

He pulled a piece of paper from his bag laying it flat on the table for the others to see. "This is the current progress of each of our students. Currently, we've kept them on a standard two-year course to apprenticeship."

"However," Sargon, the head of Thean enforcement, interjected. "We have been able to speed this process in times of stress. During the third expansion west, we were training Heirs in the span of four months."

The room went silent as the group pondered the proposition. Selyne looked over to Alfear. Finally vested in the conversation around her.

"Alfear, I've got something to ask you now," her voice came out clearer than usual, and Alfear noted the absence of the usual rosy cheeks Selyne too often possessed.

"I'll be glad to answer any questions which are within my power to do so." Alfear maintained a professional tone as he spoke.

Better to keep the air of competence around all the important people in the room. Selyne didn't have any such reservations, fidgeting with the pen given to her.

"Right. Well, my question may be more of a request." Selyne tossed the pen aside and began to sift through the papers Alfear had handed to her earlier in the week as a way to inform her of the idea before today. She clearly sat on it until now.

"Currently, your plan suggests a trip up north to one of our star forts on the border as a way to expose me and the other Angel-kin to an environment where our power could be put to practical use."

Selyne tossed the paper onto the table and began to fidget with her pen again. Alfear wasn't sure where this line of conversation was going. Selyne didn't help with the manic fidgeting she continued to do.

"Was there something which looked wrong in my synopsis, or is it something else?"

Rayal rolled her eyes at the pair, "Thea burn us all. Just say what you need to. You sound like a bunch of children with all this vanity."

Her words cut in between the conversation, effectively bringing it to a close.

Rayal turned to Selyne, her gaze matching the edge of her voice, "I'm not here to hear your complaints, so make a request or let us finish so I can get back to work."

Selyne nodded, choosing not to match the woman's gaze as she spoke. "Currently, I believe nothing is to be learned in Isel or the northern cardinal Garrison. I have the better part of my life learning of the practices and culture of both places. I don't need any more."

Rayal turned to Alfear, contemplation plain on his face. "Do you have a response, enforcer?"

Alfear thought a moment longer before answering, "I understand you may find this plan mundane, but I have other people in need of this training far more than you. They also will prove to be more useful as they lack the ties to royalty that you possess. I'm not changing a good plan like this on a whim."

Selyne rolled her eyes at his words, an unconventional response for royalty, "I couldn't give Shia's backside what the others do. I'm sick of all this. By all means, let the kids go on this trip. I am only speaking for myself when I say I don't want to do this."

"So, what would you suggest? We can't let you wander off without any protection, and I must be with the other kin."

Alfear's voice was tinged with cynicism, clearly feeling more challenged than he tried to let on. Selyne, however, remained completely above the situation, a benefit of her royal upbringing, to be sure.

"I have thought of that issue. If not from you, my mother would bring it up sooner or later. However, my plan hopes to address this question." Selyne was now leaning forward, her attention undivided.

"I've asked around, and I believe I could caravan with the Seekers in tandem with your group. We would travel north with each other until we reach the northern branch, at which point I'll go left with my retainers, and you would continue right to the northern cardinal Garrison."

One of the heads sitting in the corner leaned forward. He was an older man with greying hair and a wrinkled face. Alfear knew the man well, and the rest of the conversation slowed to a stop as he prepared to speak.

"Dear Princess, I would never imagine a time or place where I would willingly prevent a member of the royal family from doing something, but as the last surviving heir to the imperial throne, I must ask why you want to travel to the Everwood. It's not a safe place under any circumstances."

"Naturally, you would be concerned," Selyne continued, "Seeing as I'm the last living heir to Ithea's throne at this time. The stability of our government relies on my prolonged livelihood, but I'm not sure that's enough to convince me."

"If you would elaborate, Princess."

Selyne leaned back in her chair, staring at the ceiling, "I'm not ready for this. The idea of ruling doesn't appeal to me, and I'm getting tired of the political dogma this place has. I need answers, and they sure don't exist here or up north, so I'm not going."

"This plan," the department head started, "would take you into the Everwood if I understand my geography correctly."

Selyne nodded, "that's the idea."

"The Everwood is not just a place you can enter lightly. Our armies couldn't pierce its foliage for decades. It's a land crawling with old magic. Ancestors are a real and present threat there and have cost us entire battalions." The elderly man took a sip of his beer before continuing. "There are also the natural hazards. Rhinil war parties frequently travel through the Everwood, and heaven forbid you stumble into a mraven hive. It's simply far too dangerous for our only heir to the throne to travel through on some kind pilgrimage of self-discovery."

"I'd have my private security to protect me, not to mention the Seekers we'd travel with, and myself as a semi-functional Angel-kin." Selyne stared down at the elderly head and raised her eyebrow in challenge. "Do you really think anything short of a Thailian invasion will stop us?"

Rayal interjected before anyone else could, "Princess, while it may be improbable that anything could bring you harm, it's the ignorance of a child which assumes the best outcome possible."

Selyne shrugged, "I can't make you do anything yet, but I have a feeling this is what I should do."

Alfear paused, the statement halting his train of thought. He looked past the heads who were discussing what they should do.

"What exactly do you mean by that, Princess?"

Selyne met his eyes, "Which part? I've said a lot today."

"You seem adamant that you don't want to go along with our plans; I'm just having trouble wrapping my head around the reason why."

The prompt seemed to disturb Selyne, her eyes turning aside at his sudden interest. "I just have a sense that continuing the way I am isn't going to work. Something inside me keeps telling me I need to find a new path. Also, I had a dream last night."

"Really? Well, that changes things." Alfear grew silent as he processed that last statement. Everything the Princess had said up to this point could be attributed to the whims of royalty, but a dream was a different matter. It was a contentious matter in the university, but Alfear believed a dream that moved someone to act on it was not something that happened by mistake.

"What's the importance of this?" Rayal said, breaking the silence.

Alfear leaned back in his chair, running hands through his hair in a nervous habit. Rayal wouldn't get it. Military personnel rarely did.

"Alfear, we don't know what's going on. We would love to be privy to that information."

Alfear glanced about the room, trying to judge the beliefs of the people there. Despite acting like a single theological and philosophical entity, the universities were anything but that. Alfear's convictions could be met with anything ranging from approval to disgust.

They are not going to leave without an answer, though they won't want the one I have to give. Alfear groaned internally at what he was about to do. The room's eyes were on him, waiting.

"Many of you are probably unaware of something my father told me as a child. A proverb of sorts, in regards to an Angel-kin's inheritance. The line goes: An ignorant man will refuse a farmer's call for rain, but only a fool ignores the conscious voice of the Angel-kin's soul."

Alfear glanced about the room, eyes darting back and forth, judging the reactions of the group. They seemed to take it okay.

"Has this proverb ever applied with you or Lian? Surely as inheritors of the original Angel-kin, you would see this at work." Beril's voice boomed with a careful force.

He was actually thinking about what was said.

Alfear nodded, "Several times. My own and Lian's intuition have revealed many threats and treasures on our journeys."

Beril looked over to a slim man of Thailian origin. Alfear recognized the man as the Department head for Seekers here in Isel, though his name escaped him.

"This is something which most modern sensibilities would reject. What do you have to say about this?" Beril asked.

The man furrowed his brow in the thought, nibbling at the tip of his finger absentmindedly.

Finally, he shrugged, "It's possible. We know inheritances come with prior knowledge on how to use them. Also, consider the subject of ancestors in the Everwood, which implies that more than practical knowledge can be tied to a coalition of resonant power, but to have it come in the form of a dream?"

The wiry man shook his head, "I'm really not sure if that holds weight or not."

Beril turned to the other heads, "Dreia says it's possible. What are your opinions on the matter?"

The group broke apart as they discussed their thoughts on what was said. Alfear pulled himself up from his chair and made his way over to where Dreia was seated. The man looked at him, his caramel eyes flashing in the lamplight.

"You want to talk to me, enforcer?"

Alfear pulled a chair out from the table and took a seat. "I just wanted to hear your opinion on the Princess's decision; you coming from the ranks of the Seekers corps, you should know what she will be getting herself into."

Alfear watched as Dreia called a servant from the corner, requesting a drink for himself.

"I won't pretend like it's not a foolhardy plan," he said, grabbing the cup. "Though I am intrigued by what you've said tonight. I mean, using an outdated proverb as a means to legitimize the value of a dream, hardly counts as an academic source."

Dreia sipped the alcoholic beverage, face wincing at the bitter taste before setting it down. "Anyway, despite what seems sensible, I'm curious to see what you could reveal. We may have something for my Seekers to study."

Dreia gave Alfear a small smile which he tried to return, though his heart wasn't there.

"Maybe I can get myself one of those drinks." Alfear scanned the faces of each Department head. The conversation hadn't receded in the slightest. Each group was speaking over what they felt should happen. Selyne remained seated, gulping half of the vasse in her mug in a single go.

At least she isn't phased. Alfear scoffed internally. Beril turned away from the clique of people he was talking to.

"I have reached an agreement with my peers. I would like to inquire of the rest of the heads about their conclusions."

The room grew silent as people ended their conversations. Dreia stood and faced Beril, "My opinion is that we send the girl on her requested journey. Not only could it prove useful for research, but I fail to see what legal means we have to stop her if she chooses to enforce her authority."

Murmurs ripped through the room at his words.

"What about the queen? Or the emperor? Surely they won't agree to such a foolhardy plan." The elderly man from earlier added.

Alfear looked over to where Selyne was ordering another drink, a grin ghosting on the edges of her mouth. She knew exactly how this would go.

I wonder if Kalli has rubbed off on her, or if this is her environment changing her?

Beril turned to the elderly man, "The emperor is the other half of the government with greater jurisdiction in this regard. Nothing we say affects any support or lack thereof he may send."

"Of course," Dreia said, interjecting into the conversation, "This is about our funds and where we choose to put them."

Beril nodded, put off by the interruption, "I say we give support. Otherwise, we lose our claim to the expedition."

Rayal agreed, "It would be the most economical choice for our empire. The Seekers send these trips everywhere anyway."

"Seems you just need to convince the loudest voice. The rest with nothing to say will follow them." Alfear smirked as people seemed to sway.

Sliding her second cup into place next to her first, Selyne leaned back as she spoke, "If we're in agreement here, can we finish this up? I would like to begin preparations."

Rayal flinched at her words, leading Alfear to sense that something was personal between the two of them. Beril shrugged, releasing a sigh in resignation.

"Princess, you can expect us to try and sort this out. Just keep in mind that it may take a while to confirm our decision. Please try to remain calm until then."

Selyne seemed indifferent. "I will pack. I'll start from there and see where we go."

Shia, you must have given her your tongue for all the abrasive words coming from her mouth. Alfear paused as it dawned on him who he was considering. *Maybe I am beginning to see what people are so concerned about. She lacks all the propriety expected of someone born into politics.*

A knock sounded on the door before it cracked open, revealing a woman's face. She looked to Beril and raised an open watch.

"Ah. We will discuss this later. I hope we can all come to an agreement by the end of this week."

Alfear bowed to the Thean heads as each one made their way out of the office. Nothing had been decided today, leaving closed-door negotiations as the premier way to conclude the debate. Alfear smiled and bowed as another person left. He wasn't certain if that woman had even been a part of the committee. At this point, he didn't care.

Selyne stepped out of the room, and Alfear bowed. She returned the gesture, raising her eyebrow. "You really think that's necessary? I don't determine your salary."

She really looked much better than Alfear's prior interactions. He actually felt a conversation wouldn't be dangerous.

He chuckled, "That was completely sincere. You hold sway here that I do not. It makes me think maybe I should come to you for future projects."

Selyne gave him a severe glare, leading Alfear to laugh.

"Listen, you know very well why that's unacceptable," Selyne said. "The balance of Imperial power is very precarious. A Thean law enforcer receiving support from the royal family would throw the Thean heads into disarray. They might even bring in the high court."

Alfear raised his arm defensively, "I'm not suggesting we do this. We do need to keep the Thean branch happy after all."

Selyne gave a knowing nod, "Their taxes would be sorely missed."

The pair stood in happy silence. Something Alfear had thought impossible in the presence of royalty. Apparently, they were still just people after all. He peeked into the now vacant meeting room.

"Do you have a way home, Princess? I could get a carriage if you need it." Alfear said.

Selyne waved his offer away, "I had Wil go a while ago. He'll be back in a moment."

"You put a lot of trust into that soldier." He said, probing with the query.

"He's the army's strongest man," Selyne responded without looking up from her nails. "Some even claim he's the strongest man on the continent. If you read some reports, he can tear through steel lockplates with his bare hands along with catching arrows and other hyperbole."

Alfear felt the hyperbole was the thing to take away from that last statement, "Well then, I'll let you go. Hopefully, we'll see each other in a few weeks."

Selyne nodded, "If all goes as Thea intends, I will."

The pair split, and Alfear stepped into the hallway. Turning the corner, he came face to face with Wil. The man stood a good head below him, and Alfear was certain he had six years' seniority on him. Wil gave a nod of acknowledgment before stepping aside and continuing down the hall.

Alfear turned, watching his figure vanish. *The strongest man on the continent?* Alfear couldn't accept the idea. He decided to leave the matter. He wouldn't have answers tonight or tomorrow, and Kalli was expecting him for dinner. He smiled as Kalli came to mind. He'd have to cook something fancy tonight.

Alfear breathed deeply as he stepped out into the fading evening. The summer heat never bothered him, but the cool of night was something else entirely.

How many summers has it been? Twenty? Elen, help me. A sigh escaped as his age became realized. *I'm going to need to rest soon, maybe take a few decades away from the travel and politics. Maybe even settle down with Kalli. I'm sure if I kept feeding her, she'd be fine with it.* He let out a small chuckle, his voice eaten by the silent streets of the noble sector as he made his way towards home.

CHAPTER 22

Selyne breathed in the fresh air, savoring the crisp feeling as she sipped her tea. She stared out across her balcony, enjoying the cityscape beneath her.

"It's marvelous, isn't it?" she asked, turning to Kalli.

The woman sat beside her with her own cup of tea. It seemed she was around more often these days, not that Selyne minded her company. Still, it was odd having anyone as invested in her life as Kalli was. *Is this what having a friend feels like?* Selyne pondered. She glanced at Wil standing in the corner. He didn't say anything, choosing to watch the pair silently.

Kalli nodded, resting her tea cup in her lap as she took time to appreciate the view. "It's very nice. I'm a little surprised you don't spend more time up here."

"Yeah," Selyne said ponderously, "I feel like this place has too many bad habits and life experiences to be comfortable. Though with you guys, it's not like that, I swear."

"Of course," Kalli said smiling, "besides, I hear you have some good news for us?"

Selyne couldn't help but smile devilishly at the question. "Oh, do I ever."

She dug into her book bag and pulled out a letter. She slammed it triumphantly onto the small tea table, the official university seal clearly visible to everyone.

Kalli raised an eyebrow, "Is that what I think it is?"

Selyne's smile grew even wider. "I didn't think they'd get it resolved so quickly, but they've cleared us to travel with the Seekers in the next few weeks. I can only imagine the amount of hair-pulling that happened over at the university when my requests hit their desks."

"I'm sure your mother pulled a few strings," Wil said, chiming into the conversation.

Selyne shrugged, "Maybe, but that's beside the point. We're going on a journey into the Everwood. It's a real-life adventure."

Wil looked as if he wanted to say something before shaking his head and resuming his silence.

"It is shocking they let you do this honestly," Kalli said, "you've basically convinced everyone that it was ok to risk the royal line in order for you to go on a vacation."

"It's not a vacation!" Selyne said adamantly.

The thought bothered Selyne a little, but she knew why everyone felt that way.

"Think of it like this room. I'm not comfortable here because of the memories it gives me." Selyne paused as she formulated her next thought. "Much like leaving this room feels like a breath of fresh air, I feel like leaving this palace will give me the freedom to think more openly, maybe find a few answers."

"Also, it's a good opportunity for a vacation," Kalli said flatly.

Selyne laughed. "Yes, it's also a good vacation."

"So, when do we start packing?" Kalli asked,

Selyne shrugged, "I think Alfear will let us know. He is the one in charge of all of us."

"I'll talk to him tonight," Kalli said.

Selyne sipped her tea, staring out over the city. She'd have a chance to go someplace new, with new people, and new opportunities.

She looked over at Kalli. "You're a good friend, you know."

"Oh, I know," Kalli said, smiling slyly.

Selyne glanced over at Wil, "You aren't so bad either, you know."

Wil shrugged.

"I appreciate that." Selyne chortled, "it's more than I'd expected."

The group sat in a moment of silence, reveling in the moment.

I shouldn't get too optimistic, but I feel like this might just work. Selyne took another sip of tea. She'd gotten what she'd asked for, and now she just needed to sit back and hope what she'd wanted was what was needed.

* * * * * *

Fre stared blankly at the book in front of her. Three weeks spent in the library, and her mind was fried. She felt like she should understand the Ithean script, but her mind simply refused to acknowledge that fact. She yawned, stretching her arms. Honestly, how did Quintin find the motivation to do this in his free time?

Fre looked around, watching the other people studying. Despite the hour of the night, the place was bustling with students and professors busy with research or school projects. Fre found the atmosphere strange. She'd never been one for academic life despite how much her father had tried. Her gaze shifted to Lian sitting in the corner, his attention buried in a novel. He confused Fre. He was nice enough, and his teaching had been wonderful, but he never seemed quite normal. *As if he's living somewhere else whenever he stops talking.* Fre wondered what went through his mind whenever his gaze grew distant.

Lian glanced up from his novel, somehow sensing Fre's stare.

"Are you growing tired?" He asked setting the book aside, "we can stop for tonight if you're not going to get any more done. You should be excited. You've never been up north before."

Fre smiled weakly. She didn't know what to think of this whole thing. Lian had told her about it rather abruptly last week.

"I'm not sure what to think," she said, "I feel like once you've travelled a dozen different places, the sense of wonder begins to fade."

Lian shrugged, "Maybe the journey is the same, but I believe where you end up is what makes it all worthwhile."

Fre thought about those words. For the last few years, the destination had always been a dead end. It was only a matter of time before she moved on in hopes of finding the destination she'd wanted. *I've spent so much time looking for my family it's ruined the life around me.* Fre yawned again. Heavens she was tired.

"Are you ready to go?" Lian asked again.

Fre nodded, covering her mouth as another yawn broke out. Lian stood, tucking the novel under his arm. Fre followed him downstairs, marveling again at just how busy this place was at this time of night. The campus had grown silent outside the interior of the library. Fre stared up at the midnight sky. It was hard to see any stars with the city lights.

"I'll walk you over to your dorms," Lian said, looking at his watch.

Fre didn't argue as the pair walked across the university lawn towards the women's dorm.

Lian glanced at her, "Are you doing ok? You seem to have gotten distant these last few days."

Fre shrugged. She didn't know how she felt at the moment. These last few weeks had gone by in a haze of commotion; she hadn't sorted it all out yet.

"Is there a problem you want to talk over?" Lian asked, his voice more insistent than before.

Fre sighed. "I'm not sure this whole thing is a good idea."

"Elaborate," Lian said.

"It just feels like anyone else would be better suited for what you're trying to do," Fre said. "I'm not built for this, and I think we know that, so I wonder if it's even possible for me to become the person you're looking for."

Fre stared forlornly at the ground in front of her. She hadn't chosen this predicament, and as far as anyone knew, there wasn't a way to remove an inheritance. Fre would be judged under the gaze of the Thean bureaucracy as a problem for as long as she lived.

"You know," Lian began, "it's easy to believe that there is some overarching goal that I want you to reach. The Heads of the Thean institutes certainly want something specific from you, but I do not. When I look at you, I'm never comparing how much progress another student made that same week, but by how much progress you made each week."

"But it's not just education, is it," Fre retorted. "It's an undeniable fact that this power isn't something that fits me well; it was stolen for Shia's sake. Eventually, there will be no more progress to be made, and I'm going to fall short of expectations."

Lian stopped walking, digging under his shirt collar. Fre paused as he pulled out a small necklace. It was a small chain without any ornamentation and a heavy clasp to hold it together. Fre looked down at the small pendant hanging down. Its gentle glow illuminated Lian's hand as he held it out.

"Is that?" Fre gasped in disbelief.

Lian nodded. "The Seekers institute prefers we maintain the angel hearts we have. This one has been passed through my family for millennia, beginning with Amie herself. It's been mine for the better part of twenty years now."

Fre examined the small pendant, marveling at its intricate silver work. "Why are you showing me this?"

Lian pulled the pendant back, clasping it at the back of his neck. "My family line is very old, and it's common for multiple children to be born into the family, making choosing who gets the inheritance tricky. You see, my family has very heavy blood with more of the required conductors flowing through it than most people. This isn't an issue for someone who inherits Resonance; we don't know why, but for those who don't inherit, it can prove fatal."

"Did you lose someone?" Fre asked, growing somber.

"A sister," Lian replied bluntly. "However, that's not what I'm getting to at this moment. You may feel like you're a wasted opportunity or that someone else could've done better than you if given the chance. Just know that you are here, now, with a whole history behind you. We could speculate for years what could have been, but that should never change what you choose to do now, ok?"

Fre glanced around the campus. She hadn't expected this type of conversation tonight. She didn't know whether to feel comforted by Lian's words or extremely awkward.

"Just keep what I said in mind," Lian said as he began to walk again, "this trip is taking us to a place where you're going to be judged even worse than here. I believe you are fully capable of rising above it all, but only if you decide to take action."

He glanced over at Fre. She gave him a weak smile.

"I'll keep it in mind," she said reassuringly.

"Let's get you back to your dorm then shall we," Lian said.

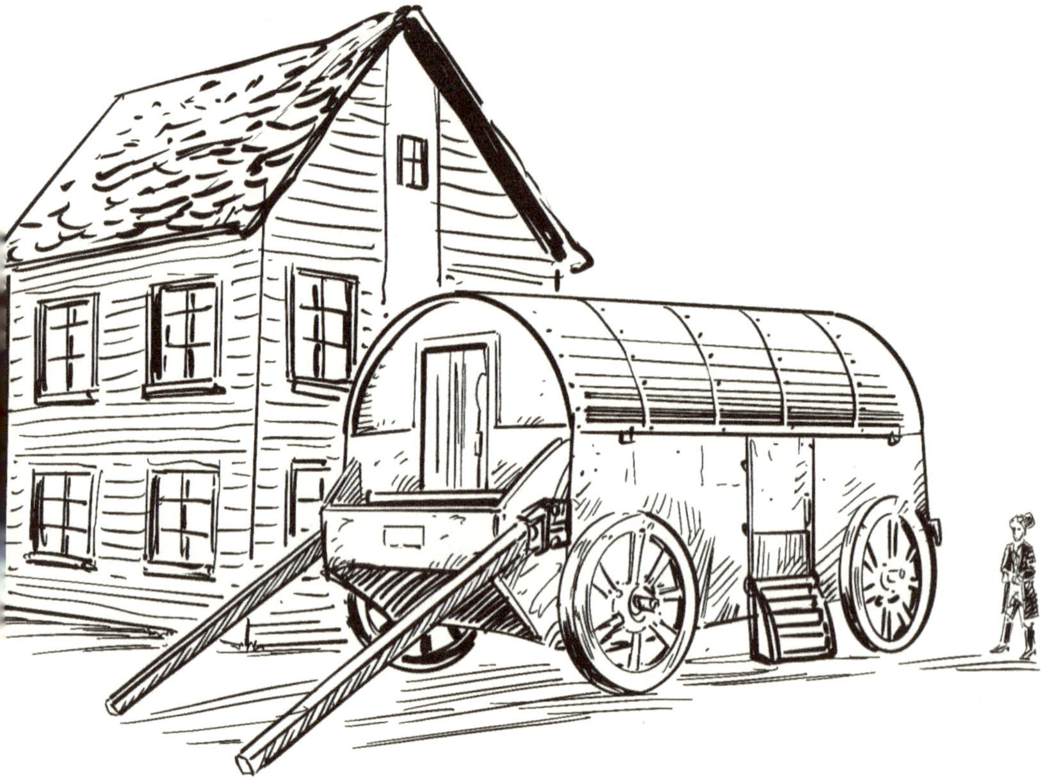

CHAPTER 23

Lian strode past the line of wagons lining the inner courtyard of the upper campus. Workers flowed past in groups, clustering around one wagon like insects to carrion, taking piece by piece until all that was left was an empty husk. Lian marveled at the uniform motion each group took, working as if they understood the goals of the other.

Some would claim it wasn't just his imagination. The Seeker division was unlike the other departments in the Thean hierarchy. Spending more time with the spirits and ancestors roaming the inner parts of Ithea's largest forest bringing back cursed and mythological items for the other departments to study.

Lian understood the feeling, if only by a lesser degree. People distrusted those with power who claimed to know more than them. The navigators were often deemed a mistrusted division, touting philosophy and theology to further their political power. It was infuriating that they were so often correct in their skepticism.

Lian worked his way to the front of the caravan, taking care not to disrupt them as he did so. As he drew near, he caught sight of Alfear speaking with a frail-looking man dressed in all gray and holding a large book out for Alfear to view. Someone moved to Lian's left, sliding up to him as he walked.

"You'd think after the work he's put in these past few weeks that the man would let us do our job."

Lian chuckled as the all too familiar voice spoke, "Indeed, if I'm not mistaken, you were supposed to handle provisions, Kalli."

The woman shook her head, raising her hands in exasperation, "The sod didn't even talk to me this morning. The indecency of some men."

Lian glanced over to where Kalli stood next to him, arms crossed, as she looked at Alfear, "I would suspect that you didn't even realize he'd neglected to visit today, or is my judgment off?"

Kalli didn't respond to the jab, instead walking towards a wagon that was in the process of being restocked, "I believe this one is where we'll be staying. I may not have worked out the arrangement, but a persistent person can get information regardless of how stubborn Seekers are."

Kalli stepped up onto the wagon, taking a seat and looking out to her surroundings. Lian walked up to the side of the wagon. Its construct was solid, making use of the newer telescopic spring system and utilizing a solid steel axle instead of reinforced wood.

"Well, our friend definitely has good taste. This will be the smoothest ride I'll have experienced with him."

Kalli stood up and looked down at the seat, dusting off her trousers before hopping to the paved road below, "Since when have you've travelled with Alfear?"

Her expression showed her confusion and a slight concern at the thought of information she didn't know. Lian thought back, the memories he'd suppressed for years, bringing a shudder to his very soul.

"In our earlier years, the Empire was all too keen on using our abilities. This was back during the last border war, and sometimes that led down paths one would rather avoid, both in a metaphorical and literal sense. It's a sensitive subject, so I ask you never to attempt to pry at the secrets hidden there."

Kalli inhaled but paused as she realized Lian's dead stare and firm hand. She brushed off his hand and turned away, her voice mumbling to herself as it often did when she was working. She'd found yet another question. Lian's body shuddered one more time to bury the memories. Kalli would sit on the question for a while, but it was only a matter of time.

Alfear returned, followed closely by a Seeker. The frail man in tow turned to face them as they drew closer, putting on the most normal face as he could manage. Lian turned into the pair, walking beside them as they discussed the last details of their journey.

"I must say, good sir, that I've never experienced a request quite like this. Many people ask for rides, but few actually wish to see the end of our journey."

"It is an odd request," Alfear conceded. "Though given how the world is taking shape, I believe it to be needed in order to train our Heirs appropriately for the future storm."

Lian continued to walk alongside in silence, listening to the conversation taking place. The frail Seeker drew the pair over to the wagons. Kalli had been inspecting them moments before.

"I've made space on these two for the number of people you provided. The one on the left will take three to the facility in the inner forest area. The other will take another three people to the northern garrison."

Alfear stepped towards the two carts, repeating many of the actions Lian witnessed Kalli making.

Alfear took one last glance at the vehicle before turning back to Lian, "So what is your summary of our situation?"

He asked the question as he surveyed his hands where he'd touched the cart. He self-consciously brushed them off on his pants before resigning them to his pockets.

"Honestly, I would take any transportation, excluding an outlander's farming cart, though Kalli seems to like this one." Lian gestured to the first one.

Alfear winced at the comment but nodded nevertheless, "I sometimes wish we could be gone sooner. Did you hear about the chaos happening in Thailia?"

Lian shrugged off the question. "Thailia is a wild place; news of famine and political unrest are constantly being sent from out west. Besides, it's not like we've dealt with their offenses before."

Alfear shook his head as Lian spoke, "This is different. The stories seem more vicious. I'm not sure how, but my intuition is telling me to be concerned."

Lian didn't respond to that. Those who obtained an inheritance from birth always seemed to hold strong beliefs about their intuition. You'd think it would be different with Lian and Alfear. Lian knew where his power came from; it wasn't some divine gift. Both came from ancient family trees dating to Heaven's War, and their power came from intact angel hearts passed down for millennia. The hearts weren't alive, not anymore at least, but they sometimes remembered that they once were. This could create memories or sensations often related to shifts in the threads. Unlike the dreams or twinges sometimes felt by Heirs, when Alfear was uneasy, it meant something old enough for his heart to remember had shifted. Sure, it could be as simple as two thieves obtaining powers familiar to their own, but sometimes…

Lian shook his head as he removed the last bit of that thought from his mind before it could finish.

He turned to Alfear, "You've spent too much time listening to the heads of the university. More than likely, it's just a hyperbolic warning sent by someone hoping to gain the attention of people at the top. Our job is to take care of our growing Angel-kin. It's what we're here for."

Alfear nodded, clearly not relaxed by the words as he fell deeper into his own thoughts.

"On a simpler note," Lian said in an attempt to move the conversation elsewhere, "Kalli caught wind of our time out east. She doesn't have any of the details, but I figured you should be aware of her curiosity before it caught you blind."

Alfear's head swung up, a look of shock mixed with just a hint of embarrassment coloring his face. "How did that come up? Wait, that's dumb; you were talking about carriages."

Alfear glanced back at Lian with cold eyes, "I've got to get the kids ready to leave by tomorrow. I appreciate the warning, and we'll have to remain watchful until we break the group at the forest edge."

Lian smiled and gave Alfear a reassuring pat on the shoulder, "I'll be sure your embarrassment never reaches the light of day. It is my embarrassment also, after all."

The pair walked away from the swarm of Seekers, heading to the right bow arm, presumably to rendezvous with Quintin. The building seemed strangely alive. Scribes scurried about the halls with armloads of books and crates full of odds and ends. Surely the Seeker haul hadn't been that interesting.

Lian followed Alfear to the Office of Hierarchal Affairs, making their way to the back of the room to Alfear's desk. As Lian continued following Alfear, he noted that his compatriot was ignoring his desk, instead walking over to where Rala sat at his own desk. Rala glanced up at the approach of the pair, quickly folding up his work.

"You here for the kids?"

Alfear nodded, "We're coming close to finishing the packing. They need to be ready to leave by tonight."

Rala pointed towards a side door in the back of the room, "I think they moved to the courtyard a few minutes ago though they could have gone to dinner for all I know."

Alfear walked past Rala, nodding his thanks as he walked by. The aloof nature of the action bothered Lian as he followed Alfear to the small door, making sure to give Rala a knowing gaze. Rala looked up and returned a smile. He knew the way Alfear got when he was concerned over something. They entered the small courtyard, the clouds obstructing the sun through the glass pane, throwing a dark shadow over the pale marble and emerald grass.

They found Fre and Quintin situated on the outer ring of marble. Fre was busy writing in the small journal she always carried with her. Absorbed with her work, she didn't register the two men entering. Quintin looked up from the book he was reading and nudged Fre from her concentration. She was startled with surprise at the contact. Her eyes darted around before landing on Lian's face.

"Is it time to leave yet? The tension around here has grown palpable. It's made me very anxious to leave."

Lian shook his head in apology, "Unfortunately, we still have a few hours. Though we could go for some food if you want to get out of here."

Fre's eyes lit up at the mention of food, and she hurried to pack up her satchel with her notebooks. Lian turned to Quintin, "Would you like to join us? I'm sure you could use some time away from your studies. At least for a bite to eat?"

Quintin leaned back into the stone bench and waved them away, "I've had a large lunch. Besides, I find this place to be quite relaxing."

Lian felt like he should push harder, but the kid was already turned back into his book. *The Tales of Angel-kin Throughout the Empire* was an odd choice to be declining dinner over. Lian wasn't sure he'd even read it before. Lian chose not to push any harder. Fre was ready to leave, and Quintin seemed more content to stay put.

"So, you're going to dinner uptown?" Alfear asked, his attention turning back to Lian.

He shrugged, "Thought we could get one last solid meal down before weeks spent on condensed and canned foods."

Alfear stepped past Lian, waving his hand dismissively as he passed, "I could care less why or what you eat. Just be ready to leave by tonight."

Lian glanced back to Fre as Alfear's body vanished behind the closing door and shrugged. "I guess it's just going to be you and me for dinner tonight. Luckily, that means we have more money to split between the two of us."

Fre gave him a rare smile, which put a smile on Lian's face.

"So, you said you like seafood, right?" Lian asked.

Fre nodded, "I heard of a place up by the Spire. Though it could be a bit costly."

Lian waved the question away, "It's just you and me. How much could we possibly eat?"

The pair's laughter echoed down the hallway before fading as they exited the bow-arm. Quintin sighed in relief as they disappeared, opening his book and reveling in the silence as he continued reading.

* * * * * *

The summer wind blew across the city of Isel, its warm currents in conflict with its brisk speed. Selyne opened her coat to let the warmth enter. It was nights like this that were precious to her. They brought back memories of racing through the forests with nothing but the moon to guide her. The memory began to hurt as reality came back to her. Those days had died even before her brothers had gone to war, back when her father had secluded himself from the family in order to lead a staggering nation.

There was no moon to guide Selyne tonight. The light above was being provided by the lamps which lined the streets of the upper citizenry. She continued walking down the marble street towards the looming structure of the university.

It had become a regular walk for Selyne, though the night sky and intermittent lamps did well to wake the atmosphere. Wil walked beside her on the left. His arms were laden with large leather bags – just the necessary items for a week-long trip to the central section of the empire. As the pair drew nearer to the large courtyard, things began to grow more and more active around them.

Dozens of men and women dressed in the heavy clothes unique to Seekers bustled about, making last-minute preparations before the caravan left. Selyne scanned the mass of heads, looking for any familiar faces in the crowd. Wil tapped her on the shoulder and gestured for Selyne's attention. She turned, following Wil's gaze.

Kalli stood by a cart, picking over a sandwich. Selyne waved to her, standing on her toes to reach out over the crowd of people. It didn't work. Kalli continued to feign interest in her food. Selyne stood down. Just as well, she needed to get to that cart anyway.

She turned to Wil, but the man had already read the current situation, stepping forward and cutting a path through the Seekers. Selyne felt like a rock sandwiched in the middle of a river, with the people seeming to flow around her with an uncanny fluidity. Something about the Seekers simply felt unnatural. Keeping a precise distance from Wil and herself, they moved about. The pair worked through the swarm, and Kalli's eyes lit up as they caught them approaching. She waved to Selyne with her free hand. Selyne waved back as she finally closed the gap between them.

"I'm so glad you decided to come with us, Kalli. I honestly didn't expect you to go along with such a harebrained idea."

"Not at all. When Alfear stopped by the house with the idea, it was all I could do to get packed."

"Really? I figured you would want to stay home with your work."

"Oh, nonsense. Any good researcher would never pass up the opportunity for some field experience."

Selyne looked up at the large cart Kalli had been looking over before being interrupted, "So, is this our carriage of fortune?"

It didn't look to be a very impressive vehicle, though judging by Kalli's face when she mentioned it, she was about to be corrected in that assumption.

"It's a marvel of Thean industrial engineering. Its suspension system is the newest available – made of the finest steel. Oh, it's also fitted with padded seats, a feature I think will interest you more than the others."

Selyne wasn't sure about that. It still looked like your average caravan vehicle. Lifting her leg up to the step on the side of the cart, she pulled herself up to view the interior. It was cozy, nothing to be elated over, but the trip should be bearable.

"When do we plan to leave?" Selyne yelled over the clamor around them.

She lurched back as Kalli poked her head through the small entrance, "Shia's breath. Don't scare me like that."

Kalli nodded, "Apologies. Currently, we're just waiting for Lian and Alfear to bring the other two Angel-kin. I'm unsure what the progress of the Seekers, but they have been finishing for the past hour or so."

A bag landed on the deck of the cart with a thud. It was soon followed by Wil carrying the other two bags along with his own rucksack. Selyne was beginning to see a problem arise with her luggage.

"Is there a place to put all of this? I refuse to have it by my feet throughout the trip."

"So glad you brought that up. Wil, if you'll bring these to the back, I'll show you where they can go."

Kalli picked up the bag Wil had left on the front of the cart and led the way to the compartment in the back. Selyne stepped out into the summer air. Her companions thought it was to work on her glyph-work with professional innovators of the field, which was partially true. However, Selyne's research through the last year was far more expansive than that. Months of searching for answers in Thean texts and histories, sometimes going into sources that some in the government would find treasonous, all while numbing the pain of loss.

Despite the haphazard nature of her work, which led to a lot of incoherent dead ends, it hadn't been fruitless. She had an idea, something found in an ancient Thailian religious scroll, written well before the border closure after the last unification war eighty years ago. It had spoken of some sort of deity in the Everwood – a remnant of Heaven's War, forgotten by Ithea but still vital to Thailian belief.

The parchment had recounted several pilgrims who had sought its wisdom, something the author suggested was common at the time.

The text was incomplete, but it had given Selyne an idea which, if everything went to plan, was about to be played out.

"Alfear!" the outburst startled Selyne as Kalli pushed past her, leaping off the cart and running to the man standing a head above the crowd.

Selyne couldn't help but smile as she watched Kalli embrace him. Selyne had her own qualms with the man, though she couldn't place exactly what it was about him that bothered her. Still, Kalli respected him, so that counted for something. *So long as we don't have to talk responsibility we should be fine.* She smiled wryly at the thought. Alfear looked over to her, smiling as he waved.

Selyne waved back absently, though Alfear had already moved on, returning to his conversation with Kalli. Selyne did her best to understand what they were talking about, and could barely hear what Alfear was saying.

"He knows when we're leaving." Alfear's voice was conversational as he spoke, "he's not going to let himself get left behind."

Kalli looked less enthused by the situation, her voice inaudible as she responded.

"What's going on now?" Selyne sighed under her breath, leaping from the cart and walking over to where the pair stood.

Two sets of eyes landed on her as she spoke.

"Apparently, Lian and Fre are still out with no recent contact." Kalli huffed, sighing internally as she spoke, giving Selyne the impression that this wasn't an uncommon occurrence.

"Sometimes, I question the Department's choice to use him. He lacks focus."

Alfear shrugged, "That may be, but you can't deny the progress they've made."

"Who are we talking about?" Selyne asked.

"It's the other Angel-kin. It would seem her teacher has been rather…lax…in his behavior."

"So, we don't know where they wandered off to? With no way of finding them? And our caravan can't leave until they arrive?" Selyne's eyebrow raised as Kalli groaned with mental fatigue at her statement.

Kalli fidgeted with her braid as she frantically looked for a way out of the hole they were stuck in. Alfear took the issue rather differently. Almost like he resigned himself to this reality long ago.

"Any chance I could help if you have a description of their vehicle or something that would distinguish them? I'll go take a look around." Selyne said, her skirt shifting as air currents began to flow around her.

"No. It should be fine." Kalli said, exhaustion seeming to finally catch up.

Wil came out of the wagon, hopping off the seat and wandering over to the group.

"I've got our things in order. What needs to happen to get us the rest of the way out of here?"

Kalli glared at him, and Alfear gave a warning look. "We're waiting for someone to get here. An Angel-kin and her guardian."

"Isn't that Lian over there?" Wil asked, pointing to a golden-haired man wading through the crowd. Alfear hurried to follow his finger's trajectory.

"By Thea, he has some gall showing his face now after all the irritation he's caused." Kalli's tone was coated in anger, though Selyne wondered if she was more relieved than anything.

Wil pushed after Kalli, the pair waiving Lian down as they waded through the crowd. Selyne watched as they collided, greeting each other. *When did he get to know that man? I didn't even know his name.* The thought unnerved her, but she didn't feel inclined to follow it up. Mostly, she just wanted to get on the road.

Lian walked with Wil, clearing the path of dwindling people as they continued back with Kalli and Fre. Alfear gave Lian a hug.

"So glad you could finally get here. Kalli was ready to give you up."

Lian chuckled, "Trust me, she made that clear. Unfortunately, we had trouble finding a cart that would carry us this far at night, so we ended up walking the rest of the way."

Alfear gave him a pat on the back, "Don't be too torn up. What matters is that you're here, and we can now begin to get on the road."

Selyne nodded at the statement. She'd been watching the crowd dwindle as the first carts departed. If they wanted to leave with them, they would have to hurry before the crowd shrank to zero.

"Your cart is the one over there. It has a storage compartment where you can put all your bags." Kalli spoke, gesturing to the cart parked in front of her own.

Lian nodded in gratitude and motioned for Fre to follow. The coral-haired girl complied, taking their bag and running to catch up.

"You would think she would buckle under the weight of a bag two-thirds her size."

Selyne watched as the seemingly frail child leapt up onto the cart's front seat and vanished into the interior. She elbowed Alfear and pointed to where she had been moments ago, "How did she become such a prominent Inheritor? I thought the sea people couldn't use Resonance without a complete burnout?"

Alfear glanced to where she was pointing, "Ah. Fre has an interesting story behind the inheritance. It's true that internal output is restricted to low-frequency burns. But Lian says she's shown great promise and resourcefulness during practice."

The words were perplexing to hear, coming from an enforcer with a lineage leading back to the middle of Heaven's War. She'd been told bloodline was everything, that the darker and heavier it was, the greater an Heir would be, and here he didn't seem bothered by a person who would clearly be a detriment to the power she held.

All this coming from the alcoholic heir to an empire? The question silenced her internal doubts. She was just as much a danger by choice, best not to grow irate over someone's birth.

A group of Seekers drew Selyne's attention, approaching Kalli from the crowd. Kalli turned to address the group.

"I see that you are all here. Can we get set up to leave, my lady?" The frontman in the group addressed Kalli as he spoke, bowing slightly to each of them in turn.

Kalli returned the bow, "Sir, we would be ever grateful if you would bring us on your journey."

Selyne stared at the strange exchange as the Seekers walked with Kalli to the carts, followed by Alfear, Lian, and the boy Selyne failed to get the name of. Wil came up beside her.

"You okay with this?" his voice seemed skeptical. "These people don't seem completely here."

Selyne sighed, "It's just the time spent in the Everwood. Culture progresses differently there, you know."

"Maybe," Wil said, unconvinced. "I've never see any people quite like these, and I've walked through outlander towns and Thailian seaports."

Selyne waved his statements off, "Seems you've spent so much time outside you missed what was in your own back yard."

Wil shook his head but let her statement stand.

"Come, we best not get left behind, else I may have to fly you there," Selyne continued, walking towards the carts.

Wil said something under his breath before following.

The summer wind blew across Selyne's face as she stood atop the wagon's front seat. A Seeker sat next to her, sorting the carriage out the gate of the Thean university. Finally, no more hair-pulling over her mother's demands or disapproving glares from the nobility. Selyne was leaving that behind, giving her a chance to truly change, and she would relish every moment.

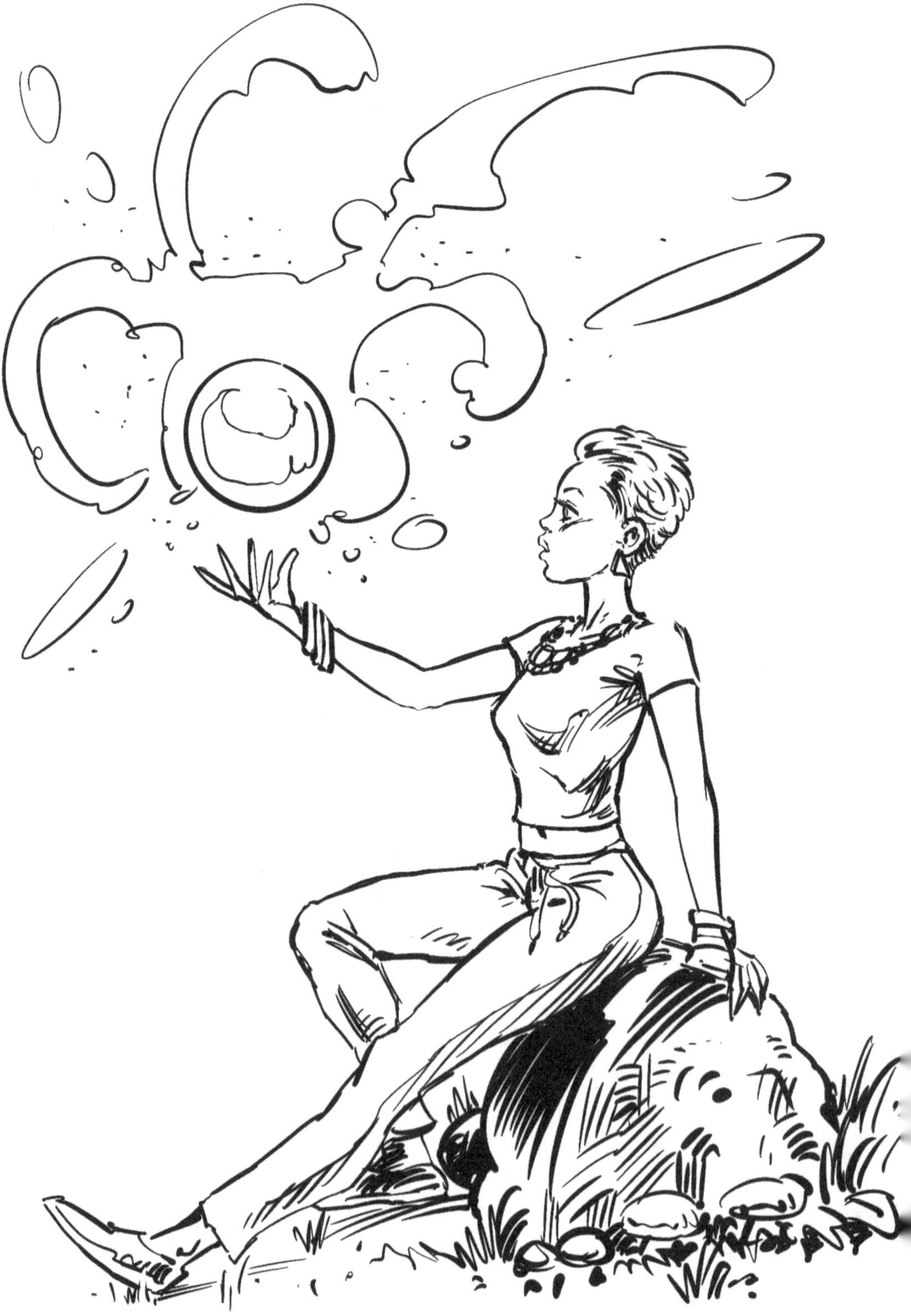

CHAPTER 24

Quintin sat at the back of the cart, staring blankly at the dust trailing behind the caravan of wagons. Several hours had passed since the pavement had receded. The light of morning brought dirt roads and endless fields with it. He yawned, body shaking with fatigue from last night's leg.

I should have taken the sleeping medicine Alfear offered. My body is so rattled I won't be sleeping comfortably for a while yet, he thought to himself.

Quintin rolled his neck, vertebrae cracking as they protested the motion. He felt like death. The cart hit a ditch, tossing Quintin's head like an egg. He groaned in despair, throwing a curse towards the inadequate performance of the spiral suspension system.

He grabbed the cylinder of water from its perch on the cushioned bench, emptying its contents down his throat. The water had grown cool overnight, the refreshing sensation excusing the metallic aftertaste it now carried.

Feeling a little better, Quintin looked back to where Fre lay, curled up on the opposite bench, sleeping like a rock. No herbs were required to convince her to rest. He smiled as he watched her. The image made him recall their early travels across the continent. He hadn't talked to her recently, his mind delving into the work Alfear was happy to supply. It felt eerily like his formative years. Constant days spent learning and helping his father manage the farm. It was getting harder now to remember what that looked like. The thought was unnerving. He'd spent too much time working on his studies. He needed to make some memories here and now, or it would fade as well.

He activated his Resonance. He only released a small amount, his body growing hazy and undefined as his inheritance converted his flesh into its individual threads. His mind reeled for a moment as his vision shifted. The familiar hues of light vanished, replaced by the swirling maelstrom he'd grown accustomed to. He sighed. The flow of energy relieved his tired body and gave him peace of mind. Ever since he'd stopped growing sick when he shifted, it had become a place to think away from the world. Sometimes vanishing felt very appealing.

Quintin banished the thought as it grew. He had things to do, questions he wanted answers to. A solitary life would have to wait. Fre turned over on the couch, her pale blue eyes shining in the morning sunlight.

"Did you sleep well last night?" her voice came out as a whisper.

Quintin shook his head.

"You never could handle travel well."

Quintin smiled wryly, "Some things don't change, despite how much pain it may bring."

Fre sat up, rubbing the last remnants of sleep from her eyes, "What's got you down?" I haven't seen you this upset in a very long time."

She leaned in as she spoke, eyes keen on Quintin's face.

She's going to keep asking until I tell her. Quintin thought. It was true, she wouldn't let it go, but he didn't want to talk about it.

"You ever think this could end badly?" he asked, meeting her gaze.

"I don't think so. The caravan is well protected, and Lian is with us. He's really strong." Fre responded.

Quintin shook his head, "That's not what's worrying me. Do you think all of *this* could end really badly?"

He gestured around as he continued, "All this studying, traveling, and other people's goals. Sometimes I think we're going to lose the good we had before."

He grew quiet, his embarrassment getting the better of him. They sat in silence; Fre staring out the window in thought. She was the only person Quintin had left. Fre glanced back at him.

"How often do you use your inheritance?"

The question caught him off guard. "Um, well, Alfear has me using it once a week. Usually for silly reasons. Why?"

Fre held out her hand. The air began to hum as she activated hers. Light filled the cabin as the sun's light refracted off the tiny slivers of what looked to be crystals floating in the air. Quintin looked to Fre, smiling as she moved them into patterns of increasing complexity. Fre smiled in return, moving the crystals into a multifaceted shape on the ceiling.

"That's amazing," Quintin said. "What exactly is it?"

Fre shrugged, "Not really sure. It's not stone if that's what you mean. The seer told me so."

Quintin stared at the pattern. It reminded him of the snowflakes they'd sometimes see out west.

"It really is a marvel. But what does that have to do with what we were talking about?"

Fre gave him a kick, "It's pretty, isn't it? A beauty beyond nature and your first action is to analyze it?"

She huffed, crossing her arms as she glared daggers from across the wagon. Quintin rubbed his shin.

"Sorry, I thought you had some big plan for that display."

"I'm getting there," she replied.

The fractal vanished from the cabin, and the sunlight seemed drab compared to its brilliance.

"We've not lost anything." Fre started again, "These last few weeks have allowed me to understand the world far better than ever before.

I've begun to wonder if we've been approaching the way we've lived all wrong."

"Can you be sure of that?" Quintin asked.

She shrugged, "If we're still friends by the end of it, then yes. Just don't vanish, and it will be ok."

Quintin nodded, "I'm not sure if that works, but I'll give it my best try."

Fre raised an eyebrow but didn't push it any further.

"Why don't we see what the others are doing," Fre said sitting up, "I'm sure it would be better than sitting in here and worrying."

Quintin sighed looking down at the book in his lap. "I think rather try and study. Alfear expects me to keep up with my required reading on this trip."

"This cart makes for a terrible place to study," Fre said.

The cart shook violently as if to emphasize her words. "Besides, don't you want to talk to a real-life princess?"

"I really don't," Quintin said dryly.

"Then what about a fellow Angel-kin?" Fre asked, watching Quintin's face intently for any sort of reaction.

I don't think she's going to leave me be. Quintin sighed, setting his book aside. "I guess it couldn't hurt. Maybe I can spend some talking with Kalli."

"Sounds like a great idea," Fre said happily. "I believe they're in the cart just ahead of us."

She pointed to the door leading to the front of the cart. Quintin thought for a moment. He was curious, but the prospect of talking to a princess felt wrong.

Fre rolled her eyes, "Come on before you pass your anxiety onto me."

She grabbed his hand, dragging him behind her as she opened the cabin door and stepped out into the front of the cart. The air was crisp, the heat of summer growing weaker as they moved further north. Their driver gave the pair a glance before returning his focus back towards the two imperial steeds pulling them.

Quintin looked out over the dozens of similar carts they had travelled with. The speed at which they moved was nothing short of amazing, covering somewhere close to a hundred and forty miles during the night. A distance impossible for any horse found on the western side of the continent.

Alfear had mentioned something about the imperial breed of horses; despite the shared name, they weren't really that closely related to other horses. Their legs were longer, with cloven hooves and a large mane far bushier and fur-like. He'd also mentioned something about their intelligence, but Quintin hadn't been listening closely enough to remember what he'd said.

Fre nudged him with her elbow, bringing his attention to the cart in front of them. Lian waved out the back window of the cart, smiling. Quintin gave a wave back. Were they eating breakfast? He caught a glimpse of Alfear and what looked to be some form of meat. He grabbed his stomach.

"You think they left any for us?" he asked Fre.

"Don't know until we look," she hopped off the cart, running up to the window.

Quintin hopped down a second later, racing after Fre. *Thea, these horses are fast.* He ran, the back of the car creeping closer at an agonizing pace. The back door opened. Lian's face was peering out at him; his hand held out. Quintin wasted no time in accepting the offer, more than happy to let the man hoist him through the air with one arm, bringing him into the confines of the cabin. He was blasted with a flurry of smells ranging from cooked meat to toasted pastries, truly something of a treasure.

The benches were packed with people, their capacity barely managing the six people seated. A tray sat in the middle of the walkway, full of what Quintin assumed had produced the previous scents.

"Quintin, glad you could make it. We have plenty of food left over, so help yourself," Alfear's voice bellowed over the conversation around him.

Quintin smiled and nodded his thanks. He took a seat, a biscuit in one hand and what looked to be a reheated piece of dried meat of unknown origin.

Kalli sat across from Quintin, speaking intently with the person next to her.

"Yeah, it's true. I find it fascinating that something as obscure as a planet could affect the frequency so much. Some scholars assume it has to do with its proximity, but I don't think that's it."

Quintin listened to the woman sitting across from him. She'd been talking since he arrived about what he was still trying to figure out. The person sitting next to the talkative one seemed to be invested, nodding along with her words and speaking occasionally.

"Interesting. So, I could increase my output of Resonance simply by flying at exactly twelve past zenith on the third month of the year. Please explain how this is practical in any sense."

Quintin watched as the first woman waved her arms almost manically as she responded, "Nonsense, Selyne. The implication that this has is massive. You know Thailia has a sky god named after that planet; Atun is his name, I believe; it's insane to imagine that's just a coincidence."

She continued with the conversation. Selyne, her companion, sat listening. Quintin figured she was about as confused as he was with the constant evolution of the conversation.

"Kalli," Lian interrupted, "Sorry to stop you, but I think you've confused my students."

Kalli stopped her speech, seeming to register the five other people around her.

"Sorry, not a subject of general interest. How are you doing, Quintin?" she asked.

Quintin fidgeted with his food, wondering how he should respond to the question.

"I've been fine mostly," he said finally.

"That's wonderful," Kalli said jovially. "I hear from Alfear that you've gotten much better with tolerating your inheritance."

Quintin nodded, "It depends on how much I use it, but it's rare for it to become too much anymore."

Kalli smiled, "You know, it still boggles my mind that you can see when you shift? I feel your extra-sensory abilities would be something truly interesting to learn about."

"It's weird and difficult to explain." He said, rubbing his head nervously as he spoke.

"We'll be sure to tell you anything we discover while on this trip," Alfear assured Kalli. "Thea knows we'll have ample opportunity to test the limits of what he can do."

Kalli sighed in satisfaction. "It's been a while since I've had a chance to take a trip like this; it feels good. It's a bit of a shame I'm not going with you all, but I won't complain about a trip to the Everwood."

Her eyes grew distant as she lost herself in thought.

Quintin shared a glance with Alfear, who smiled in return.

The conversation continued, Kalli never seeming to lack information on anything brought up. Quintin felt she must run out of material sooner or later. When the conversation lulled momentarily, Selyne took advantage of the situation.

"We've not had a chance to properly introduce ourselves." Selyne held out her hand in a greeting as she spoke.

Quintin took it gingerly, "It's good to meet you. My name is Quintin."

He felt awkward. This lady felt different in a way he couldn't describe. Maybe a conflict they hadn't resolved?

She smiled, "Same to you. I'm Selyne. I believe we've got something in common?"

Quintin nodded, "I don't know the name, so not someone I robbed."

Selyne looked at Quintin, confused. Clearly, the joke had gone over her head.

Quintin cleared his throat, "So you're an Heir as well?" he asked.

"Yes," she nodded, "An Angel-kin like everyone here, aside from Kalli. Oh, and Wil."

As she said this, she glanced toward the man in the corner with a book in one hand and a cane in the other. "My mother thinks highly of him; he's my security division on this trip. I believe you've already met Kalli. She's the smartest teacher ever, with an inheritance to boot."

Quintin smiled at her self-assured nature and guessed she might be a noble.

"I heard you and Fre grew up together. Alfear mentioned you come from the East."

Quintin felt uncomfortable with where this conversation was going.

He laughed nervously, "Yeah, I'm a noble's son. Fre's the daughter of a Thailian merchant. We've been looking for them these past few years. We hit a dead-end in Isel, and Alfear picked us up. Now we are working as full-time students at the university."

Selyne sat back in thought, "You know if you ever want to look at the royal archives, just let me know. We have every noble's whereabouts logged, and I could get you access, being a princess and all."

"I'll be sure to take you up on the offer," Quintin replied. "Do you think Fre's parents would be recorded?"

Selyne shrugged, "Not sure. If they are Ithean citizens, then maybe, but you want local information for merchants. The royal family tries to avoid too much clutter in our archives. So, we may not keep those records."

Quintin sat back. *This could be big.* He glanced over to Fre. She'd grown attentive at the mention of family. Her big eyes were searching Quintin's face. *Or, this could be a mess,* he thought. His mind began racing with all the possibilities. They still were obligated to complete service at the university. There was also the chance that their parents didn't exist.

Quintin wasn't sure if he wanted to live with that reality affirmed. They sat in silence, the meal taking up the group's focus. Quintin scooted over to the edge of the bench where Wil sat. He had buried his face into his book: *The Theory of Inheritance Amongst the Lesser Intelligent Species*. The author's name was written beneath the title though it wasn't legible from where Quintin sat.

"It's rude to stare, you know." Wil peeked over the top of the book, voice muffled by its cover.

Quintin averted his gaze, feeling awkward at being caught, "Sorry, I was interested in your choice of literature."

Wil folded the book in his hand, glancing at its title, "I find the subject interesting. However, it's more Kalli's choice than my own. I just borrow them when I'm off the job."

He studied Quintin's face, his emerald eyes shining in the sunlight, "Are you someone who enjoys reading? I hear your friend only reads Anglis."

Quintin dug into his coat pocket. He had been reading throughout the night. His hand grasped the thin paper cover, and he was relieved it hadn't fallen out while he slept.

He handed the book to Wil, "I enjoy history more than anything. If you get too technical, you'll lose my interest."

Wil set aside his book, folding the corner of the page before closing it, grasping the small paperback with a callous hand. He turned it over, raising an eyebrow, "This is a book of angel-tales?"

Quintin nodded assuredly, "I've been looking at stories all over the world, noting common archetypes or characters based on historical beings."

Wil looked to the book, still confused. "For what purpose?"

Quintin's eyes lit up at the question, "Well, actually, if what I believe is true, the implications could be immense. Angels among us as recently as a decade."

Wil's eyes narrowed as Quintin spoke, "The angels died during Heaven's War, along with the demons they fought."

Quintin shook his head, "Not exactly. I've looked through the myths along with the books accepted as historical facts. At most, only eight of the angels and demons actually died, which would leave around nine still in existence. These could be an account of our last contact. An outlander King given a magic sword by forest spirit made of gold."

Wil looked down at the cover then back to Quintin. His skepticism scrawled across his face. Quintin shrugged defensively.

"Hey, it's just a theory. I'm not trying to cause a stir."

Wil looked confused but neglected to say more.

"I told you not to do that. It hurts the pages," Kalli scolded. She grabbed the book from him, correcting the corners he had folded.

Rolling his eyes, Wil took the book back from Kalli and responded with an irritated tone, "Careful, I don't want to lose my spot in the book."

"Why don't you just get a marker board? I've got several in my bookbag. You have no excuse." Kalli glared at him, challenging a response.

Wil grumbled while opening the book to the place he had been before.

Quintin's eyes twinkled with amusement, "I take it you have this conversation often?"

Wil nodded, dejected at reality.

Quelling his amusement, Quintin responded, "It's only been a day. If you keep this up, she'll have you dead by the end of the week."

Wil stared at Quintin, "I'd like to see her try."

Quintin laughed, "You really don't budge, do you?"

"Only when I'm right."

Nodding empathetically, Quintin leaned back and relaxed. The conversation continued amongst the group. He let the feeling seep into his bones. Barring any upcoming homicides, he could come to love this.

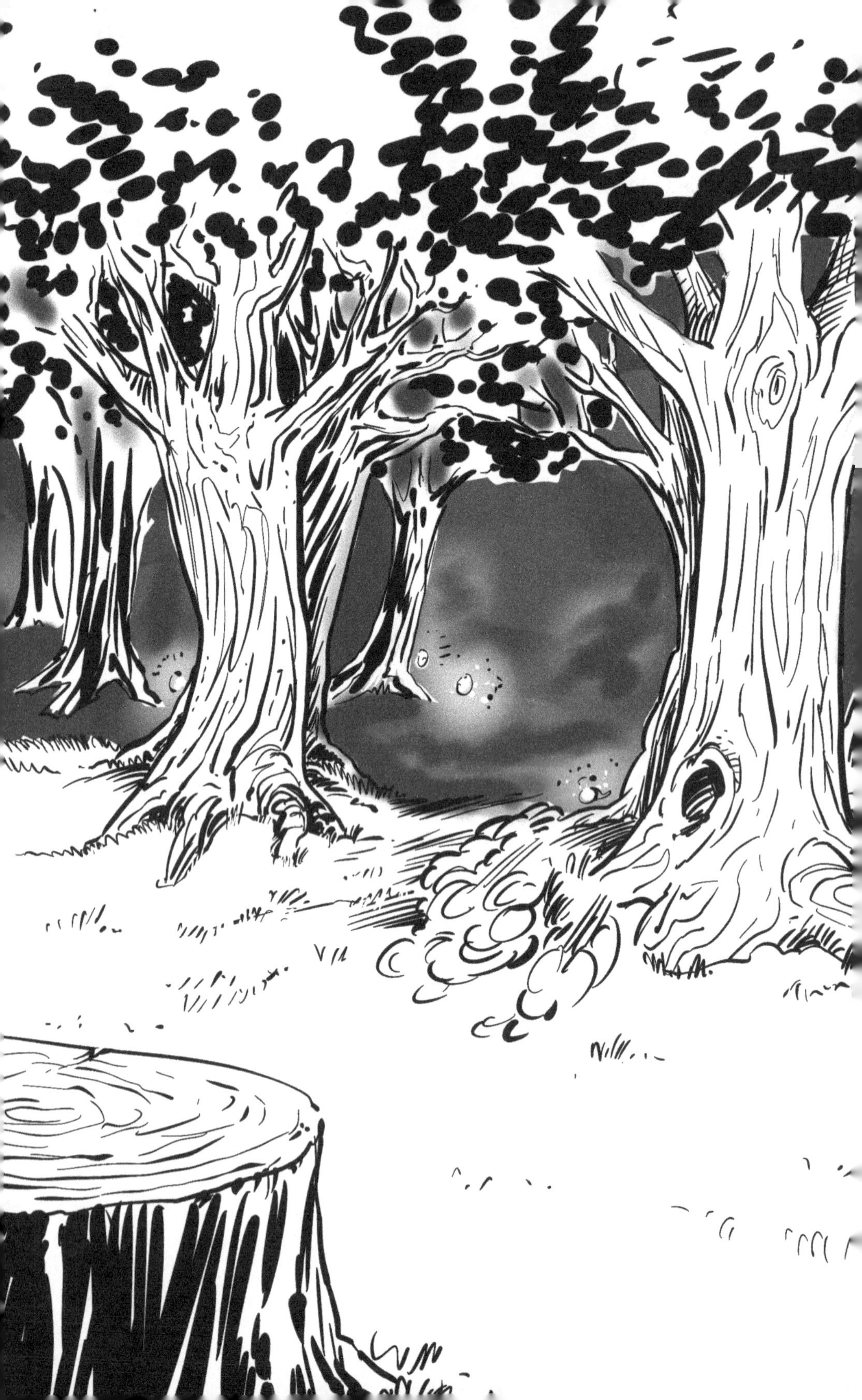

CHAPTER 25

Selyne ran in a panic. Something was wrong, and she needed to be somewhere. The world twirled in a tempest of clouds and lightning. She ran desperately, surely there would be a landmark, something to recognize in this storm-clad landscape. She stumbled over a tree root, and as she stood up, she saw something in the distance.

Pushing forward, the shape grew clearer as she approached. The building was of cera stone construction – a monolith built during a harsher time in Ithea's past when behemoths had ravaged the land. It was also a place Selyne knew well.

"I thought it was farther from the capital than this."

The thought vanished as quickly as it had appeared, and Selyne opened the oak door. The smell was unmistakable as she entered. The dust of a library and the ash of a well-used kitchen melded together to create a smell that was this place. The entryway was just like it was left five years ago: the old Rhinil pelt, now decayed on the floor, the study door was on her right. It was closed, as it had often been during her visits.

The kitchen was directly to her right. The bedrooms were beyond that. Selyne turned away from the office and walked through the kitchen. The old iron pots and stone ovens felt as if they came from a myth or fairy tale. Selyne ran a finger over the cooking table. Memories waved over her as if swept by the tempest outside. Chasing the past, she made her way to the rooms beyond the kitchen.

The halls held an eerie gray pallor. The color was worn either by time or brought on by the storm outside, sending shivers of light through its windows on the right side of the hall. Selyne's muffled footsteps were met with complete silence. Doors lined the left side of the wall. She ran her fingers over each one as she walked past the rough finish of the wood. Her hand came to rest on the brass doorknob of one of the rooms.

She could almost hear the laughter of a time gone by. Selyne paused for a moment. She wasn't sure she wanted to open the door or witness what caused the laughter in her head. She'd given this part of her life to the bottle. She didn't want it back.

"Excuse me, I've got a load of sheets to put on your bed."

Selyne jumped at the voice, releasing the door handle and turning to face the speaker. She was met with the face of her mother, but there was something off. A twinkle sat at the corner of her eyes, and her hair had a deep brown color without a hint of gray anywhere to be found. *The Shia happened to her?*

The confusion on Selyne's face didn't seem to register to Astania, who stood waiting with an impatient look directed at Selyne.

"Um, sorry. I was a little lost." Selyne pressed herself up against the wall as she spoke.

Astania rolled her eyes and walked past. "You have the strangest thoughts sometimes, Selyne. Like you would get lost in your own home."

Astania was pushed by Selyne's flattened body, carrying the basket at her side. A moment later, she was gone, vanishing into the back room. Selyne stood in the darkened space in the bedroom. It had been two years, maybe three. Little had changed. All of the blankets were folded and placed on the bed. Her toys were placed meticulously where they belonged. If it weren't for the dust, Selyne could have believed she'd only left a day ago.

"Time sure gets away from us, doesn't it? One moment we're children playing tag, the next our nation calls you to lead the people."

The voice came from the doorway. Selyne turned sharply as she tried to identify its source. The silhouette of a man stood in the doorway. His face obscured by the gray light coming from the outside. He took a step inside, running his finger over the surface of her nightstand.

"Yes, you haven't touched this memory in a long time," he said, turning to face Selyne. It was dim inside, but the face was unmistakable. Selyne recoiled at the sight, panic rising in her chest as the specter drew near.

He grinned, his teeth glowing a white crescent in the darkness. "What's wrong, sister?"

His words dripped with contempt, "You scared of what I have to say?" he spun on his heels, sword flashing as he smashed it into the side of the bed. Splinters flew around the room as Everwood met silver steel.

"Are you scared to come to grips with the fact that I'm dead?" he laughed, walking about the room and knocking over objects.

Selyne tripped over something obscured by the darkness as she tried to escape the room.

He turned back at the sound. His face was writhing, becoming more disfigured with each step.

"You're dead," Selyne cried, "You died on a battlefield on the other side of the world. You shouldn't be here!"

The sky rumbled in the distance. The room grew darker as the storm loomed overhead. He knelt down in front of Selyne. The face had stopped shifting. Its eyes had grown black like a void, and the dark hair came down like slithering snakes. The slate-colored face gave Selyne a sadistic smile.

"Trust me, darling. I know."

Shia reached out a hand, clamping onto her upper arm.

Selyne jumped; her vision blurred as light filled her eyes. She felt another touch on her arm. Yelling, she pushed away, grabbing the closest object at hand, and hurling it at the figure next to her, now only a blur of red.

Glass shattered, and she heard Wil yelp in surprise as a bottle came into contact with his head. Selyne's vision corrected, and her memory returned, along with a splitting headache. Thunder rumbled outside the cramped tent they had set up earlier that evening. Selyne looked at the empty bottle on her bed and the shattered one on the floor.

"Looks like it was one of those nights." Selyne groaned.

"Are you alright, princess?" Wil asked, concern edging his voice. "You were yelling in your sleep."

Selyne stood up, waving him away. "I'm fine. My nightmares are just being sadistic."

She stumbled over to the folding desk, holding herself up on one arm while sifting through her research with the other. "Where are those pills my mother gave me?"

She released a sigh; sometimes this whole situation was too much. *Makes me wonder why we still do it.* The voice in her mind overflowed with accusations, but she was used to that.

"Do they have food outside?" Selyne asked, turning back to Wil.

Wil stepped forward, offering his arm for her to hold, "There should be some leftover food from the last watch's dinner. Though it will probably be cold."

She took his arm, "Right now, whatever helps fill the pit in my stomach is all I want."

Wil nodded as he led Selyne out into the night air. Droplets of water covered the grass, and the faint rumbling in the distance suggested a storm had gone through recently. Selyne breathed in the cool night air, savoring the lack of arid humidity. Wil led her to the middle of the clearing surrounded by carts and tents. Several ashen fire pits sat smoldering where they'd been left hours before.

The pair made their way to a pair of camp stools left out by the watch. They had been placed around a fire pit with coals that burned hotter than the rest – their orange glow hidden under an iron cooking pot. Selyne took a seat, and Wil tapped the side of the pot.

"Looks like you're in luck." He said, retrieving a bowl from nearby. "This one is still hot."

He handed Selyne a steaming bowl of what looked to be a mixture of taff grain, broth, and spices. It was a remarkably useful food given the situation. Selyne sat there, taking quiet bites as Wil sat staring at the glowing embers.

"So did my racket wake anyone else up, or is it just you?" Selyne's voice broke the infinite calm of night as she spoke.

Wil shook his head, "No one else woke up as far as I can tell. I was already awake when you shouted."

The question piqued Selyne's curiosity. "What would you be doing awake at this ungodly hour?"

Wil looked out into the Everwood surrounding them and pointed to a spot in the darkness. Selyne followed, at first seeing only darkness. Suddenly, something flashed in the dark, a brilliant violet color beaming into the night before vanishing.

It was followed by another spectral glow. This time a constant glow of white light floated through the tree line before getting lost in the foliage. The sight made the hair on the back of her neck stand up, her Resonance rumbling gently in her chest. The rhythm hit a dissonant chord, and Selyne grabbed her head at the dizziness and pain. Wil jumped up to help at the sight.

"Easy, princess. Those creatures aren't worth breaking your head over."

Selyne pushed away his hand, trying to shake off the feeling. "I'm okay. Those things just hit an unnatural nerve, is all. It's just me being paranoid."

She looked back to where the thing had been, "What is it?"

Wil shrugged, "I'm not entirely sure. They come every night ever since we entered the Everwood."

He took his seat on his stool once again, "I've heard people say they feel unnatural. I've found them quite comforting. Like that sensation you get from visiting family."

The statement confused Selyne. She only felt unease at the thought of these floating creatures in the night. She shivered and pulled her alcohol-stained jacket closer. "You're a strange man; you know that?"

She picked up her spilled bowl of stew and refilled it.

"I could see that." Wil chuckled, "A man hailing from the southwest, going on about strange floating specters in the Everwood. I probably seem like a mraven without a head to someone like you."

"That's not what I'm talking about," Selyne said with a mouthful of taff, "I've asked around the Spire about you, and nobody seems to want to talk about you. My mother assures me you're the strongest person she could find, but your record seems rather mundane for the most part."

Selyne thought about it for a moment. "Does it have something to do with your time spent missing?" she asked tentatively

Wil leaned forward, his eyes going toward the ground. Selyne felt him growing distanced as he recalled something.

"What was it like? Living for months in the wild?" Selyne prodded further. "I hear that it isn't safe most places with the Rhinil along with dozens of other things trying to kill you. Sorry, I'm rambling and asking things that are rather personal."

The wood grew silent as her words fell off. She wondered if the prying had been too much. *Shia, this hangover isn't helping.*

"I think your mother was intrigued more than anything," Wil said, "Or maybe she just didn't want to let me go even after I was ready to be done with our nation's conflicts."

Wil laughed, "Though my time in the wild definitely played a part in her decision."

"So," Selyne began slowly, "you gave up on the military. Why?"

Wil sighed. Clearly it was a touchy subject. "I guess it was just too many dead people. Someone can only see loss so many times before he begins to question why."

"Did you lose someone?" Selyne asked.

Wil didn't say anything, though the expression on his face suggested the question wasn't far from the truth.

"I'm sorry," Selyne whispered.

"I have my fair share of ghosts," Wil said, "I've made plenty of mistakes, and there are people I failed to protect. I have no choice but to live with that."

He turned to face Selyne, his emerald eyes glowing in the firelight. "Some advice for you, don't live your life torn up by what you've failed to do. You can only do what is right at any given time, and the past doesn't determine that. Thea was kind enough to give us that much."

He brushed off his leg instinctively and stood, "Are you feeling better?"

Selyne looked at the empty bowl. Her hunger was gone, but she wasn't sure about going back to bed. "I'll stay here a while longer. I'm not very tired."

Wil nodded in affirmation and stood straight, "I'll be over in the trees. Just yell if you have any trouble."

He retreated from the fire pit, disappearing into the shadows of the Everwood. She hunched over the fire pit, her hands picking at the sparse plant life poking up between the roots of the Everwood. *That conversation was surreal.*

Her mind mulled over the conversation. It had been short, though considering the subject, she couldn't fault her partner's lack of enthusiasm. He'd talked about ghosts. She hadn't considered it all that much, but a military man would have those, wouldn't he? Selyne sighed. Her ghosts had a nasty habit of taking residence inside her head. A light flashed in the corner of her eye. She looked up to see the specter vanish into the woods. They didn't seem so bad, so long as they stayed out there, away from her.

Thunder rumbled overhead. Selyne glanced over to where Wil stood at the edge of the trees. He'd be fine, Selyne however, needed sleep.

Selyne stood up, walking to her tent. She sighed at the sorry state of its interior. It would have to wait until tomorrow; now Selyne needed to sleep. She lay down, staring at the canvas roof of her tent as her eyelids grew heavy.

Rain pattered onto the tops of the tents. Selyne cracked her eyes open. The waxed surface of her tent roof stared down at her. "Looks like I'm awake again."

Selyne turned to her desk, sitting up and looking about her room. She still wore her clothes from yesterday. The smell of alcohol and sweat had compounded overnight. *Shia, I look like death and smell like it, too.* She went to the foot of her cot, opened her bag, and rummaged around for something suitable to wear.

She produced a pair of linen slacks, a thick wax-coated rider's skirt, and a blue shirt. She also removed a heavier coat from storage, propping it on her stool for later. She wondered if a shower had been set up. She pulled off her used jacket along with her old skirt. They were the worst in terms of dirt and smell. It wasn't exactly appropriate for a noblewoman to walk around in a pair of pants, but propriety would have to wait until after the shower.

Clatter filled the campsite as Seekers bustled about, going from tent to tent, pulling down wooden structures and folding waxen tarps. The air was cool from last night's storm. Its chill covered her bare arms.

"Hey, do you know where I could find the shower?" Selyne said, waving down a Seeker walking past with a tent in hand.

The woman stopped and gestured with her free hand, "You'll find them past the cook's wagon and to the left."

Selyne nodded her thanks and moved past before the woman could give another glance. The wagons were crowded with people packing away inventory and putting away their tents in a chaotic frenzy.

Shoving herself in between Seekers, Selyne began her search for the cook's cart. Trying her best to avoid running into anyone as she did so.

"Oh, sorry," she said as she bumped into a tent pole being carried by. Another man walked past with a chest large enough to carry a man. Selyne ducked as he glided past her.

Shia, this place is a maze and a quarter. Selyne couldn't see the cook's cart anywhere, and the crowd kept growing. Her Resonance began buzzing as she stood up. Several Seekers stared at her, activating their own inheritances out of habit. Selyne gave one a smile and winked before rocketing skyward.

She held in a gag at the sudden weightless feeling which came with the change in pressure. Selyne burst out laughing as the treetops approached her view. There was no other freedom quite like flight. It was a rarity she'd been given. Her Resonance hummed evenly within her body. It felt nice to be in control.

Now, where did that cook's cart go off to? Selyne looked down on the lines of wagons filled with the heads of Seekers walking to and fro. Many of the wagons were painted deep green. Locating the blue tarp of the cook's cart only took Selyne a cursory glance to locate it. Changing the pressure difference on her body, Selyne began her gradual descent onto the ground. She touched down feet first, ignoring the glares from surprised Seekers as she made her way to the shower.

She'd been careful, making sure to keep herself oriented in the same way throughout her entire flight, keeping her previous instructions relevant as she wandered through the camp. It didn't take long until she found the stalls. They were completely enclosed and held together by easily removable bolts. Nothing to look out for on the outside, but the inside would be a different story. Stepping up to an empty stall, Selyne closed the door, finding the activation glyph on the interior and pulsing it.

Light sprung up from the glass globe above her head revealing the interior space in full. The wood walls were covered by glass wrought wires leading up to a steel disc placed in its ceiling. Kalli had explained the whole process behind it. Something to do with earth-based glyph work and silver absorber panels. Honestly, Selyne had ignored most of it.

Stowing her fresh clothes away behind a curtain, Selyne began the process of getting undressed. Tossing the old clothes into a pile, Selyne stepped into the tiny shower compartment. Several activation glyphs sat inlaid into the wall. One was dyed red, another green. Selyne decided on yellow. Water began to fall from the disc in the roof.

No rumble of pipes, and there aren't any holes in that steel disc. She held up her hand to the disc and smiled at the faint hum she felt. She stood there for a moment, simply enjoying the comfortable heat washing away the last day's travel.

What am I doing? The question had rested in Selyne's mind since she'd started this, what had she started? She had wanted answers, but would she be getting that with this trip? Of course, her mother had wanted this – that had to count for something. *Yeah, she wanted you to finally get out of the house.* Selyne slammed her head into the wall. *Let's just see where this leads. It won't kill me to do so.*

She let the glyph run out. The water slowly vanished as the Resonance destabilized and reverted back to a neutral state. She pulled back the curtain protecting the small cabinet where she'd placed her new outfit. Selyne stepped out a moment later wearing a brand-new outfit, old clothes under her arm, hair dry, and feeling ready to handle another day on the road. Turning around, Selyne noted the footpaths now clear of furniture and ware shops. Many of the wagons closed up, ready to leave. *I should get back to the tent. My paper is everywhere, and I'm not sure if Wil knows what to do with it.* Selyne looked to the sun. She had maybe ten minutes before they left. Walking to the outer edge of the camp, Selyne began the long walk back to her tent. Hopefully, this path would have fewer people.

* * * * * *

Wil stuffed the cot into its bag before tossing its lumpy mass into the lower compartment of the wagon. He'd spent the morning packing clothes and furniture into their respective compartments. All that was left was Selyne's bedframe for the aforementioned cot and the blasted folding desk. *You'd think she had a thing against paper trees with how much paper she requires. How does she store it all?*

The air grew strained, and Wil looked up to see Selyne's figure outlined by the morning sun. She floated in space for a moment; her clothes plastered to her frame as the invisible force put an unnatural strain on the fabric. The moment passed, and she continued her descent at the lazy pace she seemed to favor.

"Thank goodness you decided to show up," Will said as Selyne came to land on the forest floor. "I was at my wits end with that mess you left me on your desk."

"I figured that would be the case," Selyne said, handing Wil her used clothes. "I came as soon as possible. Bloody traffic. It's impossible to figure out."

Wil rolled his eyes at the clothes but let Selyne go as she entered the tent. Sometimes he wondered whether the job was worth his pride as a human being. *Definitely beats fighting on the southeast border. Here you only have a fifty percent chance of dying.* He laughed wryly at the thought. He could hardly argue with such logic. He found an open space in the laundry box, stuffing the dirty clothes in and slamming it shut. There would be a few more days on the road. Wil hoped they had a washboard somewhere in this caravan. Selyne stepped onto the deck of the cart, her papers rolled up and stuffed at odd angles into a small bag.

"Thanks for taking care of those," Wil said, closing the laundry. "I can now get busy with taking down the tent. Hopefully, we'll be on the trail within the hour."

He stepped past Selyne and back onto the green.

"Wil, have you managed to speak with the other Angel-kin on this trip?" Selyne asked the question, dropping her bag of writing on the seat and following after Wil.

He shrugged as he pulled the stakes from their steel rings, "Honestly, not a lot. Why, do you want to know something?"

Selyne shook her head, kneeling down to help with the tent pegs. "I just feel like I should be doing something. We're supposed to be related by angel blood or some such nonsense, yet all I'm feeling is a growing awkwardness when I'm around them."

She yanked on the tent peg in frustration. Wil had made the process look easy, but the four feet of steel barely moved a few inches with each attempt. She looked at Wil, who was busy on his next peg. He remained rigid through the entire process, back straight as he squatted down and grabbed the top of the peg. Selyne stared as he removed the full length of steel in a single motion.

"You're no angel, princess. Despite what some theologians might lead you to believe, you have immense power to change the world."

He tossed the peg aside as he spoke. "Whether it's a divine responsibility or not, I don't think feeling awkward around some children is an issue."

Selyne thought about it, sinking into the task at hand, removing the last length of peg before moving to the next. The task took less time than Selyne would have guessed. The tarp, pegs, and supports were dismantled and ready for storage before the first wagon began to leave.

She looked over to where Wil was finishing a conversation with a Seeker over the proper storage of the tent.

"Do you know where Kalli went off to? We're splitting the caravan today or tomorrow, and we need her to be with us when that happens; otherwise, this becomes a glorified vacation."

Wil turned to Selyne, coming to walk beside her as she made her way to the cart. "She said she'd spend some time with Alfear this morning. I'd recommend waiting until lunch to begin searching for her."

Selyne huffed at Wil's answer; what was she supposed to do without Kalli here? Talking to Wil was fine, but he never seemed to talk about little things. Their conversation devolved into some philosophical insight into life. It was tiresome. Selyne stepped into the interior of the cart and flopped down onto the cushioned bench.

"I'm going to lay down. Let me know if I'm needed for anything."

Selyne's voice was muffled as she buried her head into the cushioned seat.

"I'll be sure to let you know, princess." Wil gave a slight nod and grabbed his cane from its perch in the corner. "I'll just be outside."

His steps receded, and Selyne turned over to stare at the ceiling. Now it really was just a matter of waiting. "Let's hope Kalli decided to move and get back before I go insane."

* * * * *

Quintin sat curled up in the corner of the cart. He stared at the book he'd tucked in his lap, trying desperately to make out the words on the page. The cart jostled as it hit a bump in the road. The pages blurred as the cart rumbled along. Quintin sighed, setting the book aside. It had proven difficult to get any sort of studying done on this trip. He found the constant shaking of the carts paired with the constant noise outside made for a poor reading environment. Quintin looked out the small window. Dust blew up from the road as the carts thundered past, leaving a brown haze in its tracks.

"Heavens," Quintin grumbled, "I'm going insane with all this monotony."

He sat back, staring blankly out the window. It was all too much. Each week at the university was a constant rocking back and forth between subjects. Everything moved at lightning speed in order to get Quintin ready in time.

Shouts rang throughout the carts, breaking Quintin from his stupor. The wagons slowed as shouts continued to echo throughout the caravan. It seemed the lunch break had come early.

The rattle of carts stopped, its noise replaced by the bustle of men and women working on setting up pavilions for the upcoming meal.

Quintin sat up, alert, excitement exploding as the opportunity to leave the cart arose. Scrambling to gather his things, he stuffed his books into a small bag before rushing over to the exit. Sound exploded around him as he swung the door open, the muffled shouting of commands becoming clear. Quintin didn't waste a minute, leaping off the step onto the dirt road below. He sighed in relief, fully appreciating the sensation of standing on solid ground. He glanced around, trying to get a glimpse of the cart Fre had ridden in.

"Shia, what is that?" Quintin stopped dead in his tracks.

His attention focused on a large marble monolith sitting in between the crossroads. Quintin stepped forward to get a closer look, his previous mission forgotten at the moment. The crowd grew thicker as he drew closer. Quintin noticed several people bowing and folding their hands in respect towards the large monument.

"This should prove very interesting," he muttered under his breath.

His vision grew clearer as he got closer, and he couldn't help but marvel at the intricate design carved into the marble surface. It reminded him of many of the shrines found in the Anglis coastline. An obelisk capped with gold in complex swirling patterns inlaid onto the stone. Quintin noticed an inscription, though it was written in a language he didn't recognize.

"Hey, Quintin!"

Quintin turned at the sound of Alfear's voice. The large man was seated by a fire pit located beside the monument, waving his hand in an attempt to get Quintin's attention. Quintin scurried over, avoiding the crowds of people going to and from the monument.

"Hey," Quintin said, taking a seat by the fire. "What is all this?"

"This is the crossroads," Alfear said happily, gesturing with his hands to the surrounding area.

"Right," Quintin said, confused, "Why is that important?"

He glanced over at the people bowing at the foot of the monument.

"Oh that," Alfear said, "it's an old Seeker tradition that dates well back before the empire. Many pay their respects to the forest before entering in hopes of safe travel through the woods."

"It's strange, isn't it?" Quintin mused as he watched the Seekers come and go. "You'd think they'd be praying to their ratchet bows if they wanted to be kept safe."

Alfear chuckled, "Be as it may, I think they have a good sense of justice. That's not something I can judge them for."

"What does that have to do with this?" Quintin chuckled. "I'm pretty sure the forest isn't judging anyone."

Alfear laughed, his eyes glinting with amusement as he looked at Quintin.

"What?" Quintin said defensively. "It seems like a relevant question. Justice isn't a defense for irrational behavior."

"Maybe," Alfear said slowly, "or maybe it's what makes the irrational behavior rational."

"Elaborate on that," Quintin said, leaning forward in his chair.

Alfear paused for a moment collecting his thoughts before speaking. He fidgeted with his hands.

"There are many people who have struggled with the practicality of spiritual or religious actions over the years," Alfear began, "however, I think there is one way we as Helts should approach the issue."

Quintin nodded. He wasn't familiar with the realm of philosophy like he was with history or government, but he'd heard things as a child in his father's office.

"There is the worldview that you have mentioned," Alfear said, gesturing towards Quintin, "I find that to be a little reductive. A fine method for a legal system, but somewhat lacking in regards to one's own morality."

"Ok," Quintin said, "I'm still not sure how this ties back into our previous statements."

"We'll get there," Alfear reassured.

Quintin nodded, letting Alfear continue.

"Oftentimes, we see our morality as a means to maintain order in our society, like an offshoot of our justice system. The issue with this view is its removal of the individual's place in the equation. This view will, if taken to its furthest conclusion, lead towards a society with no regard towards either the law or the internal rules set up by their gods.

"You're not judging them because it's their personal duty to pay respect to the forest," Quintin replied. "I'm still not sure that's a good excuse. Surely there are more practical ways to maintain someone's moral compass."

"Yes and no," Alfear said, "What I'm trying to address is the belief that you pursue morality in order to live an orderly life within society and the moral deficiencies that occur if you really believed that."

Quintin sighed, leaning back as he tried to reconstruct what he was attempting to say. *Heavens, this is getting tedious.* It wasn't uncommon for a conversation with Alfear to regress into some sort of debate. They never felt hostile and often allowed Quintin to figure out what it was he wanted to say. It could, however, become very draining.

Quintin figured that was the reason Alfear was selected as his mentor instead of Lian. Both he and Quintin were cut from the same cloth.

"I believe that's only natural," Quintin said, "if morality causes strife in a society, can it really be moral?"

"That's a good question," Alfear said, "but tell me, would you consider the rulers of Thailia to be moral people?"

Quintin shook his head, "Of course not. Most of those nations still approve the sale of humans, barring a few examples, not to mention their constant desire for conflict on our borders. Why do you ask?"

Alfear shrugged. "Yet if you said that in the town square of most Thailian city-states, you would most certainly be regarded as a dissident. You may even end up in prison if you cause too much trouble."

Realization began to creep up on Quintin as he followed Alfear's line of questioning. "That is not what I was alluding to at all."

"Of course not," Alfear said, "though you have to admit that one's moral compass can often go against what the society around you would want."

"Yes," Quintin said, "but that doesn't mean that trying to gain favor with a forest isn't a silly endeavor."

Alfear shook his head, "It'd only be a silly endeavor if it has no effect for those who partake in it. This is what I'm trying to get at. What someone believes to be good isn't for everyone else; it's for yourself."

"Ok," Quintin conceded reluctantly.

He wasn't convinced, but he didn't want to contest it further. He wanted to move on to what Alfear really wanted to say.

"Why are you bringing this up now?" Quintin asked. "You normally aren't this adamant in our conversations."

"It's going to get more important here soon enough," Alfear said. "You're only with me for another few months before you're free to go about your own job in whatever Thean Institute you choose. Once that happens, you're going to be the only one who determines your actions. I just want to make sure you don't mess up."

"Why would I change?" Quintin asked.

His curiosity was piqued by Alfear's concern. He considered himself someone who maintained a level head. In all the years of travel he'd done as a child, it was up to him to get things done. This wouldn't be anything different.

"Heirs are given an immense amount of power both in a literal and legal sense," Alfear said.

His demeanor was serious as he looked Quintin directly in the eyes. It reminded Quintin of his father whenever he had tried coaching him on the importance of maintaining finances or good standards of living for their workers. It wasn't something Quintin had dealt with in years.

"This doesn't change who a person is," Alfear said, "but it does bring out qualities that would otherwise remain dormant. Are you familiar with the Church of Solus?"

Quintin shrugged. He'd heard the name once or twice, but out west, the larger religious institutes were less prominent as the cultural diffusion from the eastern part of the empire was pretty weak.

"I've heard about them. Can't say I've ever talked to an adherent, though."

"Well, we're about to visit a city where they are all over the place," Alfear said, "their beliefs mean they treat us almost like gods. When you're there, you will be well above reproach. That may not sound like a bad thing, but for someone as young as you, I'm worried it will be."

"You know I'm not someone who enjoys praise," Quintin said defensively, "just the idea of what you said makes me uncomfortable."

"I don't expect you to get a big head," Alfear assured, "but I expect that the same sense of fairness that allows you to refuse such praise will be difficult when everyone around you is in many aspects morally reprehensible."

Quintin paused as Alfear's words began to sink in.

"What are you talking about?" Quintin asked, "Is there something I need to know about this place before arriving?"

Alfear sighed. He seemed uncomfortable with the conversation at hand, something Quintin hadn't seen before. "To be frank, yes, this place is somewhere that dogma has taken hold very strongly in the hearts of the people. They won't hate you, quite the opposite in fact, but they are going to despise Fre."

"So, there are familial purists," Quintin scoffed, "trust me, Fre is no stranger to people like that, and neither am I."

"That may be so," Alfear said, "But you haven't seen people this militant before, trust me." His voice carried a hint of desperation as he spoke.

"I get the concern, but really it's fine." Quintin took a bite of food and looked away. As far as he was concerned, the conversation was over. Alfear sighed but let the subject go.

"Have you ever seen an ancestor before?" Alfear asked.

"That came out of nowhere," Quintin said.

Alfear shrugged, "I was curious. You took the coastal route to the capital, and I wasn't sure if you had."

Quintin shook his head. "I can't say I have, though I've read plenty. Tell me, is half of what they say true?"

"I wish I could say," Alfear said, scratching his chin. "It's a shame we'll be leaving Everwood behind us on this trip. Unfortunately, the Thean Institutes think it would be better for you to learn the more practical side of your inheritance."

"What exactly are we doing on this trip?" Quintin asked. "I was told it has something to do with our current training, but I really wasn't given the option to ask what that even meant."

"Well, it's mostly going to be field work," Alfear said. "You know, stuff like combat, research, and the sciences. I think you'll find it very enjoyable."

Quintin nodded vacantly, a smile creeping into the corners of his face. "I'll be sure to prove your concerns completely false."

Alfear raised an eyebrow before looking down at his watch. "I would hope so. It's getting time to leave here soon. I'm going to say goodbye to Kalli before we do." The large man stood up, dusting himself off.

Quintin waved him off as he left. "Don't worry about me. I'll just be waiting here."

He watched Alfear vanish into the crowd of Seekers. His mind drifted back towards Alfear's earlier concerns. "The man's got me all wrong," he scoffed under his breath, "I know what I'm doing."

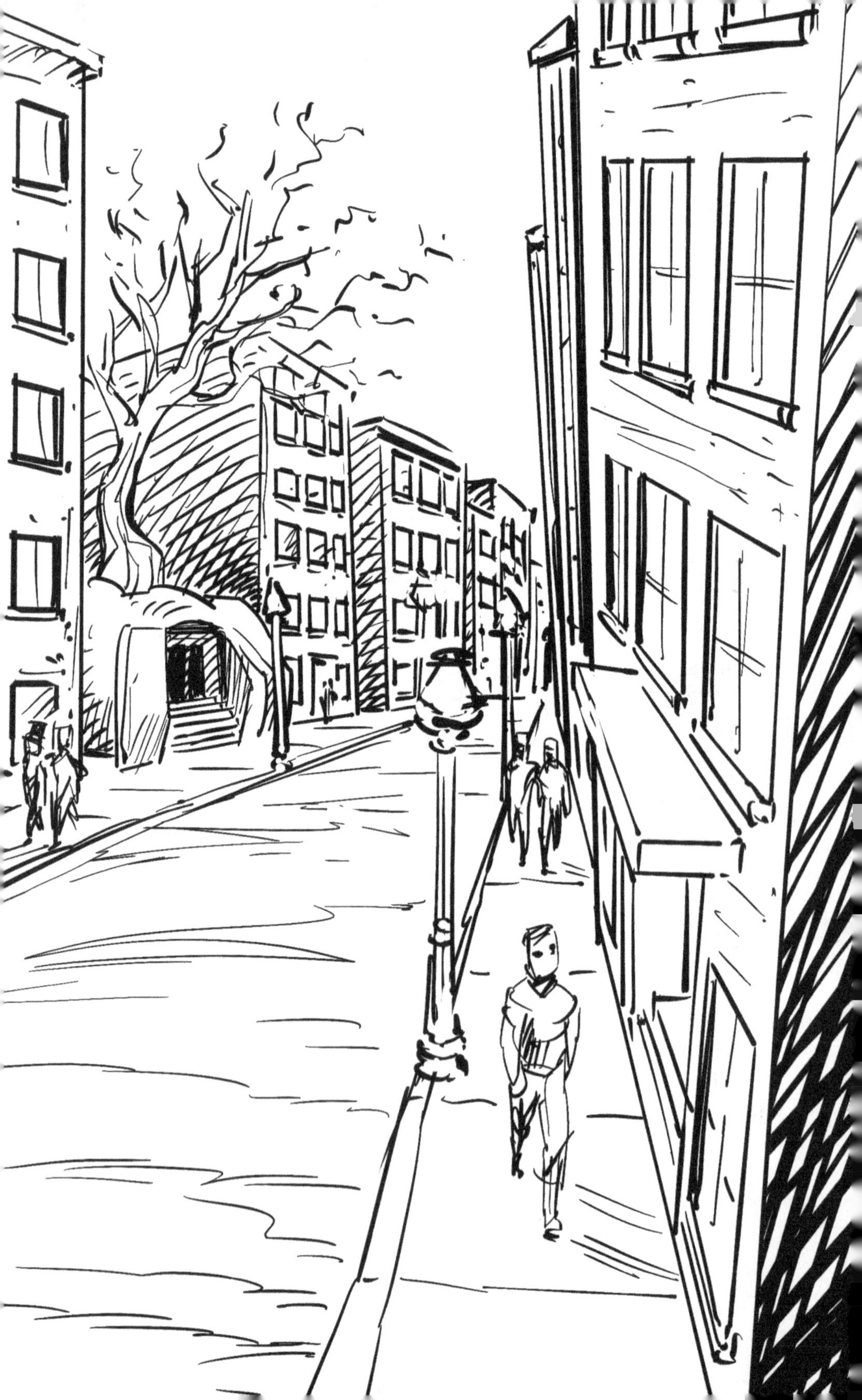

CHAPTER 26

Shadows loomed large as they travelled deep into the heart of the Everwood. The canopy created a ceiling of leaves with only the occasional beam of light reaching the forest floor. The air was cold and smelled of wet dirt. Pools of water filled the flat plains of roots that spanned most of the ground. Selyne walked beside the cart, careful to avoid the roots which crept into the edge of the road.

Three days had passed since the caravan had split. The forest grew thicker with each mile they travelled. A root frog hopped across Selyne's boot and into its namesake tangled across the dirt floor. She shivered at the sight. They, along with many of the local fauna, had made sleep a living nightmare.

Only one more day or so. Then it's a warm bed and a secure room. The thought felt odd. The Everwood was ancient. Ancestors and spirits roamed freely within its depths. The idea of a city at its center just felt wrong.

A shout echoed down from the front of the caravan, and the carts slowed to a stop. Selyne took a seat, taking care to check for any eight-legged occupants before settling.

She threw out her legs and leaned back onto the smooth bark of the Everwood. Wil would be by in a moment with food. The momentary peace was welcome. She had been walking more the past few days, and the air cleared her mind. The wagons weren't exactly moving at a leg-breaking speed. The walking had given her time to think clearly, something Selyne feared more than the ancestors living in the forest around her.

Tears began to well up at the corners of her eyes, and she brushed them away immediately. *Shia, just the thought of thinking hurts.*

She groaned and leaned back even further onto the tree. She really needed a drink. She sat up at the thought. It hadn't occurred to her to check the food wagons for any bottles. Staggering to her feet, she brushed off her dress before starting to walk to the mess tent.

Her feet protested the prolonged use on the road. Selyne grunted at the surprising ache, taking lighter steps in an attempt to alleviate some of the pain.

"Selyne?" Wil's voice carried to her from among the carts.

Not now; I just need to go a little further.

She turned in a circle until her eyes landed on the face of Wil. His emerald eyes were practically glowing in the dim light.

"Hey, I just got us our lunch for the day. Kalli is waiting if you want to come."

Selyne rolled her eyes at the cosmos's idea of a joke. "It's either I mope or eat, so lead the way."

Her voice carried a levity she didn't feel.

"Okay, we're just around the corner." Wil gestured with his cane to a spot behind a cart. He carried the cane with him everywhere now. Selyne wished she knew why.

The pair wove their way through the carts. Selyne gingerly stepped behind Wil. She would be sitting the rest of this trip. Kalli waved at the pair as they approached. Her face brought a smile to Selyne. Her beaming optimism was infectious.

"We're lucky we saw you walk by. Wil was certain he'd spend break time looking for you."

Kalli moved over as she spoke, giving room for Selyne to slide in beside her. Selyne gave a weak smile. She hadn't planned to be here until moments ago.

"I thought you were going to bring my food to the cart. Why are you here?"

Wil shrugged. "You weren't there. I caught you after talking to Kalli about looking for you."

He pulled a piece of dried meat from a bag on the ground, chewing on it as he spoke. Selyne huffed, "Did we at least get anything good to eat?"

Kalli dug into the bag, scanning over its contents.

"We've got meat and bread." She dug around a few more seconds, "And nothing else it would seem."

Selyne sighed. It hardly constituted a complete meal. "Sure, I'll have some bread, I guess."

Kalli tossed a thick-skinned loaf at her. Breaking it, Selyne noted the coarse grind of the grain, which crumbled in her hand as she pulled it apart.

"Anyone bring something to wash this down with? This bread hasn't seen the light of day for quite some time."

Wil pointed to Selyne's leg, "There's a flask down by your left foot. It should still have some water in it."

Selyne moved her leg and leaned forward. Sure enough, a leather flask rested in the roots of the Everwood. Selyne unstopped the container, taking a sip of its contents. The whole meal felt like Selyne was chewing on wood, with a bottle of grease in the case of the dried meat. Selyne spat out some gristle as her face twisted at the awful taste.

"This is pretty miserable. When are we supposed to get to our town again?" Selyne sat down the unfinished bit of jerky. "At least the bread tastes like bread, just left out in the sun a little bit too long."

She took a swig of water which helped only slightly. Lunch passed with general disdain. The group growing silent as they worked on the leathery meal. Selyne let out a dissatisfied sigh.

"I hope this trip ends early. I'm ready for a proper bed and fresh food."

Kalli nodded with a mouthful of stale bread, and Wil leaned back on the Everwood, closing his eyes.

"What do you think it's going to be like in Hayka?" Selyne tossed the question out, watching to see if either of her companions would bite.

Kalli took a swig of water, swallowing the last bites of her lunch.

"I read that it's just like your average town. However, reading material wasn't readily available on the subject. Probably has some secret research the empire doesn't want available to the public."

Selyne nodded, then looked to Wil, "How about you? Have you ever traveled to this part of the Everwood during your many military deployments?"

He shook his head, not even bothering to open his eyes. "I'm an eastern boy. The Bower woods and Thailian grassland are my stories."

Selyne pushed a little harder, "Surely you traveled through here to get to Isel? You don't look like a sailor."

He cracked one eye open, "You have a funny way of thinking, but you're wrong. One-way ticket along the coast. It's supposed to be safer."

Selyne scowled, "So, neither of you actually know where we're going?"

Her companions simply stared back in silence.

"Bloody typical," she huffed, "why did I even bring you two?"

Wil raised his hand, "In my defense, your mother insisted I come. I'm not sure why Kalli bothered."

Kalli kicked him with a frown, "Don't you feign ignorance, you outdated farm boy. I'm Selyne's teacher. She needs me to assist with learning amongst the Seekers."

Wil raised his eyebrows in disbelief, "So, you're not doing your own research while you're here?"

Kali glared at him but didn't reward the accusation with a response.

Selyne bowed her head, resting in her hands. "I should fire the lot of them. I'm sure mother could replace them."

The pair had gone silent; their attention focused on Selyne. She raised her head slightly, peering between her fingers.

"We made our Highness angry," Kalli whispered.

Wil choked on a laugh, "I blame you, but you still have to keep her."

"Both of you can rot with Shia!" Selyne hurled the empty water flask at Wil, who ducked behind his arms as it bounced away harmlessly.

She felt her face grow red as she stood up. She turned and began to walk away.

"By Thea above, she went red," Kalli gasped in awe.

Wil shrugged, "I have that effect on people. She's also got alcohol, which makes her extra volatile."

The pair chortled, whispering amongst themselves.

Just leave them be. You're better than that. The thought sounded like Selyne's mother, which didn't help her mood. She stormed past several Seekers. They scattered at the sight of her, taking care to give her a wide berth as she stomped through the wagons.

Selyne climbed up the step of their cart, face still aflame. She fell face-first on the bench letting the impact force out her breath. *I swear, they're children – the lot of them.*

Zenith begun to fade as the caravan began to move again. The carts rattled loudly as the shocks failed to absorb every root the Everwood put in their path. Selyne watched as the road appeared to be devoured behind them. The Everwood's overgrowth seemed to grow as they passed. Lights flickered in the distance, and Selyne shivered subconsciously.

"Bloody spirits," Selyne muttered under her breath.

"I thought you didn't believe in folktales?" Her mother's voice mocked her in her head, which didn't help her mood. Night didn't fall in the Everwood. Rather, the darkness just grew as the foliage absorbed what little sunlight that covered the forest floor. Selyne sat back, closing the window. Hopefully, the journey would be over soon, and she could get to work.

Darkness consumed the forest as the carts rolled to a stop. Shouts sounded outside, and Selyne looked up from her book as a knock sounded at the door.

"Come in," she yelled, closing her book and tucking it into her bag.

The door opened, revealing Kalli's small frame. Her eyes were sparkling with excitement, "We're here. You really need to look at this place. It's something else."

Selyne set aside the bag and walked to the door, swinging it open. Her eyes adjusted to the darkness as she stepped out of the cart. The city of Hayka sat enclosed by the Everwood. A quick glance revealed the small amount of land it required, only two or three city blocks. Selyne looked at the buildings silhouetted by lanterns.

"How do you think they got them so tall? Some of them threatened to overtake the Spire and that was built by angels."

Kalli shrugged, a grin plastered to her face. "I have no clue, but I fully intend to figure out how."

She hopped off the cart, grabbing the bag she'd propped against the wheel. "Come, Wil's getting our sleeping quarters set up in that building."

Kalli pointed to the towering building.

"I'll be right there. Just let me grab my things."

Selyne couldn't understand the last thing Kalli yelled as she stuffed her diary into her bag along with her pen and several other odds and ends lying about the cabin. The night air was cold, Selyne buttoning up her jacket as she walked across the stone courtyard toward the building Kalli had presumably entered. She was not met with the warm glow of torchlight. The fire cast a steady heat throughout the room, the lobby reminded her a lot of the cabins her family would visit on their spring holiday. The door closed silently, the room filled with a palpable silence.

Wil stood at a desk dominating the center of the room, whispering as the clerk pointed to a map laid out on the surface. She walked up on the group tucking herself between Wil and Kalli, peeking at the map.

"So, what are we looking at?" she asked, whispering.

Wil shouldered his bag and reached for the map, "The clerk was showing us the route to our room. They have around six stories. Any chance we could take this?"

The man shrugged, "I've got dozens in the back. Just try to keep it in one piece and bring it back when you're done."

Wil gave a nod of gratitude and looked over to Selyne and Kalli, "You two coming?"

The group traveled several flights of stairs, with Wil finally turning into the seventh level. He looked at the map, offering a pair of brass keys while he surveyed the directions.

"One of those will be room 325, and the other is 324. They should be exactly the same, so no being choosy."

The cool metal clinked gently in Selyne's hand. She looked at the number engraved on its surface.

"Which way do we go?" she asked, looking at the curving hallways going in either direction.

Wil scratched his head, still staring at the map, "Left, I think. They should be just around the corner."

"Is there a bathroom on this floor? It's been a long day." Kalli asked, peeking over Wil's shoulder.

"It's around the corner."

Selyne stepped out into the hall, following the receding figure of Kalli. She found her room on the left. The small plaque indicated the room's number. Trying the lock, Selyne was rewarded with a confirming click. The rooms up here were lit with glyphs. The inconvenience of carrying new torches up the stairs was too great.

Selyne felt around the door. Her finger came into contact with the bubble of glass inlaid in brass. Lights came on a moment later, casting the room in a white glow. Selyne draped her handbag beside the door. The room wasn't much, just a single bed in the corner with a nightstand and a wardrobe.

She began perusing the cabinet on the nightstand. She pulled a bottle out, looking at the label. Selyne popped the cap, inhaling the bitter scent. She took a swig. Selyne never considered herself to be a beer person, but the warmth was calming regardless. She sat back on the bed, taking another gulp, emptying the bottle.

Selyne sighed, setting the empty bottle aside, staring at the ceiling. She'd done it, two weeks of dry food and cramped living spaces. All in order to find some enlightenment. She grabbed a second bottle from the cabinet. The whole endeavor had built up on her; it felt good to finally have some peace.

The night grew longer, Selyne drifting further and further into sleep's embrace. Her eyes grew unfocused, and her lids felt heavy. Selyne's mind turned to her bags.

She hadn't brought them up with her. Her breath continued to slow. "Wil will grab them. Sleep comes first."

Reaching over to the nightstand, Selyne fidgeted with the glyphs on the tabletop. Eventually, she got the desired result, lights running dry, leaving her in absolute darkness.

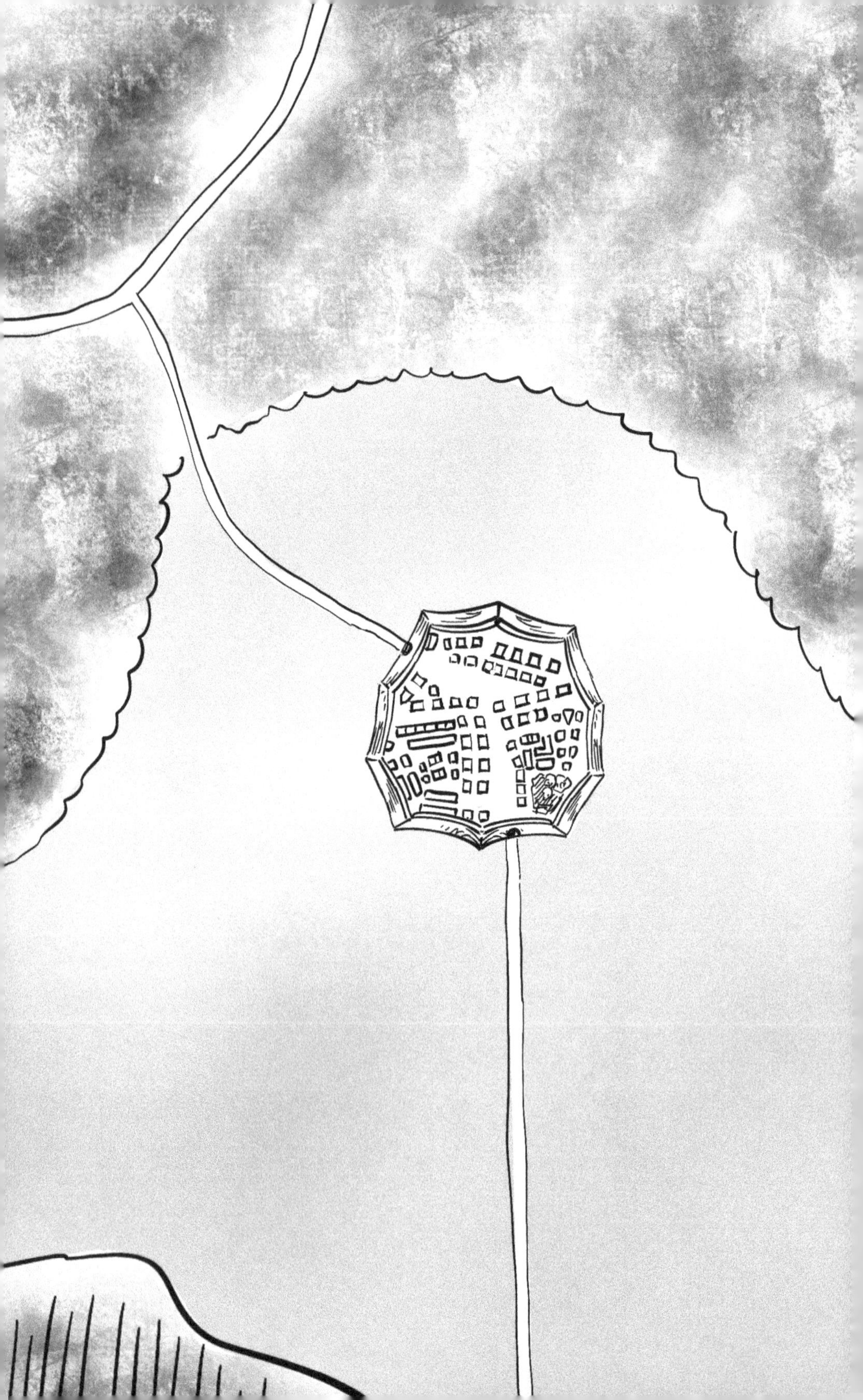

CHAPTER 27

The air had grown frigid as the caravan had continued northward. The Everwood didn't grow this far north. Only small bower trees clung to the frozen earth. Quintin shivered, pulling his carnid-skin coat tighter around his shaking frame. Alfear had mentioned that they would be traveling north. Quintin remembered the big man's reaction to his wardrobe. He'd been right to insist a heavier coat be brought, though Quintin hated to admit it.

He peeked out of the front of the cart to the behemoth which loomed before them. The northern cardinal wasn't as large as Isel by any metric, but Isel always felt like a natural structure, its walls feeling more akin to the hills around them.

The same couldn't be said for the cardinal fort. Its walls stood up from the flat forest land around it, the pitch-black walls slanting up to a spiked parapet at the top. Add the trench on top of all that, and the structure looked more like the parasitic shellfish sailors found or the larger hemasti.

Yells echoed from the city walls as soldiers called order to the men around them. The gates began to raise a moment later, the steel chains groaning as the ice broke off their surface and powdered the road beneath. The carts continued forward, the drivers moving carefully over the bridge and into the courtyard. Quintin stared, mouth hanging open as they passed through the gatehouse.

"How on earth do you think they built all this?" Fre asked, coming to sit beside him.

He stared at the large block of iron seated above them. It had to be at least a foot thick.

Quintin shrugged, "Resonance probably. It's not like anything you see out east is it?"

Fre shook her head, snuggling deeper into the white fur of her coat, "It should mean we're safe, so that's good."

Quintin nodded, the pair growing silent as the inner parts of the fortress city expanded out before them. The carts pulled to a stop – the grind of the brakes echoing throughout the quiet streets. Quintin leapt down, landing softly on the frozen cobblestones.

The courtyard was empty; the citizens presumably sheltering away from the cold. Alfear came to stand beside him, wearing full lockplate, helmet excluded. Quintin still questioned the logic of wearing steel this far north, even the guards on the walls wore heavy woven armor instead, but Alfear insisted it was warmer. Quintin felt the hum of Resonance humming faintly in the air. A factor he was sure played into the warmth Alfear championed.

The large man turned to Quintin, his face glowing with excitement, "So, what do you think?"

Alfear's breath froze as soon as it left his mouth. He gestured to the building around, "Is it as impressive as you imagined?"

Quintin glanced at the surrounding buildings. He had to concede they were impressive, made from the same black stone as everything else, with pointed roofs jutting up like the head of deformed hemasti.

He shivered, "It's bloody cold. Any chance we could talk inside where the air isn't sucking away our life?"

Alfear laughed, "Of course, I forget myself. Come, there should be an inn somewhere here."

He grabbed his large bag, gesturing with his head for Quintin to follow and grabbing his own bag from the driver's seat of the cart. Quintin followed Alfear down the street. Silence permeated the city fortress, with Quintin only passing a dozen people on his trek through the city.

The cold wind ripped through the streets and alleys, and Quintin was grateful when Alfear led them to a building with a sign hanging above it.

"The Burning Brazier?" Quintin asked, studying the painting of a small bronze bowl spewing fire pasted onto the wood.

Alfear nodded, "This was where I stayed during my last visit. It's in a safe neighborhood, not to mention I know the owners."

He strode to the door, Quintin stumbling to catch up. A large fire burned within an iron furnace set into the white plaster wall. The heat came as a welcome reprieve. The warm glow and white walls created a pleasant juxtaposition to the greys and blacks of the frozen landscape outside. Dark eyes fell on the pair as they entered. Soldiers and workers emanated hostility at their unwanted presence.

Alfear marched toward the bar, ignoring the glares and mutters. Quintin hung close. This was the type of close-knit tribal situation he avoided in the poor quarter of cities.

"I thought you said this was a safe part of town?" he whispered.

"It is," Alfear whispered back, keeping his eyes forward on alert.

Shia, what kind of place is this? Quintin thought, looking over the men and women, fingering knives and sidearms. There was always a dangerous sector in every city, but it never was supposed to be normal.

Alfear rang the bell leaning on the bar as he waited. Quintin stared at his imposing figure. Maybe the armor wasn't just here as an oversized oven. A man came out of the back as the conversation picked up a little.

The crowd turned back to their drinks. He was a short, frail-looking person, with eyes sunken into his face and a pallor approaching

Fre's in tone. Quintin got the sense he didn't get out much. He flipped open a ledger on a countertop, glancing from Quintin to Alfear.

"Will it just be you and the boy, or will your brother be joining?" he asked in a deep voice betrayed by his figure.

Alfear dug into the money bag attached to his belt, counting out silver for the night's fare. "It'll be four of us, two rooms if possible."

He handed the man a handful of pennies along with a few gold tabs.

The man raised an eyebrow, "Quite the crowd this time around."

He began counting the coins, rubbing the gold against the silver pennies as he checked their authenticity. Alfear grinned wryly but didn't humor the man with a response.

"Well, Thea, you're set up for tonight as well as the next. Your rooms are upstairs. They will be the first two on the left as you reach the top."

He handed Alfear a pair of metal bars with a small handle on one side. "These will lock your doors."

Alfear took the bolts, nodding his gratitude before motioning his head towards the door, indicating Quintin to follow. The stairway was cramped with dim glyph lights casting shadows which only added to the close feeling.

The hall ended at the second story, opening up into a corridor lined with doors. Alfear stepped up to the first room and tested the latch. It swung smoothly open, the well-oiled hinges opening without a sound. Two beds and a wardrobe were in the corner.

Alfear dropped his bag on the floor, "Well, I'll be up in this room."

He handed Quintin one of the bolts. "You and Fre will be staying in the other room. Be sure not to leave your bag unattended."

"I know how to take care of my stuff. It's not my first night in a shady place." Quintin took the bolt as he spoke.

Alfear shrugged, pocketing the bolt to his own door, "Hey, we're talking to the department head of the Seeker branch tonight downstairs. Just if you want to get a grip on our plans."

Quintin thought for a moment, "I'll be there, though you may need to convince Fre."

Alfear nodded, "Just get settled; we'll address the issue later."

Quintin shrugged before shouldering his bag and stepping out into the corridor. His room was identical to the other. Hours passed, and Quintin remained seated on his bed, head buried in a new book.

Fre entered silently, remaining quiet as they united. Night came with little change. The grey sky maintained the same level of gloom.

Quintin turned the page, staring at the illustrations on the next. The book was a historical volume detailing the formation of Ithea, focusing mainly on Amie Angel-kin. The illustration was said to be her own, an attempt to show what an Angel looked like. Quintin scowled at the oddity of the picture; the creature looked far too human. Quintin looked down at the description of the scene: *The defeat of the vengeance – the Iron Demon.*

The description was odd; the demons' titles being stated without its name. He read further into the story, the whole tale feeling more like a heroic ballad than a record of events. He came upon another illustration a few pages later. This time of Amie the first Angel-kin herself.

She stood at the edge of a cliff with the broken body of the demon-being as it fell below her.

"When I found the wreckage, there was only melted metal and burnt grease." A quote from the Angel-kin read, "Though the heart may have survived, I fail to assume that the creature could recover from such a barrage of electricity. Greater demons have fallen under less, and I am sure his mental processor was destroyed."

Quintin paused for a moment, pondering the quote. He'd held an angel heart in his hand. They were alive until destroyed. Could one maybe recover given the right circumstances? Even with their body melted into a puddle?

A knock sounded at the door. Quintin closed the book and walked over, sliding the bolt out before swinging the door open.

Lian stood with his arm raised to knock again, "Ah. Yes, we're having a talk downstairs if you're interested."

Lian lowered his head, looking at Quintin and Fre for a response.

"I'll come down. How about it, Fre?" Quintin looked over his shoulder as he asked.

She set down her notebook, one Quintin didn't recognize and grabbed her handbag. "I'll come."

Lian led the pair downstairs, back to a small table situated in the corner of the room. Alfear had seated himself with another man Quintin didn't recognize, presumably the head of the Seeker's department here in the cardinal city. Quintin pulled up a chair and sat across from Alfear, grabbing the pitcher of beer and pouring himself a cup.

The department head watched as Lian took a seat.

"Is that everyone?" he asked.

Alfear nodded before he continued, "Well then, let's get started, shall we? Can I get all of your names?"

He turned to Fre and Quintin. "I know those two, but I've yet to meet you. My name is Adran. I run the Seekers down here."

He held out his hand, and Quintin shook it. "I'm Quintin."

Adran turned to Fre. She took his hand lightly, "My name is Fre."

He nodded, sitting back in his chair.

"Adran, would you mind explaining what this is about?" Alfear interjected, "We got your message two days ago, but you were far from clear of your intentions with those."

After pouring a glass from the pitcher, he spoke, "Something has been bothering the scouts. It's nothing really, but I felt I should inform you of it."

Lian's eyes narrowed, "What exactly are we supposed to be concerned over? It just sounded like some agitated mraven nests, nothing life-threatening."

Adran downed his glass, exhaling as he set it down on the table, "It's gotten a little stranger since we've talked. Animals seem to be leaving the area, and the Seekers have reported unnatural changes in the resonant threads in certain areas west of here."

Adran seemed to shiver despite the heat. "There have been claims coming from the towns and villages closer to the forests. Talk of voices and lights in the forest, even some missing person cases. It is probably nothing, maybe the frost is getting to me, but my seekers felt it best to investigate."

He sat back, pouring another glass for himself. Quintin took a sip of his drink, processing the information being given. *This sounds like he's describing a fairy tale. Floating lights, uneasy fauna, and changes in the threads.*

The whole thing was unnerving if it was true. Lian and Alfear didn't seem to share the sentiment. Neither one showed any change to their demeanor.

"I'm sure you're going to find the problem is smaller than many people describe it," Lian reassured. "Usually, when I investigate matters of this kind, the people have combined several unnerving events into something larger than life."

He failed to sound convincing, and Adran still looked on edge before finally shrugging, "I hope you're right, Lian. My Seekers will do their best to deal with it regardless. I just didn't want you wandering too far from the city without knowing the current state of things."

The table went quiet. The words rested heavily on everyone. Alfear chimed in, "Don't be too worried. Lian and I have been through dozens of scrapes. I don't think we have anything to fear with your people around. I, for one, have full faith in your abilities."

Adran gave a half-hearted nod at the words.

"Well then," Lian said, "with the cryptic letter and intrigue out of the way, how about we talk about our stay here?"

"Yes," Adran shrugged, "Let's do that. Oh, what was it you were planning? I can open almost any facility if you give me enough notice."

"Ok. We want as much practical teaching as we can get." Lian said. "Any training on how to deal with ancestral science, apex creature families, political sciences, trade, and espionage."

Adran's brow furrowed at the list, "It sounds like you're trying to make soldiers or assassins. What is this extremely direct learning curriculum about?"

"Thailia has gotten frisky with the south-western border. Reports of warships and increased weapons production," Alfear said nonchalantly, "Not to mention reports resembling yours. Ancestors seem to be upset for some reason."

Adran seemed to deflate at the words, his age catching up with him as he took another drink, "Alright then, not an answer I probably wanted. I'll try to set up some labs for you to teach. I also will see if I can get any residents to help if you need anything."

"Thank you," Lian said, "We will be in your debt over this."

Adran shook his head, dismissing the thanks, "Don't feel like you owe me anything. You know how much just having Angel-kin helps my current situation. Knowledge of your arrival may prevent a riot yet."

The comment confused Quintin. Sure, they had a large inheritance which dwarfed what most people had, but unique forms of Resonance aside, two children didn't offer much more to help the problem.

Alfear checked the clock on the wall, "It's getting late, and you probably have some other people to attend to."

He stood as he talked, making it clear he was done with the conversation. Adran stood as well, extending his arm out, "I hope it helped. I'll do my best to give you the schedules for the university professors. Feel free to ask me if you need anything more."

The two shook hands. Alfear turned to Quintin and Fre, "We're done tonight. Any questions before this is over?"

Quintin glanced at Fre. Neither one said anything.

"Alrighty then," Alfear said, clapping his hands. He turned to Adran, "I'll be going to bed now. Let me know if anything happens."

He walked away from the table, leaving Quintin still sipping his glass of beer. This had hardly been a normal introduction. Quintin was beginning to expect that.

"Hey, child." The director said, looking at Fre, "Do you have an inheritance?"

The words sounded innocuous, but Quintin felt that there was something beneath them that made him not so sure.

Fre nodded, "I am an Angel-kin."

The director nodded absently in thought. "Take care about the city. Some people might not view your existence all too kindly. Bloody superstitious lot."

"Is she in serious danger?" Quintin asked, concerned.

The director shook his head, "Many people living in this city are part of the Solus church. They are fine enough people, but they believe in a divine purpose for inheritance. Just know that the more manic believers won't take kindly to a native of the Anglis island possessing something so holy."

Quintin sat back, confused. inheritance was valuable; he knew that, but did that warrant such a response?

"Just be aware of this while you go about the city these upcoming weeks." The man downed the last of his beer, "I'll be sure to get the things set up for tomorrow."

Quintin watched as the man checked his seat before walking silently to the door. Quintin took a sip from his glass. He'd read up about the Solus religion. Its influence was almost greater than the Thean universities here up north. He looked over to Fre who sat, drink in hand.

The last statement didn't seem to be affecting her, but Quintin had never been a good judge of her character. She met his eyes, exasperation clear on her face.

"Well, this should prove interesting," she said sarcastically.

Quintin laughed wryly, "Religious cults are always fun."

Fre rolled her eyes, "Just so long as they mind their business, then there won't be a problem."

Quintin nodded, happy to see her take control of the situation. That wasn't the case before. *She's doing better than myself in that regard.*

Quintin took a sip of beer. The thought soured his mood a little.

He gave Fre a critical glance as he spoke. Fre nodded.

"We're probably going to head up to sleep soon. I'm just going to finish my glass," Quintin said as he took a sip of his drink to emphasize his point.

Silence engulfed the room. Fre leaned back in her chair. This place just got a lot stranger and just a little more hostile.

CHAPTER 28

Selyne sat up from her bed, head pounding from the night before. "At least there weren't any night terrors this time."

Pain flared at the back of her eyes, and she clutched her head, massaging her temples. Selyne shuffled around the nightstand, searching for her pocket watch. Her fingers met the cool surface of silver, closing around the smooth surface. She fumbled with the latch, revealing the crystal surface of the timepiece. The hands sat at a quarter to zenith.

"Shia," Selyne muttered, shoving herself off the bed and dragging her feet over to the wardrobe. She swung the door open, gazing at the array of blues, greys, reds, and greens blurring together into a mess before her.

She blinked, rubbing the sleep from her eyes as best she could. She gazed once again at the wardrobe. She grabbed a new shirt, a pair of slacks, a travel dress, and socks. Setting back on her bed, she began the process of becoming socially acceptable. She didn't recall Wil ever coming in last night, though she didn't remember much of the time before bed last night.

A knock came at the door.

"Come on in," she called, sliding the riding dress over the new clothes.

Kalli stepped into the room. "I see you found the clothes I left in your closet. You know Wil isn't required to bring your stuff to your room. Taking advantage of his good nature isn't a good long-term plan if you want him to continue working for you."

Kalli gathered up Selyne's old clothes, making it clear she wouldn't press the issue much further.

Selyne sighed, holding her head in her hands. She knew Kalli was right.

Why do people have to be so bloody difficult?

She looked up, "When do we start doing stuff today? I didn't catch much of the planning last night."

Kalli looked out the door at the clock on the wall. "Wil made plans for one hour after zenith to talk to the expeditionary groups. Maybe get some hands-on experience with ancestral activity. Though with how early you're up, we may be able to push those earlier if you're feeling up to it."

She glanced at Selyne, questioning her current aptitude. "I'll be up for that, so long as there's a way to get some food to eat beforehand."

Kalli rolled up the dirty clothes, stepping out into the hall, "The third floor has the diner. Wil should still be there if you hurry. Just be sure you have your purse as you will need to pay."

Selyne looked around; she'd forgotten where she'd placed her purse.

"It's in the nightstand. Left side drawer. You left it on the floor last night." Kalli said before closing the door.

Selyne gave a small wave of acknowledgment, turning to the nightstand and collecting the small leather bag within. Standing, she threaded the small bag through her belt before putting the entire thing on her waist, looping the remainder around the other side.

Sliding on her boots, Selyne stepped out into the hall, ignoring her head and focusing on the biting pain in her stomach. The building felt like a completely different place in the light of day. Windows opened to reveal the white light of the sun. It lacked the cramped log cabin feel it had the night before.

Selyne walked around the corridor, finding the stairs, and began the trek down.

"So, what have you been up to?" Selyne asked, peering over her cup of tea at the folder of paper he was scanning. "You know, you tend to read a lot."

Wil shrugged, "What else would I be doing? Most of life is talking to people, either through speech or text. What would you expect?"

Selyne thought momentarily. She'd grown up avoiding as many social activities as possible. "I guess you'd be doing something more exciting; you just have this air of mystery."

Wil gave a slight smile, not looking away from the page in front of him, "Sorry, I'm not exciting. You're about five years too late for that."

Selyne took a sip of her tea. She wasn't done yet, "Could you still beat a Rhinil bare-handed, or is that also in the past?"

"I could still do it. I may not use my sword, but I maintain peak physical condition." Wil relayed.

"That's a bloody lie," Selyne said incredulously, "I've never seen you lift anything larger than my bag on a daily basis."

"What can I say?" Wil said, "You're always asleep before I start any form of exercise."

Selyne rolled her eyes; that was hardly a solid alibi. "You're really not that interesting to talk to; have you ever considered embellishing your life a little? Being royalty, I could give you plenty of tips if you need them."

Wil chuckled and shook his head, "I'm fine. Thanks for the offer."

They sat in silence. Selyne finished her two eggs and toasted bread the chefs had given her. Wil continued peering over the documents.

"You know, I don't think you mentioned what it was you were reading or working on," Selyne said, curiosity refueled by a well-fed mind.

Wil handed her the page he'd been looking over.

"Just this week's itinerary. I was going to bring it up later today, but now works just as well."

Selyne took a cursory glance at the page.

"Any response on the request I made?" she asked.

"Yeah, actually," Wil said. "They said you could get a guide, and you could find some interesting things that far into the Everwood."

Selyne cracked a smile, which only revealed a piece of the joy she felt. Weeks of talk and paperwork had all eaten away at her for this single week, "When's the soonest we leave?"

"That's a bit tricky," Kalli said from behind.

Selyne turned in her chair, "Why would you say that?"

"Well," Kalli said, listing off her reasons on her fingers, "First, we have to get a guide. I also need to prepare my research tools if this trip is going to be beneficial. A route needs to be charted so they can recover our remains should things go sour…"

"Alright, I get it." said Selyne defensively, "I don't need every bloody detail."

"Yes, well then, don't ask," Kalli said, sounding far more like her mother than was comfortable.

"Why don't we start our plans for today? Selyne, you're up for that, right?"

Selyne glared at Kalli, "I don't like the way you said that. But yes, I'm not that inebriated."

"Perfect!" Kalli said, clasping her hands excitedly, "How about we start with the museum? I hear the curator comes from the Thailian city-state of Ishael. He's said to collect a unique variety of artifacts that wouldn't be found in a Thean facility."

"Well, I'm glad your enthusiasm is high," Selyne said, hiding her internal despair. "Are you ready, Wil?"

The man took the last gulp of his tea, setting the empty glass onto his now empty plate. He nodded.

"We can go," he said.

Outside, Selyne took in a deep breath. She used to tell her mother she could taste and smell the autumn in the air this time of the year, which would gain her a smile from her mother. Selyne released the cool air, glad for the worst of the summer heat to be over. The city took a completely different shape under the light of the sun. It looked so clean and old. Skipping over the smoothed-out dirt and roots of the Everwood floor, Selyne let the brief moment of joy take her.

Kalli walked a step behind, talking to Wil about the architecture and history of the city.

"You'd think he would have a degree for something, or soldering gives you a better education than I thought."

Selyne looked over the crowds of people going about their day. A woman walked past with a small boy holding her hand. Did people grow up here? She turned around, walking backwards, watching the conversation behind her.

"Seekers are one of the oldest branches of the Thean government, existing as their own group of people living in the Everwood centuries before the empire," Kalli explained to Wil, who nodded, deep in thought.

"Would that explain the strange mix of beliefs they hold?" Wil asked.

"Somewhat," Kalli responded. "There are many different religious sects all throughout the empire. Mostly this decision to abstain from an imperial religion is to keep the peace, but that thought probably started when the empire reached the Everwood blockade in 651 AHW. That was where making peace with the locals proved strategically required if they wanted to conquer the kings of the west." Kalli continued. "This was before the imperial navy was formed, mind you."

Selyne marveled at the woman's willingness to go into every detail. "I thought Amie was the one to set up laws for religious freedom during the founding of the kingdom of Isel?"

Kalli nodded, taking the question in stride, "That's true. But that law wasn't ratified until later. Despite her influence on the political foundation of our empire. Amie Angel-kin was often more preoccupied with cleaning up the fallout of Heaven's War than playing politician."

Selyne paused to think about the statement. Her history classes had all emphasized a swift formation of government; it hadn't seemed so complicated, with apparently hundreds of years between decisions. "Kind of like our lawmakers now. They couldn't make a decent law if the empire depended on it."

"Here we are," Kalli pointed with her right arm, "The infamous museum of ancestral history."

Selyne turned around. It was the first stone building she'd seen in the entire city, looming over her head. Despite its jarring design choice, the museum still felt right at home among the trees, looking more like a natural stone construct than a precision-built building.

"How old is this place?" Selyne asked, still gawking.

"It's almost as old as its founder, so three hundred or so years," Kalli said.

Your knowledge is impeccable as always, Selyne thought.

Entering the cool interior, Selyne realized what was exciting her senses. Paintings covered the walls, weapons, and statues filled rooms, each one releasing an aura of energy. The whole building felt alive. The sensation resembled what she felt whenever she interacted with wisps, just more gentle. The artifacts didn't feel hostile. She walked over to one of the plaques, glancing at the artifact it described.

The Sword of Korah. The poet king of Sherma in 234 AHW. The weapon was said to contain his inheritance.

"Hey Kalli, this guy had pressure as an inheritance." Selyne said, "he made music with it."

Kalli looked over the plaque. "Well, look at that. If only you could sing."

Selyne ignored the jab; just knowing someone else used her type of inheritance for something other than factory work made her happy. The sword sang out a few notes, Selyne recoiling at the action.

"What in Shia's name was that?"

Kalli chuckled, "inheritance doesn't just give you power. I taught you that. It doesn't change for an object."

Selyne shivered, "But it can't think. Why? How?"

Kelli sighed, "inheritance is information. We build it with our minds, something that sword can't do. But it can always request patterns that it's been given."

Selyne calmed herself as best she could, "Sorry, you have told me this before. Just seeing it was shocking."

She turned, looking for Wil. He stood a room over, staring at a large exhibit. He was talking to someone.

"What is he doing?" Selyne asked, nudging Kalli.

Kalli glanced over and closed her notebook, "Let's ask."

The pair stepped out of the main lobby into the small hallway. Each side of the small hall had been modeled like a part of the Everwood. They reached Wil.

"What's this room supposed to be?" Selyne asked, her voice lowering instinctively.

Wil turned around, realizing the women were behind him.

"Your friend was just asking me that very question," the old man said.

Selyne looked the elderly man up and down. "Are you the curator of this place?"

The man shook his head, "He's a close friend. I just maintain the exhibits and answer any questions asked by any visitors."

Selyne watched as he stroked the white wisps of his beard. "So what exactly is this?"

"It's a recreation of a place held very dear to the curator's heart," he said while turning to the fake trees.

"Apparently, Alcus, the curator, made a pilgrimage to the Everwood when he was young." Wil said, "It's a common practice for Thailians, but most don't actually succeed."

The guide nodded in agreement, "Every Thailian who comes to this forest seeks the Angel of the wood. It's something I, as a member of the church of Solus, respect deeply."

His gaze moved to the statue sitting in the center of the artificial wood.

Selyne hadn't noticed the statue until following his gaze. It looked to be made from solid steel. It almost resembled a malformed tree, except this tree had a mask with two eyes and a mouth. It didn't radiate any Resonance like the other objects, being recreation, but the imagery was still odd enough to make her uncomfortable.

"I thought Thailians denounced every church this side of the ocean. Solus wouldn't mean anything to them."

"Truth remains the same, even if you denounce someone else's interpretation. Solus isn't a Thailian god, but the Angel of the Everwood bears an eerie resemblance," the guide said solemnly.

Selyne found the comment to be odd; one didn't acknowledge that their god could fit into another religion.

"So, what is the history of this phenomenon?"

The guide grew visibly excited, "The myth of Solus is very old, dating back to Heaven's War. It was said he would guide the warriors of heaven in their battles. His knowledge of the past, present, and future was unparalleled."

He gestured around himself, "It's said, after the war ended, he established the Everwood to separate himself from mankind so only the worthy could obtain his wisdom."

"Sounds like Solus isn't the only god in that myth. Why would your church worship him solely?"

Selyne knew some of the Solus theology. It was something she had wanted to know since she was old enough to read.

The guide chuckled. "A common question. Unlike Thean doctrine, we acknowledge a wider range of Angels and gods. Solus is the one we choose, but the worship of other gods is not without merit."

She struggled with the explanation, "But why would you choose one? Wouldn't his guidance fail you if you needed help with something he wasn't sovereign over?"

The museum guide simply shrugged. "We figure his guidance is all we need in life. If not, we'd be a part of some other belief."

Selyne didn't find that answer satisfactory either but figured she wouldn't get anything more from him and decided to change the subject. "So, how do you find the Solus spirit in the Everwood?"

The guide laughed, "You don't find Solus unless Solus decides you should."

She nodded, "So, it's not up to us then. That's actually comforting to consider."

The guide was nodding in confirmation.

"Could you tell us where we could find some specific items in the collection?" Kalli interjected, handing the guide a page from her notebook.

He glanced over it, "Definitely. I can show you most of these items. Though a few are archived for safety reasons. If you three will follow me."

Selyne followed behind Kalli as the guide led them through the exhibits, occasionally stopping as Kalli leaned over her notebook and wrote. Selyne glanced over to Wil. He'd been quiet during most of the day, speaking only in response to others. He stopped at an exhibit, glancing down at a silver broach set into a silver case.

"What do you think?" Selyne asked, moving towards the case.

Wil shrugged absently. "I'm not sure. The whole place feels uncomfortably familiar. Almost like the walls themselves are alive."

His voice didn't carry any fear, more like a silent curiosity. Selyne gave a wry laugh, "When it comes to anything inheritance related, I've just come to expect a sort of acknowledgment from inhuman places."

He raised an eyebrow, "What types of places are you talking about?"

She thought for a moment, "You know, I'm not really sure."

The pair followed Kalli, who had moved to another exhibit room. This one was filled solely with paintings. The place was extremely uncomfortable to stand in, with faces from bygone eras staring down from every angle.

"Shia, this is weird." Selyne hurried past Kalli into the next room.

The whole place felt like an oddity shop frequented by the nobles in Isel; only here the objects actually possessed spiritual power. The thought made Selyne wonder just how much this collection cost. The group finally moved into the last room. The lobby was visible from the entrance on the other side. They had made a complete circle without Selyne noticing.

Kalli gave the guide her thanks and said in a barely audible whisper, "Do you know where we could find the library here?"

Selyne strained to hear her. The guide wrote something down in Kalli's notebook. The group exited out of the door. Selyne released a large breath of air as she relished the open air.

"So, where to next?"

Kalli referenced her notebook, "We'll go to the library, but first I wanted to peruse some of the restaurants in town. I figure we could pick up lunch before studying for a few hours."

Selyne remembered the tightness in her stomach. Breakfast had been all protein and tea. She needed some real food. Following Kalli through the streets, Selyne passed what she assumed to be the library.

"This whole town can't be more than one or two miles wide, yet they manage to fit a population twice their size." She marveled as they travelled past the archive. The gilded wood twinkled in the sun.

"Was all this here before the westward expansion?" Selyne shouted to Kalli over the crowd.

Kalli nodded, smiling as she turned to look at the superstructure. "Ithea makes a point of not breaking things of value. We'd rather let the local caretakers maintain them. All we ask for in return is a share in the benefits."

Selyne looked away as they left the large building behind. "Shia, this place is impressive."

The buildings began to grow lower and wider as they they continued down the lane. Selyne noted the shift in smell as well. The dust and pollen of the forest gave way to cooking meat and heavy spices. Steam and smoke began to waft through the air.

Selyne couldn't help but smile at the comfort they brought. "So, what are we looking for exactly?"

Kalli turned, prying her eyes away from the various restaurant signs, facing Selyne. "I just asked the curator where the best place to eat in town would be. He gave me a name."

Kalli glanced over to the vendors, and small food joints littered around, "But I'm beginning to see how insufficient his instructions were."

The group waded through the crowded market for a few moments before Kalli finally threw up her hands in defeat.

"Alright. Who is up for some fried arboro-sti meat?" Kalli took an exploratory step towards a small food cart where a man cut off a bit of meat.

The smell of the food was gamey. It reminded Selyne of the waterfowl sometimes cooked by the Spire staff, but this meat came off a bone twice the length of Selyne's forearm.

The server grabbed a small piece of paper, wrapped the meat up, and handed it to Selyne.

"Thank you," Selyne said, smiling as she handed him several coins in return.

Selyne watched as her companions purchased their own meals. The packaging was so odd, the paper folded in a manner as to expose one side of the meat. They hadn't offered any forks either; probably they'd intended for the customers to use their fingers. Selyne raised an eyebrow, *was all street food designed this inconveniently?* The group walked about the food stalls.

Selyne marveled at just how many vendors sold some form of hemasti meat or another.

"How often do they hunt hemasti in this region?" Selyne asked as she passed another stall strong with the scent of reptilian meat.

Kalli shrugged, taking a bite of her food. "Hard to say, really. Generally, they kill what comes close to the city. We could check out the butchers if you want to take a look."

"Can we do that?" Wil asked cynically, "Is that something we can fit into the schedule?"

"Relax for a minute," Kalli reassured. "We came here to take our lessons a little slower and have some hands-on experience with the Seekers. We can afford some time to see the sights."

"It's ok, Kalli," Selyne said, "To be honest, I don't really want to watch people cut up a bunch of giant lizards."

Kalli shrugged, "Fair enough. We can begin heading back to the library. We're not scheduled to take a field trip with the Seekers until tomorrow, so expect plenty of reading for today."

Selyne sighed. The thought of digging through pages of information created a sense of disappointment.

You can't complain – this is the most freedom you've had in a long time. Selyne followed Kalli back through the crowd towards the library.

Selyne took a deep breath, letting herself absorb the strange environment around her. *Might as well enjoy the fun while it lasts.*

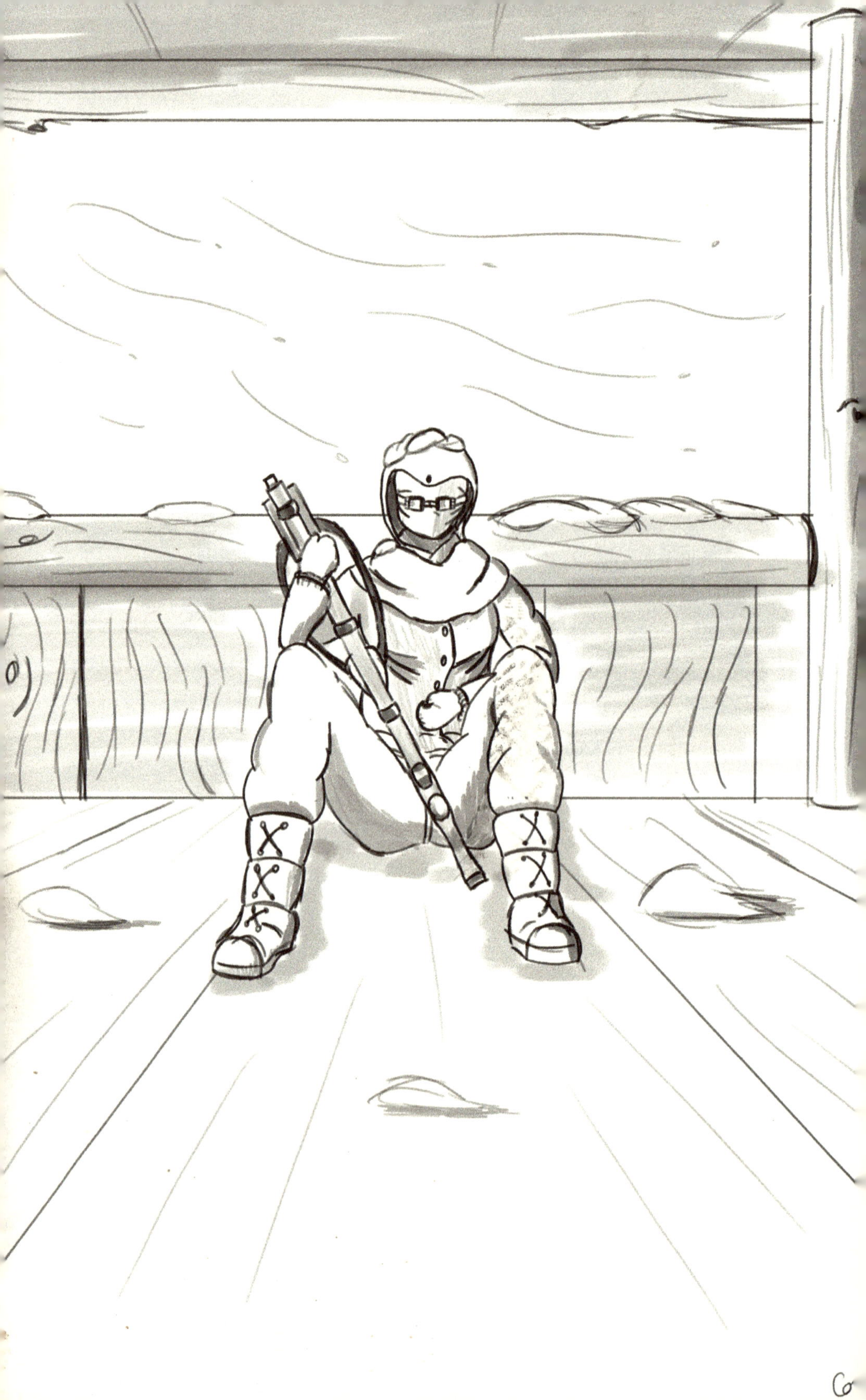

CHAPTER 29

Malta sat back, breathing in the arid air, letting the negative temperature cool her lungs. The job of scout used to be fun. North, usually, was peaceful, but now she had to deal with Solv's madness. She glanced over to her compatriot. His dark eyes darted about the forest of trees around them.

"Oh, Shia, you'll give me anxiety with your manic behavior. No ghosts are going to take your soul."

Turner stared daggers at the comment before moving his attention back to the trees, "I know you grew up in a cult, but you can't honestly think something's out there."

Malta rolled her eyes, "You southern folks don't know anything. I've seen villages disappear overnight and ancestors which defy reason."

Turner spat the words, disdain clear on his face. Malta backed off. Antagonizing fanatics wouldn't help anything.

Lights flashed in the distance. The forms of two ancestral sprites danced up through the trees. She couldn't understand why anyone would fear them. Her hood flew back as the wind rolled in from the west. Malta squatted instinctively, despite her goggles; one barely felt the cold under the gear Seekers were given.

It frustrated her sometimes. It made missions feel fake. The wind continued. Malta pulled her hood up, this time buttoning it to her face mask.

"Thea must be pissed for all the wind. Feels like a small storm."

Malta pulled her snow poncho close. It was just the season change, nothing more.

You're not going to be paranoid. She thought as the wind continued to scream through the trees above her.

Turner grew rigid, his hand moving to his ratchet bow.

"What is it?" Malta asked, growing more nervous at her partner's behavior.

His eyes moved even faster, searching for some unseen threat. "Can you feel that?"

Malta looked out the wooden parapet. The watchtowers provided a three-hundred-and-sixty-degree view of the surrounding forest, sitting a good five feet over the treetops. The night sky was clear of clouds and snow. There was nothing to see.

In an instant, an explosion sounded next to Malta, and shrapnel peppered her head.

"Shia!" she yelled, turning to the source.

Light appeared above her. Turner activated his Resonance, illuminating the forest for miles. Malta scanned the forest floor. A tree had exploded beside the tower. Its splintered stump was steaming.

"Was that you?" she asked, turning to Turner.

"I told you there's something out there. I can feel it." Turner said.

Another tree exploded further to the left. Then another, and another.

"What is this? The temperature hasn't dropped enough to break bower trees this old." Malta glanced down at the stump. It was still steaming. "I'll go get the horses. Can you make sure I'm not blindsided by whatever is doing this?"

She didn't wait for his answer before reaching for the ladder and dropping down. Stumbling as the earth gave way under the impact,

Malta staggered forward towards the stable. The horses were calm, allowing her to saddle each one without any trouble. Turner yelled something down the ladder, and Malta stepped out of the stall, missing his words in the wind.

"What?" she yelled, her voice faltering against the wind that was moving faster.

She froze in place, fear taking hold. She was sweating. The air felt too hot to breathe. Turner dropped out of the bottom of the tower, falling thirty feet to the ground.

Dust flew behind him as he pulverized the already broken earth. He raced to Malta, taking her by the shoulder and dragging her back into the stable.

She stammered to speak, "What is going on? Why is the air burning?"

Turner slammed the stable door open, letting Malta go and racing to his horse, "I've never seen anything like this. It eats the Resonance around it. I couldn't even produce a spark without pulling from my reserves."

He led his horse out as he spoke, clutching his ratchet bow in the other.

"Is that why it's boiling out there?" Malta asked. "The very air around us is being activated."

"It's like a bloody force of nature," Turner mumbled under his breath.

Malta shivered; she'd seen this man scared before but never so steely-eyed as he was before her. She could sense his demeanor through the waxed hood and goggles covering his face. Malta mounted her horse. The wind grew less manic as the air grew hotter.

Turner primed his ratchet bow, loading a white-tipped bolt manually down the barrel. The top burst into a white flame a moment later, presumably ignited using his inheritance. He turned the weapon to the sky, but another bang echoed through the forest as he pulled the trigger. The complex systems of pulleys and springs released their energy and launched the bolt into the air at near-supersonic speeds.

The chemical head burned a white line in the sky before exploding into a bright red explosion, indicating an ancestral threat of the highest order.

"We need to leave. Now." Malta said, fog now filling her goggles.

Turner pulled off his hood, revealing his sweat-soaked face underneath. "We'll head to the nearest outpost. We need to get a visual of this thing before we let it get any further."

He flicked a switch on his ratchet bow, priming the system and letting a bolt fall from the magazine down into the barrel. Malta took her hood off, the open air cooling her face.

"We'll want to head north towards outpost twelve. They should have the largest group," she said, trotting past Turner.

He looked back towards the forest. "Shia, it's close. Let's bugger out of here before it arrives."

Yanking the reigns, he kicked his horse into a gallop, and Malta followed suit. She let the animal pick the path as she turned to look behind her. The light Turner had created was starting to dissipate. The tower faded back into the darkness of night. Her heart froze as the scene receded behind her, the light had died, but she could have sworn she'd seen a pair of eyes reflecting off its last rays. It had stared right at her.

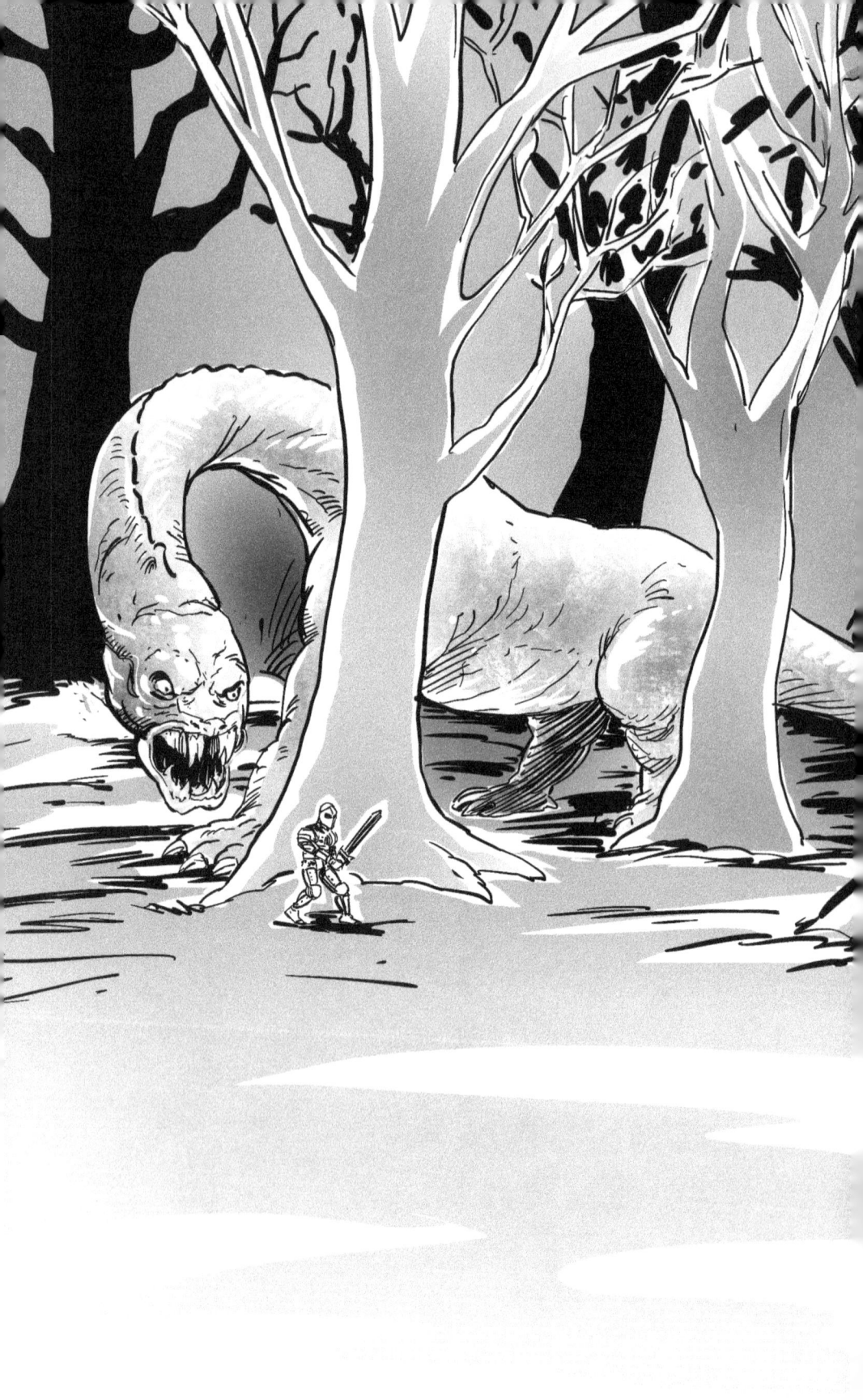

CHAPTER 30

Quintin walked through the frozen city, a sword on his side and a little steel badge on his collar. Comparing this city to Isel was like comparing the weather up north to that of the central region. Where before Alfear had set clear student teacher lines, now in this city, Quintin was treated as his own authority. The badge was a very real symbol of that, given by the Solus ministry as proof of his inheritance.

People gave way as he walked by, some even giving a slight nod of reverence. The whole experience felt unnatural to Quintin. He recalled something Alfear had said the day after they arrived. "The Thean universities do not teach one theology — you learned why during our history classes — up in the north Solus is the church, here both the universities and the church are unified."

The thought made Quintin shiver. It wasn't that Solus wasn't normal to him – out east, they believed much stranger things – but that the university was so homogeneous in its belief was scary.

Someone bowed in front of him, giving a small prayer. *Alright, that's enough of this.*

Quintin turned down a side alley ignoring the person. Why did people have to be weird? Winding his way through the city was tedious. His knowledge of the back roads was incomplete, leading to more than one dead end for Quintin. Turning another corner, Quintin was once again hit with the strange lack of beggars and homeless in the city. Alfear had said that anyone could get a high-paying job by simply joining the army. The cold weather was also a very strong motivation for those unwilling to work. He turned the corner of a small building Quintin thought he recognized, sighing in relief, as the familiar shape of the university's back door met his eyes.

He turned the knob, and the door swung inward. Nobody locked their doors in the city. Quintin pulled off his scarf and began unbuttoning his fur coat as he walked down the small hallway of labs and archives. The path was becoming almost second nature, Quintin intuitively stopping on the tenth door and entering.

Alfear sat in the corner fiddling with two metal plates from his armor, moving them back and forth like someone might do with two coins. Quintin shivered as he rid himself of the last vestiges of the frigid outdoors. He walked over and sat down at the table.

"So, how did morning patrol go?" Alfear asked, tossing aside the plates and turning his attention towards Quintin.

Quintin let out an exasperated sigh, throwing his head back over the chair and looking at the ceiling.

"I'm so done with this place," he groaned, "Everyone wants to gain your approval, and I can't walk twenty feet without some ill person asking me to fix their life."

Alfear raised his eyebrow at the outburst, "Did you help fix their life?"

"Of course," Quintin huffed, "I have cleaned multiple wells, saved a number of family pets, and stopped one theft."

He stared at Alfear, "We've been over this, but I really don't like these people."

Alfear chuckled, with a knowing nod, "I understand the feeling. These people," he paused, as he considered what to say next, "They have put very natural phenomena at the center of their moral compass, which creates very ugly repercussions when the natural world disagrees with them."

Quintin nodded in agreement.

"However," Alfear continued, "We do not."

Quintin sighed internally. He'd been hearing this for months, and it wasn't getting easier with each conversation.

"Look, I know what you're going to say," Quintin grumbled. "Can't we let the topic slide?"

Alfear looked Quintin up and down, thinking of what to say next, "Justice has a time and place. Mercy is always the first step."

Alfear grew quiet, and the pair sat momentarily in silence.

"How is Fre doing?" Quintin finally asked.

"She's remarkable. Lian has put her on a crash course like no other. Just the other day, she was able to pick a lock using only her inheritance. She didn't so much as scratch the internals."

Quintin sat up at the statement, "Really?"

Alfear smiled and nodded seriously, "Lian has pusher her fine-tuning to its very limit. She's actually been helping in the medical building, helping the surgeons with the injured soldiers coming in."

Quintin felt his mood rise as the conversation moved from heavier topics. "Do scouts get injured often out here?"

"All the time," Alfear said, "hemasti of several different species live up here, not to mention hostile ancestors. Scouts are lucky if they go an entire tour here without injury."

That was an unnerving bit of information. Quintin had always known there were scary things in the wild places of the world, but, coming up north, everything felt so much more real. It was a place where humanity didn't really have jurisdiction.

"Do Rhinil live this far north?" he asked.

It would be a perfect godless place if they did. He was a little relieved as well as disappointed when Alfear shook his head. "Rhinil and mraven-cor tend to prefer warm climates, so they stay south of the Everwood though perhaps if given motive they would come up here."

Alfear's voice drifted as he speculated the prospect, "So Rhinil are like the mythology says they are? The whole talking and planning isn't just poetic license?"

Shaking his head adamantly, Alfear replied, "By no means are they fake. Speaking from experience, they were very clever and capable of human-level thought."

"Really."

The door opened as the pair continued to talk. Lian and Fre entered and removed their ice-covered coats.

"We're back. How was your day?" Lian asked, his voice filling the room.

Alfear shrugged, "I've been good. Mostly just spending time studying as Quintin did morning patrol. How about you?"

The pair continued with the new conversation, leaving Fre and Quintin to themselves.

"So, I heard you were learning surgery in the hospital?" Quintin asked. "How is that going?"

Fre shrugged, "It's cool. I haven't been allowed to work on anything vital yet. Just getting used to using my inheritance in tandem with other tools."

She brushed the question off. Quintin floundered to say something to spark interest.

"I heard you're getting better at that. Alfear claimed you're not accidentally cutting things when you use it."

She nodded, "Yeah, the doctors were impressed by that. They claim I'll be heaven-sent to anyone I treat should I get the proper practice."

The image of Fre in one of the doctor's bulky robes and hat popped into his head. He smiled, "What do you do for a uniform? Do they fit or…"

Fre blushed slightly, clearly embarrassed. "We roll up the sleeves. I don't fit the trousers, so they let me off with my own."

Quintin nodded, "We'll have to fix that before you go professional. It's unacceptable."

"Seriously," Fre huffed, "Why does everyone have to be so bloody large in this country?"

She thought about it for a moment before shaking her head, "Anyway, how has your week been? Any serious progress?"

Now it was Quintin's turn to roll his eyes, "Not really. My inheritance seems to have plateaued. Alfear has just kept me busy helping this city of fanatics."

"Well, that sounds fun. Did the status of divinity not suit you?" The sarcasm dripped off Fre's question.

"Not even remotely," Quintin said. "I swear if someone asks me to bless their dog or to come to the sanctuary, I'm going to lose it."

Fre chuckled at his pain, "I wonder if you jumped off a cliff if they would follow?"

"The scary thing is some of them probably would," Quintin yelled, "It's terrifying."

Fre nodded, "You should spend some time at the university. The crazy is diluted there."

Quintin shrugged. He hadn't considered the option.

"You just have to wonder about people sometimes. They believe some scary things."

Fre laughed, "This coming from the guy who believes in fairy tales."

"Hey," Quintin felt himself getting defensive. "There's history hidden in myths. Even the ones found in the church of Solus. I'm just not taking that possibility as far as they are."

"Sounds like an excuse to me," Fre said, unconvinced.

Quintin wasn't sure how he could convince her, so he simply dropped the matter.

"So, what do you think they're talking about?" Fre asked, gesturing to Alfear and Lian.

Quintin shrugged dismissively, "Nothing of interest. Maybe it even runs parallel to our conversation."

"They do like to talk about us, don't they?" Fre said, watching the pair in speculation.

Alfear turned around to face the pair, "Hey, you two, we're heading over to the university to sort out plans to shadow some scouts this week. Are you two okay staying here?"

He glanced between the pair, judging their reactions. Quintin shrugged before glancing at Fre, "I don't see any issue with that."

Fre nodded in agreement.

"Alright then," Alfear said, clasping his hands, "Tomorrow we'll start our weapons proficiency classes, but until then, enjoy the rest of today freely as you choose."

He turned to Lian, and the pair exited out the door. Quintin sighed as they left. He'd been hoping for some indoor study after days of walking the city. He looked over to Fre, who had tucked herself into her chair and was now busy reading.

"I guess that works, too." Quintin walked over to the bookshelf at the corner of the office, hands running across the leather spines as he read the titles. He had stopped on a large book. It had a wooden cover, unlike the others, and looked to be much older than the others.

Speeches and Poems from the Florize Kingdom

Quintin didn't know where Florize was, though it beat much of the other titles on the shelf. Sitting back in his chair, he cracked the first page and began to read.

* * * * * *

Quintin felt his body tremble as the wind seeped through his fur coat into his bones. The sun never seemed to rise this far north. Quintin's sense of time vanished what seemed like days ago, though he couldn't be sure. He blew into his hands, hoping to restore some warmth to his body. The university was just around the corner and he reminded himself he could warm up once there.

He broke into a jog, his muscles resisting the movement. Running through the cold air made him feel even colder. He consoled himself with the approaching rooftops of the university, Quintin spent most of the time in this city working with the Thean Guards, shadowing the professionals and helping where he could. It was a rather freeing experience. If only the citizens weren't such psychos.

Quintin figured he'd seen everything there was to see with the religious zealotry. He'd clearly been wrong. Quintin shivered as he yanked the university doors open. He didn't come here to get angry. He hadn't seen Fre all day and wanted to see if he could catch her at the infirmary. Quintin passed another city guard as he wandered the hall. The man gave him a small nod of acknowledgement as he passed. Quintin returned a wry smile as the man passed. Heavens, it's too cold outside. Quintin shook out his arms in a feeble attempt to rid them of the cold.

The layout of this university was an entirely different beast from the one in Isel. It had none of the vaulted ceilings or large windows, opting instead for a low squat design probably built to retain as much heat as possible. It also lacked any separate buildings. The entire complex linked through large hallways. It had its perks. It meant Quintin could get to the infirmary from the enforcers quarters without going outside. The air grew sterile as Quintin continued through the complex, the ever present smell of antiseptic hanging in the air. The infirmary was often a very relaxed place. Despite the ice on the street, injuries were uncommon unless the garrison had a recent skirmish with some of the tundra's fauna. Quintin glanced over the rows of beds trying to spot Fre from amongst the nurses.

"Can I help you with anything Angel-kin?" A nurse walked up beside Quintin looking over the beds as if to find what it was he was looking for.

"I'm looking for Fre," Quintin said clearing his throat, 'She's a fellow Angel-kin."

The woman nodded. "The Pale-blood is in the back,"

She gestured for Quintin to follow as she spoke, "We do most of our surgery work out of view of other patients."

Pale-blood, huh? Quintin found the term was used rather freely throughout the city. He'd even heard it whispered amongst the garrison. He followed the nurse to the back rooms. These were more specialized, with each room supplied with its own set of medical instruments. Quintin also noticed the implementation of doors on each room along with rather thick walls. A measure taken to prevent any noises from these rooms from disturbing the patients in the main hall no doubt. The nurse stopped at one of the rooms on the left.

"You've got a visitor," The nurse said, smiling awkwardly.

Quintin peeked into the room. Fre was busy sorting through medical equipment, rolling up bandages and storing various clamps and cutting implements. She glanced up at the sound of the nurse's voice, smiling as her eyes met Quintin's.

"Hey you," she said jovially, "I was beginning to wonder if you would stop by."

Quintin laughed wryly. "They've been keeping me rather busy around the city. I spent this afternoon helping store ammo at the armory."

"No kidding," Fre said, tucking away another box of equipment. "It's been a similar story over here. Never a dull moment, isn't that right Sheryl?"

The nurse nodded nervously, glancing between Fre and Quintin.

"That's good to hear," Quintin said, "Have you seen any progress since our last conversation?"

The room began to buzz as Fre activated her Resonance, a devilish smile plastered on Fre's face. "I wouldn't have imagined that surgery work could translate to something more practical, but look at this."

Fre unrolled the bandage and tossed it into the air. Quintin watched as it fell to the floor. His mind paused as it registered what exactly had happened. The length of cloth was now four pieces.

"What?" Quintin gaped, "when it was moving so fast?"

Fre's smile broadened further. "It's been remarkably easy to get the hang of it. Lian told me it just takes repetition for most heirs to figure out the limitations of their abilities."

"Well, he wasn't wrong," Quintin said. The cloth reminded him of his first experience with Fre's inheritance. He still had the scar from that day.

"So," Quintin continued, "Are you doing anything else today?"

Fre sighed, picking up the cut-up bandage from the table and placing them into a bin. *Heavens, I think she cut those into equal sizes.* Quintin shook himself gently back to attention, focusing on Fre.

"Unfortunately, I think we're going to be rather busy tonight," Fre said, "I've been told we have another scout group coming in tonight and we're supposed to do a checkup on all of them before they're ok to go about their lives."

Quintin pursed his lips in irritation. He understood the importance of her work, he just wished they could talk a little more.

"When do you need to be ready?" He asked.

Fre glanced at her pocket watch, and Quintin wondered where it came from.

"I've got maybe an hour before they arrive, Sheryl, is there anything else for us to do?" Fre glanced at the other nurse.

"I believe room seven still needs cleaning," Sheryl replied.

Fre shrugged helplessly. "Well then, we should probably get started on that."

She looked at Quintin with a smile. "Will I see you around?"

Quintin nodded.

"Good." Fre gave a slight nod to Quintin as she exited the room. Sheryl moved to follow after her. Quintin grabbed her arm, staring at her intently.

"Um sir?' Sheryl said confused, "is there something I can help you with?"

Quintin nodded. "That girl has a name. If you want to avoid my ire then you should all learn how to use it."

Sheryl gulped, nodding nervously.

"I'm glad you understand, " Quintin said, releasing her arm.

Sheryl gave one final nod of respect before shuffling off after Fre. Quintin stepped out of the room, walking back towards the armory. *If only I could convince everyone in this entire city as easily as that.* Quintin sighed. He was growing tired of this place. Fre at least seemed happy.

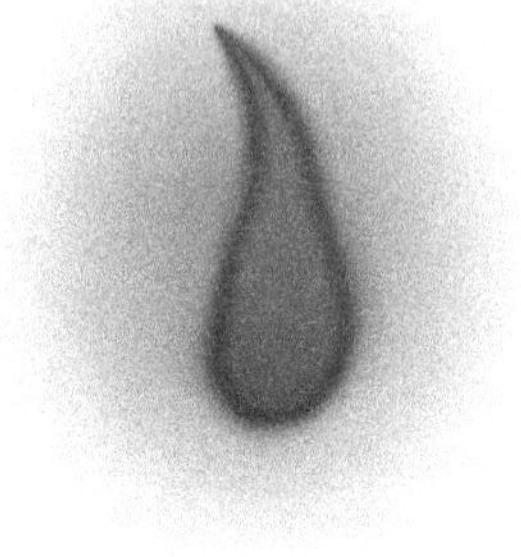

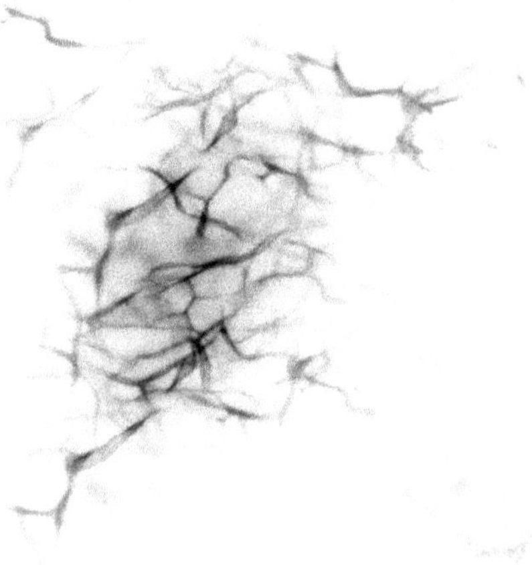

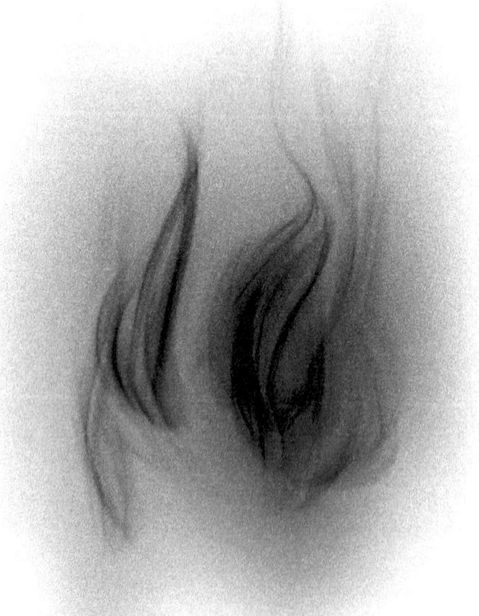

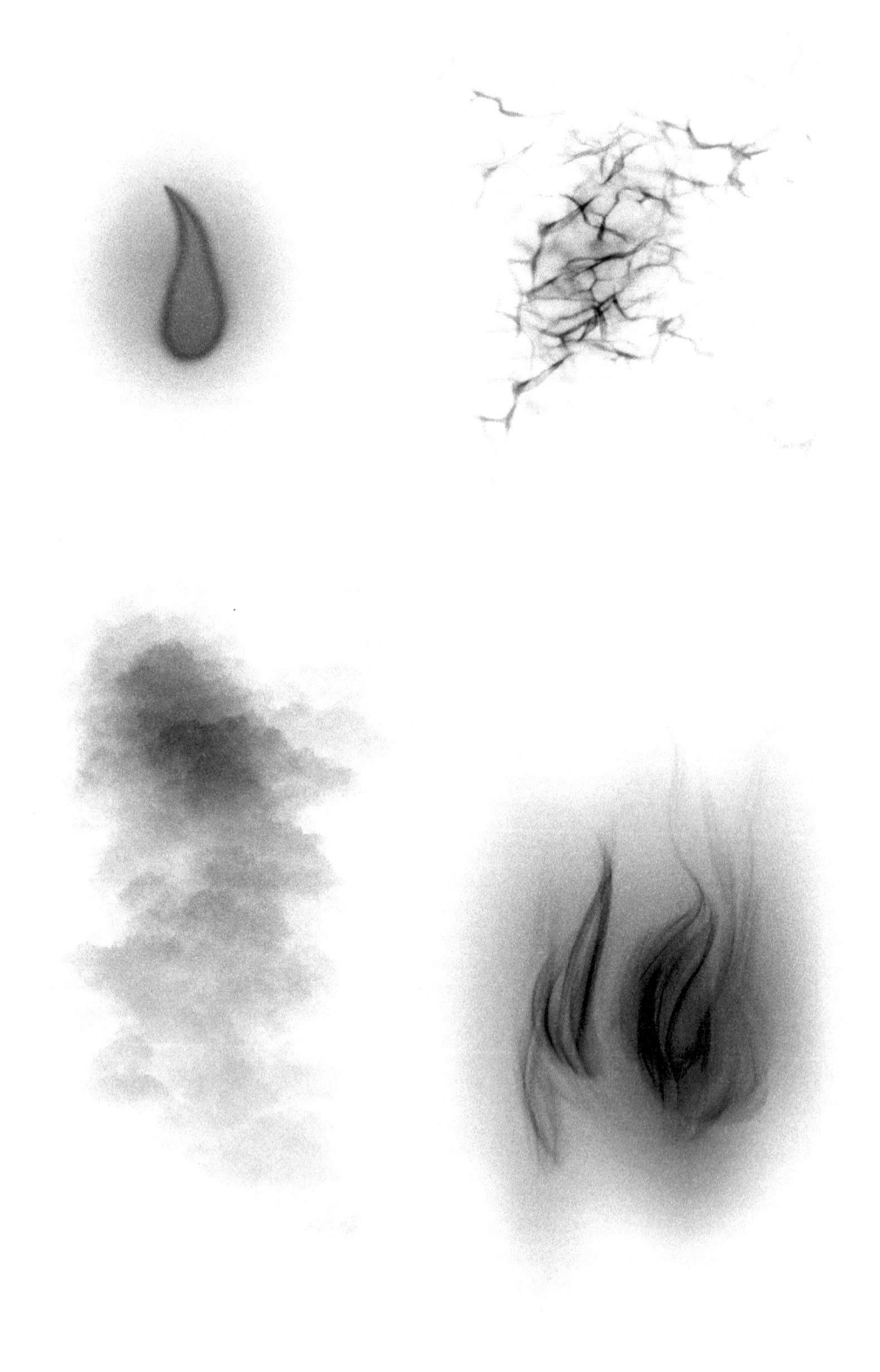

CHAPTER 31

Quintin took a deep breath as he looked down the rail of the crossbow. His finger twitched in anticipation. The shot would be perfect. He pulled the trigger, eyes closed and hands sweating, despite the winter air. The bolt rocketed through the air, lodging itself head deep into the wooden frame at the target.

He rolled his eyes. It wasn't even a proper ratchet bow, and he shouldn't be scared of it. Sighing, Quintin grabbed the string with his left hand, priming the weapon in one swift motion. The weapon had a remarkably light draw weight, only several hundred pounds, but getting a ratchet bow built to withstand the cold was too expensive to give a kid to use for target practice.

"Just remember to try to keep your eyes on the target," Alfear said as he adjusted Fre's stance.

"Both will overcome the issue through safe exposure, so keeping a mental note to keep them open is just to give you something to accomplish."

Quintin marveled at the man's words; his filter seemed to have fallen over more than usual.

Quintin tightened his grip as his eyes burned a hole in the center of the target.

"Easy there, Quintin. You aren't strangling it to death."

He ignored Alfear's suggestion, pulling the slack in close. The bolt flew from the rail, this time, Quintin caught a glimpse of its trajectory through squinted eyes. It buried itself into the bottom left of the circular target.

"You're too tense," Alfear admonished, "I can see every muscle in your body tighten. That will adjust where your arm is in space, throwing your aim off. But good job with the eyes."

Alfear turned to watch Fre, who had managed to land another bolt within the blue ring. Quintin set down the crossbow. He was sick of the daily torture routine. Did he really need to learn this? He seated himself under an overhang, taking a gulp of frigid water from his cylinder.

Day in and out, they had gone through dozens of military drills, combat training, and weapon proficiency. They had spent two total hours on science and history. Quintin had counted.

He pulled his coat tighter around himself as the wind moved through the courtyard. Quintin shuffled over to where Alfear stood.

"You're improving," Alfear said. "Before long, you'll be able to shoot at an average level."

Quintin shrugged indifferently. He wasn't planning to use this practice, but it was part of the program which he wanted to finish.

"That's all I need, right?" he asked Alfear, closing his cylinder and setting it to the side.

Alfear gave him a pat on the back, "Don't take it lightly. Someday you're going to need this."

His speech quieted as his eyes focused elsewhere. Quintin followed his gaze.

"Scouts?" Quintin asked as a group of soldiers dismounted and marched hurriedly toward the garrison.

He noted the urgency that they moved and looked up at Alfear, whose demeanor had completely shifted.

"Those horses are lathering," Alfear said, walking towards the courtyard.

Quintin watched him leave, confused.

"Where is he off to?" Fre asked, setting aside her crossbow and walking up to stand next to Quintin.

"I'm not sure. Some scouts came in, and he got nervous about something." Quintin watched the stable hands lead the horses away. The creatures seemed just as nervous.

"So," Quintin started.

"So? What was that about?" Fre asked as she took a sip from her cylinder.

They watched as a frantic crowd buzzed around the new arrivals. Quintin watched with narrowed eyes as he tried to make out what they were doing.

"Not sure," he said finally. "Alfear said something about the horses before storming off."

Bells began to ring out over the city. The heavy sound instinctively filled Quintin with a sense of dread. He looked to Fre, dumbfounded. She grimaced as the sound continued.

* * * * *

Alfear stormed into the gates garrison, pushing through curious soldiers and ignorant nurses as he made his way over to where the scouts were. The pair sat across from a man Alfear didn't recognize. He looked up as Alfear approached, face growing dark.

"What's going on here?" he asked, addressing the scouts.

"Well," the woman stuttered, glancing from Alfear to the man sitting across from her.

"Who has given you the right to march in here and ask questions?" the man said, glaring at Alfear.

He pulled out his badge, tossing the silver pin onto the table, "Alfear Bassan – from Isel's enforcers unit. Now, what has caused the panic?"

The woman looked to the man, who simply grumbled. She looked back to Alfear. "We're here to report some abnormal ancestral activity."

Her voice shook as she shivered uncontrollably, "We located it outside the twelfth outpost last night."

Her partner cut in. He was shaking almost as much as she was. "We need to evacuate the city now."

Alfear softened his demeanor, speaking evenly, "Why do we need to evacuate?"

The man's eyes grew wide. Alfear grew steely as he did so. Whatever they'd seen caused panic just to recall.

"We grouped up with outpost eight before coming here, and we sent up a flare, but we couldn't do anything." He stopped as tears came to his eyes.

The Garrison commander leaned forward, "Soldier, can you tell me where the others are? Outpost eight has up to fifty scouts. Did none of them come with you?"

The man didn't say anything, simply choosing to shake his head. The commander cursed, running his fingers through his hair. Alfear sat down, pursing his lips as he thought, "So you engaged the creature?"

The woman nodded, "Our Heirs engaged first. But I took several shots myself."

Alfear nodded solemnly, "It survived that, I presume?"

She nodded again, "I confirmed thirty direct hits from explosives and armor breaking rounds with no effect. My partner tried to hit him with Resonance. He didn't make it."

Alfear looked to the Garrison commander, "Can you sound the alarm? The city needs to evacuate now."

The man released a string of curses but nodded all the same. "I'll mobilize the guard. The citizens can be out in several hours."

Alfear gave a nod of gratitude before turning to the shaken pair, "Can I have your names?"

"That's Malta. I'm Dien," the man said.

"Ok. I'll be sure to have you taken care of." Alfear gave a knowing stare to the commander, who understood.

"Ok, you lot," the commander yelled to the crowd which had formed. "We've got a maximum level threat we need to alert the city and prepare for combat."

The room exploded with a clatter as the commander continued to hand orders to others. Alfear stepped away. He needed to find Lian and get the kids out of the city, walking out into the frozen air. He looked to where Quintin stood with a confused expression on his face.

"Shia, this has gone sour fast."

* * * * * *

Lian made his way down towards the gate. Bells boomed overhead as people stepped from their houses and shops, confused. Lian shared the sentiment, confused at what was happening to cause the ruckus. Soldiers filled the street as he neared the gate, all armed and looking scared.

Scanning over the crowds of people, Lian thanked Thea for making Alfear a head shorter than a giant. The big man stuck out like a tree in a wheat field. His instincts tingled a little as the pair met each other's gaze.

"This may be finally happening. After all these weeks." Lian didn't know what this was, just that it had tickled the back of his mind for months. Splitting the crowd, he waded over to Alfear.

Lian noticed Quintin and Fre standing next to him. "What's all this about? My nerves have been practically buzzing. Are we being invaded?"

Alfear shook his head, eyes steely, "Your instincts have it right. We're in a situation with a hostile ancestor. The city is primed to evacuate."

"Do the troops have the city protected?" Lian asked as he watched the soldiers begin to fill the streets.

"They are doing their best. They can get everyone out before this thing arrives, but actually dealing with the ancestor is another story." Alfear approached Lian, concern shadowing his face, "We need to get the kids out of the city. I need to know you'll stay with me until we're out."

Lian looked into Alfear's eyes. They were unwavering in their determination. Lian put his hand on Alfear's shoulder, "Don't worry. I know my priorities."

Alfear raised his eyebrows but said nothing in return.

* * * * * *

Quintin followed Alfear through the flooded streets. Men and women dragged children to wagons while soldiers held back the panicked masses. Alfear split the crowd, his tall figure covered in full lockplate, ensuring people gave a wide berth. Lian followed from the rear, ensuring the group didn't get separated. Wind began to move through the street. Screaming in Quintin's ear drowned out the sound of the crowd.

This feels like Armageddon, he thought.

He looked up at the university building, squinting as the wind continued.

"Funny how such a combination of events can make an environment feel hostile," he smirked a little at the thought.

Alfear pushed open the door, shoving himself inside. The halls felt eerily quiet. The sound of footfalls echoed throughout the stone corridor as they made their way to the office.

"Grab what you need," Alfear said, slamming the door open. "We're leaving the stuff at the inn. Lian, could you grab the weapons?"

Lian nodded sharply, continuing down the hall. Quintin grabbed his bag from its perch on one of the chairs, making a rudimentary attempt of scanning the rest of the room.

"The books will be left," Quintin sighed as he stared wistfully at the collections. So many original works were going to be lost.

He pulled his bag closed, turning and rushing behind Fre out the door. A rumbling echoed from the roof of the building as if a waterfall had been unleashed above them. The sound continued for a moment before ending in a crash. Alfear raised an eyebrow keeping his pace relentless. The group marched through the central plaza of the university, circling the central desk towards the armory.

"We'll take the east exit to the gate," Alfear said, holding open the door, "The Thean stables should be still open."

The pair followed him through the armory, passing the empty lockplate lockers and weapon racks.

This armory could supply a kingdom with enough hardware to challenge the empire, and they were evacuating?

"There you guys are," Lian said, appearing from the empty cases. "I have all our stuff."

Lian tossed Quintin his sword-breaker and handed Fre her glyph blade. He had donned his lockplate and carried his own sword at his side.

"Thanks," Alfear said, taking his sword from Lian. "These aren't objects we can afford to leave behind."

"Naturally," Lian said, smiling wryly. He turned to Quintin and Fre, "You two take up the rear. We're picking up our speed, so please keep up."

Quintin nodded in understanding. The group began running down the empty corridors. Quintin marveled at the speed of mobilization. They burst out of the side exit and began running toward the east gate. The roads were small and were adjacent to university housing. Alfear stormed ahead, following one of the larger streets.

Quintin watched as the silhouette of the exit gate grew closer. Thean workers bustled about the gatehouse, Seekers panicking as they loaded carts with supplies while enforcers maintained order in full lockplate, creating a wall of steel leading the scribes and speakers to their intended ride.

"We need to find the head of enforcement. He'll be able to find us a seat," Alfear said, turning to Lian. "We need to leave this city as soon as possible."

He seemed to pose a challenge with the word, looking Lian up and down critically.

"Of course," he said, brushing past. "Do you remember his name?"

Alfear puffed his cheeks out in irritation. "I believe it was Adin. I don't know, though."

"Well then, let me ask." He said as he marched over to one of the enforcers explaining the situation.

The enforcer waved his arm and pointed to a building. Lian saluted and marched back to the group. "He's in that inn over there. He's leaving soon, so we need to hurry."

The group walked into the darkened interior. The dining area had been cleared of tables with a group of soldiers standing around a single desk moved to the center of the room.

Alfear stepped up to the soldiers, "Hey, I need to talk to the head." He motioned his thumb over his shoulder to Quintin and Fre. "These two need to get out of the city the soonest available time."

"We're busy at the moment." One of the soldiers said, holding Alfear back. "Talk to the Seekers if you want to find them a seat."

Alfear brushed off the soldier's hand, peeling off his badge from his bracer and handing it to the soldier. "I hate pushing people around, but as an enforcer of the First Order of Isel, I demand to speak to the head."

The soldier glowered at the badge. "I'll see what he says."

He took the badge and retreated behind his comrades, leaving Alfear and Lian behind. Quintin looked up at the soldiers' faces hidden behind the helmets. He couldn't tell what they thought behind those tinted visors, but their body language was tense.

The previous soldier returned shortly, gesturing for them to follow. "The head said he'll hear you out, but make it quick; we're short on time."

Alfear nodded his assurance to the man. They followed the man behind the line of soldiers. Several men and women sat around a large desk with a large map on display across the desktop.

"Ira, I need you to move your artillery to the citadel square," a large man said, pointing to a section of the map, "See if you can hit the gatehouse from there."

The woman standing next to him nodded, "I'll see what my soldiers can do. We'll move to the ramparts if needed."

The woman saluted before departing. "Alright, who is next?"

The man looked around the desk Alfear stepped forward, meeting the man's gaze.

"Who are you?" the man asked, confused.

Alfear gave a small salute, "I'm a First Order Enforcer for Isel. My name is Alfear."

The head scratched his chin, looking at Alfear, "What's your concern? I have men to lead, so make it snappy."

"Sir," Alfear responded, "I have two Angel-kin with me in need of evacuation."

He shrugged, "Talk to the Seekers about transportation. Did you want some men? Go with Irwin and see if you and her can find some free troops to send."

He glanced over to Alfear, eyebrow raised. "Five guys sound good to you?"

Alfear nodded, "Thank you."

The head turned away immediately back to the people around the table.

"Alright, I need the third and first Infantry battalions on the rampart. Marza, Brigen, tell your men that they are to use resonant bolts only, clear?" The head gestured to the remaining commanders. "You all will be in the streets. Make sure to keep the caravans moving and clear of the action."

He looked around and took note of the ubiquitous nodding, "Good. Then clear out."

Alfear marched back to the door of the inn as the group disbanded. He checked over his shoulder for Quintin.

Alfear's eyes met Lian's as he approached. The golden-haired man looked dangerous, "I know that pained expression."

Lian was about to do something dumb. He stepped forward, meeting Alfear halfway. "We need to stay."

His voice was sharper than his gaze. Alfear groaned.

"Shia, Lian. You know we can't do that. You know this." His voice grew strained as he pleaded.

Lian shook his head, "I just overheard some of the soldiers. The Solus church has locked its doors and refuses to leave."

Alfear held up his hand. "We talked through this; the kids take priority. We can let the garrison deal with it."

Lian shook his head even more firmly, "The garrison left with the citizens of the city, along with most of the Thean force."

Alfear grew steely-eyed, jaws clenched. "We have a duty beyond our personal desires. Don't break that rule now."

Lian chuckled, "But duty lies beyond the Thean desires. Justice must be served."

Alfear grew hot in the face. He could feel his Resonance growing agitated. *They're a bunch of godless pagans. Justice burns them.* He wanted to yell that to Lian's face.

Alfear looked to Quintin and to Fre. The fear was plain on their faces.

What have you been saying this whole time? Alfear paused, his mind clearing. He sighed in resignation. Lian was right again.

"Shia, burn you man," Alfear said, looking at him.

Lian smiled, relief plain on his face, "Thank you."

Alfear grimaced. "Don't thank me yet. We still need to address this issue."

Lian nodded, running his gauntleted hands through his hair. "We need to get them out if possible. A freighter cart seems impossible to win, given the military's response."

Alfear nodded, "One of us should take the kids to the church. The others can try to assist the vanguard effort if needed."

Lian turned to Fre, "You okay with that?"

Fre froze, thinking intently. She nodded. Alfear glanced to Quintin. The boy nodded.

"Okay," Alfear said, clasping his hands. "You two follow me to the church. Lian, you'll catch up."

Lian nodded, "Send a sign when people start moving. I'll get out when they do."

Alfear reached out his hand. Lian paused before reciprocating.

"Step one?" Alfear asked.

Lian nodded, "Step one."

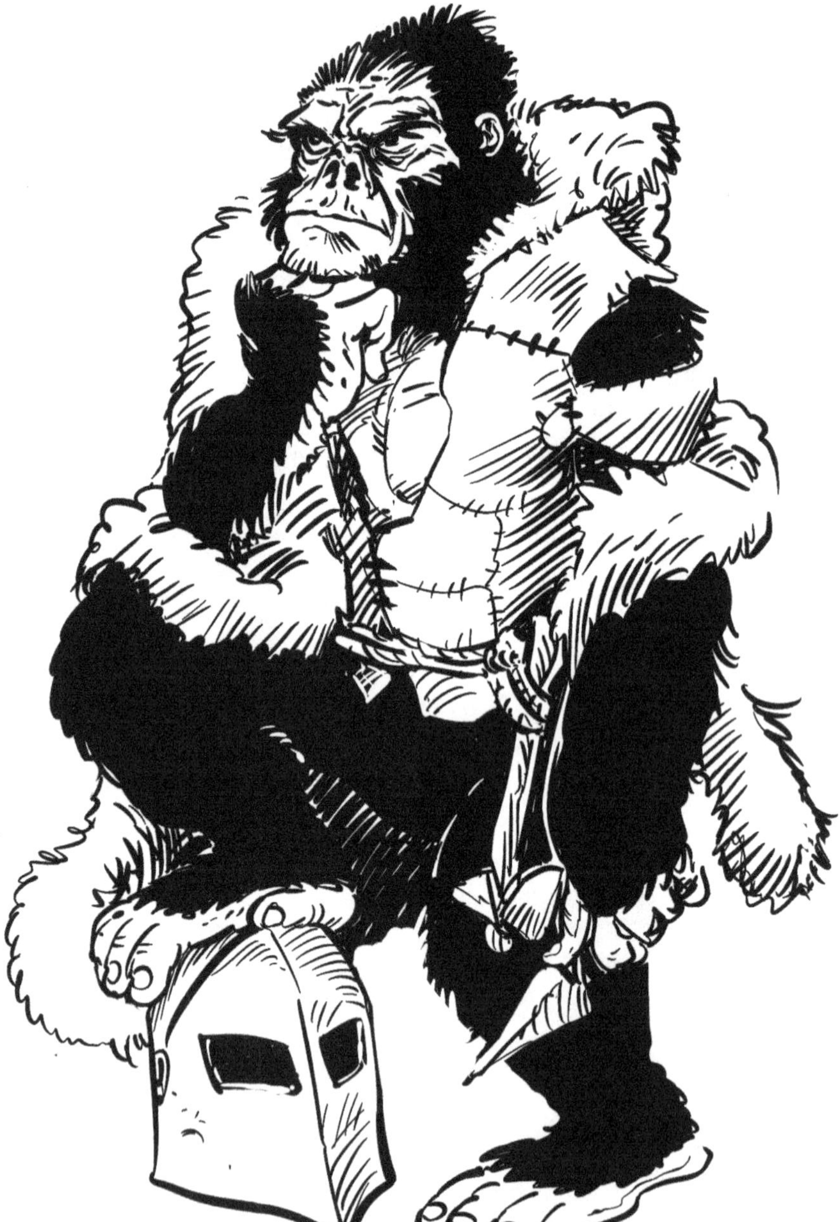

CHAPTER 32

Selyne sat, looking at the ceiling of her bedroom. The moonlight had faded hours ago, and the sun was just beginning to spread its rays out across the Everwood. She hadn't slept all evening, and now it was almost time to go. Pulling off the covers, Selyne went over to her wardrobe to get dressed, fumbling around the dark interior for the light.

Kalli said the research team left at dawn. I think I have a little time before they wake up.

After slipping on a traveler's dress over her shirt and trousers, she took a gulp of her water from the bedside pitcher. Selyne began to feel just a little more human. Selyne opened her window out into the foliage, the mild sunlight giving a comfortable glow easier on her eyes than the white glow of glyph lights.

Selyne grabbed her bag and scanned the room for everything she wanted to bring. This was only supposed to take two days out and two days back and would take up the majority of their stay in the city. Selyne slipped on her boots before stepping out of the door.

The city streets were silent, the buildings just dark masses down here where the sun didn't reach. Selyne noted several Seeker guards on patrol but not much else. The air had grown colder the farther north they had travelled, so much so that Selyne's nose burned with numbness as she breathed in the morning air. She looked up at the canopy. The urge to fly grew as the darkness of the forest floor grew in her mind.

The hum of Resonance buzzed around her as she prepared. The guards wouldn't appreciate the panic she was about to cause. Selyne smiled, *let them panic.*

The air twisted around her as the familiar feeling of pressure spread throughout her body. The task was far from simple, the balance constantly shifting and in need of adjustment, yet to Selyne, it was the one ability she hadn't needed to practice. All the hours with Alfear spent trying to throw objects or make them float when her greatest ability came freely.

Selyne floated upwards, careful to navigate the twisted branches as she reached the canopy roof. Sunlight began to peek through the cracks as the leaves grew less and less dense. Pushing aside a large branch, Selyne blinked as the sun's surface burned into her retinas. Selyne gasped quietly as she marveled at how much the view changed in the fifteen minutes spent on the ground. The morning mist caught the glory of the sun, sending a red and pink haze over the sea of dark green.

Selyne wasn't alone either. Wisps danced among flocks of birds through the trees and around the buildings which jutted up from the forest floor. Selyne couldn't help but smile to herself. She looked around for a branch she could sit on and watch the whole image unfold before her eyes. The sun continued its trek across the sky, and the building came to life. People opened their shutters, signifying the beginning of the day.

"What in Shia's name are you doing out there?"

Selyne jumped as the voice hit her from behind like a freighter cart. She turned, Resonance flaring subconsciously as she looked to locate the origin of the voice.

She looked to a building sticking up from the tree line about forty feet away from where she sat.

"Did you even sleep last night? You look like a nighttime terror," Kalli sat, leaning out her window, her eyes glowing with either irritation or shock. Selyne couldn't differentiate the two.

She chuckled wryly, "Sorry. The plans for today got to my head, and I just…"

Selyne pondered her predicament for a moment, "Didn't sleep?"

She shrugged. Kalli groaned, clutching the bridge of her nose as if she was dealing with a headache. "I'll be down in a minute."

Kalli finally said, "Just be down soon, ok?"

Selyne nodded in affirmation. Kalli didn't wait for any more of an answer as she turned away into her room. Selyne smiled as she watched her go.

"She really does sound like my mother."

A wisp floated by her face, and Selyne brushed it away. The sun had completely cleared the horizon, and the mist had begun to dissipate.

"I guess I should probably head down," she thought, "The sky has grown boring."

Stepping off her branch, Selyne began the complicated process of navigating the branches down to the forest floor. The temperature was chilly beneath the trees. Selyne shivered as she left the heat of the sun. People had begun to go about their daily routines, and several carts had already formed a caravan going out and deeper into the Everwood.

Selyne got more than a couple of hard glares from citizens as she floated down, though, at this point, Selyne simply tuned it out as white noise.

Coming to rest on the cobbled drive, Selyne began her scan of the road for her compatriots. It was a moment before Wil stepped out of their complex's door. Bag over his shoulder, and his cane in his right hand, his eyes met hers, and he changed course, walking over to her.

"I hear you didn't sleep last night?" he asked, looking her up and down.

Selyne laughed, "Yeah, the nerves got to me. Though I swear, I'm not tired."

He gave her a critical look, "Just be careful. I've stayed up for longer, so you shouldn't be in any danger now. But it's a habit that can hurt you if not cared for."

Selyne nodded. "On the bright side, no headache this morning. I'm feeling fully capable and ready for action."

Wil nodded, "Hence the anxiety."

Kalli stepped out of the building, catching the pair in her gaze and marching over, "I see you're both getting along."

She gave Selyne a glare but said nothing more.

"Yeah, sorry about that," Selyne said wryly, the woman's judgment making her uncomfortable.

Kalli waved a dismissive hand, "Don't worry too much about it. Honestly, having you awake now may be a blessing. Better early than late, right?"

Selyne chuckled awkwardly and nodded.

"So, Kalli," Wil said, gesturing toward the carts, "Which one is ours?"

The group turned their attention towards the fleet of carts sprawled about the area.

Kalli looked over them, "We're looking for cart number twenty-eight. It's the only cart going into the part of the Everwood you requested. Selyne looked over the fleet. Many had obvious numbers painted on their sides, but others were less overt.

Kalli called over a Seeker, "Hey you, could you tell us where coach twenty-eight would be?"

The man turned and gestured vaguely behind him. "All deep forest excursions are supplied by the building over there. You should find twenty-eight parked somewhere."

"Thank you," Kalli said, bowing slightly in gratitude. "We wouldn't have found it otherwise."

"Anytime," the man said before turning and walking away.

Kalli yawned, meandering towards where the man had pointed. Selyne stepped in behind her, gingerly trying to avoid Kalli's feet as the woman continued her agonizingly slow pace. Selyne tugged at her traveler's dress in irritation.

Why is she so slow? I'm the one who didn't sleep. She huffed her cheeks.

They came up to the row of carts, taking a minute longer than required. Kalli perked up a little, rubbing her hands together in anticipation.

"Okay, people. Let's find this cart."

Selyne began to work towards the other end, Wil shadowing her. Selyne stared at the carts.

"Do you know where the numbers are on these things?" she asked, scratching her head.

Wil took a once over of the cart in front of them and shook his head, "Not a clue."

Selyne pursed her lips. She glanced back at Wil, "I'll go low; you go high?"

Wil shrugged, "Works for me."

The pair began their search. Selyne checked around the wheels for any sign of a number. She stepped around the to the other side of the wagon. She stopped, staring at the golden number emblazoned on the side.

"Well, Shia, that's easy." Selyne almost laughed at the stupidity.

"Wil, I found it!" she yelled. Wil popped out of the cart's interior.

He followed her eyes, "Uh, well, okay then. On to the next one," he smirked.

"Hey, you two," Kalli yelled into the conversation, "Our ride is this way."

Selyne pivoted on her heels. Kalli started waving them down. Wil shrugged, hopping down from the cart.

"This is why we brought her, I guess."

Selyne smiled, "We're barely qualified for cart acquisition."

Wil waved his hand, "Of course, we have much more important things to do, like tasting the local booze."

Selyne glared at him, which only broadened his grin, "Let's go see what Kalli found."

She growled, and Wil continued smiling though he obliged Selyne's request. The pair found Kalli sitting on a red cart instructing several men with the bags they had prepared the night before.

"Watch how you hold that. The books in there are worth more than your yearly pay." Kalli yelled at one of the Seekers, who grumbled in compliance. Her eyes gleamed as she finally had something to do.

Selyne came to a standstill. Crossing her arms as she watched the woman oversee the project with an eagle's eye.

"She does like ordering people around," Wil mused.

Selyne nodded, "She'd wither away if she didn't have something to do."

She caught someone else in the corner of her eye. She nudged Wil, pointing, "He doesn't seem to be enjoying her tirade as much as we are."

Wil looked at the muscular man fidgeting as if looking for answers in his mind.

"Our caravan leader, no doubt." Wil mused.

Selyne looked at the man. He was now with the Seeker. He remained rather calm, given the situation.

"Should we go talk to him?" Selyne asked.

Wil scratched his chin, "Yeah."

"I imagine Kalli didn't explain herself." Selyne shrugged. "It's a noble thing, I'm sure."

Wil glared at Selyne, raising an eyebrow. Selyne ignored him, walking over to the flustered man. "Can we help you, sir? I'm Selyne. My escort is Wil."

The man eyed her as if his anxiety seemed to go away.

"Is that your researcher?" he gestured to Kalli as he spoke.

"Would you please excuse our companion?" Selyne smiled wryly, "Sometimes she gets overzealous."

The large man looked at Selyne for a moment, "Don't worry, it seems well intentioned. She's got my men working overtime, which they never do. Just make sure she doesn't interfere with our tasks on the road. We may be traveling together, but we aren't beholden to you."

Selyne nodded vigorously, "Of course. Could I get your name if we're to travel together?"

"I'm Seeker Ingrid," the large man said, holding out his hand.

Selyne took it tentatively. "Pleased to meet you, Ingrid. Could you tell me when you expect to get us out of here?"

Ingrid placed his hands on his hips, speculating over the Seekers packing the carts. "Given our current pace, I'd say we have another hour at most before departing."

He scratched his stubbly chin, "Yeah, I'd say that was about right."

Selyne gave him a slight bow, "Then I leave the rest up to you. I'll collect my companion if that's ok with you."

Ingrid chuckled, "You do that."

* * * * * *

Selyne moved over the Everwood's floor, stepping gingerly over the tangled roots as she found her way to the caravan. The undergrowth was sparse this deep into the Everwood, with nearly every inch of the ground covered in tree roots so thick that they'd begun to meld together.

It created a strange wooden surface that stretched for miles. Selyne stepped up to one of the carts, taking a seat on its step. She looked out into the forest, watching as swarms of lights flitted in lazy circles through the trees.

The appearance of wisps had only gotten more common as they'd travelled deeper into the Everwood. Selyne shivered as one flew particularly close by. *I don't care what Wil has to say; those things will never feel normal.* Selyne glanced around for Kalli. The surrounding forest was dotted with Seekers. Some were simply talking with one another, while others chased after the floating lights trying to document behavior or measure some phenomena.

"Where did she wander off to?" Selyne grumbled, pushing herself off the cart.

She passed by the other carts, checking each one as she passed. She found more Seekers busy with various scientific instruments, many of which Selyne didn't recognize. Selyne sighed. *Just how far could one woman wander?* Selyne walked past the wagons, making a circle.

"What are you up to?" Selyne turned towards the voice to find Wil leaning against a tree, chewing on a piece of jerky.

"Thank Thea, I found someone I recognized." Selyne gasped in relief. "I've been all over this place looking for Kalli, but she seemed to wander off somewhere.

Wil nodded, looking down in thought as he processed the problem. "My best guess is she is somewhere in the forest. I can't imagine she'd get lost in this camp."

Selyne looked out into the Everwood. A wisp zipped through the trees.

She shivered. "Do you think you could come with me? I really don't want to wander out there alone."

"I think following you is sort of my job," Wil said, standing up from his perch, "I don't think I'd see the light of day if your mother learned I let you go into the Everwood without supervision."

"Thank you," Selyne said, relieved. "So, where do we start?"

Wil glanced around for a minute. "I think our best luck is in that direction. Most Seekers are over there. Kalli may be absent-minded, but she's not stupid. She'll be careful to stay with a group this deep into the Everwood."

Selyne didn't object to the assessment. Following behind Wil, she walked towards the forest edge. They passed by a group of Seekers coming in the other direction.

"Excuse me, gentlemen," Wil said, waving the group down, "But have any of you seen Kalli?"

One of the Seekers gestured behind her with her thumb. "The noble is a dozen yards or so back looking at some wisps."

Wil gave a small bow of thanks. "We appreciate the help."

The lady shrugged before continuing to walk back to the caravan.

Wil turned to Selyne. "Looks like we found her."

The pair continued further into the overgrowth. Selyne stepped around a small sapling shooting up from one of the roots only to stumble into a puddle.

"This place somehow made a forest consisting of one tree into a nightmare worse than most hedgerows," Selyne grumbled, pulling her foot out of the water.

Thank Thea I decided to wear boots today.

Wil glanced back, making sure Selyne was okay. "The forest has to grow somehow. The Saplings which grow up are able to put down more roots which create more saplings and so on."

"I know how the Everwood works," Selyne said dryly, "trust me, Kalli wouldn't stop talking about it."

Wil laughed quietly. "Speak of the devil."

Selyne looked up to see Kalli seated beside a small sapling. Her notebook was resting on her arm as she watched a small glowing orb perched on one of the sapling's leaves. Selyne stepped quietly over to where the other woman was seated. Kalli gave her a quick glance before returning to her notebook.

The air around Kalli buzzed with Resonance. Selyne focused, trying to see the threads.

"What kind of Resonance is that?" She whispered.

"It's electrical Resonance," Kalli said plainly, "I've found that it's the frequency this wisp likes the most. The Resonance I can produce that he likes most, to be exact. His frequency is a little different."

"You called it he?" Selyne asked, "Does he have a name also?"

Kalli smiled at the question. "No, no name. I'm not sure why but wisps seem to carry themselves a certain way. This one just felt like a he."

Selyne looked at the strange little entity. She'd been told they were creatures made of pure Resonance, not unlike how many Seekers thought of an ancestor. She stared into the blue center of the glowing orb.

"It looks alien to me." Selyne sighed, "Though that doesn't seem to be the consensus with most people."

Kalli shrugged. "I hear a lot of people aren't comfortable around wisps or ancestors. Though most of them aren't Heirs, I think it has to do with the sharing of information. Take this wisp, for example…"

Sparks flew from Kalli's hands as she increased her Resonance. Selyne always forgot this woman could do that; she used it so rarely. The small orb grew agitated, shivering as the Resonance increased around it. The air grew still as Kalli stopped Resonating suddenly. The wisp stopped shaking and began floating lazily in the air.

"That's odd," Selyne said warily.

Kalli turned to her notebook. "I've been playing with this one all afternoon. I've tried several different frequencies and documented the wisps reaction to each."

She handed Selyne her notebook. Selyne glanced over the pages, trying her best to decipher Kalli's crooked script.

"So, how do you think this explains my hatred for wisps?" Selyne asked, thumbing through the pages, "it looks like you've just been tormenting a wisp for the past few hours judging from these notes."

"Hardly," Kalli said dismissively, "consider that this is Resonance travelling from one creature to another. If we then consider that Heirs are in some way related to these creatures, wouldn't it make sense that they could send signals to us?"

Selyne raised her eyebrows in skepticism. "I'm not so sure we're built like these things. We have a lot more fleshy parts to deal with."

Kalli rolled her eyes. "Of course, we don't interact on a biological level like we do with pets or animals, but what about a spiritual level?"

Selyne shook her head. "I don't know if that's the case, but hey, I'm also not an expert. Maybe run it by the Seekers and see what they think."

"They've said their part," Kalli said, "some of these notes are in fact theirs."

Selyne glanced down at the notebook again. The pages were crammed with words, many of which were hardly legible.

"Do all scientists have poor handwriting?" Selyne asked, "I can't distinguish your chicken scratch from the others."

Kalli chuckled. "It's rarely important who gets credit out here, though if you can figure out who wrote what, I'd be thoroughly impressed."

"Don't hold your breath," Selyne scoffed, glancing down at her watch. "Hey, would you like to grab some food here in a minute? I was meaning to ask you before I got distracted."

Kalli watched as the wisp she'd been studying floated up through the trees before disappearing in the foliage.

"I guess," she said, sighing, "I'm not really inclined to try and capture another wisp. Besides, it looks like the others aren't coming back anytime soon."

"Perfect!" Selyne exclaimed, "I hear the cook is preparing some fine travel rations just for us."

Kalli chortled, "They do spoil us, to be sure. I don't think I've ever eaten anything better before in my life."

Selyne laughed at the comment, the pair sharing a moment of joy. Even Wil cracked a small smile.

The camp was quiet when the group returned. Seekers sat around the cook fires, enjoying calm conversation over lunchtime. Selyne marveled at the behavior. She'd travelled with these people for several weeks now, and they never seemed to lose their silent aura. Selyne was pretty sure one could yell and have it sound like a whisper.

Wil looked for an empty spot by one of the cook fires, offering the seats to Selyne and Kalli as he stood.

"I'll stand if that's ok," Selyne said, "I'm too anxious to sit at the moment."

Wil shrugged as he took the seat for himself. Selyne was handed a plate full of reheated meat and grain porridge. She nodded thanks as she took the plate and wandered over to the edge of the campsite.

Selyne leaned up against a tree trunk, taking a bite of her food as she stared out into the Everwood. The conversation murmured behind her, but she only gave it half an ear.

The wisps darted close overhead, with several pausing in front of Selyne before zipping away into the forest. They seemed agitated by something, the last ones seeming to shiver with manic energy as they streaked across the forest floor.

Strange, I've never seen them act like that before. Selyne set aside her now empty plate. She stepped into the underbrush, her curiosity getting the better of her.

The forest floor was barren. The wisps had vanished entirely.

"Selyne!?" Wil yelled into the forest behind her. "Something is off. Are you okay?"

"I'm fine," Selyne yelled back, "something has spooked the wisps, though."

She began to turn back towards the camp when something moved in the corner of her eye. Selyne froze, turning her head to get a better look at what had caused the motion. Shadows obscured her vision. Selyne squinted desperately. Something was there; she just couldn't see it. Selyne's heart froze in fear. The shadow had begun to move, a pair of glowing eyes shining in the dark as the creature stared directly at her.

"Selyne?" Wil asked, walking toward where Selyne sat frozen.

The creature let out a blood-curdling shriek, its teeth flashing a brilliant white in the darkest of the Everwood. Selyne felt her Resonance flare as her survival instincts activated. The creature leapt at her, fangs bared. Air warped around it, throwing the large creature against a tree trunk. Selyne flared her Resonance, even more, the hum of energy growing painful. The creature tried standing, but its legs snapped as the air twisted them out of shape. Selyne watched the creature tumble in the air, crushed by the vortex of pressure she'd created. The shrieking stopped, and the animal fell to the ground, lifeless.

"By Shia, what happened?" Wil's voice came out steely as he stared at the lifeless creature.

Selyne gasped as her lungs drew in a shaky breath. It had all happened so suddenly. She hadn't processed what she'd just done.

"Ah Shia, that's a Rhinil." Wil turned to Selyne. "We have to get out of here quickly. We can't have any of the others coming."

As if on cue, the forest erupted in a cacophony of shrieks. Dread consumed Selyne's mind, and she felt her throat constrict as she panicked.

"Hey, snap out of it!" Wil said, grabbing her hands, "Right now is not the time to freeze."

Wil paused, his hand moving to his cane, turning towards the underbrush. Rhinil burst out from the collection of saplings. They loomed over Wil as they rushed forward, their arms reaching out to rip the man apart. Wil brought the hardwood stick up in an instant. Shattering the first Rhinil's arm, he shoved the creature to the side as he turned to face the second.

Selyne rushed forward as Wil fended off the second creature. She grasped his arm, flaring her Resonance.

"Hang on!" she shouted, the air billowing under the pair.

Wil barely had time to look behind him before they shot up into the air. Selyne felt the branches tearing at her arms and head as she shot through the forest canopy. She grimaced, the pressure pushing her upwards growing painful as it pulled at her. They broke through the canopy. Selyne's burst of energy threw them into the atmosphere. She looked down to see Will still clinging to her hand. Her Resonance faded as the threads she'd ignited grew still, and the pair began to fall towards the ground.

Shia, I forgot we needed to land. Selyne grimaced at the thought. She had plenty of Resonance in reserve. Her body, however, was reaching its limit. The forest canopy began to approach. Selyne took a deep breath, Resonance beginning to thrum painfully through her body, collecting air beneath her and Wil as they prepared to land.

Remember, keep it gentle. We have another person to get to the ground. Selyne pulled Wil close, watching the forest floor intently. The descent was slow, Selyne taking care to navigate the foliage.

"We should be in the clear," Selyne said, touching down on the forest floor.

Wil brushed himself down. "That was surprising. Are you feeling okay after taking off like that?"

"I feel ok," Selyne said, "I just need a moment to rest."

Selyne stumbled as her vision began to blur, the world spinning. "Maybe I could use a little…"

Selyne failed to finish her thought, her vision tunnelling as the edges grew dark. *It hurts;* Selyne groaned internally. Darkness fell on her consciousness.

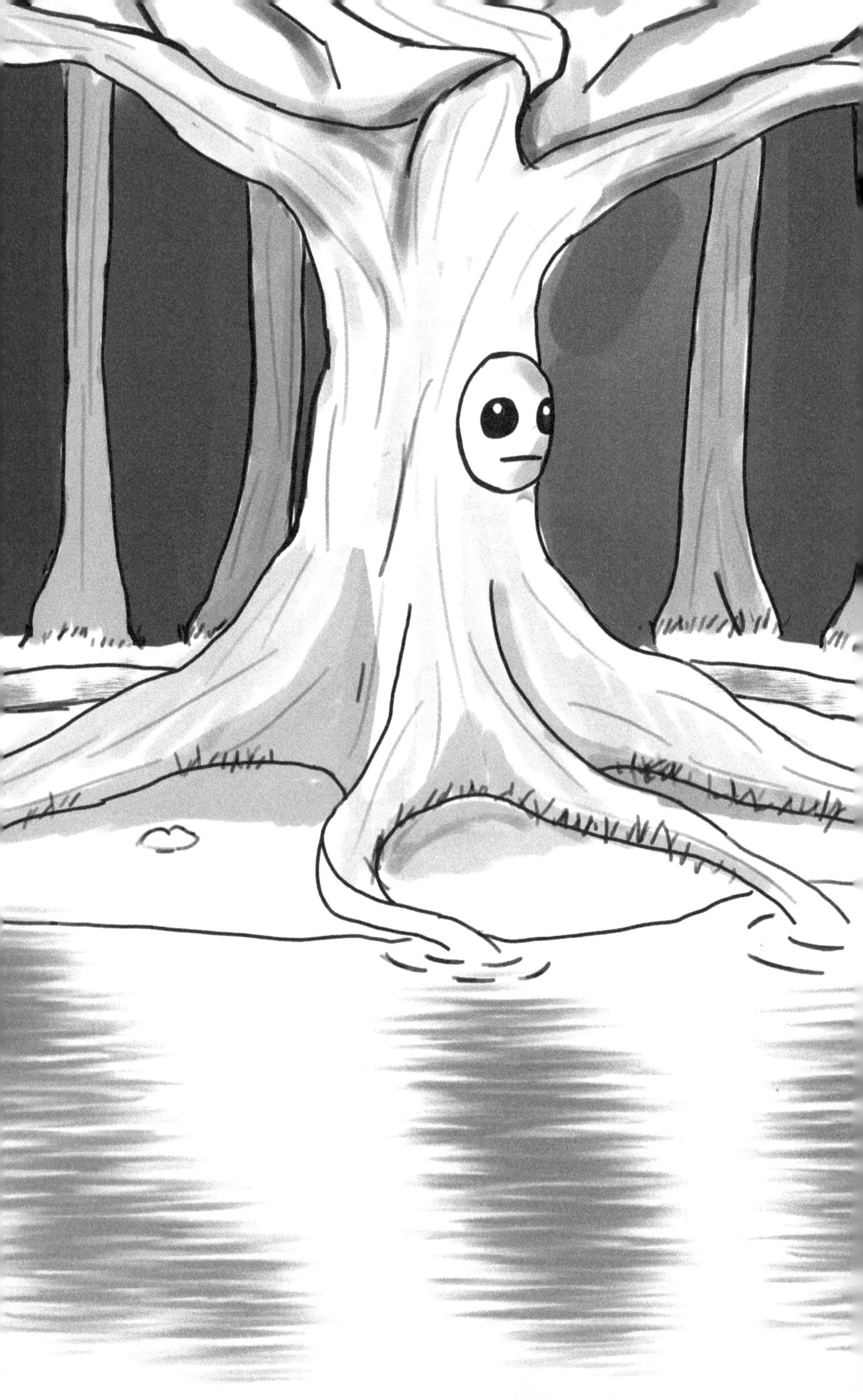

CHAPTER 33

Selyne coughed as she stood. Her head was pounding from the crash. Her vision hurt, and waves of pain moved through her as she tried to sit up.

"I think I'm okay," she thought, prodding her chest for any cracked ribs. Her arm was still sore where the Rhinil had tried to grab her, but otherwise, she seemed unharmed. "The question now is where did we land?"

Selyne recalled the screeching preceding the attack. She had panicked when it happened, throwing herself and Wil away from the conflict at dizzying speeds. Heaven only knew where she'd ended up.

She leaned back against the stump of an uprooted Everwood sprout. Rocks clattered next to her, followed by a fit of coughing. Wil stumbled out of the brush a moment later, his jacket torn from the Rhinil attack, but otherwise unscratched.

His eye met Selyne's, and a visible wave of relief washed over him. "Thank Thea, you're alright."

Wil walked over to her and knelt. "Do you have any cracked or broken bones? You carried us quite a way into the air."

Selyne shook her head, "I'm alright. Just a serious headache and bruised pride."

Wil nodded and sat beside her.

"Do you know where the caravan is?" she asked.

Wil shook his head, "I've looked several miles in each direction. There aren't any signs of others."

Selyne groaned, trying to determine how far she could have carried them – it could be miles, for all she knew.

"Alright, so we're alone. Do we know where the trail is?" she asked, though she knew what the answer would be. Wil looked up from where they fell and shook his head.

"There's a ridge that is something like five hundred feet in height. After that is just the Everwood. Clearly, we're very lost."

Selyne sighed, cradling her pounding head in her hands. "This isn't looking too good, is it?"

Wil didn't say anything, choosing to sit silently as Selyne mulled over her options.

"Well, waiting around for what caused this won't get us anywhere," Selyne said as she stood up, dusting off her dress. "What do you say to a walk?"

Selyne gestured to the forest in front of her, "It can't be that scary out there, right? Besides, I have you."

Wil chuckled at the statement but stood nevertheless. "It won't be a problem. Though we'll need to be careful, the Rhinil will be more active now."

His eyes scanned the dense foliage around them warily as he spoke.

Selyne shrugged. "Don't worry too much. If anything goes wrong, I can always fly us away again. Besides I trust you to deal with anything that I can't."

Wil nodded, "That may be the case, but how exactly do we intend to find the way back?"

Selyne paused, thinking as she surveyed their surroundings. She could fly them above the canopy, but with no metric to judge their position, searching for the caravan would be a shot in the dark.

Selyne looked up at the large ridge Wil had mentioned earlier. Everwood roots poked out from the embankment and seemed to stop.

"What exactly is this place?" she asked, looking at the sparse bower trees and rocky soil around her.

The ridgeline seemed to have protected the area from the ever expansion of the Everwood; its roots unwilling to take hold in the rocky soil.

Selyne looked to her left and her right. The rocky embankment seemed to curve inward on either side.

"Shia, this feels like a crater," Selyne said, awestruck.

Wil hopped over the rock, tilting his gaze toward the cliffside. "Could be. This place has a sense of otherworldliness."

Selyne shook her head. The sensation wasn't just in Wil's head. "The Resonance here seems agitated for some reason."

Selyne recalled the way she felt while entering the museum back in Hayka. The strange tension felt back there wasn't unlike what she felt now.

"Do you think it's dangerous?" Wil asked nervously.

Selyne shook her head. "It's not hostile. I kind of want to try and see what's causing it."

"Princess, I'm not sure now is the time to start looking for trouble," Wil said wryly. "Keep in mind we still have to figure out how to find the others before it gets dark."

Selyne ignored Wil's urge to let the issue go.

"This could be something big," Selyne said excitedly, "I wouldn't want to miss out on discovering something that no one else has."

She stepped over the rocky landscape, looking into the bower trees in front of her. The sensation seemed to grow stronger as she did. As if whatever was resonating so strongly wanted her to come and find it.

"Princess, this isn't a good idea." Wil's voice seemed to be pleading now.

"You don't have to come with me," Selyne said as she began to walk into the woods.

Wil grumbled for a moment before jogging to catch up to her.
Selyne looked at him, smiling, "So, you do care?"
Wil grimaced, glancing toward the forest. "It is my job."
"Well then, let's continue on," she said.

* * * * * *

The forest grew even more dense as the pair continued. Selyne pushed underneath a web of thorns hanging from the trees. Wil took up the rear as they walked. What Selyne had once felt as a tug on her mind was now a steel rope wrapped around her mind. She needed to be here. Wil had grown silent, perhaps sensing the oppressive atmosphere despite not having an inheritance.

Selyne paused a moment. They'd walked for hours now, and her legs were beginning to fail. She slumped onto a tree root and waved for Wil to stop.

"Let's rest a moment. We're almost there. I just need a few minutes."

Wil paused and sat down beside her, "It's a shame we didn't bring a water cylinder. You look like you could use some."

Selyne groaned, "And you look exactly like you did six miles ago."

Wil smiled, "That is why I am the bodyguard."

She stretched her legs as her muscles screamed. "This was a bad idea. Why do you let me do these things?"

Selyne grimaced as she pulled her legs in. Wil leaned back against the trunk of the tree, gazing off into the foliage.

"I feel like it's worth it. Don't you?" he asked.

Selyne winced, "Mostly, I feel like it hurts more often than not."

Wil smiled vaguely, "It's good for character, trust me."

He yawned as he spoke. Selyne rolled her eyes. Silence took the pair, and the sounds of the forest took their place.

It sounds happy here, Selyne thought. *The baggage of time doesn't affect this place like the Everwood.*

She noted that there was a lack of ancestors of any kind in the trees. Before she couldn't walk a hundred feet in the Everwood without seeing at least one wisp.

"Should we keep going?" Selyne asked, sitting forward.

Wil shrugged, "I'm waiting on you, princess. It depends if we want to reach our destination before it gets dark."

Selyne scowled, "How do you know how long this is going to take?"

"I've felt something for a few miles now. It's been getting oppressive recently."

Selyne stared at him in disbelief, "You've never once told me you have an inheritance. What can you do?"

Wil shook his head, holding up his hands. "It's not like that. You look at my records, and they'll show I never acquired an inheritance. I don't know why but this feeling is here, and it won't go away."

Selyne stared at him critically for a moment, "I think it's time for us to go."

Selyne pushed herself up. The ache of her joints had receded toward a manageable level. Wil tucked his legs under him and stood in one swift motion. The pair wandered further into the forest. Selyne was beginning to feel hungry. Her stomach clenched at the lack of food.

"Don't stop yet. We're almost there."

Selyne could feel the presence even greater than before. Selyne glanced to the sky. They had an hour of daylight left at most.

"Shia, what is this?" Wil's voice trailed behind Selyne.

"What's up?" She asked as she looked into the forest. "Oh…"

Her voice trailed off. The waning sun cast shadows over the forest.

"I presume roots aren't supposed to glow like that."

Wil shook his head, "I've yet to see anything like it. If not for the time of day, I'd have missed it completely."

Selyne crouched down, hand trembling as she reached to touch it. "Hello."

Selyne recoiled as the voice echoed through her head. "What in Shia's name was that?"

Wil tensed, "What is it?"

He reached instinctively for his cane. Selyne let out a shaky breath, regaining as much composure as possible.

"I think the roots just spoke to me."

Wil crouched down beside her and poked the root with a tree branch.

"Does it feel like what we're looking for?" he glanced up at Selyne.

She held her hand to her mouth, processing the shock, "Trees don't bloody talk!"

She shuddered at the thought. She regained control, steeling herself, placing her hands on her hips.

"Let's follow it," she said, forcing her strongest voice.

Wil shrugged, dusting off his pants as he stood. "I'll follow wherever you want to go."

Selyne stared at the glowing tendril leading deeper into the wooded area. She took a deep breath, "Let's go."

* * * * * *

Night extended over the forest, yet the light continued to grow. The tiny tendrils they had found earlier had grown considerably thicker. Selyne felt they should arrive at their destination soon. Wil stepped over the root gingerly. The moon seemed strangely indifferent to the alien situation. Selyne recalled that happened to many soldiers who spent long amounts of time on the battlefield.

They seemed to lose any sense of self-preservation as well as a strong sense of empathy. Selyne figured he wasn't too far from that. "You did see his record, and it's definitely the case."

Wil looked up at her as she averted her gaze, "What's the matter?"

Selyne looked back at him, "Nothing. Just reconsidering my choice of security."

Tremors rumbled throughout the forest. Dirt shifted beneath the pair as the massive tendril began to move. It began to approach Selyne, attempting to wrap around her. Wil reacted immediately, leaping onto solid ground. Selyne sprung into the sky with blinding speed, branches tearing at her arms as her inheritance screamed in panic.

The tendril followed her up but slowed its approach. Selyne looked back at where it hung motionless in midair.

"Shia, what exactly are you? What do you want?" Selyne yelled, glaring at the floating tendril.

"That wasn't a good form of introducing yourself." The voice hummed in the air. It seemed confused.

"So why are you now taking an interest in us?" Selyne panted as she tried to catch her heart racing in her chest.

The tendril swirled around as if trying to think of an answer. It approached Selyne. She pulled herself back. Building up pressure between her hands. "Don't do that. It's not helping."

She growled.

The tendril stopped, motionless. "Now what?"

Selyne released the power stored up in her hands, waiting. They sat there a minute or so – the impasse growing redundant. Selyne tensed as the tendril began to retreat back down. Selyne relented, staring intently as the thing went back down below the tree line.

"What?" Selyne let all the pressure out from her hands, letting the wind buffer her as she sat in the air. She released some of the pressure in the air, letting gravity take her downward slowly. The trees, now stripped of leaves from her panicked flight upwards.

At least it makes the descent easier, Selyne thought wryly.

Selyne descended, scanning the forest floor. "You have to be bloody joking."

Selyne's face flushed with anger at the image in front of her. Wil had seated himself on a spot farther inward, away from the initial contact area. The tendril had situated itself across his legs and seemed to be talking to him.

"What in Thea's name are you doing?" Selyne slammed into the ground, stomping over to Wil, fuming.

Wil looked up at her, jumping to his feet.

"Wait, Selyne, it wants to talk." He stood in front of her, barring her way. "I know what it wants."

Selyne growled, "You expect that to make me any less angry? Because it's not working."

Wil held up his hand in defense, "I'm not saying anything of the sort. Just don't try to kill him."

Selyne huffed, pushing past Wil. The tendril stood erect, pointed towards her.

"You had something to say?" Selyne grabbed the tendril.

"I apologize for scaring you. I lost your presence a little while ago. I guess I was excited to finally be able to speak to you."

The entity spoke with an accent Selyne couldn't place, but her gut told her it was probably more authentic than hers.

"Hell of a way for you to get excited. I thought you were going to kill me for a second."

Selyne watched as the tendril seemed to shiver. "God, no. I wouldn't dream of such a thing."

"So, you have something to say to me?" Selyne asked.

"Yes. So much." The entity rumbled. "If you and Wil would follow me, we have a lot to talk about."

Selyne shivered as the chill of night seeped through her bare skin. The forest had receded behind them, leaving her and Wil walking through a rock flat. The tendril remained motionless as they followed its path. Selyne noted it wasn't the only one of its kind, as other areas of the rocky terrain glowed with a similar bluish hue.

She looked down at where her feet were stepping. The stones seemed to be mostly obsidian, making the broken shards hazardous to step on.

"How does a place like this come to exist?" Selyne whispered under her breath.

Wil looked over the vast field of rock. "There are many places that don't make sense in this world. My guess is we're standing on a battlefield."

Selyne stepped onto a section of stone. Its surface was completely smooth. "This doesn't seem man-made, too unnatural." She gazed at the stone a moment before turning her attention back to walking.

Wil snorted at the sentiment, "You've never seen a determined Heir burn away a hundred men in an instant. Ask Alfear about it sometime. He's versed in heat-based combat."

Selyne's mind reeled at such a calloused and self-assured statement. "Well then…that's disturbing."

Wil shrugged, "Most wars are."

Selyne walked in silence, unsure of what to do.

"The stone is pretty, though."

To think that it likely formed during some forgotten conflict gave it a sense of sanctity. She felt like she should be there. Selyne paused momentarily as her eyes registered where exactly the entity was leading them. To what seemed to be the center of the glass flat. Here grew what seemed to be a tight group of trees in which the tendrils all came to a center. Selyne stepped up to the tree line, looking back at Wil, eyes raised.

Wil nodded, "We came this far. It would be stupid to turn back now."

Selyne didn't need any further encouragement. The tendril beneath her feet shivered, rising up to interact with her. Selyne raised her eyes, placing a hand on the large root-like tendril.

"What is it?" she asked, agitated.

The tendril seemed agitated as well, growing rigid. "Princess, I need to ask one of you to wait outside as I talk to the other."

Selyne placed her free hand on her side, "Why is that required?"

The tendril grew calmer. "I know a lot about you. Your companion too. Do you want to bring things up with him?"

Selyne crossed her arms before realizing she needed to maintain contact. "What do you know?"

She looked to Wil, who looked uninterested, which was fine with her.

"We could talk about all sorts of things," the creature hummed, "So many questions throughout your life. What do you want, Selyne?"

The entity spoke the words as if beckoning Selyne to give an answer. Selyne tensed, grinding her teeth. This wasn't an opportunity she wanted to pass up.

"I'll speak with you." She turned to Wil, "Can you wait here? I want to talk to this thing alone."

Wil paused, tossing aside the piece of obsidian he had been fidgeting with in his hands.

"Can you get out if needed?" his voice held a hardness he rarely used.

Selyne nodded, "I'll be sure to remove myself should the situation get dangerous."

Wil sat back, running his hand through his hair. "This isn't a safe situation – you get that, right?"

Selyne brushed off the comment with her hand, "I get that. But I want answers. That's why I'm here after all."

Wil hesitated as if halting what he was about to say. "I thought this was supposed to be a practice in the Seekers' life. Maybe a small hike in the woods."

"Excuses get you places." Selyne said, "Reality tends to scare people."

Wil raised an eyebrow, "Well then, just be sure to yell if you need help."

Selyne nodded, turning her attention back to the creature in the glass forest. She gestured to the tendril, "If you'll lead the way, we can get this over with."

The creature quivered before retracting into the glass columns. Selyne squeezed into the close corridors, the frigid stone taking bites out of what little warmth she had left. The discomfort didn't last long as she stumbled forward, feet splashing into a lake stretched out before her.

Selyne yelped, sinking knee-deep into the icy pool, sending ripples over the pristine surface.

"Shia, the water burns." Selyne ignited Resonance, pulling herself out of the water.

Selyne froze as her attention was caught by the creature in the center of the lake. Light glowed out from the tendrils, not unlike the ones Selyne had followed. Each one came together at a large tree-like trunk seated on a large obsidian pedestal in the center of the crater. Selyne floated gently over the water to the creature's body.

"Greetings Selyne," it hummed. "You've made a stir throughout the world. I'm so glad to finally have a chance to speak with you."

The voice echoed out from the center of the glowing body; it didn't seem to actually have any sort of mouth.

"You're the one causing disturbances in the Resonance here," Selyne said, landing on the obsidian island. "Would you mind telling me why?"

The creature began to writhe, the bark-like structure flowing like oil as a head appeared to come into view. It wasn't human. The face reminded Selyne of a lot of the masks used by the horse people in the northeast of the empire.

"I will explain everything here and now," the creature said, a faint glow emanating from its eyes and mouth as it spoke. "If you'll take a seat, we can begin."

"Let us start with names," the creature said, "I am Solus. Many treat me as a god. Some do not."

"Hold up," Selyne said incredulously, "What allows you to make such a claim? I've heard many of the older tales. Many claim the name of Solus, so why should I believe you?"

The creature, Solus, remained unchanged in either expression or demeanor. "You've been having dreams, correct? I can tell you why."

How on earth? Selyne's mind reeled at the offer, "How on earth do you know about that? I haven't told anyone about that."

The creature hummed, his light pulsing in what Selyne felt was a thoughtful way.

"There are many things that carry through the Resonance," Solus began. "Much in the same way information is stored in an inheritance and passed to the next generation, an Heirs emotions and thoughts carry through the threads as information which is picked up by entities like myself."

Solus paused in thought. "Who have you seen in your dreams?"

"Give me a moment here," Selyne begged, sitting down on the obsidian pedestal.

This was all too surreal. She'd wanted a journey of self-discovery, a chance for some fresh air. She hadn't asked for this.

She glanced up at the creature's mask, its expression unchanged. "I've been dreaming of Shia, though I didn't think it was anything more than my own nightmares."

She noticed Solus tense slightly before it responded, "She would be the one to try and communicate with you. That creature's whole goal is discord. Hopefully, she wasn't too hostile."

Selyne pinched the bridge of her nose. This whole thing was too much to comprehend at one time.

"How does someone enter your dreams?" Selyne asked, "That shouldn't be possible. How on earth does Resonance even store energy."

Selyne picked at the obsidian, tossing a flake into the water.

Solus's color shifted slightly. "You are an Angel-kin, that much I know based on the way the Resonance trembles around you. I could not explain to you how information is stored in the threads of Resonance. Just know that certain entities can tap into this information. Entities like myself, Shia, and even Angel-kin are such entities. Though as you are a human, sleep is the easiest time for you to receive this information."

Selyne mulled over the information. Something, Shia, had found her mind in the Resonance. It was absurd, but the way Solus explained it seemed so reasonable.

"So, you're telling me something sent me a message over the threads?" Selyne asked.

Solus hummed. "Yes, Shia, to be exact."

"Why hasn't anyone told me about this?" Selyne asked, "Alfear and Lian are Angel-kin, and I've never heard of anything like this."

Solus hummed. "Your connection to the threads is weak. Only your strongest ideas and emotions could be heard."

"So, I'm noisy?" Selyne said.

Solus hummed. "Relatively speaking, yes."

"Why didn't you try and speak to me? You would've been far better company than Shia."

Selyne saw Solus's lights flicker gently as if embarrassed.

"I do not have convictions strong enough to send out for people to hear." Solus said, "I merely listen and remember."

Selyne stood up, fanning out her dress in order to remove any obsidian flakes.

"Well, you have me here now," Selyne said, "mind telling me why you called?"

"I cannot," Solus said.

"What?" Selyne said in disbelief.

Solus seemed to grow agitated. "You called for me. I responded. Do you have a question to ask?"

Selyne couldn't believe it. After what she heard of Solus, she would have expected him to be more divine? Selyne held her head in her hands. What on earth was she supposed to do with this?

She sat there for a moment. Selyne didn't know what this creature knew or whether it was even telling the truth. However, if what it said was accurate, then it could offer some answers to Selyne's questions.

"Why has Shia been in my dreams," Selyne asked, "I get she's got a thing for chaos, but why me and not somebody else?"

Solus seemed happy at the question, his humming growing faster.

"That is difficult to explain," he said slowly, "Shia knows you're important and sees you cracking under pressure. I think she wants you destroyed before you can be a threat."

"Really," Selyne said, shocked, "I don't think she needed to do anything if she wanted me breaking under pressure. I was doing that just fine without her."

Solus hummed curiously. "Care to elaborate?"

Selyne sighed, the thought of the last few years of her life giving her pause.

"I'm not sure you'd understand, being a god or whatever." Selyne paused for a moment, trying to figure out her next words. "Have you ever wanted to stop being a God – to just detach from the world and become something less?"

"If I were to stop giving wisdom to the people who seek me, then what would I be?" Solus said as if to himself. "I feel my meaning would fade if I ever did something like that."

"So, am I meaningless if I step away from the purpose others decided I would accomplish?" Selyne asked bitterly, "Isn't that a twisted way of viewing your life?"

Solus grew dim as if disliking what Selyne had said.

"Your life is your own, I assure you," Solus said, "but wouldn't life be so much better if we could get control of it? You could dig your heels into the ground and try to change who you are, but understand you cannot deny the truth forever, and eventually, it will come for you."

Solus hummed excitedly. "Maybe if you accept who you are here and now, embrace reality. Then maybe you could work to become the best you possible, and your life wouldn't be one somebody else chose for you."

"That's not being in control, and it's just agreeing with the people who decide your life for you," Selyne groaned.

Solus seemed to shrug. "Maybe those people have control over your life because you've relinquished it. You are a princess and an Heir regardless of what you would want. No one decided that for you."

"So that's it then?" Selyne said, "I'm supposed to go back and accept it all?"

"I cannot make you choose," Solus said, "only tell you what I think is right. When you leave here, it will be your decision."

Solus watched Selyne, his eyes seeming to burrow into her through the mask.

"Do you think I can actually do this?" Selyne asked, "I'm not ready."

Solus hummed in approval. "I do not know. However, staying here won't help. If you want to figure that out, you'll have to go out there and see."

"Will I ever see you again?" she asked, looking into the creature's mask.

"No," Solus said.

"Then this is goodbye," Selyne said curtly, "I'll consider what you've said, but I'm not convinced."

She turned and floated away across the surface of the pool. "The steel arm of vengeance? I'll have to ask him about that."

The sun had begun to rise when Selyne stepped out of the strange crater. Wil sat where she'd left him earlier, tossing flakes of obsidian into the distance.

"Are you ready to go?" Selyne asked.

Wil turned around, smiling as he saw Selyne.

"Did you get what you wanted?" He asked.

Selyne shrugged. "We'll see. It was strange, to say the least."

Wil nodded, "Considering why we're here, that makes a lot of sense."

Selyne laughed gently. "Getting here is not something I want to replicate, though the way you bodied that Rhinil was something else."

Wil laughed wryly, running his fingers through his hair nervously. "It was uncomfortable for sure. Speaking of which, I think it's time we begin searching for the rest of the party. I can't imagine that attack went well."

"Of course!" Selyne exclaimed, "I'd almost forgotten. Heavens, they must be worried."

Wil stood up, tossing aside the pebbles in his hand. "Should we get moving?"

Selyne glanced up at the tree canopy.

"Come here," she said, beckoning Wil to her, "I'll fly us out of here."

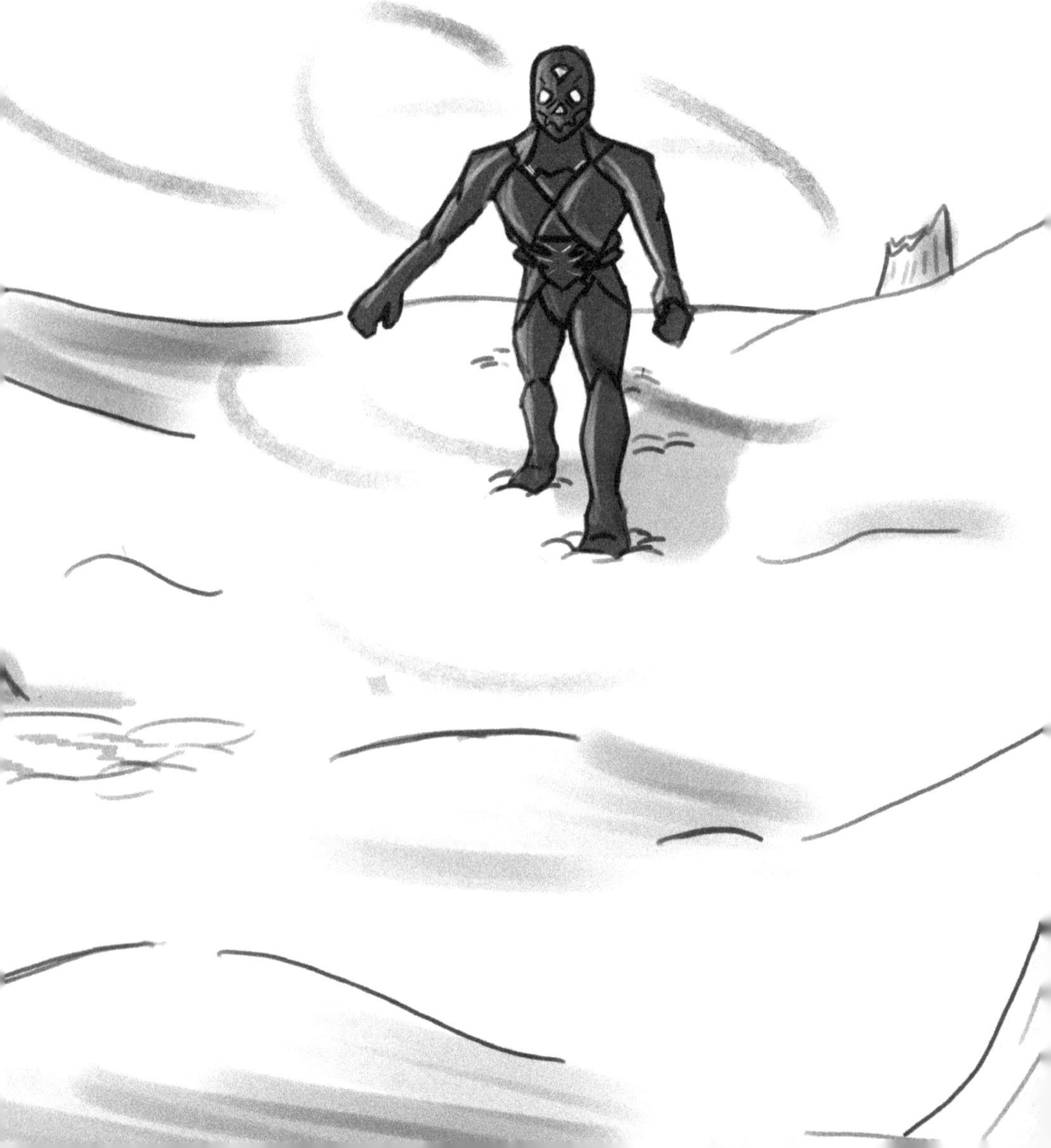

CHAPTER 34

The sky burned above the cardinal city as blazing cannons burned to life on the rooftops. Lian flinched as another cannon fired above him, followed by soldiers shouting orders frantically to reload it.

I need to find a way up there. Lian looked around for an entrance to any of the large buildings. No access existed on the streets, which made sense for a military complex that didn't want civilians knocking on their doors.

Lian decided to try one of the adjacent alleys, stepping out of the main street and into the cramped space. Water dripped from somewhere above him, ice cracking ominously as the heat continued to spread and grow. Lian splashed through puddles. There didn't seem to be any door inset on the wall.

Onto the next one. Lian turned the corner, coming face to face with an imperial soldier.

The man yelped, grasping for his sword, startled by the imposing figure in lockplate in front of him.

"Easy soldier," Lian called, raising a reassuring hand, "I'm with the hierarchal units, a Seeker."

"Oh, thank Thea!" the soldier exclaimed, registering the brass badge inlaid into Lian's armor. "What do you need, sir."

Lian glanced to the alley behind the soldier, "I'm looking for the one in charge of the city batteries. Do you know where I can find them?"

The soldier stepped back, gesturing down the alley, "Follow me, sir, I can get you to her."

Lian nodded his thanks, following the soldier down the alley. They reached a small building that jutted off the larger tower with several guards standing outside a heavy iron door, carrying full-length ratchet bows. The guards stood up straight, growing alert as Lian approached.

"Branson, why'd you leave your post?" one of the guards asked Lian's guide, "Who in Shia's realm did you bring with you?"

The man eyed Lian up and down, unfazed by the badge. Lian's guide, Branson, shuffled nervously.

"He's with the Thean Seekers. He wanted to talk to the colonel."

The guard paused, thinking. "What's the purpose of this request? Shouldn't you be on the ramparts?"

Lian nodded, "I'm going there shortly, but I need to address a flaw in the strategy you've been given. I really can't explain it here; it needs to go to the top."

The guard shrugged, probably knowing he couldn't stop Lian with his level of authority and power, "Branson will take you up. You won't miss the colonel, but Branson will know her face."

The guard moved out of Branson's way as he led Lian through the heavy door into the fortified building. They passed several other guardsmen as they reached the stairwell. The interior seemed to have the sole purpose of a munitions facility, with rooms stacked to the roof with lattice rods and extra cannon barrels.

There's enough ammunition here to supply a small war, Lian marveled at the preparations, *we're not even bordering contested territory. What is all this for?*

The sounds of explosions at the gatehouse answered Lian's question a moment later. *Hell is at our doorstep. Let's hope we can convince it to choose another day to seek vengeance.*

Lian stepped out onto the flat rooftop. Such a structure would be odd in a frozen city like this without the context of a dozen blaze cannons seated on its surface. Lian didn't know what kept the ice off the roof, but he could walk freely without fear of slipping. Branson pointed over to a group of people standing behind the spotters, clearly the ones in charge of the battery. Lian nodded his thanks to Branson.

The man, in turn, saluted, "May I return to my post?" he asked.

Lian saluted back, "Of course, don't let me keep you waiting."

Letting the young man go, Lian turned towards the group of officers. He singled out the woman with the braided cord attached to her uniform. Lian wasn't familiar with every insignia the empirical army used in their armed forces, but a more complicated setup usually indicated importance. The woman noticed Lian as he approached.

Kind of hard to miss, the only man in full lockplate is bound to attract eyes.

He gave a quick salute, which she acknowledged with her own. "What brings a Seeker here?" the colonel asked, "Hopefully, some good news for a change."

Lian smiled wryly and shook his head. "Unfortunately, ma'am, the situation at the gate is as bad as it seems."

The woman sighed, "Are we withdrawing then?"

"We still have time to turn this around," Lian said hopefully, "Tell me, what range are you firing at the moment?"

The colonel waved over another officer, he handed her the chart of numbers in his hand. "Currently, the target sits a mile and a half outside the city," she said, glancing over the data, "moving a pace of about four miles an hour, pretty slowly, honestly."

Lian nodded. *Probably an ancestor of a higher order. It probably needs to collect as much Resonance from the area as possible before continuing forward, perhaps explaining its lethargic speed.* Lian looked over to one of the spotters. "Any chance I could borrow a glass?"

The colonel turned to a spotter behind her. "Hadre! I need your glass for a second."

A younger woman looked up from her glass. She said something to her gunner before standing to answer the colonel's call. "You needed something, ma'am?"

"Yes, dear, your glass?" the colonel held out her hand.

Hadre fumbled with the strap of her glass, "Of course, give me a second."

She handed the colonel the tool. "Thank you. You'll have it back in a moment."

The colonel gestured to Lian to follow her to the edge. "Take a look."

Lian obliged, taking the tubular object, putting the lens to his eye. The landscape looked completely alien. Once covered in ice, the shattered trees stood like bones sticking up from a mist-covered terrain, like an image of Shia's realm on earth.

"Look to the right; the creature lies at the edge of the woods." the colonel pointed.

Lian adjusted his gaze, *"What on Thea's earth?"*

His heart burned with emotions he couldn't explain. The creature wasn't anything he'd seen before. Made of some form of black stone, with eyes glowing white. Its figure was vaguely humanoid, yet it was off, the proportion just different enough to set alarms off in Lian's head.

"It looks so alien," Lian pondered, *"but why does it feel so familiar?"*

The creature turned its gaze, staring at Lian. An iridescent light filled the glass's field of view as a cannon landed a blow on the creature. Lian stumbled back a little, taken aback.

"Are you okay, sir?" the colonel asked, concerned.

"Prepare to use your Heirs to power the cannons rods," Lian said with iron resolve, "I'm about to ignite all the Resonance for several miles, it'll render any lockplate or glyph based weapons unusable, but it will remove that thing's source of power."

He watched the colonel blanch at the prospect, "Thea above, you can do that?"

Lian nodded, "Prepare your soldiers for a cold engagement, and try to enjoy the light show."

* * * * * *

Quintin followed Alfear through the empty streets of the city.

"It's so quiet on this side," Fre said beside him, "Almost like the city has died."

Quintin shivered. He didn't like how well that she voiced his feelings. Their goal was the Solus temple. Fortunately, the religion liked to flex its wealth. Quintin could make out the spire of the building even here in the upper city, where structures reached dozens of feet high. Alfear turned down another side street. His mood had been sour during this entire trip, and he kept glancing back at Quintin and Fre.

It had bothered Quintin the entire time. Alfear seemed to have a hatred of many of the followers of Solus throughout the city, much of that Quintin could rationalize, *but to leave them here without aid?*

The sentiment seemed to go against everything Quintin had been schooled in these last few weeks. His thoughts were interrupted as the group turned out into a large courtyard. The temple stood several dozen feet above everything around it, its spires cut from the same dark stone as the city walls, a stark contrast to the greyish-white of the marble which built the majority of the building.

Alfear paused at the large iron door. "Are you two sure you're going to be okay in here? You may see something you don't wish to."

Quintin nodded in unison with Fre. Curiosity had taken both of them, fear only coming as an afterthought.

Alfear shrugged, "Then let's go. Fre stay close to me, and we'll try to get these people to leave as quickly as possible." He looked to Quintin, "I'm going to need you to search the back rooms. We don't want anyone left behind."

Quintin nodded, adrenaline rising. The door swung inward silently, the well-oiled hinges creating an unearthly notion as something so large moved so fluidly. Whispers came from the dark interior as citizens reacted to the foreign presence. Alfear stepped forward, causing excitement as people saw his lockplate.

"Have you come to save us?" a woman asked.

Alfear began addressing people as they closed in on him. Quintin used the opportunity, sliding to the edge of the pavilion.

Look for the back rooms, the area was dimly lit, small glass spheres lining the walls providing the only light. He found a door at the back. Giving the handle a shake confirmed its lock had been activated. Quintin didn't bother asking for help, activating his Resonance.

Immediately his vision shifted, the world becoming the swirling storm of energy. Touching the door, he found it didn't have any sort of silver lining. He didn't know why but that felt strange to him. He stepped into the room beyond, releasing his Resonance as he did so. He materialized into a hallway seemingly carved into the earth beneath the building, the walls lined with activated glyph lights. Sounds echoed in the darkness, Quintin barely discerning the forms of voices. Blood began to rush in his head as Quintin approached the area of noise.

He was met with yet another door, this one clearly lined with an inch of pure silver. *Do I knock?* Quintin took a tentative step forward, hand poised in front of the reflective surface.

"Louder," a voice said beyond the door, "I suspect we'll have to deal with that angel soon enough."

The voice was accompanied by another shortly. "We'll have to deal with the people upstairs, there's no guarantee we can protect them here."

"Don't worry," the first voice assured, "I'm sure one of the celestial fragments will show devotees such as us mercy in these end times."

Quintin knocked on the heavy door. The sound echoed throughout the close corridors, followed by a silence Quintin found uncomfortable.

"Sora, is that you?" the second voice called out.

"No, I don't know who that is," Quintin yelled as confidently as possible. "My fellow Angel-kin and I are here to get you out."

Mutters came from the other side, shocked and uncertain. The sound of bolts unlocking rang out, followed by the door swinging tentatively inward. Quintin was met with a dozen or so faces peeking out at him from the room. "How did you get here? Did one of the wards let you in?"

The large man stepped forward, taking a defensive stand in front of Quintin as he demanded an answer.

Quintin chuckled, "No, no, I simply let myself in. If you didn't want me here, you should've considered investing in more silver for your doors."

The large man brushed past Quintin, giving him a dangerous look before going to check the door. Quintin glanced awkwardly at the other people in the room, waving halfheartedly at the woman and children beyond.

"Shia below, there's not so much as a scratch." the large man returned, looking paler than before. "The door hasn't been tampered with; the boy seems to have walked through it."

The room burst out into a cacophony of chatter. Quintin noted several men and women dressed like the elders he'd seen walking throughout the city. *Are these people their families?*

One of the elders turned away from the group to address Quintin. "Which one are you, the spirit of deception, or perhaps connection?" the elder stepped forward, her eyes glowing in the glyph light.

Quintin didn't have a clue what she was talking about, "I'm not sure what you're talking about, but my teacher needs you to leave now. He can ensure your safety."

The woman shook her head, pointing to the interior of the room. "We cannot leave this place. Decades of research and collecting would be lost." She paused as if searching for words.

"Whether you leave here now or not won't decide the outcome of this place. We have Angel-kin putting their necks out in order to get you people to safety," Quintin continued, "My teacher has already begun moving the people outside to someplace safer."

The woman returned to her peers, the group discussing the matter in hushed voices. Quintin shook his hands out in agitation, glancing nervously about the room. The whole situation made him uncomfortable. *If only they could see how I do, my thoughts make more sense than the words coming from my mouth.*

"Will you be with us while we leave?" one of the elders asked, uncertainty clearly painted on his face.

Quintin nodded, "I'll be right behind you, and you'll have other Angel-kin waiting to escort you outside."

The elders glanced around at each other, judging each other's expressions.

The elder shrugged, "We'll see how it goes, but we will return at the earliest signs of insecurity."

A little paranoid, but I'll take it. Quintin gestured to the door, "Lead the way; I'm right behind you."

Lian arrived at the gates of the city, greeted by the frantic shouts of soldiers. Lian wiped his forehead as the heat continued to increase. He would need to deal with that as quickly as possible.

Time to finish a proper ignition; seems like the Heirs present haven't had much luck, Lian noted, the area was dotted with dozens of unstable threads, probably forming a circle around the target.

It was a basic tactic to try and stem the flow of Resonance being pulled by an ancestor, though it wasn't working in this situation. Lian climbed the ramparts, brushing past confused soldiers, pausing as he reached the top looking over the forest.

No time to waste, Lian began activating his reserves of Resonance. *I wish we had time to warn the infantry, but that thing is within spitting distance. Hopefully, they catch on.* The air began to thrum with power as the latent threads began to resonate with the frequency of Lian's own. He continued pushing, burning through more and more of his reserves as he spread his influence further. At that moment, Lian felt like a god, becoming aware of each particle his power touched, creating a picture of reality in its entirety within the mile or so he could reach.

The soldiers had grown silent, probably sensing something wrong about the air around them. The ancestor had also stopped, pausing its rampage to watch Lian. Arcs of electricity flew through the air as Lian struggled to maintain his influence over such a vast space.

Just a little longer; I need you to move just a little further. Lian pushed harder, half his reserves having vanished and the other half following close behind. He could let the threads go, they'd be expended as intended and leave the creature bereft of a constant source of energy, but Lian wouldn't leave this up to chance. The threads began to comply, slowly at first but growing in speed as Lian's ability began to overcome the initial inertia. More and more arcs of lightning flashed as the massive amount sought escape, though at this point, it didn't matter. Lian had it moving too fast for any sudden change in direction.

Lian came back to himself, his awareness growing smaller as the power grew and condensed in front of him. He met the creature's inhuman gaze, his gaze unwavering as he focused his power on that one image.

The ancestor began to break into a sprint, no longer concerned with collecting power, racing along a beeline towards Lian. *Nice try,* Lian thought, *but it's time for you to burn in the light of justice.*

He could see all the threads he'd collected, focused into a single line, in reality, placed directly over the creature's head. Lian let go of his control, releasing the power as if from the rail of a rachet bow. Light split across the sky, the sun paling in comparison as the bolt struck its target. Lian winced as the wave of concussive force struck him on the ramparts, deafening him. He noted several soldiers falling over beside him.

I probably should have warned about the light, Lian noted as he saw the other soldiers reel at the loss of their vision. Lian ignored them for the moment. He needed to ensure the job was done. His tinted visor had spared his vision, though the darkened glass now made it difficult to distinguish shapes amongst the roiling clouds of dust on the field.

He had looked in the eyes of this thing and felt the same connection that bound him and Alfear. He would know if it ever died.

"So good to see you again, son of justice. Are you going to stand in my way today." the voice came out of the clouds of dust, though Lian felt like it was speaking in his mind.

"I don't know you," Lian said, "though if you come for these people, I will stop you."

"Protecting pagans even to this day," the ancestor said, amused, "some things don't change, I see."

The creature appeared from out of the dust, stepping up to the city wall, a smile clear on its inhuman face. "I'm not stopping," the ancestor said, opening its arms in invitation, "So let's settle this now so I can move on with my job."

Lian leaped off the ramparts, steel boots sinking into the muddy earth. He pulled on what little ability he had left inside, activating his inheritance.

"We're both working on residual power," Lian said, drawing his sword and taking a stance, "Let's try to keep this civil."

The creature smiled and rushed forward towards Lian, the light of Shia glowing in its eyes.

* * * * * *

Quintin sat back as the elders tried their best to usher out their families from the large safe rooms. Quintin had only found one of many safe rooms down here in the tunnels, and the elders were taking their time with moving everyone upstairs.

Quintin blew air into his cheeks as he looked about the room for anything to occupy his mind. The place was loaded with jars of food to last a few months, along with the various eating utensils and seating options. It made for an unremarkable place to be. His fingers caught something as he leaned back on one of the tables. Quintin pulled his weight away as he turned to see what he'd touched.

Hello, what are you doing here? A book set on the table, pages open to the world. Quintin picked it up, noting its weight. He flipped to the cover taking his time to read the old Thean – *inheritance, The Origin of Mankind's Divinity.* Quintin raised an eyebrow, his curiosity growing; this wasn't someone's cookbook.

Quintin glanced around to make sure nobody was watching. Clearing the room, he activated his inheritance, and the book became incorporeal to the rest of the world in an instant. Moving carefully, Quintin placed the now unreal book onto his back.

Let's hope Kalli is correct about this. If she wasn't, he'd have some explaining to do. Quintin let out a sigh of relief as the book remained in place and he moved his hand away. Hopefully, it would stay there until he wanted it later. The lines of people began to move, and Quintin gladly stepped in line. The book felt integral to the beliefs these people had; perhaps reading it would give Quintin some insight into what was going on between Alfear and Lian.

* * * * * *

The ancestor slammed into Lian with the force of a thousand hemasti, moving faster than any normal man as it threw Lian backward. His lockplate was the only thing saving Lian from having his chest cave in, and his limbs pulled out of their sockets, the armor flaring the current running through it, creating an unbreakable bond between each piece of steel. Lian timed his movements perfectly, moving as soon as the current normalized, bringing his blade down on the forearm of his adversary.

His arms shuddered as steel slammed into solid stone, chips of obsidian flying in every direction as the weapon bit into the creature's skin. The ancestor didn't waste any time with his retaliation, bringing his other arm forward for another strike.

Neither of us is willing to use our reserves first. Lian grimaced as another hit landed on his chest, this one less forceful than the last. It was a painful truth during a conflict between Heirs, but generally, it was the one who struck first who lost, often leading Heirs to risk a fistfight rather than suffer the guaranteed failure of losing the advantage of Resonance. Lian couldn't wait for this ancestor to strike first. Pouring Resonance into his sword, Lian brought the weapon in for another strike. The blade crackled with electricity, glyphs coming to life along its edge.

Lian pushed for a central attack, aiming for the torso in hopes of shattering the consciousness along with the body. Ducking beneath another strike, Lian brought the sword upwards, driving the tip of his weapon into the ancestor's chest. He felt steel crack along his back as his enemy's hands overwhelmed the glyphs holding the lockplate together. Lian ignored the preceding pain, driving his weapon further into the creature's stone skin.

He smiled as he saw the ancestor's eyes harden with anger as Lian's blade released the energy stored in its lattice. The ancestor flew backward, arcs of plasma propelling him into the muddy ground. Lian pushed the advantage, grimacing as he felt something give in his back. The ancestor stood up, legs skating as it righted itself. Obsidian skin fell off in shards from its chest, though Lian could see the damage wouldn't last long.

Lian clutched the angel's heart. It had grown warmer against his chest. *Maybe it's time to let go; take me in, and it will assure victory.*

Lian recognized the voice in his head, like an extra conscience talking alongside his own. *Not yet,* was the reply, *not yet.*

The ancestor came towards Lian again, eyes glowing brighter than before. Lian positioned himself carefully, hiding the exposed portions on his back, preparing his aching body for the next assault.

* * * * *

Quintin stepped out into the courtyard surrounding the large church. The atmosphere seemed dead around him as if the threads had gone silent in the world. The cold had also begun returning. Quintin found Alfear standing at the front of the large group. Fre stood behind him, seeming more guarded than usual.

Quintin approached the pair. "What's our plan from here?" he asked, looking at Alfear, "There are well over a hundred people with us."

"I've talked to the Elders, and they are getting things organized." Alfear surveyed the crowd as if ensuring what he said was true. "If only we had some wagons. Lian really didn't think this through."

The crack of electricity traveled up from the gatehouse as if contesting Alfear's judgment. Quintin almost smiled as Alfear rolled his eyes at the coincidence.

"Hey, you!" Alfear yelled, grabbing a passing elder, "What's the situation? Will we be getting out of here on time?"

The younger man reeled at Alfear's looming form, "We're trying to find wagons, sir. We'll let let you know when we've got the members ready to leave."

Alfear let go of the man, and he scuttled away. "Shia, this is cutting it close."

For once, Quintin agreed with how he spoke. This whole situation hadn't been thought through. Another crack came from the gatehouse, sounding more metallic than the last.

"Is he going to be ok?" Quintin asked worriedly.

Alfear glanced up at the sky as if looking for something. "He's ignited the atmosphere, which will help subdue the creature, but he can't have much juice left himself."

He wistfully glanced over towards where the fight was taking place.

"Are you going to join him?" Fre asked, interjecting into the conversation.

Alfear paused, then shook his head, "He's ignored you both in favor of other responsibilities. He has the freedom to do so, but for me to leave would be a failure for both of us."

"Seems likes you primed yourself to fail, safety for everyone?" Fre said, confused, "Seems you should shrink your horizons."

Alfear chuckled wryly, "You say that, but with the power I have, it's impossible to abandon people I know will be hurt or even killed without me."

Fre raised an eyebrow, "Even these people?" she asked, glancing skeptically at the masses of people in front of them.

"Especially them," Alfear said.

"Why?" Quintin asked; he still didn't have a serviceable answer.

"Don't grab the head of a mad serpent; better to let it swallow its tail than risk its venom."

Alfear paused for Quintin's next question, holding up a hand as the man from earlier approached.

"Do we have good news?" Alfear asked.

The man nodded, "The elders found some wagons left by the commanding lord of the fort. There are enough to move everyone, especially if the younger men and women walk."

Alfear gave the man a bow in respect, "Thank you for the information. Have people started loading?"

The man nodded, "The elders are organizing everything now; they should be leaving soon."

Alfear glanced to Quintin, "I'm going to make sure they don't mess this up. You stay with Fre, and I'll be back soon."

* * * * * *

Lian stumbled as he stood up once more. Bones creaked in protest, his armor failing to protect them from the last barrage. He spat out a molar, wiping the blood off his face. His opponent didn't share the pain. The ancestor had slowed in its regeneration of material. Its reserves wore down by the artillery barrages and Lian's attacks.

However, Lian wasn't going to last. His last pauldron fell free as he stood straight, its glyphs strained beyond their stress threshold. It was only his chest plate protecting him, which wasn't effective without the other components to disperse the force.

"You ready to finish this?" the ancestor asked, walking lightly across the muddy field.

A bolt smashed into the ancestor's head, molten Resonance burrowing into his face as another blaze cannon struck true. The creature barely slowed its gait, its head reforming moments later.

"Can I get your name?" Lian asked, wincing at the pain speaking brought.

The creature laughed, "If you don't remember, then it isn't worth your time."

The creature swung, and Lian produced an arc of plasma in defense. The flash of light was blinding without his tinted visor, and the noise deafened. The ancestor flew backward from the blast.

You don't have many of those left, Lian's other conscious said, sounding worried. *The cannons will take care of him, watch.*

Lian tried to assure it, though he didn't entirely believe it. Another volley came down from the city, scorching everything around the ancestor's feet. Lian turned away, shielding his eyes from more damage.

"Those accursed abominations," the creature growled.

Lian turned and sprinted towards the woods.

The air grew hotter around him, steam rising off the ground as melted snow evaporated. Lian just had time to duck behind a fallen tree before the creature unleashed its fury. It was the first resonant attack the creature had unleashed. Earth melted like wax, the air burning red with heat as the ancestor unleashed a wave of heat towards the city walls. Lian grimaced as soldiers reeled from the blast, falling from the ramparts. The silver ore stone glowed a brilliant white as it melted and warped. *Heaven protect them.*

Lian couldn't see if the wave had hit the artillery batteries. He could only hope the walls had stopped most of the energy. The creature let out a sigh as if relieved.

It turned back to Lian, "Shall we finish this?"

Lian groaned, leaping over the fallen tree. He'd lost his sword in the last confrontation, a pity. He could really use the silver. *It's time. Let me go.* Lian winced, shaking his head.

The ancestor moved in for yet another strike. Its jagged hand came forward, seeming lethargic compared to its earlier attacks. Lian let the hand move past his shoulder, coming up and grabbing the creature's wrist, he poured another charge into the creature's body. The ancestor's arm exploded, obsidian flecks tearing into Lian's arm and face.

The creature stumbled backward, and it seemed to actually be hurt. The ancestor stared down at its jagged stump, the stone taking much longer to reform than before. Lian smiled, adrenaline masking his pain. This thing would break.

"I suppose I need to end this," the creature hissed, forearm now mostly reformed.

Trees burst into flames as the air began to heat up again. The creature's fury was concentrated wholly on Lian, the murder intent on its inhuman face.

You can't stop this, please, let me go. Lian looked down, finally acknowledging his tattered arm.

If this doesn't work, we'll both be gone. Lian felt affirmation come from the other voice.

The ancestor released its reserves, another wave of fiery death rolling towards Lian. Lian leaped forward; his entire resonant reserve transferred into his hands and arms. His body began to absorb some of the heatwaves, the metals in his body absorbing the energy, but it wouldn't last long. A wave of energy this big would need a lot of extra power, forcing it into such a small direction.

If Lian could stop this creature soon, he might just survive. Tearing the buckles on his gambeson, Lian reached for the necklace around his neck. His hands touched something cold, and he yanked it out, snapping the silver bands. In his hands sat a single dimly glowing stone encased in a silver cage. Lian grew ill, staring at the angel's heart in his hand.

It's okay. I will still be here, just a little fractured. The voice didn't reassure him. *I'm more scared that I'll never be rid of you. My vow will never be broken. I am the heart of justice, and my word will not be broken.*

Lian didn't have any more time to argue with the voice in his head. He came upon the ancestor, blistered fists crackling with the fire of divine judgment. Lian had a moment of satisfaction looking at the shocked expression on the ancestor's stone face. His fist contacted the creature's skin, and it exploded. Every last ounce of power left in Lian's body traveled through the creature, breaking apart the stone. Lian released the heart as his hand entered the middle of the ancestor's torso. He gave the creature one shove before everything went dark.

* * * * * *

Quintin peeked out from his hiding place behind one of the carts. He'd been shielded from the blast of heat; others hadn't been so lucky. The first dozen wagons sat in flames in front of them, and thankfully their occupants had managed to escape with minimal burns. Quintin looked over at Alfear, hoping for answers.

"The gatehouse has gone silent," Alfear said, concern plain on his face.

"The cannons have stopped as well," Quintin noted.

Alfear nodded, turning to Quintin. "I'm going to try and find the battery commander. You make sure these people are safe."

He looked at Fre and Quintin, respectively, as he spoke. They nodded, and the big man walked down the road in search of someone in charge.

"It's eerie, isn't it," Fre said, looking to the abandoned buildings, "everything has gone so quiet."

Quintin followed her gaze, taking in the empty streets. Excluding the slight crackle of burning wood, everything was silent.

"I don't know why everyone else is keeping silent," Quintin said, looking to the citizens huddled in the wagons.

"It's like they don't want to wake the conflict up," Fre said ponderously.

Quintin shrugged. He found it confusing. Minutes passed, Quintin scribbling notes into his journal. His mind drifted to the book on his back. It had stayed incorporeal throughout their ride through the city, staying firmly where he'd placed it. *Make a note to look at that later.* He jotted a few memos in his book before closing it.

Alfear hadn't come back. Quintin didn't know how to take that. Fre jumped as bells began to toll behind them.

"What on earth is that?" Quintin asked.

The wagons around them erupted with cheers, men and women climbing out and hugging each other on the street.

Quintin grabbed a passing stranger, "Do you know what that is?" he asked, pointing to the bell tower.

The stranger laughed. "That's the all-clear sign, Angel-Kin; we've protected the city."

Quintin looked dubiously at the melted stone and shattered roof tiles but decided to let the man have his celebration.

"You think we could go look for Lian?" Fre asked as she tugged at Quintin's sleeve, looking worriedly at the gatehouse.

Quintin paused. The people being safe now was what he needed. He let himself go with Fre, following her further down the city street. Buildings looked more and more like puddles of glass the further they traveled down the road. Soldiers milled around the gatehouse, treating men and women covered with burns and melted silver. The image was straight out of a fairy tale, as if Heaven's War came and visited the world.

Fre pulled Quintin over to where Alfear stood, talking to several officers. It seemed that no one had avoided burns of some kind. The two officers having a wrapped arm and bandaged head between them.

"We still have soldiers guarding what's left of the body," the female officer said, "my gunners will turn it into a puddle if it so much as moves."

Alfear turned to the other officer, eyes critical. "How is Lian?" he asked. "Right this way, and I'll show you."

The man gestured for Alfear to follow.

Fre reached Alfear's side, grabbing his arm. "Is he going to be ok?"

Alfear turned, shocked by Fre's sudden appearance. "We'll have to wait and see," he replied reassuringly.

"He isn't gone yet, young one," the officer said, stepping into a hospital tent.

Fre stepped forward, walking alongside the medical cots. She found Lian towards the back. His entire body was wrapped in bandages with multiple splints holding arms and legs.

Lian looked over, eyes meeting Alfear's. "You should see the other guy," he spoke through gritted teeth.

Alfear shook his head, partly in anger, another part in relief. "I would put you into a cast if you weren't already in one," he said, laughing in disbelief.

Fre seemed to calm down after hearing Lian's voice, taking a seat beside the cot.

"He should be out of here in a few weeks," the medical officer said, "probably won't even have any noticeable scars."

Alfear clasped the man's hand, shaking furiously. "Thank you, sir. You have no idea how much that means."

The officer shook his head, "you should have seen this man. He took took that creature on his own."

Quintin looked at the immobile figure of Lian on the bed. *He could have died.*

Quintin felt the book on his back as if it had grown heavier at the thought. Quintin shrugged to himself, *maybe I'll get some answers in here, though that will have to wait till later.*

* * * * * *

Selyne ascended above the treetops of the surrounding Everwood. The light of the morning sun had revealed the landscape of the crater they'd wandered into, causing Selyne to wince as the obsidian earth reflected its glassy surface up to where she hung in the air.

"How are you holding out?" Selyne asked, glancing back at where Wil clung to her shoulders.

They'd risen well above the surrounding tree line. From here, they'd hopefully be able to spot evidence for their camp. She heard Wil yawn, seemingly unfazed by the situation or her previous question.

"You know you can be one of the least interesting people to talk to sometimes," Selyne said irritated.

Wil shrugged in resignation, "I can't help it if the conversation isn't going anywhere," he glanced downwards, "Which is saying something given our situation."

"Well, sorry for not entertaining you," Selyne said.

Wil smirked, taking joy in her irritation, "Whatever you say. Kalli would be able to think of something."

Selyne ignored the jab making an obvious effort to check the tree line for any signs of life. "We're looking for smoke, correct?"

He nodded, pointing over her shoulder, "I'd check over by those trees. They look promising."

Selyne looked to see if she could make out why he'd recommended them. *They just look like any other group of trees.*

Selyne decided to humor the suggestion, swooping down for a closer look. The smell of burning wood wafted through the branches as the pair approached, a good indicator of human life. Selyne looked at Wil, surprised.

"How on earth did you smell the smoke from up there?" she asked.

"I didn't." he responded, "The smoke created a darker haze of the trees than the mist."

Selyne wasn't sure whether that was a valid answer, but currently, she didn't care. Descending downward, navigating slowly through the heavy foliage of the Everwood, careful not to tear their clothes any further. Voices sounded up towards them as they approached, men and women shouting frantically about something.

"Sounds dangerous," Selyne said, looking back at Wil, concerned.

The man nodded, "Get me down there; I'll see what's the issue."

Selyne didn't hesitate despite several questions, moving quickly to reach the panicked people below. The caravan had circled up with Seekers standing watch at the forest beyond with ratchet bows locked and ready.

Wil leapt off of Selyne's back, falling the last twenty feet, landing next to an unsuspecting Seeker. The hooded man jumped at the surprise, turning and releasing the steel bolt loaded in his weapon. Wil dodged back, avoiding the metal rod by a hair, raising his hands in assurance.

"Easy," he yelled, "it's Wil. I've arrived with Selyne."

Seekers turned their heads as he called out, whispering frantically at the change in circumstances.

"Where have you been?" the Seeker hissed, "We've been staying put to see if you'd arrive."

"What's the matter?" Selyne asked, landing beside Wil.

"Princess," the man stammered, "we've got a serious situation on our hands."

A shout came from the other side of the camp, causing the group to tense.

"Let's go," Wil said, taking Selyne's hand, "They're going to need us over there."

"What, why?" Selyne said, dragging behind Wil.

"Rhinil."

Wil hopped one of the wagon's harnesses, cutting through the circle of carts. Civilians were situated here, mostly cooks and researchers. Kalli was probably somewhere close.

"The Seeker said they had waited the night," Wil said, "Rhinil don't like us staying in place for too long. They see it as an attempt at settlement."

Wil parted the crowds of people, coming to the other side of the wagons. The Seekers had formed up, situating themselves where they could retreat behind the wall of wagons quickly. Selyne followed Wil to the front of the group, standing ready for whatever was coming from the woods. The surrounding area was dark, shadows creating monsters in the foliage. Selyne guessed that wasn't far from the truth.

A horn sounded from within the forest, an eerie sound driving a spike of ice into Selyne's soul. The forest came alive a moment later, shadows rising and stepping into the clearing. The apelike bipeds came to stand a dozen feet away from them, their dark eyes staring intensely at the humans.

"They don't look friendly," Selyne whispered, noting the swords hanging on many of the creature's belts.

Wil nodded, "Looks to be a roving war party, a pit. The communes are much more reasonable."

Selyne shivered as one of the creatures met her gaze. "Are we going to need to fight?" she asked quietly.

Wil shook his head, stepping forward. "Let me talk to them. They will listen to me."

He stepped away from Selyne, approaching the line of Rhinil. "Stand back."

One of the Rhinil growled, stepping forward and hitting its chest once at Wil. Wil stopped, showing his unarmed hands.

"We just want to move through this place, please." He stepped forward slowly.

The Rhinil struck with terrifying speed, its arm coming up to smash Wil's skull. The man moved like water. Moving inside the creature's guard and smashing its face inward with his fist. The Rhinil crumpled where it stood, the others frozen in shock.

"Steel-son!" one of them yelled, followed by a cacophony of others yelling throughout the forest.

Selyne stared, dazed at what she'd just witnessed. Time had seemed to shift around Wil as he moved as if he'd separated himself from reality.

"By Shia below, I couldn't even see him move," one of the Seekers gasped.

The Rhinil slowed their shouts, coming to a stop as they shuffled about.

"Calm yourselves," A voice called out from the Rhinil ranks.

A smaller Rhinil appeared from amongst its peers, approaching Wil. The ape stared angrily at his fallen comrade. "You know I can't afford a loss like that."

Wil shook the blood off his hands, shrugging. "I'm familiar with your troop. It was expected."

The Rhinil growled but didn't deny the statement. "You visited the tree father?"

Wil nodded.

"Burn that silver beast," The Rhinil growled, "Constantly it refuses to speak with us."

"You know why," Wil said.

The ape nodded, "Soon, that will change, son of vengeance, the time for humanity will end; I've heard it from the angels."

Wil shook his head, "I don't care. As of now, you will let us through, and you know you can't beat me."

The Rhinil sat for a moment as if unwilling to let the matter slide.

"We move out!" it finally yelled, "Tonight, we rest in bower trees of the southern forests."

A rumble of dissent echoed through the woods as the war band was deprived of its chance at a fight.

The smaller Rhinil turned back to Wil, clearly upset. "I understand the situation you've put us in, and your history with the red band affirms what you've said."

Wil gave the Rhinil a bow in respect. "Thank you until we face each other again."

The Rhinil chuckled, "Your wish may come sooner than you may desire."

The war band vanished as quickly as it had appeared, armed Rhinil fading into the shadows they appeared from.

"What on earth were you thinking!" Kalli yelled, storming out from the ranks of Seekers, glaring daggers at Wil.

The man turned around, confused. "What's the issue? I had it completely under control."

A crack echoed out as Kalli smacked Wil in the face. "I don't care what reports say about you; that was stupid."

Wil placed a hand on his face. It didn't seem to have hurt, though he was shocked. Selyne walked up to the pair, leaving the Seekers to their conversations.

"It felt like you knew that creature," she mused, "care to explain what I just witnessed?"

Wil scratched the back of his head. "The Red Band is the war band I had the pleasure of running from during my time missing in the field."

Selyne nodded, still unsatisfied with the answer. "Steel-son? Care to explain that?"

Wil looked up, contemplating his next words carefully. "Can we answer this when we get back? I can tell you everything then."

Kalli raised an eyebrow. "You sure about that?" She asked skeptically.

Wil nodded. "I'll let you hang me if I don't."

"Ok then," Selyne conceded, "We can wait until then."

"Until then," Wil agreed.

EPILOGUE

Selyne took in a deep breath, condensation puffing out in front of her as she released the frigid air from her lungs. Winter had turned over the hold of autumn, bringing relentless storms in the city of Isel. Selyne pulled her coat closer as she opened her bedroom door. The hall was eerily empty, the servants sent home early as the snow and ice had begun to fall.

She found the whole situation surreal. Summer had fallen into autumn, which in turn had frozen into winter. Three entire seasons come and gone in an instant. Selyne walked down the hallway towards the dining hall. Had she changed at all in that time? Selyne didn't feel different.

Sounds echoed up from the kitchens where the cooks would be busy with tonight's meals. Unlike the other staff, the cooks lived in the lower half of the tower just above the garrison. Selyne continued down the hallway past the kitchens, stepping out of the way as servers passed with trays of food. A man brushed past her, fumbling for a moment as the tight confines of the hallway threatened his balance.

Selyne ducked out of the way of the man's arm.

"I am so sorry, ma'am," the servant stammered nervously, "pardon me."

The man gave a quick bow as he shuffled off towards the dining hall. Selyne gave a faint laugh.

"Don't mind me," she said as the man vanished down the hall.

He probably hadn't heard her. Selyne shrugged, letting out a sigh. The dining hall was empty as she entered, her parents having eaten earlier in the evening. Selyne walked over to the head of the table where two plates had been set out. Pulling out a chair, Selyne seated herself and waited for her companion to arrive. She pulled out her watch, looking at the hand sitting over the ruby, indicating noontime.

The door opened as if on cue, Wil entering silently.

"Help yourself to some dinner," Selyne said, gesturing to the seat. "We've got something to talk about."

Wil nodded, closing the door behind him as he took a seat at the table. "I should congratulate you, Princess. I hear you're now the emperor's regent in Isel."

He took a bite of his food before continuing, "But I figure you didn't ask me here to celebrate."

Wil searched Selyne's face for any hint of what was coming next.

"You still have a question to answer," Selyne began, leaning forward to rest on folded hands. "I think at this point I may be due a few more than that, actually."

Wil leaned back into his chair, tugging at his beard nervously. "I had hoped you'd forgotten that, to be honest," he said.

He gave Selyne a critical look. "Though I suppose this won't get me in much trouble now that you're your father's regent."

He went silent for a moment, looking intently at the open air as if searching for answers. "You remember Quintin's abilities with Resonance?"

Selyne shrugged. Her father was very interested in what he could do. "Not really. He could could turn himself invisible, right?"

Wil nodded. "More importantly, his power was an internal ability. An inherited Resonance rarely seen anywhere in the world."

Selyne raised an eyebrow, curiosity growing. "What exactly does that have to do with anything I've asked you in the last couple of months?" her eyes narrowed, "You seem different right now."

Selyne couldn't place the sensation. A sense of familiarity paired with the sensation of dread.

Wil chuckled wryly, "I guess that's a little obvious, isn't it?"

Selyne's mind raced as her jaw dropped. "How long has this been a thing? Did my mother know about this!?"

Selyne felt her face grow hot as the man nodded in affirmation, and she shook her head in anger. "Heaven burn that woman."

"If it's any help, it wasn't just you," Wil said, perhaps to give her some reassurance. "My current situation is supposed to be kept hidden for national security. Not even my father knows about it."

Selyne wasn't convinced, "Why are you telling me this now?"

Wil shrugged, "I keep my word with people I trust."

He said it so easily as if that sentiment didn't break a dozen of his imperial oaths.

"So, your father doesn't know about this?" Selyne queried, " Did you break someone's heart like Quintin?"

Wil raised an eyebrow at the venom in Selyne's voice. He shook his head, "It's more complicated than that."

"Are you a late bloomer, like me then?" Selyne asked.

Wil shook his head again.

"Well, then please enlighten me." Selyne huffed impatiently.

Wil took a deep breath as if readying himself for what he was going to say next.

"My inheritance," Wil began, "if that's what you want to call this, comes from an oath I made."

Selyne didn't know what that meant, "An oath with my father?" she asked, growing uneasy.

Wil shook his head solemnly before continuing in a whisper. "No. With an angel."

Selyne sat back, trying to comprehend the idea. "How? What does this mean exactly?"

"That's a long story," Wil said, looking down at his watch. "Do you have an afternoon to spare?"

Selyne opened her hands in an invitation, "I've got all day."

Wil nodded, "good, let's start from the beginning…"

* * * * * *

Alfear leaned out the balcony window, savoring the chilly breeze blowing through the city of Isel. Winter had always been his favorite time of year. He'd seated himself pretty high up in the university library. Here one could see the entire cityscape sprawling out below them. *It really is something to behold.* Alfear sighed in satisfaction. It was a time like that where he realized just how good life could be.

Someone tapped on the glass door of the balcony, drawing Alfear out of his peaceful contemplation. The large man turned, smiling as the face of Quintin looked back at him.

"Come on in," Alfear said, inviting Quintin onto the balcony.

Quintin cracked open the glass door. "Are you busy at the moment? I can always come another time."

"Not at all," Alfear said, "quite the opposite, actually. I'm just appreciating the view. Did you have something to talk about?"

Quintin took a free seat and sat down. "I wanted to talk about two weeks ago. I have some questions that need to be answered."

He fidgeted nervously as he spoke. Alfear hadn't seen the boy this nervous before.

"What exactly is on your mind?" Alfear asked.

Quintin dug into his bookbag, pulling out a large leather-bound book. "I managed to grab this from one of the rooms in the cathedral up north and have spent some time reading through it. Can you tell me why I should care for anyone who ascribes to the beliefs in this book?"

Alfear raised an eyebrow in surprise. "That's a heavy way to start a conversation."

"Do you have an answer," Quintin said sharply, "this isn't something I can excuse."

Alfear nodded in understanding. "I know the reasons you're angry. I struggled to figure out that same question."

He looked into Quintin's eyes. They were colder than the frozen tundra up north.

"Did you feel the threads grow stale in the city when we were trying to evacuate the church?"

Quintin shrugged, "I think I noticed; why?"

"That was Lian's doing. He ignited every thread in the surrounding atmosphere in an attempt to shatter the ancestor's body." Alfear steepled his fingers as he formed his next sentence. "There was enough power in that blast to level the city and then some."

"Ok," Quintin said, "I think we've been over this before."

Alfear shook his head. "I'm not sure you've really understood why I keep bringing it up. Tell me, was it good for Lian to do what he did? He sacrificed nearly everything, including the ability to safely pass on his inheritance to someone of his choice to protect those people."

Alfear waited for Quintin's response.

Quintin shrugged. "Honestly, I'm not so sure. That's really hard to come to grips with."

Alfear thought about his next words carefully. The kid was right, but he was missing something crucial. Alfear had to figure out how to say it.

"What if someone from the church of Solus was in Lian's position, and we replaced the church with an Anglis temple. Would it not be a good thing if they set aside their hatred aside to save those people?"

Quintin clenched his jaw. It was clear he saw where Alfear was taking this and didn't know if he liked it.

"I guess I'd prefer it if they tried to save the citizens," Quintin conceded.

Alfear nodded in agreement. "That's what I want to tell you. Heirs can't be so reckless with our judgment. We aspire to something greater than that. Where others would spit in the face of those they find reprehensible, we do the opposite. Otherwise, we'll end up being judged the same as those we hate. We are supposed to aspire to something higher."

Quintin sighed. "You know I don't ascribe to Thean theology; this feels awfully preachy."

Alfear shook his head, "No, you have a very strong sense of right and wrong. Regardless of what you believe, I think that needs to be controlled, or you'll end up hurting those around you."

"So, we just let it go?" Quintin said indignantly, "that's not justice either."

Alfear nodded, "You'd be right; however, we have a place for judgment as well as a time. The Department Heads want to send you out as soon as possible. That's your opportunity to really make a difference. Could you just promise me you'll try and save people before you decide they should be destroyed?"

Quintin shrugged. "I'll give it some thought."

Alfear's smile broadened. That was about all he could ask the boy to do after all.

CPSIA information can be obtained
at www.ICGtesting.com
Printed in the USA
LVHW091114220723
753083LV00001B/96

9 781957 262109